THE WESTMINSTER INTRIGUE

TRACY GRANT

ACKNOWLEDGMENTS

The Westminster Intrigue is the first full length novel I wrote entirely during the COVID-19 pandemic. I am so grateful to have had the Rannochs and their friends for company in this unprecedented time, and so grateful to all the people who support my writing and the Rannochs' world in so many ways. As always, huge thanks to my wonderful agent, Nancy Yost, for her support and insights. Thanks to Natanya Wheeler for once again working her magic to create a truly amazing cover that captures Mélanie Rannoch and my image of the ball sequence that is central to the story, and for shepherding the book expertly through the publication process, to Sarah Younger for superlative social media support and for helping the book along through production and publication, and to the entire team at Nancy Yost Literary Agency for their fabulous work. Through the trials of the pandemic, we all stayed connected and everything stayed wonderfully on track. Malcolm, Mélanie, and I are all very fortunate to have their support.

Thank you to Eve Lynch for the meticulous and thoughtful copyediting. I love sharing the Rannochs with you and so appreciate your care for getting their story right.

Thank you to Kristen Loken for a magical author photo taken in one of my favorite places, San Francisco's War Memorial Opera House, on one of my favorite occasions of the year, the Merola Grand Finale. Your brilliance never fails to amaze me, Kristen! Missing the Opera House and live theatre, I particularly love to look at this picture as a reminder of times that were and will be again.

The solitary work of writing is even more solitary these days. I miss my writer friends and am grateful for the chance to keep up with them virtually whether on FaceTime or Zoom or just with an Instagram post that brightens the day. Thanks to Veronica Wolff and Lauren Willig, who both understand the challenges of being a writer and a mom. To Penelope Williamson, for sharing adventures, analyzing plots from Shakespeare to *Scandal*, and being a wonderful honorary aunt to my daughter. I'm so glad we got to actually see you while I was writing this book. To Jami Alden, Tasha Alexander, Bella Andre, Allison Brennan, Josie Brown, Isobel Carr, Catherine Coulter, Deborah Coonts, Deborah Crombie, Carol Culver/Grace, Catherine Duthie, Alexandra Elliott, J.T. Ellison, Barbara Freethy, Andrew Grant, C.S. Harris, Candice Hern, Anne Mallory, Monica McCarty, Brenda Novak, Poppy Reifiin, Deanna Raybourn, and Jacqueline Yau.

Thank you, Deirdre, Chris, Sierra, and Piper for being wonderful neighbors and supporting my writing. Special thanks to Deirdre for the extra three hours the weekend I was finishing the book.

Thank you to the readers who support Malcolm and Mélanie and their friends and provide wonderful insights on my Web site and social media. Talking with you about the series has meant more than ever this past year.

Thanks to Gregory Paris and jim saliba for creating and updating a fabulous Web site that chronicles Malcolm and Mélanie Suzanne's adventures. To Suzi Shoemake and Betty

Strohecker for managing a wonderful Goodreads Discussion Group for readers of the series. Thanks to my colleagues at the Merola Opera Program who help me keep my life in balance—I could not imagine a better group to spend virtual work days with.

As I wrote this book, I thought a lot about my mom, Joan Grant, with whom I first wrote about Queen Caroline's trial in *Frivolous Pretence*. I finished up the book listening to *The Chocolate Soldier*, which we both loved. I still remember her taking me to see it one evening after work when I was a teenager. We got stuck in traffic, missed dinner, but made it to the show, and then had a late dinner afterwards. A special night. I miss you, Mummy.

And finally, thanks to my own daughter, Mélanie herself, for inspiring my writing, being patient with Mummy's "work time", adapting to the past year, sharing her precious Yorks the night I was finishing the book, and offering her own insights at the keyboard while working on her own stories. This is her contribution to this story –"I am so proud of my mommy for finishing her book! I know it must have been hard but in the end she got it done and I am so proud of her so so so so so so so so so so so so so proud!"

DRAMATIS PERSONAE

*indicates real historical figures

<u>The Rannoch Family & Household</u>

Malcolm Rannoch, MP and former British intelligence agent
Mélanie Suzanne Rannoch, his wife, playwright and former
French intelligence agent
Colin Rannoch, their son
Jessica Rannoch, their daughter
Berowne, their cat

Laura O'Roarke, Colin and Jessica's former governess
Raoul O'Roarke, her husband, Mélanie's former spymaster, and
Malcolm's father
Lady Emily Fitzwalter, Laura's daughter from her first marriage
Clara O'Roarke, Laura and Raoul's daughter

Gisèle (Gelly) Rannoch Thirle, Malcolm's sister

Miles Addison, Malcolm's valet

Blanca Mendoza Addison, his wife, Mélanie's companion
Pedro Addison, their son

Valentin, footman
Mrs. Erskine, cook
Giles, groom

The Davenport Family

Lady Cordelia Davenport, classicist
Colonel Harry Davenport, her husband, classicist, and former
British intelligence agent
Livia Davenport, their daughter
Drusilla Davenport, their daughter

Archibald (Archie) Davenport, Harry's uncle, MP, and former
French intelligence agent
Lady Frances Davenport, his wife, Malcolm's aunt
Chloe Dacre-Hammond, Frances's daughter from her first
marriage
Francesca Davenport, Frances and Archie's daughter
Philip Davenport, Frances and Archie's son

The Mallinson Family

Arthur (Julien St. Juste) Mallinson, Earl Carfax, former agent
for hire
Katelina (Kitty) Velasquez Mallinson, Countess Carfax, his wife,
former British and Spanish intelligence agent
Leo Ashford, her son
Timothy Ashford, her son
Guenevere (Genny) Ashford, Kitty and Julien's daughter

Hubert Mallinson, spymaster, Julien's uncle

David Mallinson, MP, Hubert's son
Simon Tanner, playwright, his lover

The Langdon/Pendarves Family

Viscount Pendarves (Pen)
Sophia Langdon Prescott, his sister
Philippa (Pippa) Langdon Haworth, their sister
Phoebe Langdon Molyneux, their sister

Lord Prescott, Sophia's husband
Lord Molyneux, Phoebe's husband

Cynthia Haworth, Pippa's daughter
Katie Haworth, Pippa's daughter

The Blayney Family

Edmund Blayney, journalist
Captain James (Jamie) Blayney, his brother
Margaret (Daisy) Blayney, Jamie's wife

Captain Edward (Ned) Royston, Jamie's friend
Mrs. Jasper Fullingham, Jamie's landlady

Others in London

Edith Simmons, classicist and former governess,

Bertrand Laclos, French émigré and former British intelligence
agent
Rupert, Viscount Caruthers, his lover, MP and former British
intelligence agent
Gabrielle, Viscountess Caruthers, Rupert's wife and Bertrand's

cousin

Kit Montagu, Leveller
Sofia Vincenzo Montagu, his wife

Humphrey Smythe, Lord Beverston, Elsinore League member
Barbara Smythe, Viscountess Beverston, his wife
Benedict Smythe, their younger son
Nerezza Russo, Benedict's beloved
Roger Smythe, the Beverstons' elder son, MP and Leveller
Dorinda Smythe, Roger's wife

Juliette Dubretton, novelist
Paul St. Gilles, painter, her husband

Manon Caret Harleton, actress
Crispin, Lord Harleton, her husband

Jennifer Mansfield Smytheton, actress
Sir Horace Smytheton, her husband, former Elsinore League
member

James Fitzwalter, Duke of Trenchard, Laura's first husband's
son

*Lord Fitzroy Somerset, Wellington's secretary

Letty Blanchard, actress
Jack Tarrington, actor

Henriette Varon, former seamstress to the Empress Josephine
Lisette Varon, former agent, her daughter

Jeremy Roth, Bow Street runner

*Sir Nathaniel Conant, chief magistrate of Bow Street
*Lord Sidmouth, British home secretary

Danielle Darnault, opera singer
Ilia Darnault, her daughter
Grace Arbuthnot, Danielle's lady's maid

Pierre Ducroix, journalist

*Emily, Countess Cowper, patroness of Almack's
*Harry, Lord Palmerston, Secretary at War, her lover
*George Lamb, her brother
*Caroline (Caro George) Lamb, his wife
*William Lamb, Emily's brother
*Lady Caroline Lamb, his wife

*Granville Leveson-Gower, Viscount Granville, politician and diplomat
*Harriet Leveson-Gower, Viscountess Granville, his wife

*George IV, King of the United Kingdom of Great Britain and Ireland
*Caroline, his wife

*Henry Brougham, MP, Queen Caroline's lawyer

*Lord Fitzroy Somerset, secretary to the Duke of Wellington

Hon. Thomas (Tommy) Belmont, Elsinore League agent
Frederick Talbot, Marquis of Glenister, Elsinore League member

If this were played upon a stage now, I could condemn it as an
improbable fiction
—Shakespeare, *Twelfth Night,* Act III, scene iv

CHAPTER 1

London
September 1820

New arrivals were always a source of interest at the Chat Gris. Men were a source of potential revenue. Certainly to the women who worked the rooms above the common room, but also to men and women who played games of dice and cards at the cracked tables or lifted a purse, a watch, a snuffbox, or an embroidered handkerchief in the course of a game or while serving ale or gin or moving between the tables. Or upstairs in the rooms over the common room before or after —or even during—bed sport. New male guests were also potential rivals for the pickings on offer. Or for the women who worked the tavern. New female guests were less likely to come to the Chat Gris plump in the pocket, but they too might be rivals for the night's pickings, whether those were purses or watches or other trifles to be lifted or wealthy gentlemen to be enticed upstairs. So the women who worked the Chat Gris eyed female new arrivals with suspicion. And the men who frequented the tavern surveyed them with the interest posed by novelty.

When a tall man in an olive drab greatcoat that could keep most of the denizens of the Chat Gris in funds for weeks came through the door, shaking raindrops from his beaver hat and the four capes on his coat, he drew gazes from all round the common room. He made his way to a table in the center of the room, set down the hat, and shrugged out of the coat to reveal the high shirt points, padded shoulders, and nipped-in waist affected by a dandy. They all knew the type. Sort who fancied himself daring for drinking a pint of ale in St. Giles. The newcomer with the high shirt points ordered an ale and joined a game of cards, then laughed when he lost heavily. Several women sidled up to him but he showed no interest, though one helped herself to his purse. He also showed no interest in three women, also new to the Chat Gris, who arrived not long after. Despite the fact that they were a striking trio—one dark, one with guinea gold ringlets, one a redhead. Their sarcenet and lustring gowns had once been fine, but any of the discerning women in the tavern could recognize hems that had been turned and lace and ribbon that had been added to cover stains and wear. That and the low-cut necks and spangled scarves said they came from a different world from the gentleman in the caped greatcoat, even if they were all new to the Chat Gris tonight.

The three women sauntered up to the bar and ordered gin. Then they separated and moved about the room with the air of those going to work, something nearly every other woman in the Chat Gris recognized well. The red-headed woman attempted to catch the eye of the man with the greatcoat but had no more luck than the Chat Gris's regulars. Then she fell into conversation with a man in a bottle green coat who was also new to the Chat Gris. Not long after, they wandered upstairs, the man's arm draped round her shoulders and his hand slipping between the green velvet ribbons on her bodice. The dark-haired woman cast a look of annoyance at her redheaded friend, who was having better luck than she was herself, then tossed down the last of her gin and ordered another. The blonde woman was bent over the man in the padded coat, who actually looked up and gave her a smile. Emboldened, the blonde woman dropped down on his lap.

Five seconds later, the door opened to admit another man, taller even than the man with the high shirt points, though he slouched more and his swagger said he was more at home in St. Giles. He cast a look about as though in search of something. His gaze lit on the blonde woman. He pushed his way between the tables, grabbed the blonde woman's arm, and pulled her off High Shirt Points's lap.

"Take your bloody hands off my woman."

"Take your bloody hands off me." The blonde woman wrenched away from the new arrival. "What do you think you're doing, Will?"

"I should be asking you that, witch."

"No offense meant," High Shirt Points said. "I had no notion—"

"He doesn't own me." The blonde woman yanked her arm from the grip of the man she called Will.

"I've spent enough on you." Will grabbed her again.

"That doesn't give you rights."

"Here now." High Shirt Points pushed his chair back. "I believe the lady asked you to leave her alone."

"Mind your own business." Will dragged the blonde woman closer.

"Here now, Julie." The dark-haired woman, who had been watching with apprehension, broke away from a stout man she'd been flirting with and ran over to the blonde woman. "You know what he's like when you set him off."

"He had no business following us," Julie said.

"How the bloody hell else am I supposed to know what you're doing?" Will jerked Julie into his arms. Julie pulled away from him and stumbled into the next table. When Will reached for her again, High Shirt Points stepped between them.

"Leave the lady alone, sir."

"The lady is no lady, she's a—"

High Shirt Points drew his fist back and aimed a blow at Will's jaw. A surprisingly strong blow ("Must train at Jackson's," someone murmured). Except he got his booted foot tangled in the legs of his chair and the folds of the greatcoat he'd flung over it. So he lurched into Will. Will drew his fist back to counter, but instead the two of them went down with the chair and greatcoat in a tangle of broken wood and torn wool.

"Now look what you've done," the dark-haired woman said to Julie.

"Serves him right," Julie declared, pulling her skirt out of the way to reveal silk stockings worked with clocks and cherry-red satin ribbons tied round her ankles.

Will yelped.

"Oh, Will, are you hurt?" Julie flung herself down beside him.

Will put a hand to his face. "That devil fair near broke my nose."

"Poor darling." Julie looked up at High Shirt Points. "You beast."

"See here, madam—"

"Oh, Will." Julie now had his head in her lap. She bent down and kissed him.

High Shirt Points stared down at them. "I suppose all's well —I say!" He clapped a hand to the side of his closely tailored coat. "My purse is gone."

"Don't look at me." Julie was smoothing Will's hair, gaze locked on Will's own.

"Julie." The dark-haired woman caught her arm. "Let's get out of here."

"Not before—"

"Hunh—" Will sat up and shook his head. "Did you accuse my woman of stealing?"

"No. That is—" High Shirt Points straightened his padded shoulders. "My purse is gone. And I had it when she sat down."

"Don't remind me that you were pawing her." Will scrambled to his feet.

"I was not—"

The dark-haired woman tugged Julie to her feet and pulled her towards the door.

"Here now." High Shirt Points grabbed Julie's pink satin sash. "Don't start running off."

"Unhand her." Will lunged at High Shirt Points. High Shirt Points blocked the blow and struck back. They lurched into the table, upending High Shirt Points's tankard of ale. The dark-haired woman dragged Julie through the crowd of interested onlookers. Julie's skirt caught on a splintery chair leg and tore. The dark-haired women pushed open the door and pulled Julie into the street. High Shirt Points lurched after them. Will grabbed him and the two of them tumbled out into the street after the women, grappling as they went, to the accompaniment of shouts and calls of encouragement from the onlookers.

Someone threw a tankard after them and someone else slammed the door shut on the wind and rain and mêlée.

MALCOLM RANNOCH CURSED the tight-fitting coat of his costume as he stumbled into the street. He aimed another blow at Harry Davenport, the supposed Will. Several stitches gave way in his coat, which made it easier to move. Harry hit him back as they both staggered in the mud. Mélanie and Julien had already run down the alley at the side of the Chat Gris. Malcolm pushed himself up on one hand before he could collapse in the mud, and lurched to his feet. He and Harry stumbled into the alley after Mélanie and Julien.

The alley was darker than the street, the ground squishy with rotted food from the Chat Gris kitchen and most likely worse. Julien paused below a window, the skirt of his filmy pink gown held up, and gave an owl call good enough to have fooled Malcolm had he not been watching. An answering call sounded and then the casement window above swung open and the candle within the room caught a gleam of tawny hair. A leg clad in a silk stocking and ribboned garter swung over the sill, and with almost no sound, Kitty Mallinson let herself out the window, climbed down the upper story, and dropped down into Julien's arms in a stir of green skirts and lacy petticoat.

"Good timing," she said. "I'd just secured the papers and our target is out like a light. Everything go all right on your end?"

"As much like clockwork as an improvisation can." Julien steadied her and put his hands on her shoulders.

"I think we put on a good enough show that no one was thinking about what you were doing upstairs," Malcolm said.

"Thank you." Kitty flashed a smile at him.

"Good to be back at work," Julien said. "Though I'm rather sorry I didn't get to play your part, Kitkat."

Kitty's grin flashed in the moonlight. She touched her fingers to Julien's blonde hair piece. "There's a limit to how far you could have carried the masquerade, darling, however good you are at it. And no, I didn't have to go particularly far with him before the drug took effect."

Julien grinned. "I didn't ask."

"Your husband kissed me." Harry was stripping off his side whiskers, which were coming loose in the rain. "Quite convincingly."

"I should hope it was convincing." Julien pushed his blonde ringlets back from his face. "I try not to do things that aren't convincing on a mission. Hopefully that report will throw off anyone who happened to be there or who hears about it later and remotely guesses it might have been us. My apologies to Cordelia."

"Oh, Cordy won't mind that." Harry stowed the whiskers in his pocket. "I don't think she's quite forgiven all of us for going off without her, though she claims to understand it was risky for someone not trained to fight."

"Speaking of which, we should get home," Malcolm said. "Before Cordy and Laura lose patience. And before we run more risks." He looked at his own wife, who was grinning with the excitement of a successful mission. Which he admitted he couldn't but share himself. He reached for her hand. Just as three men rushed down the alley.

Harry, who was closest, knocked one to the ground first. Another rushed at Malcolm. A glancing blow to the shoulder knocked Malcolm backwards. He stumbled, then used the force of his weight to throw the attacker off balance. A third man screamed as Mélanie tossed the contents of her scent bottle in his eyes.

Malcolm glanced over his shoulder and saw that a fourth man was holding Kitty at the opposite end of the alley, a knife to her throat. Julien had gone still. Kitty fell back as though in a faint, knocked her attacker backwards and twisted free. Julien grabbed the man and forced his knife hand away. The man screamed and the knife went flying. Julien twisted the man's arm behind his back and pushed him to his knees. "Who sent you?"

Kitty snatched up the knife and tossed it to Julien. "Who sent you?" he repeated, the knife now at the man's throat.

The man made a hoarse sound. The man Malcolm had been fighting broke away and darted down the alley towards Julien and Kitty. The man Julien held slumped to the ground, a knife protruding from his chest.

The other attackers scattered. Julien dropped down beside

the man who had attacked Kitty and gave a curt nod. "Gone. Damnation. I should have seen that coming. I'm getting rusty." He pushed himself to his feet and touched Kitty's arm. "You all right, Kitkat?"

"Just wounded pride because he got a jump on me."

Harry looked down at the dead man now spilling blood onto the grimy cobblestones. "Rather proving the point about needing a team versed in fighting tonight. But why the devil—"

"Explanations at home," Mélanie said.

Julien looked down at the dead man, brows drawn, eyes glassy.

"We can't move him," Malcolm said. "Or alert anyone."

"No. I know that." Julien seemed to shake himself. "Let's get home."

CHAPTER 2

It was far from the first time Mélanie Rannoch had returned to her husband's beautiful Berkeley Square house—their beautiful Berkeley Square house, as Malcolm would be quick to say—with a ragtag group of allies. On more than one occasion they'd encountered the watch on their return. In fact, the experience was so familiar she'd had her story ready for the watch tonight. On other occasions she or Malcolm or another of the group had been wounded. Tonight, they avoided the watch and none of them was seriously hurt, so they trudged up the steps to the fanlight and Ionic portico merely wet and bedraggled.

She opened the door and ushered their friends into the entry hall just as Laura O'Roarke, Malcolm's stepmother, and Cordelia Davenport, Harry's wife, came running out of the library. "Thank goodness," Cordy said. "We were starting to worry." Then she went still, her gaze going from one of them to the other. Laura, who was just behind her, did the same.

Malcolm had a bruise beginning to form on his temple. Harry was caked with mud. Kitty's dress was torn. They were all dripping water onto the black and white marble checkerboard of the floor, but it was less their appearance that caused the reaction than what their faces betrayed, Mélanie suspected.

"No one's hurt?" Laura asked.

"Just wounded pride," Julien said.

"Come into the library and get warm," Laura said. "I'll make coffee and Cordy can pour whisky."

Mélanie went to the kitchen to help Laura with the coffee. It was late enough that they had sent all the servants to bed, and they had all got accustomed to doing basic tasks on their own during their exile in Italy two years ago. Or re-accustomed, in Mélanie's case. She had certainly not grown up an aristocrat. Laura flashed a smile at her but said, "I won't ask questions until you can tell Cordy too. I promise."

Cordelia had supplied everyone with whisky by the time they brought the coffee to the library. Malcolm and Harry had scrubbed their faces. Julien had changed into a shirt and breeches, though he still had traces of rouge and eye blacking on his face. "I forgot how constricting a corset is," he said, going to take the coffee tray from Mélanie.

"Why do you think I avoid one myself whenever possible?" Mélanie said.

They settled round the fire to face the results of a mission that had seemed, as missions go, relatively straightforwards. Gisèle, Malcolm's sister, who was undercover with the Elsinore League, a mysterious group dedicated to advancing their own interests, had reported that a League agent was buying papers from a man named James Blayney at the Chat Gris. They had gone to the Chat Gris with the aim of intercepting the sale.

"And it all went quite according to plan," Kitty said, accepting a cup of coffee from Laura. "Well, as according to plan as these things ever do. The drug in his wine took effect right on schedule. I didn't even have to prevaricate. Or go particularly far. And unlike when we tried to take the papers off George Dalton in June, I found the papers right away. He was still out cold when I got out the window. The others were all there."

"After staging quite a nice little fight," Harry said. "Malcolm still has an excellent right hook. Only then in the alley we encountered a real fight."

"The League?" Cordelia asked.

"I don't see how they could have known we had the papers that quickly." Malcolm was frowning into his whisky glass. He set it down and reached for his coffee cup. "Even if their agent went upstairs the moment Kitty dropped out the window and realized the papers were gone, there's no way he—or she—could have alerted the men who attacked us."

"I was thinking the same thing," Kitty said. "It looks as though someone else knew the papers were being exchanged tonight. And was trying to intercept them."

"Just like your ball," Cordelia said.

"Just like nearly everything involving the king and queen," Mélanie said. The former prince regent, George IV since his father's death at the end of January, though he had not yet been crowned, was determined to divorce his long-estranged wife Caroline. She was being tried before the House of Lords on charges of carrying on 'a most unbecoming and disgusting inti-macy' with her courier, Bartolomeo Bergami. The Tories, as the party in power, were firmly aligned with the king. The Whigs were backing the queen, at least in part because they hoped the defeat of the bill would cause a rift between the Tories and the king and loosen the Tories' grip on power. The queen's lawyers, Henry Brougham and Thomas Denman, were aligned with the Radicals, like Malcolm and Julien, and the opinion of the masses was on the queen's side. With the city on edge, Mélanie had thought they might be assumed to be protesters tonight if the watch saw them. They had seen a group demonstating outside Lord Castlereagh's house on their way home. The jockeying for power and debates over the witnesses and evidence—much of it

involving salacious details, such as information about bedsheets
—had been the talk of London for months. The trial had been in
progress since August. They were now at the end of a three-
week recess between the prosecution's case and that of the
defense.

"What is in the papers?" Laura asked.

Kitty drew the packet of papers from the bodice of her gown
and spread them on the sofa table. Chairs creaked and clothes
rustled as everyone gathered round.

There were several sheets, written in a flowing hand.

*Italy was a surprise in many ways. I had thought to escape and
recover my equilibrium in a gondola or beside the sea. But I
hadn't reckoned on the people from my past who would follow
me there. Or on the new people I would meet. I'm not sure
which was the more dramatic in retrospect, but Alexander
Radford certainly made an indelible impact.*

Multiple indrawn breaths showed they had all got to the
name at the same time.

"Surely Nerezza didn't write this?" Cordelia said.

"I doubt it," Malcolm said, "though it does look like a
woman's hand. But I doubt Nerezza was the only woman the
man known as Alexander Radford was entangled with during
his time in Italy."

Alexander Radford was the name, or more likely the alias, of
the mysterious man trying to take control of the Elsinore
League. Nerezza Russo had been involved with him in Naples
and the League had tried to have her killed, though Malcolm
and Mélanie and the others hadn't understood why until they
connected Alexander Radford to the League. Radford also
seemed to have infiltrated negotiations in Italy with Malcolm
and Kitty's former spymaster, Lord Carfax. His real identity
seemed to be a matter of some secrecy.

"Now we know why the League wanted the papers," Kitty said. "But who wrote this? Do any of you recognize the hand?" She looked at her husband, then at the others.

"No." Julien glanced at Mélanie, at Malcolm, at Harry.

"It hardly proves anything," Malcolm said. "I wouldn't recognize the hands of most agents I've worked closely with."

"We don't know this was written by an agent." Cordelia glanced through the papers again. "It sounds more like she's a courtesan."

"She could be both," Kitty said. "But that hardly narrows the possibilities a great deal." She looked at her husband again.

"Why are you looking at me?" Julien inquired.

"Because you've been the most active in those circles recently."

"Which circles? Intelligence or—"

"Both," Kitty said.

"I think you overrate me, sweetheart."

"I doubt it."

Julien looked down at the papers his wife had retrieved. "I wouldn't recognize the hand of all sorts of people I've known even as intimately as my wife is inferring. But it is an interesting question. As is how Blayney came into possession of the papers."

"I didn't spend much time with him," Kitty said, "but based on the time I did, he struck me as not at all in the league of the woman who penned those words."

"There's no obvious connection to the queen and king," Laura said. "But it is Italy."

"Quite," Malcolm said. Princess Caroline, now the queen, had lived in exile in Italy for some years, and her life there with Bergami was at the heart of the case against her. Years before he was king, the regent had set up a commission, chaired by the vice-chancellor, to collect evidence against Caroline. The vice-chancellor had sent three commissioners to Milan to talk to Caroline's former servants. In June, the day after Caroline returned to England demanding her rights as queen, king had presented this evidence to Parliament in two now notorious green bags. A number of those who had given evidence to the 'Milan commission' had been brought to London to testify in the trial.

They scanned the papers Kitty had recovered again for anything relating to the queen, but there were few details, and they left off abruptly.

"These were just a teaser," Malcolm said. "Proof Blayney was offering the League's agent that he had something legitimate to sell."

"Which means we need to get the rest of the papers," Harry said. "You didn't find out where Blayney lodges, did you, Kitty?"

She shook her head. "I went through his coat looking for more, but I didn't find anything. But we should be able to make inquiries. It's a simple trace."

"We should show the papers to Nerezza," Mélanie said. "I agree it's unlikely she wrote them—the words don't sound like her—but she may have an idea of who might have done. I wonder—" She broke off as the sound of the front doorbell reverberated through the house. She shot a quick glance at the mantel clock, though she knew it was long past midnight. If Raoul, Laura's husband and Malcolm's father, had returned early from his trip, he'd have used his key.

Malcolm pushed himself away from the table. "I'll see who it is. At least we're all more or less presentable." He glanced at his discarded, padded-shouldered coat, shook his head, and went out into the hall in his shirtsleeves. Kitty snatched up the papers and tucked them back into her bodice. Harry and Julien got to their feet. Just in case it was an attack. In general, their enemies didn't ring the doorbell. But stranger things had happened.

Voices sounded in the hall, Malcolm's easy, then a few moments later he returned to the library accompanied by Jeremy Roth. Roth, a Bow Street runner, had worked with them on a number of cases and was now a good friend and a frequent guest in their home.

"I'm sorry to call so late." Roth took off his damp greatcoat and laid it on the marble library table where it wouldn't make a water mark.

"You know we don't retire early, Jeremy." Mélanie poured a cup of coffee, black, as she knew he took it, and carried it over to him. "And we're entertaining friends, as you can see." She didn't add explicitly that they'd been on a mission, but Roth would surely guess it. She was still wearing her spangled sarcenet gown and paste diamonds and Kitty was also still in her costume. Julien was back in a shirt and breeches but still had rouge and eye blacking on. Harry had pulled off his side whiskers but his hair was still darkened. Malcolm's high shirt points still flopped about his neck.

"I know," Malcolm said, moving back to the fire. "We've either been rehearsing a play or on a mission. Without going into details, let me say Mel is still the only one of us employed at the Tavistock."

Roth gave a faint smile, but his eyes were serious. "I was called to St. Giles this evening. To a tavern called the Chat Gris. Have you heard of it?"

"We don't generally frequent taverns in St. Giles," Malcolm said. "Except on missions."

"Yes, I know." Roth's gaze swept the room. "A man was found knifed to death in the alley beside the Chat Gris. People remembered a fight in the tavern earlier in the evening involving two men fighting over a woman and another woman who seems to have been a friend of the first." His gaze swept the room again, obviously taking in details without lingering on any of them. "But the dead man doesn't sound like either of the men who were described. A dandy in a padded coat and a man with side whiskers and a spotted neckcloth." His gaze settled on Malcolm's coat, thrown over the back of one of the Queen Anne chairs, and then on the spotted neckcloth now hanging loose round Harry's throat.

"All right," Malcolm said, "we were there. The fight was a set-up to cause distraction. We fled into the alley, where we were attacked. One of the attackers killed the dead man."

Roth nodded. "To be honest, I couldn't connect you with the description I got. Well, not until I saw how you were dressed. I came because I can always use help in an investigation. Do you know why you were attacked?"

"Most likely to get the papers I'd retrieved," Kitty said. "That was the reason for the distraction. I had just dropped down from an upstairs window when we were attacked."

"You were upstairs at the Chat Gris?" Roth said.

"Retrieving the papers from another guest at the tavern," Kitty said, as coolly as though she'd been talking about meeting someone to view paintings at Somerset House rather than essentially being in a brothel.

"Was he in the room when you left?" Roth's voice was even, not shocked but intent.

"Sound asleep. Or, more accurately, drugged."

"Do you know his name?"

"James Blayney. At least, that's the name we were given."

Roth nodded, gaze still intent. "Sandy hair, mid-thirties, wearing a bottle-green coat?"

"Yes." Kitty's brows drew together. "Was he still at the Chat Gris when you got there?"

"In a manner of speaking." Roth hesitated for a moment, as though choosing his words with care. "He's actually the reason I was called there. In addition to the dead man in the alley, we found a sandy-haired gentleman in a bottle-green coat dead in a room upstairs at the Chat Gris."

CHAPTER 3

Silence gripped the room, sharp with the tang of shock. Rare for this group. Julien edged closer to Kitty.

Kitty scarcely moved a muscle, but her eyes had gone very dark. "How did he die?" she asked.

"He'd been knifed."

Kitty's fingers curved round her coffee cup, but her gaze stayed steady on Roth's face. "Do you think he was still unconscious when he was killed?"

Roth met her gaze without flinching, though his own gaze seemed to soften. "I can't be sure."

"It's not your fault, Kit," Malcolm said. "No one could have known you were going to drug him, and if someone was planning to kill him they'd have found a way somehow."

"Dear Malcolm." Kitty spared him a brief smile. "We can't really know that, can we?"

"No," Julien said. "But you certainly didn't intend for him to end up dead. Any more than I intended for the man in the alley to do so." He looked at Roth. "I didn't kill him, as it happens. He grabbed Kitty and put a knife to her throat. Kitty got away and I got hold of him, but one of his companions stabbed him before I could get him to talk. Not my finest moment on a number of levels."

"You all survived the attack. I'd say that makes your response a success." Roth surveyed the group. "I don't suppose you'll tell me what it was you were after."

A crossfire of looks shot across the sofa table. Roth was a friend and an ally. He was also in the employ of the Bow Street Public Office. And the chief magistrate of Bow Street reported to the home secretary, Lord Sidmouth. With whom Malcolm's politics frequently put him at odds. Leaving aside the fact that Mélanie had once been a Bonapartist spy and Julien had spied for both sides during the war.

"We were intercepting papers the Elsinore League wanted to buy," Malcolm said.

"To do with the queen's trial?"

"Not on the surface. They seem to have to do with the identity of a man called Alexander Radford who is connected to the League."

Roth nodded. He knew when not to ask too many questions. "James Blayney appears to be the victim's real name," he said. "Captain James Blayney. My patrol ascertained that he had rooms in Percy Street. I'm on my way there. I was hoping Malcolm would come with me. I could use your insights."

"Gladly," Malcolm said.

"And perhaps Mélanie as well. Another opinion is always of value, and it could be particularly helpful if we have to interview a woman."

"I'd be happy to," Mélanie said. "But I think Kitty would be a better choice, if she's willing." She glanced at Kitty.

Kitty drew a breath, part surprise, part hesitation, part acknowledgement, part perhaps relief. "Yes," she said. "That is—"

"An excellent idea," Julien said, over his wife's unusual hesitation.

Kitty's gaze locked on his own. "Thank you."

"Sensible decision," Julien said. "You know more about Blayney than any of us."

Roth nodded as though quite unaware of the undercurrents. "We also got the name of a friend who had accompanied Captain Blayney to the Chat Gris in the past. A Captain Royston, who lodges in"—Roth flipped through his notebook—"St. Martin's Lane. I'd like to interview him without delay as well." Roth looked at Harry. "I thought a military man connection might be good."

Harry nodded. "Of course. Perhaps Mélanie would come with me."

Mélanie shot a look of gratitude at their friend. "Happy to."

JAMES BLAYNEY HAD LODGED in a narrow house in a quiet part of Percy Street. Noise and lights came from a tavern at one corner and a coffeehouse at another, but the house itself was shuttered and dark. Roth, Malcolm, and Kitty traveled there in one of the Rannochs' carriages. It wouldn't have been a difficult walk, but it was late and raining and speed was important.

Roth rang the bell. Malcolm glanced at Kitty as they waited. She had changed out of her spangled green gown into a claret velvet dress trimmed with black braid and a black velvet cloak, as he had put on a black coat cut for comfort and with shoulders blessedly free of padding. Kitty had also exchanged her sparkly paste jewelry for a pearl necklace and earrings and wiped off some of her rouge and eye blacking. All done with the speed and consummate care of an agent. But the light of the lantern over the door caught the shadows in her eyes beneath the shade of her hood. He'd been on a number of missions with her, most of them nine years ago, when they'd been in Spain. When he hadn't yet met Mélanie. When Kit hadn't been to Julien what she was now. When Malcolm and

Kitty had been lovers. But he'd never seen quite that look in her gaze.

"It wasn't your fault, Kit," he said, as he'd said in the Berkeley Square library.

Kitty gave a faint smile beneath the hood of her cloak. "You know you'd be blaming yourself in the same circumstances."

"Probably. But since when have you always agreed with me?"

She gave a strangled laugh. "Dear Malcolm. You always know just what to say."

"And you know better than to let self-recrimination interfere with a mission."

Kitty tugged her hood into place. "Certainly not with a mission."

The door was opened by a woman of indeterminate age with her hair in curl papers, wrapped in a voluminous pink silk dressing gown and paisley shawl. The light of the lamp she carried caught the surprise and indignation in her blue eyes. "What do you mean disturbing decent people at this hour?"

"My apologies, madam. I am Inspector Roth of Bow Street. My associates Mr. Rannoch and Lady Carfax. We would not have disturbed you were the circumstances not extraordinary. If we might have a word with you in private?"

The lady coughed, stared from Malcolm to Kitty, blinked, gaped at Kitty. "If you—did you say, Lady Carfax?"

"Mr. Rannoch often assists Inspector Roth," Kitty said. "My husband and I sometimes do so as well. As does Mr. Rannoch's wife. Perhaps we could talk inside? Mrs.—"

"Fullingham. Mrs. Jasper Fullingham. Of course, my lady."

Mrs. Fullingham led them down a narrow hall papered in a faded trellis pattern that flashed in the lamplight as they passed to a small sitting room that smelled of floral potpourri and lemon oil. She set the lamp on a table and lit two tapers. "I'm afraid there isn't a fire. Would you like tea?"

"Please don't trouble yourself." Kitty took the lead in speaking, which seemed best as far as the results they were receiving.

"Do sit down." Mrs. Fullingham pushed one of her papered curls behind her ear. She appeared torn between delight at entertaining a countess and anxiety at what they might be about to tell her.

Kitty sank into a chair opposite Mrs. Fullingham. When the ladies were settled, Malcolm and Roth sat as well.

Kitty cast a glance at Roth. He inclined his head. "Do you have a tenant named James Blayney?" Kitty asked.

"Captain Blayney? Oh, dear, is he in some sort of trouble?" Mrs. Fullingham pushed another curl into place. "Such a charming man, but I did sometimes wonder—What has he done?"

"I'm afraid he was found dead this evening, Mrs. Fullingham," Roth said, in a kind but steady voice.

"Dead?" Mrs. Fullingham's hand jerked, pulling the paper from the curl and sending two hair pins thudding to the Turkey rug. "Good heavens. Footpads? What is London coming to?"

"He was in a tavern. We are endeavoring to discover who killed him," Roth said.

"A brawl?" Her fingers closed on the curl paper, which had fallen in her lap. "I wouldn't have thought—"

"Not a brawl, so far as we can tell. But he was knifed. It would help greatly if you could tell us what you know about him. And if he had any enemies."

"Good heavens, do you imagine I would rent lodgings in my house to a gentleman whom I knew had enemies?" The curl paper crackled as her fingers tightened on it again. "He always seemed a most well-bred young man. He fought at Waterloo. He'd been on half pay since, but he told me he had excellent prospects. He was always very kind and obliging, but I did sometimes worry—"

"About his associates?" Malcolm asked.

"Yes. No. He rarely had callers. His people were from Shropshire. They didn't come here. I gather there was some estrangement from his family."

"You said prospects," Kitty said. "Was he perhaps planning to marry?"

"Oh no. That is, I never heard anything of the sort. There was a lady who called on him once. Very elegant, you could see she moved in the first circles. Her gown alone—"

She hesitated, gaze on the folds of claret velvet showing beneath Kitty's cloak.

"I know just what you mean," Kitty said. "Did Captain Blayney mention her name?"

"Oh no. He merely said she was an old friend with some news for him. And of course, I wouldn't presume to ask questions."

"What did she look like?" Malcolm asked.

Mrs. Fullingham frowned. "She was slender and of average height. I assumed she was about Captain Blayney's age because he called her an old friend, but I can't be certain of that. Or of her hair or eye color. She wore a beautiful bonnet with heavy veil."

"Obviously at pains to conceal her identity," Roth said.

"I'm sure I couldn't say. The only other lady—" She broke off, her fingers working over the curl paper.

"Mrs. Fullingham?" Kitty said in a gentle voice. "Was there another lady who called on Captain Blayney?"

Mrs. Fullingham's brows knotted, her gaze on the frayed curl paper. "I don't know that I'd call her a lady."

Kitty leaned forwards, confiding friend more than great lady now. "Dear Mrs. Fullingham, pray don't hesitate to be candid on my account. I'm a married woman. Did Captain Blayney have a mistress?"

Mrs. Fullingham flushed and looked up to meet Kitty's gaze. "I'm sure I don't know the nature of the relationship. But there was a lady—a woman, for I don't believe the term lady applies. She called on him, though usually they spoke in the sitting room, quite correctly."

"Did she also arrive veiled?" Roth asked.

"Oh no. Her attire was perfectly respectable and of quite good quality, though it appeared to be a few years old."

She looked at Kitty's gown and cloak again as though noting details of fashion Malcolm and Roth would be blind to. Malcolm had noticed copies of *La Belle Assemblée* on the console table across the room. "What did she look like?" he asked.

"Fair hair. A bit brassy. I couldn't say about her eyes for sure, but I think they were blue. Not in the first blush of youth, but not much more than thirty, I suspect."

"Height?" Roth was writing in his notebook.

"Not very tall. But not slender. That is—" Mrs. Fullingham sniffed. "Her waist was pulled in, but she—"

"Filled out her corset?" Kitty said.

"Precisely, my lady." Mrs. Fullingham sniffed again. "I'll warrant it took a great deal of lacing to make her waist so tiny. I often thought poor Captain Blayney must be quite taken in as to her character."

"Did she do anything that made you suspicious?" Roth asked.

"No." Mrs. Fullingham's overplucked brows drew together. "Not precisely. But one could tell she was no better than she should be, if you'll pardon my speaking bluntly, ma'am. I worried that a gentleman like Captain Blayney was wasting time on her, when he should have been thinking about setting up his nursery with a respectable girl."

"Perhaps he saw this young woman as a respectable girl," Malcolm suggested.

"Oh no. I'm quite sure not, Mr. Rannoch. She was certainly not the sort of woman who makes a man think about marriage. I'm sure you will appreciate the type."

"To my mind, intense love makes a man think about

marriage. Are you saying Captain Blayney didn't appear to love this lady?"

"Oh, dear no. That is, I'm sure I couldn't say how he felt. But this young lady—"

"Did you ever hear her name?" Roth asked.

"He never introduced her to me. He described her as a friend. But I did hear him call her Grace once. Assuming that was her real name."

"Did anyone else call on Captain Blayney?" Malcolm asked. "Or did he send particular letters?"

Mrs. Fullingham frowned. "No. That is—He sent letters, but then he had a number of military friends, which gave him a voluminous acquaintance. Some of his friends called on him on occasion, but I'm sure I couldn't give an accurate description. They were gentlemanly men. Quite a different sort from Miss Grace whatever-her-name-is."

"Did you get names?" Roth pulled out his notebook.

"A Captain Royston. A Major Willingham. Or perhaps Willoughby. They were both about Captain Blayney's age. I assume they were comrades from Waterloo and before. I daresay they had many military reminiscences to share."

Roth jotted down the names in his notebook. "Did Captain Blayney appear to be in funds?" He closed the notebook over his finger. "I'm sorry, but I have to ask."

Mrs. Fullingham twitched a curl smooth. "He was never late with the rent. Well, not more than a few days, except the one time, and he had a most understandable explanation. He'd actually asked me for a week's extension just two days ago, but he was quite sure he was coming into funds soon, so I didn't think anything of it."

"Did he say where the funds were coming from?" Roth asked.

"No, and of course I didn't pry." She frowned, as though realizing the funds would now not be forthcoming. "And he dressed beautifully. I know it can be difficult for former soldiers in these times, but he seemed to manage better than most." She sniffed, this time as though with sorrow. "He really was a most unexceptionable man."

"Could we see his rooms?" Roth asked.

Mrs. Fullingham raised her brows. "Why on earth—"

"They may contain information connected to whyever he was killed."

She drew back in her chair. "But surely this was some sort of dreadful accident. A robbery gone wrong or a woman of no—" She broke off, gaze sliding to Kitty.

"It's difficult to know what it is at this point," Roth said. "And we need all the information we can get."

Her hand went to her throat. "Do you think I need be alarmed?"

Roth exchanged a look with Malcolm. "I shouldn't think so, but there are people searching for papers Captain Blayney had. We'll retrieve anything that seems significant, but I'll have a patrol keep watch on the house."

Mrs. Fullingham shivered, then led them out into the passage and up the stairs. She unlocked a door and opened it onto a darkened room. The smell of brandy spilled out into the passage. Even before she raised her candle, Malcolm had his suspicions. He stepped into the room and nearly tripped over a pile of books. Mrs. Fullingham raised her candle. The books had spilled from a shelf. Broken glass crunched underfoot. A drinks table had been upended, shattering a set of decanters. So had a low bookshelf. Drawers were pulled from a writing table, papers scattered over the floor, ink pooled from a tipped-over inkwell.

"Merciful heavens." Mrs. Fullingham clutched the doorframe.

"It's unlikely they're still here," Malcolm said. Though without meeting Roth's gaze, he knew they were both remembering the intruders they had surprised searching Lewis

Thornsby's rooms the night Thornsby had been killed last January.

"Lamp," Kitty said. She'd always had keen eyes in the dark. "On the floor to the right."

Malcolm retrieved the lamp, which was tipped over but unbroken. Kitty produced flint and steel and they lit the lamp. The flare of light illumined wreckage throughout the room and a half-open window letting in a chill breeze.

"One of us will stay with you," Malcolm said to Mrs. Fullingham.

"I'm all right," she returned, in a surprisingly brisk voice. "Just make sure there's no one in here."

They separated and explored the room and the one adjoining. Everything in the room had been turned over, smashed, cut open. Malcolm pushed up the partially open sash. "Mud on the wall," he said to Kitty, who was nearby. "Footprints below."

"The mattress is slashed," Roth said from the bedchamber doorway.

"A lot of crumpled, yellowed bills," Kitty said, her hands full of papers. "Nothing so far to identify 'Grace.' A love letter from someone signing herself *S. I miss you desperately. Will never forgive my sister.* Which raises some interesting questions, but it isn't dated and it's a bit yellowed, so it may not be recent." She looked round at the destruction. "If whoever searched found anything, it must have been in about the last place they checked."

"Assuming someone else didn't find it first," Malcolm said. "But even so, we should search ourselves."

They flipped through books, pulled off bindings (Malcolm always felt a qualm at doing so), tapped paneling and floorboards. Nothing.

"Has anyone been through the front door today?" Malcolm asked Mrs. Fullingham.

"Certainly not. I keep a respectable house. I'm very aware of comings and goings."

"So anyone would have had to break in."

"Surely that's what this man did. You said someone came in through the window."

"Assuming that person was the only searcher," Malcolm said.

"Merciful heavens. What are we in the midst of?"

"An excellent question," Roth said.

CHAPTER 4

*H*arry looked at Mélanie as they climbed the steps of Edward Royston's lodgings. "Well done."

Mélanie smoothed the skirt of the mulberry sarcenet pelisse she'd put on. "Kitty's feeling guilty. She shouldn't, but it's understandable. She needed to be doing something. And she has more knowledge of Blayney than any of us. She'll have better insights."

Harry nodded. "Sensible. And I'd like to think I'd be as forbearing sending Cordy off on a mission with one of her ex-lovers."

"You've been remarkably forbearing about Cordy's getting information from several of her ex-lovers." Thank God she could be frank with Harry.

"Not much other option, is there? Anything else would be lack of trust, which could unravel a marriage."

"Precisely."

Harry squeezed her arm briefly and rang the bell. A bleary-eyed porter admitted them. After they evoked their names and also handed over considerable coins, they found themselves in a small sitting room with Captain Edward Royston. He was in his mid-thirties, about Blayney's age, with sleek dark hair, a once trim physique starting to run to fat, and the look of one who would prefer to spend his days putting hunters over fences and drinking good port, but who hadn't managed to muster the funds to do so. His cravat was off, his shirt open at the neck, his coat rumpled as though he had hastily shrugged it on. His breath smelled of brandy. But then, Mélanie reflected, theirs no doubt smelled of whisky. And they had looked far more disreputable than Royston did before they put themselves to rights to pay the call.

He stared from Mélanie to Harry, as though trying to determine if he knew them.

"No," Harry said, "we've never met, though we may have been at some of the same entertainments in Brussels. You were with Maitland, weren't you? I was on the duke's staff. And Mrs. Rannoch's husband was an aide to Stuart."

Royston nodded, though he still looked a bit confused. But the mention of Waterloo had a way of creating an instant bond for those involved, even five years later.

"Our apologies for the late call," Mélanie said. Bad news was often best delivered quickly. And taking people off guard could be helpful. "We thought you would wish to know at once. It's about your friend James Blayney. I'm afraid he was found dead earlier this evening."

"Jamie's dead?" Ned Royston stared from Harry to Mélanie as though expecting one of them to deny it. "Christ." He ran a hand over his hair. "Your pardon, Mrs. Rannoch. Part of me's expected to hear Jamie was dead from the moment we first met. But I suppose part of me thought he'd survived so much he was half-immortal. I mean, anyone who got through Waterloo—"

"I know," Harry said. "I ended up face down in mud. I'd have been done for if Mrs. Rannoch's husband hadn't got me off the field."

Royston held Harry's gaze. "I took a bullet to my leg.

Surgeon wanted to amputate, but I begged him to hold off. He told me I was a damned fool, but it healed after a fashion. Still feel it when it rains. Jamie got a lock of his hair shot off but came through without a scratch otherwise." He frowned at the toe of his boot for a moment, then looked up at them. "What happened? Did he take a knife in a tavern brawl? Or fall afoul of footpads?"

"It was in a tavern, but it seems to be a bit more complicated," Harry said. "Perhaps we could sit down. Inspector Roth of Bow Street asked if we could have a word with you."

Royston's gaze narrowed, then shot to Mélanie. "Rannoch. You and your husband are the ones who go about Mayfair investigating crimes."

"Not just in Mayfair," Mélanie said. "And we have no official capacity. But we wanted you to get the news at once. And we thought you might prefer to talk to us."

Royston gave a rough laugh. "I have no idea what Roth looks like, but I imagine most men would prefer to talk to you. By all means, come in." He took a lurching step into the room and flung out an arm towards a faded damask settee and pair of armchairs near the fireplace. "May I offer you anything?"

They declined and settled themselves in the armchairs. Royston glanced at a half-full glass of brandy on an end table, snatched it up and tossed it down, then sat on the settee facing them.

Mélanie snapped open the steel clasp on her reticule and pulled out a notebook and pencil. Now that she was a writer, she always carried them, as Roth did. She flipped past her notes on Act II of her new play to a clean page. Appropriate that the book had bits of her life jumbled up. There was a draft of one of Malcolm's speeches too and a drawing her son Colin had done. "Did you know Captain Blayney was frequenting the Chat Gris tonight?" she asked.

Royston shifted in his chair. "The Chat Gris was always one

of Jamie's haunts. He'd play dice. Or—well, there's more than one sort of game played at the Chat Gris. Begging your pardon, ma'am."

"No need. This is an investigation, not a social call. And I see no need to pretend to sensibilities I don't possess." Really, it was so much easier now she wasn't trying to keep up the façade of a Mayfair wife and could just be frank. Except of course that at times the façade of a Mayfair wife could be useful for opening doors.

Royston regarded her for a moment, as though trying to determine what sort of animal she was. "Er—yes. That is, thank you. That is—I didn't know Jamie was going there tonight. To the Chat Gris. The last time I saw him was two days since."

"Did he seem concerned about anything?" Harry asked.

"Concerned? No. He seemed excited." Royston frowned, as though conjuring the words. "Said if all played out as he thought, he'd be able to pay me the ten quid he'd borrowed and even stand me a loan."

"Did he say why?" Harry asked.

"No. And, truth to tell, I didn't ask or think much of it. Jamie always had some scheme in mind that was going to make his fortune, and they almost always came to naught. When I first met him, he was trying to persuade all the chaps in the regiment to buy shares in a company trading in Jamaica."

Harry leaned back in his chair. "You met in the army?"

"When we both got our commissions."

"An immediate bond." Harry gave an easy smile, and for a moment Mélanie would have sworn he was perfectly at home in the military fraternity, though she knew quite the opposite was true. He stretched his legs out, like a man relaxing at his club. "Interesting the reasons we all have for going into the army. Duty. Ambition. For me it was an escape. I'd made rather a mull of my marriage. But no matter why one joins up, no matter where one comes from, suddenly everyone's equal. After a fashion, anyway." Even in the service of an investigation, there was only so far Harry would go in a masquerade.

"An uncle helped me to my commission," Royston said. "Only thing he ever did for me. Made some sort of promise to my mother, he said." He met Harry's gaze and gave a short laugh. "Not sure how she twisted his arm. Jamie was the second son of a clergyman from Shropshire. He went home occasionally, but after his father pegged off, less than a year after he lost his mother, he and his brother quarreled. Haven't heard him talk about his family since."

"Was he still close to anyone in his family?" Mélanie asked.

Royston frowned. "Not particularly. I think he was closer to the manor children growing up. They all played together, as he tells it."

"Whom did his father have the living from?" Harry asked.

"Lord Pendarves. From what Jamie said, he helped send Jamie and his brother to Eton. I think that and hanging about the manor probably helped cement Jamie's expensive tastes. He never quite said so, but I don't think it was easy to grow up and realize his playfellows had a great many more options in life than he did. Lord Pendarves helped buy his commission, I think, but there didn't seem to be a lot of money forthcoming thereafter. And there was some sort of quarrel a few years after Jamie joined up."

"With Lord Pendarves?" Mélanie asked.

"Yes. Father of the present Pendarves. Jamie wouldn't talk about it, but when he came back from leave, reaching out to Pendarves didn't seem to be an option anymore."

"Was he still close to the Pendarves children?" Mélanie asked.

"Langdon, that's the family name. I saw him talk with one of the girls at the theatre. There are three or four, I think. Never could keep them straight. And he tried to interest one of the husbands in one of his schemes. Didn't come to anything."

"And his brother?" Harry asked. "Did they ever patch it up?"

"Depends on what you mean. They talked every now and again. Jamie said his brother was always his last resort when he needed something. But he seemed to come through with a bit. I think it was mostly that Jamie couldn't bear to be lectured. And that his brother didn't have a lot."

"Is he a clergyman like their father?" Mélanie asked.

"God no. Runs some sort of newspaper. Always going on about the evils of the ruling class and emancipating this and that group, that sort of thing. Called the *Claribel* or something."

"The *Clarion*?" Mélanie said in surprise.

"That's it." Royston stared at her, brows raised. "You've heard of it?"

"I've read it. They have some excellent articles. They wrote quite a good one about one of my husband's recent speeches, though of course I'm a bit biased."

Royston shook his head. "Never could make sense of his and Jamie's being from the same family. One of them trying to claw his way into society, the other trying to tear it down. But Jamie did mention seeing Edmund—his brother—a month or so ago. So you'll want to talk to him. Maybe he knows about this latest scheme of Jamie's." Royston shook his head. "Damned if I could make head or tail of Jamie, for all we were friends."

"What about women?" Harry asked in an easy voice, quite as if Jamie Blayney's connections to whomever had written the papers he had been attempting to sell to the League weren't a matter of considerable moment.

Royston coughed.

"Please, Captain Royston," Mélanie said. "I move in Mayfair society. I'd be a fool not to think there were women. Unless he only favored those he found at the Chat Gris."

"What? Oh, no. Jamie favored—er—a wide variety. From all backgrounds."

"There was no one in particular, then?" Mélanie said.

"Wouldn't quite say that. Wouldn't say that at all. There were a number—over the years."

"And lately?" Harry asked. "Had he been seeing a particular young lady?"

Royston gave a short laugh. "I suppose you could call it that. Pretty thing. Hardheaded too. Seemed to keep Jamie's interest, if not exclusively."

"What is her name?" Mélanie asked.

"Grace. Never heard her last name. Lady's maid, I think, from something she said, though I couldn't swear to it. Guinea bright hair. And a trim little figure—" He broke off and coughed again.

"Given what you said of Blayney, I would have assumed as much," Mélanie said.

"Always did have an easy time with the ladies. Easier than I did. Not that I've—" He coughed again.

"Could this Grace have had anything to do with Captain Blayney's claims of fortune?" Mélanie asked.

Royston laughed. "She's a lady's maid. Or something of the sort. Hardly has a fortune to offer."

"But she might have had means to a fortune," Harry suggested.

Royston's frown deepened, and for a moment Mélanie was quite sure he was sorting through how much to tell them. "Doesn't seem likely. But of course, I can't know for sure. For all Jamie's open manner, he didn't reveal that much about himself." He stared into the cold grate, as though just realizing how much this was true. "But then, one doesn't, does one? I mean, one shares a bottle or a hand of cards or—er—meets up with ladies. Or talks about the ladies. Or maybe tells stories from the war. But one doesn't really talk much about life. That sounds a bit ghastly, doesn't it?"

Harry shifted in his chair. "It certainly sounds unsurprising. God knows I don't talk easily."

Which was true, Mélanie thought. Except he did talk to Malcolm. And Malcolm talked to him. Probably about things he couldn't even share with her.

"Is there any one of the family Captain Blayney is still in touch with, if he's not close to his brother?" Mélanie asked, jotting down in her notebook. She lifted her gaze to Royston with a smile calculated to charm. "Who would be the best person for more information about him?"

Royston dragged his booted toe across the floor. "I probably know him as well as any of his friends. There's Willoughby and Shaughnessy, but he probably confided in them less than me. And then—well, they haven't lived together for years, but I suppose you could ask his wife."

"His wife? "Mélanie cast an involuntary glance at Harry. Why the devil hadn't it occurred to them to ask sooner if Blayney had a wife? It should have been an obvious question, whatever life he'd been living. And then, close on, came the question she might once not have thought to ask. "Does he have children?"

"Scads of them." Royston scraped a hand over his hair. "That is, three or four. Maybe five. He met Daisy—Margaret—at Brighton or Worthing or Bath or somewhere on leave. Five—six —no, seven years ago now. '13. Came back announcing he was married. We all thought he was funning until he actually showed us the announcement in the *Morning Post*."

"Did Mrs. Blayney accompany him to the Peninsula?" Mélanie asked.

"God no. No place for a lady."

"I was in Lisbon with my husband," Mélanie said. "But he was a diplomat."

"Different thing that. Following the drum's not at all the thing for a gently bred woman. Didn't take your wife, did you, Davenport?"

"No." Harry stretched his legs out. "I couldn't very well. We weren't speaking at the time, and I joined the army to get away.

But should I ever rejoin the army—which seems exceedingly unlikely—I'd take her with me. Cordy's quite intrepid."

Royston shook his head. "Can't see if myself, for all the fuss about Juana Smith. After all, she's Spanish. Makes a difference, I think." His gaze lingered on Mélanie.

"I'm half Spanish," she said. "And half French."

"Ah." Something in his gaze said that accounted for a lot of what was odd about her. Mélanie hid a smile and thought of Kitty.

"In any case," Royston said, "Daisy was breeding by then. And I gather the bloom was already a bit off the rose. She managed to get in a delicate condition whenever Jamie came home, but they didn't live together long after Waterloo. So you could say they never properly set up a household at all."

"Were they on speaking terms?" Harry asked, with the bluntness of a man who has been estranged from his wife.

"Oh yes. Shouting terms, perhaps, but Jamie still went down to Chelsea to see her on occasion. Still saw the children. I'd be shocked if he confided in her, but she might know something." Royston flung himself back in his chair, brows drawing together. "Marriage still counts for something. Though looking at the royals, damned if I know what."

"I KEEP THINKING about Captain Blayney's children," Mélanie said, as she and Harry navigated the blue-black pavement. Royston's lodgings were even closer to Berkeley Square than Blayney's, so they had elected to walk. The rain had slackened to a drizzle, not enough to warrant putting up her umbrella.

"It's a hard thing to lose a parent," Harry said, "even an absent one. To my eternal shame, I had no idea how much I meant to Livia until I actually met her. Of course, Cordy had kept my memory alive. We don't know that Mrs. Blayney has done as much."

"No. But Blayney has actually seen the children. I wonder—"

Mélanie went still and felt Harry's stillness beside her. They didn't look at each other or quicken their steps, but then, without glancing to the side to indicate their intention, they ducked into a narrow alley between the brick walls of two shops, overhung by the jutting first stories of both. Mélanie pulled her skirt up away from the slops as the stench of animal and human waste washed over them. The alley gave on to a court with smoke-blackened walls and overhanging beams, smudges in the moonlight.

She stepped to the side, her senses keyed to pursuit from the street. The clatter of carriage wheels. Footsteps. Slowing? And then the press of steel against her back, through the merino of her pelisse. "Don't move," a rough voice said. "Or I stab your pretty friend."

CHAPTER 5

*H*arry went still beside her. Mélanie spun round, caught her attacker's arm, and jabbed her umbrella in his face. The man yelped. The knife went flying; Harry flung himself on it, seconds before a second attacker ran from the shadows.

Mélanie swung the umbrella at Rough Voice as he lunged back at her. Rough Voice staggered. Harry sprang to his feet, caught Rough Voice from behind, and threw him against the wall. The second man lunged at Harry from behind. Harry spun round and got him in the hand with the knife.

A third man, dressed in a more fashionable coat, ran down the alley from the street. Mélanie stuck out the umbrella and he went sprawling on the cobblestones.

Harry caught her hand and they raced across the yard and down an alley on the opposite side. Harry put his shoulder to a cracked wooden door and they stumbled into a close room that smelled of damp and wood rot. It was pitch dark, but from the air the walls were close. They inched forwards. Then went still as footsteps pounded down the alley outside the door. One at least of their attackers, but he didn't stop. Harry pushed open another door and they stepped into another small room, with a cracked, grimy window that looked onto the street and let in light from street lamps and the moon. A narrow bedstead stood against one wall, a three-legged stool had a chipped looking glass and a flowered basin and ewer atop it. Harry pulled out his purse and spilled coins beside the looking glass, then opened a door onto a narrow passage with crumbing wallpaper and another door that led to a quiet street.

"We'll send money to pay for the door," Harry murmured as he pulled the door to behind them. They hurried down the street, turned into the broader precincts of the Haymarket and then into Piccadilly, and didn't slow their pace until they reached Berkeley Square.

"Someone thinks we know a great deal more than we do," Mélanie said, reaching for the door handle.

"Pity they didn't enlighten us." Harry followed her into the hall. "Let's hope the others can help put the pieces together."

"What do you think they wanted?" Cordelia asked, after a quick survey of Harry and Mélanie that seemed to reassure her that neither was hurt. "It's not as though you have any papers."

"They might have thought we did." Mélanie undid the frogged clasps on her pelisse and slipped it off. It needed a thorough brushing, but she'd managed not to tear it. She and Harry had returned home to find Malcolm, Kitty, and Roth not yet back and Cordy, Laura, and Julien waiting anxiously for news.

"Or they might have been trying to warn us off," Harry said. "Or eliminate us entirely."

"If so, they didn't know whom they were dealing with." Julien, who was lounging about the room with the elegant insouciance of a caged tiger, refilled Mélanie's coffee from the fresh pot he and Laura and Cordy had made. "It will be interesting to see if Kitty and Malcolm and Roth are attacked as well."

"I do applaud the way you don't fuss over your wife, Julien," Mélanie said.

"Well, obviously the three of them could elude any attackers." Julien refilled Harry's coffee.

"It sounds as though Captain Blayney's wife would have reason to want to be rid of him," Cordelia said.

"But she'd have been unlikely to be at the Chat Gris tonight. Though stranger things have happened." Mélanie dropped down on the settee and took a sip of coffee.

"Interesting about Captain Blayney's growing up with the Langdons," Cordelia said.

"Do you know them?" Mélanie asked. Cordy seemed to have grown up with half the beau monde. So did Malcolm, but unlike Malcolm, who tended to retreat, Cordy had maintained active friendships with many of those she'd known from childhood.

"A bit." Cordy blew on the steam from her coffee. "I was friends with Pippa Haworth—Pippa Langdon that was—when we came out. We were both a bit discontented even when we made our debuts. Which gave us something in common, and made Pippa seem more interesting than most girls in our season. I don't think Pippa was very happy in her marriage."

"Neither were you, at first," Harry said in an equable voice.

"Pippa didn't choose nearly as well as I did." Cordelia reached for her husband's hand. "Haworth had about a quarter of her understanding and less than a tenth of her imagination."

"Most definitely." Harry took a drink of coffee. "I did go out with you on occasion that first year we were married. I remember the Haworths, though I'd forgot she was a Langdon. Interesting woman. And quite wasted on her husband."

"Pippa and I were both rather preoccupied after we married," Cordelia said, "but Pippa was one of my former friends who didn't cut me when I was in disgrace, which I'll always be grateful for." She frowned. "We rather drifted apart when I was living abroad. Not for any particular reason. But she stopped writing as much, and I confess I didn't write as much as I should."

"You were busy nursing the wounded and reconciling with your husband," Mélanie said.

"Still. I should have found time to do more. And I wondered if Pippa perhaps had reasons not to want to be in touch. I've seen her a few times since we came back to London, but not much at all since Italy. Haworth died. A riding accident. Quite dreadful, for all I never cared for him. It was while we were in Italy. I wrote and Pippa wrote back. Then by the time we returned to London, she'd gone off to Paris. I called on her last spring when we were finally both in town at the same time. Always a bit hard to catch up after so long." Cordy frowned again.

"What?" Mélanie said.

"Pippa and I had always found it easy to pick up through the years when we hadn't seen each other for a time. She was perfectly kind on that last visit, but I had the oddest sense she was holding something back. As though she didn't want to talk a great deal because there was something she didn't want to reveal. I'd have put it down to her husband's death, but she'd always been perfectly able to talk about the challenges of her marriage before. And she didn't strike me as grief stricken. More as though"—Cordelia's brows drew tighter together —"more as though she was hiding something."

"Did she ever mention Blayney?" Julien asked.

"No. At least not that I remember. She hasn't seemed to go about in society as much lately and neither have I, so I haven't seen her more than a handful of times. And after that last visit I haven't called again."

"Is she the eldest sister?" Mélanie asked.

"The middle one. Sophia's the eldest, though only by a year or so. She's married to Lord Prescott."

"Good God," Mélanie said.

"Do you know him?" Laura asked.

"Not at all well. He's a Tory politician. Malcolm's mentioned him in connection with the queen's divorce trial. He's playing an active role in trying to keep Tory votes in line for the king."

"Sophia wasn't so friendly during my disgrace," Cordelia said. "But I can't really blame her. We'd hardly been friends before and associating with me undeniably had a social cost at that point. No sense in mincing words. Phoebe—she's the youngest—was still in the schoolroom when I made my debut, and by the time she was out in society I was hardly considered appropriate to associate with young debutantes. She wasn't long married when I went to Brussels, just before Waterloo. She's married to Molyneux now. So she and Sophia are both married to politicians."

"Interesting, particularly now with everything happening in the Lords." Mélanie looked at Julien. "Do you know either of them?"

Julien was frowning into his coffee cup. "I daresay I've seen them in the chamber, but I can't claim to know them. I did meet their brother Pendarves once years ago."

"Years?" Mélanie said. Julien had been in exile for twenty-five years. "When you were children?"

"No." Julien took a drink of coffee. "In '14. On a mission. I was in disguise, and I'm not sure he'd recognize me now."

"Not that we have any sense Pendarves is involved," Cordelia said. "He hadn't seen Blayney recently, from what it sounds."

"No," Julien agreed. "Not from what we've heard so far." He frowned and took another drink of coffee.

Mélanie watched him for a moment. But then, they'd all learned not to press when someone was concealing something. How else were agents supposed to remain friends?

"I can talk to Pendarves, if need be," Julien said. "But it sounds as though we have other leads to pursue first. Blayney's widow, at the very least, and possibly more, depending on what Kitty and Malcolm and Roth learn. Perhaps—"

He broke off at the sounds of the front door opening. "Speaking of which," he said, as his wife, Malcolm, and Roth came into the library.

From the taut energy about all of them, it was clear they'd learned something, but then calling at Blayney's lodgings they could hardly have failed to do so.

"Out of curiosity," Julien said, "by any chance were you attacked on the way home?"

"No." Malcolm's gaze shot to Mélanie.

"Only a bit of mud on my pelisse," she said.

"And no chance to learn what they wanted, more's the pity," Harry said.

"The same group as in the alley by the Chat Gris?" Roth asked.

"I don't think so," Mélanie said. "Not unless they changed their clothes. We didn't get a good look at faces."

"No one attacked us," Malcolm said, "but someone had gone through Blayney's rooms very thoroughly. Kitty was masterful at getting his landlady to talk."

Kitty unfastened her cloak and tossed it over a chairback. "He was perhaps in somewhat straitened circumstances, though he was at pains to appear otherwise. His people supposedly came from Shropshire. He had callers including a mysterious veiled lady who was well dressed. He also had a mistress named Grace."

"We heard about her too," Mélanie said. "She may be a lady's maid."

"Interesting," Malcolm said.

"He does seem to come from Shropshire," Mélanie added, as Julien and Laura poured coffee for the new arrivals. "He's the younger son of a clergyman, and grew up on the Pendarves estate playing with the Langdon children. And he has a wife in Chelsea. Though apparently they haven't lived together in years. Also a brother in London who publishes the *Clarion*."

"Christ," Malcolm said. "Edmund Blayney. I should have put it together."

"Yes." Mélanie met her husband's gaze as he sat beside her. "Odd the way bits of one's life collide."

"Do you know him?" Roth asked.

"Only from his words in print," Malcolm said. "Which are quite impressive. I think Raoul may actually know him."

"He does." Laura set down the coffee pot. "Though I've never met Mr. Blayney. Raoul has a great deal of respect for him."

"He should know about his brother," Roth said. "As soon as possible. As a journalist, he'll have sources all over the city, so he may get the news quickly. Better for us to break it."

"And we want to see him get the news," Malcolm said.

Roth met his gaze. "Quite. The same's true of the wife. But it sounds like the brother was in closer touch, and we can get to him sooner."

"And he's getting a newspaper out," Malcolm said. "He'll still be up."

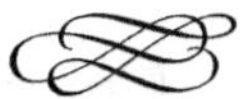

CHAPTER 6

Mélanie pulled the nursery door closed as she and Julien stepped onto the landing. All the adults had been going up at various times all night to the nursery, where Kitty and Julien's and Cordy and Harry's children were staying along with her own and Malcolm's and Laura and Raoul's.

"They're having a much more peaceful night than their parents," Mélanie said.

"Mmm." Julien leaned against the wall by the stairhead. "I expect a lot of questions in the morning. I'm surprised Leo and Colin and Emily and Livia at least haven't woken up to demand to know what's going on." He pushed his hair back from his forehead. His eyes were more shadowed than usual. "Everyone was very understanding about our need to be doing something, even if it was only climbing the stairs and making sure the youngest contingent was still asleep." He watched Mélanie for a moment. The light from the candle sconces on the stair wall caught traces of blacking round his eyes and rouge on his cheekbones. "Well done."

Mélanie scooped up Berowne, their cat, who had slipped out

of the nursery after them. "The attack wasn't that difficult to foil, and Harry and I didn't learn that much."

"You learned quite a bit, even if we can't yet make sense of the pieces. But that isn't what I was talking about."

Mélanie settled Berowne against her shoulder and pressed her face into his soft fur. "I could say the same to you."

His mouth lifted in a half smile. "I'll confess I'm not used to sending my wife off with her former lover. But then I'm not yet used to having a wife or anyone to whom I'm tied in any way, legal or emotional or otherwise." He frowned at the Rannoch crest etched on the crystal of the whisky glass he held. "Whatever 'otherwise' might mean. It's a novel experience. But then I do recognize that being able to pull it off is an important part of maintaining a relationship. Not to mention friendships. And one could say if I wasn't comfortable with Kitty's going off on a mission with Malcolm, I wasn't ready to marry her."

"It's one thing to be comfortable with it in the abstract. It can be rather different when one is faced with the reality in person."

"Probably just as well to get used to it, considering the lives we all lead. But then how often have Malcolm and Laura seen you and O'Roarke go off on missions?"

"Point taken," Mélanie said.

"Of course, one might say there's no better way to demonstrate trust," Julien said. "I rather think that's what Malcolm would say in his maddeningly reasonable way. Or perhaps that one realizes that it's the only way to make both the relationship and the friendships work. One either goes mad, or one learns to trust."

"That's remarkably insightful, Julien. Did you think this way when you were acting cold-blooded?"

"On occasion." He stared at the flames in the wall sconces that ran down the stairs. "Blayney's death shook Kitty. Going to his lodgings helped. At least I sincerely hope it did. It seems to have done. On a purely practical level, she actually talked to

Blayney earlier tonight. She had insights I didn't. Better for the investigation for her to put them to use."

"You've learned things about marriage it's taken some of us years to figure out." Mélanie stroked Berowne's head. His purrs reverberated through the lustring of her gown. "Malcolm's forbearance is amazing. Raoul never bothers him. Or at least he never admits to it."

"Perhaps he realizes not admitting to it is the secret to making it work. Of course, O'Roarke is his father." Julien frowned. "All things considered, I'm rather glad you're not Kitty's mother. Or my mother. I imagine that makes it both easier and harder." He glanced sideways at her. "I imagine having Kitty and me about does a bit of both."

She turned her head and met his smile. "More easier than harder."

"You're very kind." He shifted his shoulders against the wall. "It means a lot. What we all have."

It was clear "we" meant more than him and Kitty and her and Malcolm. "Yes," she said. "It does."

Julien's gaze fastened on the candle flame reflected in the polished wood of the stairs. "Kitkat's happy. At least, she seems to be. I wouldn't want her to be with me if she wasn't. At least I know enough to know I *shouldn't* want it. So there's little sense in worrying about how she might feel about the past. As for Malcolm, it's quite clear he made his choice."

"He never chose to give Kitty up." It was something Mélanie had never put into words before with anyone.

"Not in so many words, perhaps. But I think they both knew it wouldn't work. Or perhaps it makes it more comfortable for us to think so." Julien dug his shoulder into the ivory plaster. "I imagine Malcolm does the same when it comes to you and O'Roarke. Or perhaps being Malcolm, he's ruthlessly honest and doesn't allow himself to do so."

"Malcolm is—remarkable. In many ways."

Julien gave a crooked smile. "Jealously does little good. Which doesn't mean one doesn't feel a twinge. For what it's worth, I think Malcolm's more over Kitty than Kitty is over Malcolm."

"Perhaps it's not a question of being over." Mélanie looked down at Berowne's gray fur against the shiny gray of her gown. "Relationships change. Without one's quite realizing it's happening. You don't care less, you just care differently."

Julien gave a crooked smile. "Kitty used to tweak me on how I felt about you. Which wasn't—entirely inaccurate."

She looked at him in the flickering light of the candle sconces. "We weren't ever much of anything, Julien."

"We were friends, which counts for a lot. Though I wouldn't have used the term then." He hesitated. "You made me see things differently. You made me see possibilities."

"Possibilities I didn't acknowledge myself. At least not on that journey with Hortense." Years ago—almost a decade, though it seemed longer in terms of how they had all changed— she and Julien had accompanied Josephine Bonaparte's daughter Hortense when she traveled to Switzerland to give birth in secret to her child with her lover.

"Not in so many words, perhaps. But you never denied what you believed in. And later I saw the life you were living."

"And mocked it, as I recall." She pulled Berowne closer and put her lips to his head.

"What better defense than mockery to a truth one is trying to avoid? If I believed in what you had with Malcolm, I had to admit the possibility for myself, and that was rather terrifying. It still is, in a way. It's just more terrifying to imagine being without it." He smiled at her. "Thank you."

～

As MALCOLM HAD PREDICTED, despite the hour, a light showed in the window of Edmund Blayney's print shop. Malcolm rapped at the door. A few moments later it was opened by a broad-shouldered man in a printer's apron. The lamplight caught the strong bones of his face and the burning light in his deep-set eyes. His shoulders tensed, as though he was about to draw back his fist and plant them a facer. Malcolm tensed in response, fingers curling inwards.

"Our apologies for the late hour," Roth said. "I'm Inspector Roth of Bow Street and this is Malcolm Rannoch."

"That was quick." Edmund Blayney's shoulders relaxed slightly. "How the devil do you know about it? I hadn't sent word yet."

"Word?" Malcolm asked.

Edmund stepped back and flung out an arm towards the print shop. The printing press was knocked over. Strings of clothesline hung with newsprint dangled loose by one end from their moorings. Drawers had been pulled from a desk, scattering papers, sealing wax, pieces of type, bits of twine, and assorted type letters over the floor. "Someone broke in tonight while I'd popped round to the Dove & Raven for my dinner. I've been trying to clean it up. And to decide whether it was worth summoning you lot or whether that was more likely to bring the home office down on my head."

"I take a flexible approach to what I tell the home office." Roth stepped into the print shop. "And Rannoch considers them the opposition."

Edmund regarded Malcolm as he followed Roth into the print shop. "You're the Rannoch who sponsored the anti-capital punishment bill, aren't you? And who spoke on habeas corpus?"

"Yes. I'm also a reader of your paper."

Edmund's brows rose. "You surprise me. I didn't think our readership ran to Mayfair."

"I know a number of people who follow what you have to

say. I think you may know my friend Simon Tanner. And my—Raoul O'Roarke."

"I do. And have a lot of respect for both of them. I have a lot of respect for what you've done in Parliament."

"Tried to do would be more accurate." Malcolm glanced at a drying newssheet dangling from a clothesline. He could see a headline: *The Case for the Queen.* "You must be particularly busy now."

Edmund gestured at the drying newsprint. "Royal shenanigans sell far more copies than cogently argued—at least in my view—debates about Corn Laws, abolition, habeas corpus, and the general ills of the country. But it's news. It's gripped the country and it has people protesting. It will help pay for the other articles. Ideally, it will bring in some readers who will actually read the other articles. Assuming I can get tomorrow's paper out."

"Do you have any idea who did this?" Roth asked.

"None. I was hoping you did. How the devil did you know about what happened?"

"We didn't, as it happened," Roth said. "I'm afraid we have some news about your brother."

Something flashed in Edmund Blayney's eyes that might have been fear or wariness.

"I fear it's bad news," Roth continued without preamble. "Your brother was killed tonight."

A muscle tightened beside Edmund Blayney's jaw. Otherwise, he did not move. "Was it a fight?"

"No, it appears more complicated. He was knifed, but it seems premeditated. At a tavern called the Chat Gris in St. Giles."

"Christ." Edmund glanced to the side. "Part of me's expected to hear this ever since Jamie left home. And part of me never thought his actions would catch up with him. You don't know who killed him?"

"No. We're attempting to discover who. And why. When did you last see your brother?"

Edmund passed a hand over his face. "A month since. Maybe more. He borrowed five pounds. That was generally when I saw my brother. When he wanted to borrow something."

"He didn't send you anything more recently to keep for him?" Malcolm glanced round the chaos in the printshop.

"You think that's why this happened?" Edmund's eyes widened, then narrowed. "Someone was looking for something of Jamie's?"

"Your brother's own rooms were turned upside down tonight as well."

"And you think that strains coincidence."

"A bit."

"You have a point. I don't have anything of Jamie's. But as to whether the ransackers thought I was hiding something for him —I admit it's likelier than any explanation I've been able to hit on."

"Did they take anything?" Roth asked.

"Not that I've been able to discover so far. Not even the little bit of money I had tucked away."

"It can't be easy," Malcolm said. "Running a newspaper doesn't tend to pay well."

"I manage. Easier for me than most of the people I write about. But no, I don't have a lot. Which is probably why Jamie didn't apply to me more often."

"Your brother was trying to sell papers," Roth said. "Could they have contained information he got from you?"

Edmund's brows snapped together. "First you accuse me of hiding information for Jamie, then you suggest I was feeding him secrets."

"The two might be connected," Roth said in a steady voice.

Edmund gave a mocking laugh. "My trade is to convey information to as many as possible. While I freely admit I don't have the circulation numbers I'd like, I don't keep secrets. That would be unconscionable for a journalist."

"Even if bartering those secrets could give you the power to achieve other things?" Roth asked.

Edmund's eyes narrowed. "I can see why you'd wonder that. I don't play those games. Though there's no particular reason for you to believe me. I expect I wouldn't, in your shoes. Or Rannoch's." He looked between them. "What was in these papers?"

Malcolm cast a glance at Roth. "They appear to be personal. The papers your brother had on him were only a teaser. He was negotiating the sale."

"And the person he was selling them to killed him?"

"That's one possibility," Roth said. "It's not clear what happened. Or why."

"Whom was he selling the papers to?"

"We aren't sure," Malcolm said.

"And you don't want to tell me." Edmund gave a short laugh. "Again, I wouldn't in your place. But the truth is while it's a journalist's instinct to trace a story, I wouldn't publish my brother's peccadilloes. Less for his sake than for that of whomever those papers belonged to in the first place. Blackmail's a dirty business." His mouth tightened. "I take it that's what Jamie was involved in?"

"It looks that way," Malcolm said.

Edmund grimaced. "I'd like to say I thought better of my brother. But it's not a surprise."

"Had you known your brother to attempt blackmail before?" Roth asked, pulling out his notebook and pencil.

"No. Which doesn't mean he hasn't. Jamie had no end of money-making schemes and not a great deal of scruples about what he'd try. I don't know the details of most. The truth is Jamie and I hadn't been close since we were boys. Assuming we could have been called close then."

"You grew up in Shropshire?" Malcolm said.

Edmund gave a curt nod. "Our father held a living from Lord Pendarves."

"I know his son," Malcolm said.

Edmund nodded. "Yes, I can see your interests would align. Though you're willing to go considerably further than Pen—young Pendarves. My father and old Lord Pendarves had gone to school together. Pen—Pendarves now—and his sisters played with us as children. Odd, we didn't seem that different in those days."

"Perhaps because you weren't," Malcolm said.

Edmund gave a wry smile. "So speaks the Radical politician. Who happens to be a duke's grandson. Fundamentally, no. But our choices and expectations in life were poles apart. One only had to step into the small parlor at Pendarves Chase and then walk back across the park to the vicarage where our drawing room was half the size to know the difference. Jamie grew up aspiring to that life. I grew up wanting to overturn it. Which may be one reason Jamie was always more charming than I was, though in truth I think he just possessed more charm from the first. Old Lord Pendarves was fond of him. Fond enough he paid our school fees at Eton. I'm not sure he'd have done it just for me. And I, of course, didn't stand on my principles and refuse."

"You were a boy," Malcolm said.

"I was old enough to know what I believed and to express it with the self-righteous certainty of the young. But I accepted his patronage. He got me a place at Oxford as well. And bought Jamie a commission."

"Giving your brother a fortunate start in life."

"So it seemed. Though I expect it was challenging to be with other officers who had considerably more wherewithal at their disposal. The sort who took crates of china and crystal and port into the field. But for the first few years Jamie still had old Lord Pendarves to support him."

"Jamie's friend Royston told us your brother and Pendarves seemed to have had a falling out, but he didn't know the particulars," Malcolm said. "Do you know what changed?"

Edmund glanced away and grimaced, as though debating how much to say. "Sophia. The eldest Langdon daughter. She fancied herself in love with my brother."

"And old Lord Pendarves's fondness for your brother didn't extend as far as Captain Blayney's marrying his daughter?"

"I expect it might not have done, but Sophia was already married at the time her feelings for my brother became an issue."

"Undoubtedly a complication," Malcolm said. "They were lovers?"

Edmund drew a breath.

Malcolm felt Roth give him a sharp look. But investigations could require questions he'd abhor in everyday life.

"You're a plain-speaking man, Blayney," Malcolm said. "And we need information about your brother's past."

"It's Sophia I'm thinking about." Edmund glanced at the drying newsprint, then looked back at Malcolm. "But yes. That is, I can't claim to be in the confidence of either, but that was certainly the impression everyone had. Sophia was married to Lord Prescott and apparently bored in her marriage. She saw Jamie when he was in London on leave. Eventually it got back to old Lord Pendarves. He threatened Jamie with all sorts of things. Got him packed back to the Peninsula. The Prescotts have apparently managed to go on with their marriage. There was no open scandal. But from then on, Jamie was on the outside. Our father had died two years before, and old Lord Pendarves died not long after. Pen—Pendarves now—our boyhood playfellow was much more resistant to Jamie's charms than his father had been. I think he actually did help Jamie out once or twice, but then they seem to have quarreled as well. Or perhaps Pen just got tired of Jamie's entreaties. Jamie always had some plan or another for making his fortune, but they tended to come to nothing."

"And you were in London when this happened?" Roth said.

"Yes, but I moved in very different circles from the Langdons or the Prescotts or my brother. I left Oxford and earned my keep writing articles and pamphlets. Old Lord Pendarves left me a bit. I used it to start the *Clarion*. I'm not sure he'd appreciate the use his legacy was put to. Or perhaps he would. He was fairly tolerant of my ranting. After Waterloo, Jamie's debts were worse and he had fewer sources to appeal to for aid. Occasionally he was desperate enough to appeal to me. Those were the only times I saw him in recent years."

"You said you saw him a month since," Roth said. "Did he mention anything he was engaged in?"

Edmund frowned and rubbed his fingers across his forehead, then scrubbed at the ink stain. "He claimed he was on to something that could change his fortunes, but as I said, that's the way he always tended to talk, so I didn't think much of it. He did ask some questions about the press. How many copies I usually circulated, how long it took to get something into circulation."

"You think he was going to ask you to publish something?" Malcolm said.

"I didn't at the time. In retrospect—perhaps. But I don't see how that relates to his selling something."

"Perhaps it was a backup plan if the sale fell through."

"Following through on blackmail?" Edmund grimaced. "I could see his using the threat, but there'd have been no fortune to make from it. Not unless he could sell a great many copies indeed." His head shot up and he looked from Roth to Malcolm. "He didn't offer to sell these papers to me. Whatever they were, I couldn't have paid him much. Believe that if you won't believe I don't have the stomach for profiting off human misery." He glanced at the drying newssheets again. "I suppose we're all profiting off the king and queen's misery in a way, but then when their misery's an issue for Parliament there's little avoiding it."

"A lot of people think the trial could change the government." Roth said.

"I know. And I'm all for anything that could give the Whigs an edge. And even more the Radicals. Aside from the fact that the queen strikes me as ill-used. But even with protests in the streets, I'm afraid it will take more than this to pull down the Tories."

Malcolm met Edmund's gaze. "For what it's worth, so am I."

Edmund inclined his head. "You seem too sensible a man to think otherwise."

"Royston told us your brother had been seeing a young woman," Roth said. "Called Grace. Gold hair. May be a lady's maid."

"I suspect he was seeing more than one young woman. I can't claim to have met any of them. Or to know their names. But my brother almost inevitably had more than one string to his bow."

"Was he still in touch with Sophia Prescott?" Malcolm said.

"You'd have to ask Sophia. I don't think theirs was a deathless love, but I may be a bit biased, having seen them both with scraped knees and snotty noses." Edmund frowned suddenly. "Has anyone told Daisy?"

"Who?" Roth looked up from his notebook.

"Jamie's wife."

CHAPTER 7

"*I* like him," Malcolm said. "I can see why Raoul likes him. But I don't think he's telling us the whole truth about his brother."

"Nor do I." Roth sank back on the sofa in the Berkeley Square library and glanced at the clock on the mantelpiece. "Probably better to wait until tomorrow to call on Mrs. Blayney. We can go to Chelsea in the morning. And someone will need to talk to Sophia Langdon. Lady Prescott. Who may be the *S.* in the love letter we found in Blayney's rooms." He looked round the group. "Is it too much to hope one of you is connected to her?"

"Lady Prescott?" Kitty said. "I know her. We're related—that is, her husband is my first husband's cousin. She called on me when I first came to London a year ago. Which was kind, though I got the sense that she was relieved I wasn't quite so wild as whatever her idea of the Argentine suggests. I also got the sense Edward and her husband hadn't been on the best of terms, but I returned the call. She wrote me a very pretty note of congratulations on my marriage to Julien."

"Before or after she knew who I was?" Julien said. "That is, that I was Arthur Mallinson."

"Before, to her credit. Then she wrote again paying her compliments when it was clear we were the Carfaxes. They came to our ball."

Julien frowned. "I'd have sworn I shook hands with everyone that night, but I don't believe I met them."

"Probably not. Convention didn't have you standing at the head of the stairs for hours while the interesting work of investigation went on. But in any case, though I'm usually the outsider, for once I can be of help." Kitty looked at Cordelia. "You know her. Would it help if we called on her together? Oh, I'm forgetting about your ball tomorrow night."

"I wouldn't let a little thing like giving a ball stand in the way of an investigation. But in Sophia's case I don't think I'd help," Cordelia said. "She still sees me as a scandal. I think I can do better calling on her sister Pippa and seeing what she can tell me about Sophia and Captain Blayney."

Kitty looked at Mélanie. "Would you like me to take you to call on Sophia?"

Mélanie smiled at her friend. "Can you doubt it?"

"I can't say she'll confide in me. She doesn't strike me as the sort who's likely to confide in anyone. But she's also too well bred, I think, to show us the door."

"Sometimes that's all it takes," Mélanie said. "Perhaps—" She broke off as a rap on the front door echoed through the library. Brisk and decisive, even through the thick walls. Malcolm pushed himself to his feet. "I know that knock."

"So do I." Julien gave a cross between a wry smile and a grimace. "Probably inevitable. I'll let you do the honors as we're in your house."

Malcolm went into the hall. A few moments later, he returned to the library with Hubert Mallinson, his, Kitty's, and Julien's former spymaster, Julien's uncle, Mélanie's former opponent. And now, in the fight against the Elsinore League, the reluctant ally of all of them.

"I might have known I'd find you all here. Convenient, actually." Carfax's—Hubert's, Mélanie could never get used to it—gaze swept the small group gathered in the Berkeley Square library. "I take it you were all at the Chat Gris tonight?"

"Not all of us." Laura gave him a cup of coffee. "Someone had to mind the hearth. I'd love to say it was Malcolm and Julien, but not in this case."

"Hmph." Hubert set his hat and gloves on the library table and moved to one of the Queen Anne chairs. "I was suspicious the moment I heard there was a brawl at the Chat Gris, before the bodies were discovered."

"How the devil did you know it was us?" Julien demanded. "I kissed Davenport rather to make sure you wouldn't."

Hubert's brows drew together. "I thought that was Lady Cordelia."

"I was here with Laura," Cordelia said.

"Thank God I can still shock you, Uncle."

"Who says I'm shocked?" Carfax accepted a cup of coffee from Mélanie. "A good agent should be prepared to kiss the devil himself."

"Thank you," Harry murmured.

Hubert took a drink of coffee. "And I'd have thought you were all broadminded enough not to find it shocking in the least. If you're assuming I'm narrow minded, that's very short-sighted of you."

"An excellent point," Kitty said. "I've never found you narrow minded in the least."

"Thank you, my dear. You've always been eminently sensible. Part of why I was so glad Julien married you."

"You never fail to amaze me," muttered Julien, who'd been convinced his uncle hadn't wanted him to do anything of the sort and would try to stop the marriage.

"Hmm." Hubert looked at Julien, then at Kitty, then at Harry, then settled back in his chair. "I admit I probably wouldn't have been suspicious if I hadn't known a League agent was at the Chat Gris tonight." He took another drink of coffee. "Can someone give me some brandy or whisky or whatever I have no doubt the rest of you have in your coffee?"

Malcolm grinned and moved to the drinks table.

"What were you after tonight?" Hubert asked.

"Do you really expect us to answer that?" Malcolm poured brandy into Hubert's coffee.

"We're supposed to be allies now," Hubert said.

"Like when you tried to buy papers from the League four months ago?" Malcolm stoppered the decanter.

"That was different." Hubert took a drink of brandy-laced coffee. "That was politics."

"And the League aren't?" Malcolm returned to the other Queen Anne chair and settled himself beside Mélanie.

"Not in the same way."

Malcolm picked up his own coffee. "We could debate that."

Hubert settled back in his chair. "We're going to need to be allies now. Who was with Captain Blayney when he died?"

"None of us," Julien said.

"Interesting." Hubert regarded his nephew. "I thought I'd detected your handiwork."

"I'd have managed it much more neatly."

"There is that." Hubert's gaze swept the room. "One of you went upstairs with him."

"I did," Kitty said. "He was alive when I left. But drugged." She looked at Julien. "Roth already knows."

"Your talents are undimmed, Kitty," Hubert said. "I'm glad to see being Lady Carfax isn't holding you back."

"Thank you. Though I don't think you're being entirely forthcoming, sir."

"On the contrary. There aren't many agents of your calibre. I hate to see those talents go to waste, whoever's uses they're being put to. I don't want you to get rusty, in case we need you again."

"You said the same to me once," Malcolm said.

"And I meant it."

"Kitty and I both stand warned." Malcolm flashed a look at Kitty.

"You and Kitty both have your priorities straight."

"So we do. It remains to be seen whether that will ever include putting our talents to use in your service."

"We're talking about Britain's service."

"Who says you can tell the difference?" Malcolm inquired.

Hubert settled his shoulders against the high chair back. "I never do things in my own service. You know that."

"Ha." Julien tossed down a swallow of coffee.

"And just now we're talking about fighting the League, which is broader even than Britain's interests." Hubert met Roth's gaze. "I know you've been an ally of the people in this room at the expense of Conant and Sidmouth. I'm assuming that for present circumstance I count as one in this room."

Roth inclined his head. Sir Nathaniel Conant was the chief magistrate of Bow Street. Lord Sidmouth was the home secretary, to whom Conant reported. "If the Rannochs are working with you, then I am as well, sir. To the same degree."

Hubert's mouth twitched. "You're a brave man, Roth. And probably dangerous."

Roth gave a faint smile. "Thank you, sir."

Hubert's gaze settled on Julien. "What about the man found knifed in the alley beside the Chat Gris?"

"That wasn't me either. We were all attacked. One of the attackers pulled a knife on Kitty. Kitty and I disarmed him and I got a knife to his throat, but one of his confederates killed him before I could persuade him to talk." Julien stared at the cup in his hand as though the gold rim held secrets. "Yes, I realize I'm getting rusty."

"I wouldn't quite say that." Hubert took another drink of coffee. "What were the League trying to buy from Blayney?"

"Papers," Malcolm said in an easy voice.

"Yes, I generally assumed that. I'm not entirely rusty either. What sort of papers?" Hubert's gaze went from Malcolm to Julien to Mélanie to Kitty. "We are supposed to be allies."

"In some things," Malcolm said.

"Against the League. So can I assume this situation is like last June and crossed over into the case against the queen?"

"Not apparently. Not so far." Malcolm shot a look at Mélanie, then at Julien. Mélanie nodded and saw Julien do the same. Malcolm took a sip of coffee. Mélanie, curled beside him in the chair, wondered if Hubert knew just how carefully Malcolm weighed each step he took in the complex chess game between them. "On the surface, the papers appear to be letters or a diary or memoir written by a woman who knew Alexander Radford abroad," Malcolm said.

Hubert set his cup down. Coffee and brandy spattered in the saucer. Which was about as close as Hubert came to showing he'd been disturbed. "Do the papers reveal who Radford is?"

"The papers Blayney had on him tonight don't reveal much of anything except that the writer knew him," Kitty said. "They were just to prove he had the real goods, we think."

"And he either didn't have the rest of the papers in his lodgings, or someone else got to them before we searched," Malcolm said. "The lodgings had definitely been searched. Torn apart." He settled back in the chair beside Mélanie. "We were giving even money on your being behind it."

"If I had the papers, I'd hardly be here now," Hubert pointed out.

"No, but you might be if you'd searched for them and failed to find them," Julien said.

"My agents don't tear things apart. You should know that."

"You've lost a lot of your good people. You can't afford to be so picky. And we don't know how many people searched Blayney's rooms tonight."

"I didn't know of the existence of these papers until just now." Hubert adjusted his spectacles. "Talking of being rusty." He reached for his coffee. "Who's the woman who wrote these papers?"

"We don't know." Malcolm looked at Kitty.

Kitty pulled the papers from her gown, where she had hidden them when she changed, without embarrassment. She held them out to show Hubert without relinquishing her hold on them.

Hubert smiled at her over his spectacles. "You've become so cautious."

"I was always cautious where you were concerned, sir. And now I don't have to worry about working for you."

"I thought we agreed you'd call me Hubert." Hubert adjusted his spectacles and quickly scanned the pages as Kitty flipped through them. "You're right, they don't reveal much."

"Do you recognize the hand?" Malcolm asked.

"No." Hubert looked up at him. "I truly don't. Though there are a number of agents whose hands I wouldn't recognize." He settled back in his chair. "I don't know much about Blayney. A half-pay officer?"

"Son of a Shropshire clergyman. Always with a money-making scheme, according to his brother and a friend we spoke with tonight."

"Oh, God. Is his brother the one who publishes the *Clarion*?" Hubert's fingers froze on his right earpiece. "I suppose you're friends with Edmund Blayney."

"No, but Raoul is."

"Of course he is. Well, that might prove useful." Hubert frowned. "Where is O'Roarke, by the way?"

"Coordinating," Laura said. "He should be back in a day or so."

"I assume he's coordinating somewhere other than Spain if he'll be back so soon. Interesting. And no, you haven't revealed anything dangerous. You never do, Laura." Hubert set down his cup. "Still difficult to work out how a half-pay officer came by such sensitive information. I assume you've talked to Edmund Blayney by now. What else did you learn?"

"His print shop was searched as well. Presumably by someone who thought he had his brother's papers," Malcolm said. "But he doesn't seem to have done. Their father held his living from the late Lord Pendarves. They grew up on the Pendarves estate playing with the children."

Hubert's brows drew together. "Was James Blayney still close to the Langdons?"

"Not a great deal, apparently," Malcolm said. He did not lightly reveal secrets about other people's marriages.

Hubert looked at Julien. "You dealt with the younger Pendarves."

Julien leaned back in his chair and crossed his legs. "I don't know what you're talking about."

"Don't play games, Julien. You were working for Talleyrand."

Julien picked up his coffee cup. "No comment."

"Idiot," Hubert said, with surprising affection. "I'll admit I applaud your loyalty to your employers. But actually, Talleyrand told me himself. When we saw him last year."

"You mean when we were cleaning up your plot about the dauphin," Julien said.

"Russia," Hubert said in repressive tones. "When Tsar Alexander and Grand Duchess Catherine were here in '14."

"Yes." Julien's voice was easy, but his gaze was perhaps slightly more armored than usual. He looked at the others. "In '14, during the peace celebrations when Bonaparte went to Elba and the tsar and the grand duchess were here." He looked at Carfax. "I didn't think you knew about that."

"I knew you were in London. I didn't see any reason to interfere. I suspected it had something to do with the Russians. Frankly, I didn't mind Talleyrand's getting information. It takes more than one country to control Tsar Alexander." Hubert leaned further back and tented his fingers together. "Pendarves was tasked to support the Russian delegation while they were here. Make sure they felt important, answer questions, smooth ruffled feathers. It wasn't his fault the visit went badly. The regent didn't like being outshone by Russian royalty any more than he now likes being outshone by his own wife. But Pendarves's role made him an excellent source of information."

"Have you spoken with him since Blayney's murder?" Hubert asked.

"It's only been a few hours."

"You've spoken with a number of other people in those hours, it seems."

"There's no reason to think Pendarves should even come into this," Julien said. "He hasn't been close to Blayney since they were children, according to his brother."

"No, I suppose not. Would he recognize you now?"

"I'm not sure. I've been in the same room with him in Parliament and at Brooks's and he hasn't seemed to."

"Perhaps for the best. Though it could still be a useful connection." Hubert frowned. "Still trying to make out how Blayney might have come by the papers. What are you doing to recover them?"

"As we trace Blayney's movements, we'll get more ideas of where he might have hidden them," Malcolm said. "Or who might have taken them."

"Best to have all of us working on it."

"If you get any leads, for God's sake share them with us, Uncle Hubert," Julien said. "The last thing we need is to deal with your minions on top of everything else."

"We need to recover the papers," Carfax said. "And you're best positioned to do it. I'd be a fool not to render any assistance possible. Whatever you all think of me, I don't think any of you would call me a fool."

"Not precisely in those words," Julien said. "But I wouldn't say you're good at letting others do your work for you."

"On the contrary." Carfax settled his elbows on the chair arms and reached for his coffee. "If you can get them to do it satisfactorily, it can be highly efficient. Could I have a bit more brandy, Malcolm?"

CHAPTER 8

"**I** think I am going to have to talk to Pendarves." Julien frowned into his whisky-laced coffee. He, Kitty, Mélanie, and Malcolm had lingered in the library after Malcolm saw Carfax and Roth out and the others went upstairs. He'd made a remark about finishing their drinks, but Kitty was quite sure her husband wanted to talk. Just as she was sure the Davenports and Laura had sensed that when they went upstairs. "Given that we now know Blayney had a penchant for blackmail," Julien continued. "We don't know he tried it on Pendarves, but it's a possibility. And I also feel I should warn him."

"You think he's ripe for blackmail?" Mélanie set down her cup. "Julien, was Pendarves an agent?"

"No. Not that I know of." Julien turned his cup in his hand. "One can never be sure, but I'd be quite surprised if he proved to have been an agent. As Uncle Hubert said, Pendarves was working with the Russian delegation in '14."

"I remember," Malcolm said. "I was in a number of meetings with the Russian delegation, but I didn't work with them anything as closely as Pendarves did." He looked at Julien. "Did I see you?"

Julien gave a faint smile. "We were at one or two of the same receptions."

"And at Ascot," Mélanie said.

"I wasn't sure you noticed."

"Unlike Malcolm I'm used to seeing you in disguise."

Julien took a drink of coffee. "I'll confess the challenge of being back in Britain lent interest to what wasn't a very complicated assignment. Talleyrand wanted to know what the Russians and British were talking about in hopes of keeping them from making an alliance at the expense of France—and Europe, he'd argue, given Alexander's ambitions. He wanted me to keep track of the negotiations and of what was happening behind the scenes. Pendarves was spending a lot of time attending to the tsar and Grand Duchess Catherine, so he was an excellent source of information on what was happening in their rooms at the Pultney Hotel."

Julien was prevaricating uncharacteristically. Even Kitty wasn't quite sure why, though she was beginning to suspect.

"Julien, are you saying you had a liaison with Lady Pendarves?" Mélanie asked. "Or with—"

"Quite," Julien said.

"Well, that complicates things," Kitty said.

Julien met her gaze with a crooked smile. "Mmm."

Kitty smoothed a crease from her gown. "I was wondering which of us would be in this situation first."

"Sorry, sweetheart."

"No need to apologize. But you should undoubtedly warn Pendarves. Would he recognize you?"

"I'm not sure. I was telling Uncle Hubert the truth about that. My hair was a different color and I had my brows darkened and I was using a different name. But we were certainly closer than Uncle Hubert realizes." Julien kicked his foot against the chair leg. "Uncle Hubert's story of my working secretly for crown and country all these years is supposed to explain this sort of thing in my past. But in this case—"

"Is there anything in writing?" Kitty asked. "Or anyone who may have seen you?"

"When have you ever known me to put anything in writing?" Julien said. "Or let anyone see anything I didn't want them to?"

"Just being cautious, my darling. But there must have been others before you. No doubt going back to when Pendarves and Jamie Blayney knew each other. So if Blayney was given to blackmail—"

"Yes," Julien said. "That's why I need to speak with Pendarves. If Blayney was amassing blackmail documents, he could have information about Pendarves that someone got hold of tonight, along with the papers about Alexander Radford by the mystery woman." He tossed down the last of his whisky and coffee. "And if Jamie Blayney was already trying to blackmail Pendarves, Pendarves had a motive to have killed him. I should see him tonight before he gets the news from someone else. And because we don't know who else got into Blayney's papers. It's just not the easiest thing—"

"To admit one's been spying on someone," Mélanie said.

"As you say."

Malcolm watched Julien as Julien set down his cup and pushed himself to his feet. "Are you all right?"

"Hardly the first time I've interrogated a suspect." Julien reached for his coat, which was still draped over a chair from before they'd gone to the Chat Gris. "Whatever he may have done, I'm quite sure Pendarves isn't the most dangerous person I've faced."

"No, but it's not easy when a suspect is also—"

"An ex-lover?" Julien shrugged on his coat. "I imagine you know about that. At least, to the extent you ever suspected Kitty. God, that must have been awful. Sorry, old chap." He settled the coat on his shoulders. "This is nothing in comparison. Don't worry, I'll manage. This liaison was conducted in the course of a mission, after all. Awkward, but what agent hasn't learned to be pragmatic in the face of awkwardness?"

Kitty followed her husband into the hall. "I'm sorry, Julien."

"You're sorry?" He looked at her in inquiry and apology as he pulled on his gloves. His face was insouciant in that way it only got when he was holding things at bay. It had taken her years to learn to read the signs.

"It's uncomfortable," she said.

"I'll manage." He tugged on the second glove. "I'm sorry for putting you through this."

"I might say the same." She walked up to him, pulled out her handkerchief, and wiped off the traces of eyeblacking and rouge on his face. "Do you want a waistcoat and cravat?"

"No, a coat will make me presentable enough. It's one of the advantages of being Lord Carfax. I can get away with things."

She smoothed the front of his coat, and set her hands on his shoulders. "It seems to be a night for sending each other off with ex-lovers in one way or another."

"Yes, well." He lifted her hands from his shoulders and kissed them, each in turn. "If it's any comfort, I was never in love with Pendarves."

"But it was more complicated than some of them."

"My darling." His gaze settled on her own, glinting with ironic honesty. "How do you know?"

Kitty took his face between her hands and pulled his mouth down to her own. "I know you."

DESPITE THE HOUR, a liveried footman answered the door of the Pendarves house in Belgrave Square within seconds. Probably had been dozing on the bench just inside the door, Julien concluded. None of the eccentric business of the family's answering the door themselves after a certain hour, which the Rannochs had adopted after their time in Italy, and which a number of their friends copied. When Julien and Kitty had moved into Carfax House, it had never occurred to Julien to do anything differently. He could still remember the perplexed reaction of the long-time Carfax butler and footmen. But they now seemed quite happy with the arrangement.

The Pendarves footman didn't blink at the late hour or Julien's lack of a cravat and waistcoat. He took Julien's rain-spattered hat and conducted him down a marble-tiled hall, not unlike that in Carfax House, to an oak-paneled library, also not unlike that in Carfax House, though slightly smaller. The whole house was reminiscent of Carfax House. The same post-Civil War era bones, the same updates, obviously by Robert Adam, to mantels and ceilings and friezes, similar arrangement of the rooms, with the library on the ground floor at the front of the house and the study behind it, similar mix of Sheraton and Hepplewhite furniture with Jacobean and Elizabethan pieces brought in from the country house, and modern additions like Chinese and Japanese cabinets and tables that were lacquered or inlaid with ebony or zebrawood.

Unlike at Carfax House, there were no toys or small boots or coats lying about, though Pendarves had two or three children. Perhaps more now. Julien frowned, sifting through memories. Pendarves had mentioned his children with restrained affection, but it hadn't been something they dwelt on. It hadn't been something Julien had thought about a great deal. He wouldn't have noticed the lack of evidence of children in the public part of the house six years ago. He'd been a different person then. In so many ways. Odd, when Leo and Timothy and Genny were such a fundamental part of his life now.

The Pendarves library was bare of personal touches of any sort. The woodwork and gilding were handsome, the books plentiful, bound in the finest morocco, and an excellent selection of titles from what Julien could make out. But the furniture, upholstered in the leather and velvet one would expect in a library, looked little used. Pendarves was fond of books, but this did not appear to be a room he or his family relaxed in. Assuming Pendarves relaxed at all. From their prior acquaintance, Julien was not at all sure he did. Except on seemingly rare occasions when he let himself indulge his true impulses.

The door opened, with the well-oiled soundlessness of a prosperous house run by a plentiful staff. Julien turned and faced the man who had been his lover.

A shock of familiarity went through him. Pendarves's eyes were a familiar blue that somehow defied the contained set of his face. He was tall, half a head taller than Julien. His bearing was rigidly correct, as though he'd been born in a starched cravat and tightly buttoned waistcoat. An appearance belied by curling hair, the color of burnt umber, that would never quite behave. Julien could remember running his fingers through that hair.

Julien hesitated, gaze locked on Pendarves's own, thrown back to a time when he'd still sold his services. When whom he slept with had been part a question of business, part a matter of novelty. When novelty and choice had both intrigued him. When he hadn't been—well, besotted came to mind, but even more fundamentally, when he'd been able to entertain the thought of anyone but Kitty in his bed. Odd how all that had changed. When he'd met Pendarves, a new mission had still quickened his blood. Well, that hadn't changed. But he'd grown a bit more fastidious about what he'd do. And in the service of what. And he couldn't imagine intimacy with anyone but Kitty. Or even the counterfeit of intimacy.

"It's been a long time," Pendarves said.

Julien leaned one hand on a Hepplewhite chair back. "I wasn't sure you recognized me."

"I wasn't sure I was supposed to admit it." Pendarves stepped forwards but checked himself after a few paces. He'd always let Julien make the first move. In any number of ways. Odd, Julien realized. He always let Kitty make the first move. A legacy of what he knew of her past, but it had started before he was aware of her past. A certain care for what she wanted. A reticence about what he could expect. Fear, perhaps, of botching the whole thing at the start.

"I recognized you the first time I saw you in Parliament," Pendarves said, with the formality of one choosing his words with care. "From some feet away, in fact." He smiled and a bit of the old Pendarves broke through. "I suppose it's all right to admit that now? I assumed I wasn't supposed to say anything. Considering the stories that have been going round about your activities on the Continent—"

Oh God. Uncle Hubert and his schemes. Which, as usual, worked better than Julien credited. "I was—"

"It was to do with the Russian delegation, wasn't it?" Pendarves said. "Your needing information. It's all right." He gave another smile, half ironic, half self-deprecating. "I always suspected you had some reason for wanting to get close to me. I'm no spy, but I should have been better on my guard. Or perhaps I didn't want to ask questions."

Julien swallowed the bitterness that welled up on his tongue. God help him. When had he learned what guilt was? And how the hell had Mélanie managed this for so long? "You're too good a man for this sort of intrigue, Pendarves."

"I'm in politics. Some would say that means I live in the gutter." Pendarves gave another smile, this one twisted. "I should be relieved you were working for Carfax—the former Carfax— and not someone worse."

"That's one way of looking at it." Odd to think of Uncle Hubert as cover. No need for Pendarves to know he'd been working for Talleyrand. At least not at this point. "I'm sorry, I know it's late," Julien said. Not that he hadn't called late during their past association, though he'd been more likely to climb in through a window.

"I don't retire early. As you know." Pendarves gestured to two carved chairs by the fire. "Can I get you something? Whisky?"

"Thank you." It would give the conversation a touch of normalcy he could play on. And he needed it. Far more than he wanted to admit.

"Perhaps I should have guessed from your fondness for whisky." Pendarves filled two glasses. "That you were British."

"I don't know about that. I know any number of those born on the Continent who can appreciate a good highland malt." Including his wife and Mélanie Rannoch. Julien took the glass Pendarves was holding out to him.

"It must be a relief," Pendarves said. "To be home."

Julien bit back a laugh. That was oddly true, but only because Britain and Carfax House had become home, thanks to Kitty and the children, in ways they never had been before. "I'm very fortunate in my life," he said with unfeigned sincerity. "I never thought to be back here, and certainly not to be back here under such happy circumstances." As Mélanie said, it was amazing how often one could fall back on the truth. He dropped down in a carved velvet-covered chair. The sort of chair everyone—no, not everyone at all, not most of the population, but most everyone he had grown up with—had had in their family for generations. "I'm constantly amazed that it has worked out."

Pendarves seated himself in the chair opposite Julien. "My felicitations on your marriage."

"Thank you." Julien had responded to those words dozens of times, in dozens of drawing rooms and libraries and ballrooms, since he and Kitty had married. But not to an ex-lover. Which was surprising, actually, considering the number of ex-lovers he had.

Pendarves hesitated. "It looks to be a happy one."

"It is. Something I never thought to find." Julien stared at the candlelight playing off his glass. How odd to speak the unvarnished truth. "It can happen. Though as recently as a year and a half ago, I'd have sworn it wasn't possible."

"I'm glad. Glad you've found it is possible, that is." Pendarves hesitated again. "I'm very fond of my wife. I thought when I married her it would be enough for me."

It was more than Pendarves had said about his wife during the time he and Julien had been—together, if the word could be used for what had passed between them. If the word "together" could be used for Julien's relationship with anyone before Kitty, which he wasn't at all sure it could. But Pendarves's very protectiveness round his wife had told Julien a great deal. A great deal that perhaps Julien hadn't noted as much as he should have done, given his own thoughts at the time. And that unfortunately strengthened Pendarves's motive to have got rid of Jamie Blayney, should Blayney have threatened his family. "There are all different sorts of marriages," Julien said. "Until recently, I never thought to attempt it myself. But Kitty's enough for me. In all sorts of ways. I only hope I prove to be enough for her."

Pendarves gave a faint smile. "I shouldn't imagine you have cause to worry."

"You haven't met my wife. She's brilliant and quite remarkable and wonderfully self-sufficient. It was a distinct battle to persuade her to consider marriage at all. Not because of me so much as because of general principles. Difficult to persuade a woman into an institution in which she gives up so much of her freedom. At least legally."

Pendarves frowned. The frown of a man for whose sisters marriage had been the only possible aim in life. "But without marriage—"

"Women retain a good deal more control. Especially widows in comfortable circumstances, as Kitty was. A wife gives up control of her person, her fortune, unless she ties legal bows round it, control of her children. Quite unconscionable, really. I'd hesitate to do it myself. Fortunately for me, Kitty had at least a moment of blind sentimentality. She told me she trusted me, which is perhaps the most amazing thing anyone has ever said to me. And she was willing to risk it. Risk marrying me. Even though it meant becoming Lady Carfax."

Pendarves raised his brows. "Surely, to be Countess Carfax—"

"If you knew Kitty, you'd understand it's not something she'd jump at. She had a very good life without me." Julien took a drink of whisky and settled back in his chair. "But perhaps that makes marriage easier. One doesn't expect to find everything in the other person. I'd never want to burden anyone I loved with the need to provide everything to make me happy."

"But you are happy." Pendarves made it not quite a question.

"Yes." It was not something Julien was used to thinking about, but the answer came unbidden. Amazing, he was happy as Lord Carfax. Despite the challenges of that life. Despite the echoes of the past.

"I'm glad." Pendarves looked into the depths of his glass. "I know my life—our family life—I know who I am—presents challenges for my wife. I've tried to protect her as best I can."

"Are you sure she wants to be protected?"

"Surely—" Pendarves's head jerked up. He stared at Julien. "Can you imagine what the truth would do to her?"

"That depends on a number of things. Including if she's in love with you."

Pendarves passed a hand over his face. "We never talked about that. No. I suppose it was implied at the start. One used the words, at least. They're almost as much a part of a proposal as the actual marriage vow. 'Will you make me the happiest of men?' Every man is supposedly the happiest of men on his wedding day. I don't think Catherine expects romance from me now. I'm not even sure she'd want it. It might—er—seem like a demand. But she does see me in a certain way." He straightened his shoulders against the red velvet of the chair. "In any case, that's my problem. And of course, none of that is why you're here. Our past—association—isn't why you're here."

"No." Julien's fingers curved round the chair arm. "James Blayney was found knifed to death in a St. Giles tavern this evening."

Shock, seemingly genuine, filled Pendarves's gaze. "Good God. Do you know—"

"We know very little. We're attempting to learn more."

"You're working with the Rannochs."

"We're all assisting Bow Street."

Pendarves took a drink of whisky. "He was always reckless, but I never thought—you know we grew up together?"

"Malcolm Rannoch saw his brother tonight."

Pendarves nodded. "Haven't seen Edmund in even longer than Jamie. Odd, when we were once all so close."

"Did Blayney know?" Julien hesitated, searching for the right words. "About your past?"

Pendarves's gaze locked on his own. "You mean about my depravity?"

Julien pushed himself half out of his chair, then sat back. "You're too sensible to use such words about yourself."

Pendarves's gaze remained steady. "It's a plain term."

"It's nothing of the sort."

Pendarves tossed down the last of his whisky. "There's no reason to think Blayney knew anything about us."

"I'm not concerned about that." Julien set his own glass on the table beside his chair. "I am concerned about how he might have tried to use personal details against you."

Pendarves flinched, but met Julien's gaze. "I wouldn't succumb to blackmail to protect myself."

"Or to protect your wife and children?"

Pendarves drew a hard breath. "Not even to protect them."

Julien held his former lover's gaze. "But Blayney did try?"

Pendarves pushed himself to his feet and strode back to the drinks table. He refilled his glass, tossed down half the contents, refilled it again, crossed to Julien and refilled his glass. "Jamie was born with the gift of charm. A gift that quite bypassed me." Pendarves set the decanter down on the table between their chairs, rattling the crystal. "And no, I never fancied Jamie. Difficult to imagine fancying someone who's been an imp in one's life since you were both in leading strings. And I certainly never confided in him about my romantic life or anything else. I suppose we might have been called playfellows. Maybe even friends." Pendarves took a drink of whisky and frowned over the rim of the glass. "Yes, I'd have called him a friend when we were boys. I enjoyed playing with him. I envied how at ease he was. I worried about the trouble he got into. I knew my father was fonder of him than he was of me. I don't mean that as a complaint. It's a statement of fact. Jamie was far more like Papa than I was. Papa had an ease of manner and a way of persuading people to his thinking that I quite lack. Jamie enjoyed riding and shooting and all the pastimes my father enjoyed. But even when I thought of Jamie as a friend, it would never have occurred me to confide in him." Pendarves swirled the rest of his drink in his glass and dropped back into his chair. "For one thing, we never talked enough about me for the subject to come up." He set his glass down on the table between their chairs, a few inches from Julien's. "But Jamie knew. About me. Or at least guessed. Not sure how. I don't think you'll be shocked to know I haven't had a very varied career. I don't find intimacy easy with anyone. Even my wife. Especially my wife. And I knew the risks of indulging my—inclinations."

"So how do you know Blayney knew?" Julien kept his voice even.

"I didn't realize it until a few years ago, when he came round asking for money. When I refused—because it was far from the first time he'd asked—he worked hints that he knew—about me —into the conversation. Without directly threatening anything."

Julien felt himself give an inwards flinch. Odd. And foolish. It had been likely from the start. That was why he'd come, after all. "Clever. He must have known if he'd directly threatened you, you'd have thrown it back in his face."

"Yes, probably. I don't lose my temper easily, but when pushed to it—" Pendarves looked at his hand. His fingers had curled inwards. Julien had seen him spar at Jackson's once. He was very creditable with his fives.

"So you paid him?" Julien asked.

"I came up with something. Not what he wanted. But enough to send him on his way with things still on an amicable footing between us. And the next time he asked, I did the same. Before he had to threaten."

"Did he have proof?" Julien sat forwards in his chair. "Anything in writing?"

"No." Pendarves reached for his glass and then froze, fingers taut round the crystal. "That is, he certainly never said—"

"Because Blayney's things have been searched. By Malcolm Rannoch and Jeremy Roth, a Bow Street runner he works with. No one found anything of yours, but someone ransacked them first. Perhaps more than one person."

Pendarves's gaze locked on Julien's own. "I don't—commit things to writing. But—"

"Your sister might."

Pendarves drew back in his chair. "Oh, God, I suppose I should have guessed you'd find out." He hesitated, as though waiting for Julien to confirm what he knew.

"We heard Blayney fell out with your father over your sister Sophia. Lady Prescott."

Pendarves released his breath. Almost as though he were relieved to have it in the open. "Yes. Father'd always been able to forgive Jamie a great deal, but he drew the line at that. I didn't even know about it until after he'd confronted Jamie and sent him packing back to the Peninsula. He warned me we needed to steer clear of Jamie, but we couldn't make a complete public break or people would ask questions."

"So you continued to meet Blayney and receive him. And you gave him money."

Pendarves picked up his glass and looked into it. "From time to time. Never a great deal. But enough, if I'm honest, to keep him from being a threat." He tossed down a drink. "And yes, I'm more than a bit disgusted with myself."

Julien watched his former lover. Who might also be his friend, though at the time they'd been lovers he wouldn't have admitted to having friends. "It's not easy facing exposure. It's all very well to disdain ridiculous conventions, and thank God you don't deny who you are. But you shouldn't be disgusted with yourself for considering what the revelation of the truth would do to your family. You could be faulted if you *didn't* consider it."

Pendarves's gaze settled on Julien's face. Almost like the brush of fingers. "You didn't used to talk like this."

"Yes, well, being a father and husband has changed me. As have other things. And the risks are undeniable. I could see that my wife was aware of it tonight."

"Your wife knows?" Pendarves said on a note of shock.

"I'm sorry. It was unavoidable. She won't tell anyone. She's an agent herself. There are few people I'd trust so well to keep secrets."

"Yes, but—" Pendarves stared at Julien, gaze wide with incomprehension. "How long—how on earth did you—"

"Oh, she's known about my—past for some time. From the first, really. I never tried to hide it. But I didn't enumerate my past lovers any more than I expected her to enumerate hers. Much better to leave that in the past, unless the past intrudes on current matters. Which happens more often than you'd think.

Kitty didn't know about you until tonight. I may not appear to have a great deal of delicacy, but I do try to respect friends' privacy."

"And you can simply go on—"

"It's in the past," Julien said. "That helps. Kitty's not much concerned with who was in my bed before we met—before we —committed, I suppose you'd say—any more than I'm concerned with who was in hers." He met Pendarves's confused gaze and gave a twisted smile. "Probably franker than any conversation you've had with your wife. But Kitty and I are quite different people."

"Yes." Pendarves passed a hand over his face. "I can see that."

"On the other hand, I'd be rather distressed at the thought of anyone else in her bed now."

"My dear fellow. She's your wife."

"That doesn't seem to concern a number of our colleagues in the Lords. And the Commons. And the world in general. And more power to those for whom the arrangement works. But I realized it wouldn't suit me. I don't intend to have anyone else in my bed either. In fact, I find I don't want to."

Pendarves met his gaze for a long moment while memories danced between them. "I didn't ask."

"No, you wouldn't." Julien returned Pendarves's gaze. "I love my wife, and I have no desire to be with anyone but her. But I wouldn't give up my memories for the world."

Pendarves gave a wry smile. "It was an assignment."

"It wasn't just that," Julien said, in a moment that revealed more than he was wont to show to anyone. "Speaking as one who knows the difference."

Pendarves swallowed and released his breath. "Thank you."

"It's the truth. It's part of why I came tonight. Because I was concerned Blayney's death could expose you to comment and worse. I wanted to warn you right away."

"I appreciate that." Pendarves reached for his glass, but his fingers stilled on the crystal. "Part?"

Julien picked up his own glass and took a sip. "Blayney was murdered. We need information from those who knew him."

"Of course. And I've admitted he was blackmailing me without either of us ever acknowledging it. Which doesn't mean I didn't find it tiresome. That he might not have escalated it or I might not have decided to put a stop to it without his escalating it." Pendarves met Julien's gaze, his own clear and steady and yet harder than Julien had ever seen it. "In other words, I've just given myself an excellent motive for murder."

CHAPTER 9

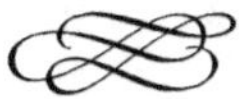

itty dragged a cloth dipped in face cream over the blacking round her eyes. It was taking longer than usual to clean her face with the heavier cosmetics. And things weren't where she was used to, though Mélanie had laid everything out for her on the brown-veined ivory marble top of the pretty satinwood dressing table in the bedchamber they were occupying in Berkeley Square. Mélanie was the perfect hostess. She was perfect at so many things. It would be so easy to dislike her if she weren't such a good friend.

Kitty glanced at the cradle where her toddler Genny was sleeping, then looked back in the glass. Her own eyes stared back at her. It must the traces of blacking that made them appear so shadowed, and the flickering light of the tapers beside the glass that put such a haunted look in their depths. She started to dip the cloth in the rose-flowered bowl again when a movement caught her eyes in the glass. Her husband leaned in the doorway. She wasn't sure how long he'd been there. Julien moved like a cat.

Kitty turned round and met his gaze. "Did you see him?"

"Mmm." Julien moved to the dressing table and put his hands

on her shoulders. "I'd forgot how difficult it is to confront someone one's deceived. Or maybe I simply haven't done it much. Fortunately or unfortunately, he seems to believe Uncle Hubert's story that I was undercover for Britain and assumes I was getting information for Uncle Hubert about the Russians. I didn't tell him that the truth was worse—or perhaps better. He says Blayney didn't know about our relationship."

Kitty released her breath.

Julien cupped her cheek. "Craven."

"You can't blame me for being worried about my husband."

"There are a lot of things people could hold against your husband." Julien dropped down on the dressing table bench and turned sideways to face her. "Fortunately, the proof is murky. But apparently Blayney did have knowledge of Pendarves's affairs that he tried to use against him. Did use against him. Apparently he made vague not-quite-threats that prompted Pendarves to lend him money for years."

"Affairs with whom?" She scanned his face.

"He didn't say."

"It gives them both a motive. Pendarves and his lover. Lovers, perhaps."

"Yes. I'll have to try to work it out of him. I don't think he's been pining for me, but I think our association probably meant more to him than it did to me. Poor devil. He's a good man." He gave a crooked smile. "I didn't used to talk that way. What have I come to?"

Kitty met her husband's gaze. "You like him."

"Yes, I do. He cares about his wife and can't tell her or their children the truth of who he is. He has the life David might have had. That Rupert would have if he hadn't managed to talk to Gaby." He tucked a curl behind her ear. "You're right, I do like Pendarves. And I kept thinking tonight—he doesn't have anyone he can be himself with. At least, not that I know of. Which makes what I have with you even more of a miracle."

"My love. It's a miracle in any number of ways. Not least because we're managing to make it work."

"Yes, I imagine a number of those at our wedding would have given even odds or worse.

"Oh, no. Our friends are very supportive. And rather more inclined to romantic delusions than they admit."

Julien pushed himself to his feet and poured two glasses of whisky from the decanter on the pier table by the windows. "Kind of them to leave us this."

"Mélanie thinks of everything."

"Mélanie went undercover as the perfect wife almost a decade ago. In many ways, she's just coming up for air." He put one of the glasses into her hand, then stared into his own glass. His brows were drawn, his gaze hooded, as though he didn't like what he saw in its depths.

Kitty pushed herself to her feet and touched his arm. "Darling?"

"I'm all right. It's not Pendarves."

"It's the earlier part of the night."

Julien took a drink of whisky and nodded, as though he didn't trust himself to meet her gaze. "It's just—been some time."

Kitty slid her arm round her husband. One night in Argentina, he'd killed a man in a knife brawl. A man who had been attacking both of them. She remembered the economy with which he'd pocketed his own knife, his brisk inquiry if she was all right, his professional disposition of the body. There'd been the briefest flash of acknowledgment in his eyes, but otherwise nothing to betray he was anything other than a professional who had done this countless times before. But a lot had changed since then. "You didn't kill him." She reached up to touch his face with her free hand. "You wouldn't have."

"No, that would have been foolish." Julien tossed down another drink of whisky. "We needed information. Which is why his companion killed him before we could get it. It's a long time since I've been that close to—anything of the sort. Not since—"

Not since a year ago, when he'd killed Malcolm's brother, Edgar Rannoch, who had been trying to kill Malcolm. Who had once taken Kitty by force. Whom Julien had known since they were boys. Whom Kitty had asked Julien to help her with on the night that had brought them back together and in a sense set them on the path to where they were today. That night had ended with their lying on her bed, both fully clothed, holding each other against demons past and present.

Kitty didn't say more but slipped her arm tighter round her husband. "It's not that I thought we were out of danger. It's not that I even wanted to be, frankly. But I didn't think we'd confront this so quickly. At least, I don't think we need worry being Lord and Lady Carfax will render us dull."

"Yes, we've managed to stake out our own territory." Julien took another drink of whisky. "Are you all right, Kitkat?"

"Oh, yes." Kitty took a sip from her own glass. "All he did was grab me and put a knife to my throat. I've been through far worse."

"That was enough. But it's not what I was thinking of." Julien laced his fingers through her own. "Perhaps it's just the fact that I'm replaying the events of tonight myself."

Kitty turned towards him. "Damn it, you know me too well. I don't particularly care for the idea that James Blayney is dead remotely because of me."

"We don't know that he is."

"Says the man who's brooding over the man who attacked me."

Julien frowned down at their clasped hands. "I suppose this is what it is to have a conscience."

"You've always had a conscience."

"A working conscience. It always seemed to me that Malcolm and Mélanie and O'Roarke—who has more scruples than anyone, much as he tries to deny it—spent far too much time dwelling on their past actions. But the devil of it is once one starts, one can't seem to stop." He glanced over at Genny's cradle.

"I know," Kitty said, "It's different, wondering what they'd think of you. But perhaps more wondering what you think of yourself."

Julien nodded. "Odd. I didn't used to care much what I thought of myself. On the whole, that was easier. And then there's the fact that I now have to worry about what my wife thinks of me."

Kitty tightened her fingers over his own. "I can't imagine why you would."

"Possibly because her opinion matters to me. Not that I'd admit it. Mostly for fear of sending her shrieking in the opposite direction."

"I love it when you talk nonsense," Kitty said. "Unless it's in the midst of a mission." She turned her head to kiss him, then said, "If I weren't Lady Carfax, Roth might have arrested me tonight."

"Roth's too sensible to have done that."

"He might not have had a choice. He arrested Laura."

"Laura was found with a pistol in a room with a murdered man. But you're right, if you were the woman you'd been playing tonight at the Chat Gris, there might have been pressure to arrest you."

Their conflicting worlds came rushing over them. As had always been inevitable. She'd just been hoping idiotishly that it wouldn't happen so soon. "It's not going to be easy for you if the truth comes out."

"I'm not beholden to anyone. They can say what they like about both of us. I'll still have a seat in the House of Lords. And it would drive Uncle Hubert mad. Which is a rather agreeable thought."

"Uncle Hubert knows perfectly well what we were both doing tonight."

"Oh, yes." Julien grinned. "He just counts on it not becoming public." His grin faded. "Odd how one's perspective can shift. There was a time when a mission that ended with one or two dead bodies wouldn't have given me pause."

"Nor me. But we're not in the midst of a war. And somehow —I feel more responsible."

"So do I." He tucked a strand of hair behind her ear. "Perhaps I don't like confronting the person I used to be."

"Oh, my darling, who does?" Kitty rested her head against his shoulder for a moment. "I certainly don't, at least at times. But we wouldn't be here without the people we used to be." She'd never been so aware of that as she had the night they'd reunited.

"A good point. And I'm immeasurably grateful for the woman you are. I'd be quite satisfied if I ever become half as worthwhile a person." He stared down at his fingers in her hair, the smile leaving his eyes. "Someone stabbed his comrade tonight, a handsbreadth away from both of us. Seemingly without a second thought. In the service of a mission. The man who did that is closer to the man I used to be than I care to admit. And the fact that I even talk about the man I *used* to be indicates quite a significant change."

Kitty tilted her head back and put her hand against the side of his face. "I know you, Julien. I know the person you've always been."

"That's more than I do, my darling. I'm still trying to work out who I am."

"I expect we're all doing that too. But I know a great deal about who you are. Among other things, my husband. Our children's father."

He put up his hand and gripped her own. "And I'm trying to do my best to live up to both."

CHAPTER 10

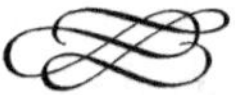

Chelsea was only three miles from Charing Cross yet still a rural village, surrounded by pastures where cows chomped at the grass, orchards in turning autumn gold, and meadows sloping down to the river. Malcolm pulled his curricle up before the Blayney house, a brick villa with door and window frames sorely in need of a fresh coat of paint, and a front garden that looked as though someone had stopped caring about it some months since. A child's wagon filled with rainwater lay forgot beside weed-choked flowerbeds that hadn't been pruned for autumn. He glanced sideways at Roth.

"Whatever Blayney was up to, he doesn't appear to have been supporting his wife," Roth said.

"No." Malcolm tethered the horses to the gatepost and they rang the bell. A maidservant of indeterminant years with tired eyes opened the door.

Malcolm offered her his card. "Is Mrs. Blayney at home?"

The maidservant nodded and led them down a cramped passage to an overstuffed sitting room choked with the smell of cheap potpourri.

"Blayney was living a very different life in London," Malcolm said. "Of course, they're hardly the only married couple to lead separate lives. We have the king and queen as an example."

Roth looked at a red-painted top that had rolled under the settee. "It's more complicated when there are children involved."

Malcolm shot a quick look at his friend. Roth's wife had left him and their two sons years ago. Malcolm still didn't understand the reasons. For all they had shared, Roth had never confided them, but the wound obviously cut deep. "Yes," Malcolm said, in an even voice. "This will be hard for Blayney's children." Easier, perhaps, paradoxically, if he'd been an entirely absent father.

"Do you think—" Roth bit back whatever he had been about to say at the sound of footsteps in the passage. The door opened, admitting a child's cry from the back reaches of the house and the person of Mrs. Blayney. She was a woman in her early thirties, with a rounded figure that might once have been trimly voluptuous, dark hair haphazardly dressed, and a face sunk into premature lines of disappointment.

Her gaze darted from Malcolm to Roth. "What can I do for you?"

"Mrs. Blayney." Malcolm inclined his head. "My name is Rannoch, and this is my friend Roth. I'm afraid we have some unfortunate news. It's about your husband."

She pushed the door shut, rattling the sagging frame. "You can skip the pleasantries. How much does he owe you?"

"You are mistaken, madam," Roth said. "Neither of us has met your husband."

"Ha. That wouldn't stop Jamie from owing someone money." Her gaze shot between them. "What is it?"

"Perhaps we could sit down?" Malcolm said.

She dropped into a chair and gestured to the settee opposite her, uncertainty in her gaze. "About the only time I hear from Jamie is when someone comes to me needing something. Or when Jamie comes to me needing something. What is it?" Her voice was sharp and weary but held an undercurrent of anxiety.

"I'm very sorry to tell you that your husband was killed last night, Mrs. Blayney," Roth said.

"Killed?" She blinked. Not with grief or shock or horror, but with disbelief. "He couldn't have been. Jamie is the most hard-headed man imaginable."

"I'm afraid there's no doubt, Mrs. Blayney," Roth said, in a gentle but inexorable voice. "Your husband was positively iden-tified. I realize this must be a great shock."

"But—" Her gaze shot between them. "Jamie survived the Peninsula. He survived Waterloo."

"As I did myself," Roth said. "It's a tragedy to get through that hell and meet death at home."

Her fist shot to her mouth. She doubled over, shoulders shaking.

Malcolm got to his feet and went to a cabinet that held an array of decanters. He poured a glass of sherry and put it into Mrs. Blayney's hand. Her fingers tightened round the glass, as though she were holding on to her sanity. She stared into the glass for a moment, like one searching for answers, then gulped down half the contents. "What happened?"

"We aren't entirely sure," Malcolm said. "He was knifed."

"In a fight?"

"No. He'd been drugged first." He hesitated a moment, but there was no point in avoiding the truth. "He was in a tavern called the Chat Gris."

"He was drugged at a table?"

"No." Malcolm returned to his chair and kept his voice level. "He was in a room upstairs."

She gave a rough laugh. "You mean the Chat Gris is a brothel."

"It seems to be something of the sort," Malcolm said in a

matter-of-fact voice. "Though apparently your husband was there to sell information."

"Jamie?" Her brows drew together. "You're telling me my husband went to a brothel to conduct business? That's rich."

"According to his friend Ned Royston, he had a number of schemes for making money," Roth said.

"That he did." She sobered and grimaced. "One more foolish than the last. But—What was he trying to sell this time?"

"Information, apparently," Malcolm said. "Some papers written by a lady whom we haven't been able to identify."

"Jamie was selling love letters?" Mrs. Blayney took another drink of sherry. "That's rich."

"They aren't love letters," Malcolm said. "They aren't letters at all. They appear to be some sort of diary or memoir."

"Jamie was selling a lady's secrets?" She frowned. "Was it one of the Langdons?"

"What makes you think so?" Roth asked in a neutral voice.

"Jamie grew up with them. And their brother. Their father was Lord Pendarves. Their brother is now."

"Yes, we learned that from Captain Blayney's brother last night."

"So you've talked to Edmund?" Her lip curled. "Can't imagine what he told you about me."

"He seemed concerned," Roth said.

"Yes, I suppose he would be." Her fingers slid along the stem of her glass. "Edmund has a core of decency that Jamie quite lacked, I'll give him that."

"He told us Captain Blayney had once been close to Sophia Langdon. Lady Prescott," Malcolm said.

Mrs. Blayney gave a grim smile. "You could put it that way. Being a gentleman, I suppose you would. She was mad for Jamie. More fool her."

"And Captain Blayney?" Malcolm asked.

Mrs. Blayney's brows drew together. "Jamie had a knack for

making a woman feel she was the love of his life. I'm sure he did that with Lady Prescott. And I think he'd more than half make himself believe it. Maybe Lady Prescott meant more to him than some. The affair was over before I met him, but she still meant something to him. But truly, I think it's more that he was obsessed with the whole family. With what they had that he didn't. He took me to see their grand house in Shropshire once, when we were first married. The family were all away and a housekeeper showed us about. Jamie showed me the rooms where he played as a child. The stair rail he slid down. Sometimes I'm not sure anything would satisfy him but having that house for himself. Which of course he was never going to."

"What makes you think he might have had a diary or memoirs belonging to one of the Langdon sisters?" Malcolm asked.

"Just that everything to do with that family seemed to fascinate him. Though if he wanted something for papers written by one of them, I'd think he'd want it from the family."

"The lady who wrote these papers lived or at least had lived on the Continent. Which I don't think is true of any of the Langdon sisters," Malcolm said. And the tone of that excerpt implied a woman less of a decorous wife than any of the sisters appeared on the surface.

Mrs. Blayney frowned, her gaze more focused. "Jamie hasn't been to the Continent since Waterloo." She took another drink of sherry. "At least, not that I know of. Sometimes he's gone long enough he could have been to Timbuktu for all I know. When did he get these papers?"

"We don't know," Roth said. "We were hoping you could tell us more."

"Me? Surely if it wasn't clear to you at the outset it's clear now that Jamie and I weren't on close terms. Which is putting it mildly. He hadn't spent a night here in months." She froze for a moment, perhaps at the realization that that night was the last night she'd ever spend with her husband.

"It must still be a great challenge to be without him." Malcolm leaned forwards, gaze steady on her own. "I would like to give you a sum to see to your family's protection."

Her eyes, blue with a violet undertone, widened and then narrowed. "Why in God's name would you want to?"

"You've clearly been left in a bad way. You seem a capable woman, but you have limited options for earning money. I don't like to see children and their mother at risk."

"Oh." She drew a breath. "Well, in that case, I suppose—" She got to her feet, walked to the cabinet, and refilled her sherry glass. Action as prevarication. Malcolm admired the tactic. He hadn't been embroidering when he said she was a capable woman.

She lifted the glass to her lips and took a sip, but the action was more thoughtful and less desperate than before. "We haven't had much for a long time. But sums would come in from time to time. Jamie would appear and leave something, or send money or gifts. He wasn't good with money, as I said, but he had some success. I didn't ask questions." She turned from the drinks cabinet. "Best not to talk about money, I always thought. Are you married, Mr. Rannoch?"

"Yes."

"Do you discuss finances with your wife?"

"There isn't a great deal I don't discuss with my wife."

She surveyed him for a moment, her gaze unexpectedly clear and sharp. "I don't know whether to envy or pity you. What about you, Mr. Roth?"

"I don't discuss anything at all with my wife. We haven't lived under the same roof for years."

"For which you are perhaps to be congratulated." Mrs. Blayney returned to her chair. "Jamie and I were a watering place romance. Bath. We met at an assembly at the Pump Room and were married a fortnight later. Marry in haste, repent at leisure. I was there with my great-aunt, who needed me to fetch her a glass and carry her shopping parcels and read aloud to her. I didn't care, it was the first time I'd been further than my village in Hertfordshire. Jamie was in his regimentals. I had a new frock and a pearl necklace, thanks to Aunt Mathilda. We each thought the other had more than we really did. We learned the truth before we'd been married a month. It didn't make for an easy first year. It didn't make for an easy much of anything." She swallowed half her second glass of sherry, then set the glass on the table beside her chair and gripped her elbows. "But I confess I—I'm sorry he's gone. I think I'll be sorrier when it properly sinks in. God." She pushed loose strands of hair out of her eyes. "As for any payments he may have received—I can't answer for a certainty. But there is one thing—"

"Yes?"

She drew a breath. One could see the pretty, prattling girl who had captivated Captain Blayney at Bath, overlaid by the more wary woman she'd become. "Jamie wasn't here often, as I said. Less and less the last year. He had a woman in London, I think. Probably more than one." She seemed to catch something in Malcolm's and Roth's gazes. "I'm right, aren't I?"

"Yes." Malcolm said. Softening the truth would do no good, especially when she'd already guessed it. "Her name is Grace. She may be a lady's maid."

"Hmm. He's come down in the world. My first rival was an actress. I suppose I should thank her for taking him off my hands. But in any case, Jamie made one of his rare visits here a week since. The first in almost two months. He left me five pounds and said he'd soon have more. Said he was on to something that would make our fortune."

Malcolm cast a glance at Roth. "Did he say what that might be?"

"No. He was always so full of schemes, I didn't take him seriously. Told him to get along and I'd believe it when I saw it. He said"—she frowned—"Jamie said he'd prove me wrong, but that the children and I should be ready to leave quickly, just in case."

"Did he say why?" Roth asked.

"Not in so many words." Mrs. Blayney swallowed the last of her sherry. "When I asked him if it was so bad he thought the duns were going to throw us out, he said that wasn't it at all. But that it was possible things could get very dangerous very quickly." Her gaze shot between Malcolm and Roth. "Are we in danger?"

"People are looking for the papers your husband had," Roth said. "His rooms in London were searched last night. So was his brother's print shop. Anyone looking into his life would likely know he didn't spend much time here. But it's possible someone would try to search here. I'll assign a patrol to keep watch on the house until we know more. I'll bring him down myself later today."

"Thank you. But if there's such a fuss—what in God's name is in these papers he had?"

"That," said Malcolm, "is what we're endeavoring to discover."

CHAPTER 11

"Cordy." Philippa Haworth got to her feet and came forwards across her sitting room, both hands extended. "What on earth are you doing here when half of Mayfair will be descending on you in a few hours?"

"I had to get out of the house or drive myself and everyone else mad double-checking things. Harry and the footmen are moving furniture, and Harry told me to get out for a walk while I could." Cordelia took her friend's hands, then after a moment gave her a quick hug, as she would have done in the old days. "I'm sorry, it's been too long. Somehow we get so wretchedly busy."

Pippa smiled. She looked much as she always had, her dark hair twisted into a nonchalant knot that seemed to threaten to escape its pins but didn't, her side curls falling round her face with artful abandon, her green eyes lined with blacking. But for all the elegant bravado, there was something more contained about her expression. "Yes, and you're hurrying about London investigating crimes and all sorts of exciting things," she said.

"Not really." Cordelia hesitated. She was rather tired of playing it all down. "Well, yes, all right. I suppose we are, in a way. I have to say it's very satisfying to actually do something productive."

Pippa grinned, and for a moment looked like the old Pippa. "Yes, I should think so. You don't know how I envy you."

Cordelia's surprise must have shown on her face. Pippa smiled. "Do I seem so shallow?"

"No, of course not. I'm the one who always seemed shallow. I suppose, in a way, I was shallow. I was bored, I think. Restless. I should have realized—"

"That you weren't the only one?" Pippa smiled. "Pity we didn't talk about it, perhaps. Not that I have much patience for whining, but I could have done with more rational conversation. Do sit down and let's have some tea, like in the old days."

They moved to the chairs and sofa round the fire, which, typically for Pippa, were covered in a vivid paisley print that conjured Laura's stories of India but also had comfortably padded cushions and gracefully curved backs that invited one to relax and didn't insist on posture that made stays bite into skin.

The footman brought tea and Pippa poured out two cups. "I'm sorry I wasn't better at writing," she said, as she handed a cup to Cordy across the sofa table. "I was in low spirits much of the time you were in Italy. I know that makes me sound dreadfully missish. But it's true. Not the blue devils, like Caro Lamb. Just—out of sorts with myself."

"I'm sorry," Cordelia said. "I know a bit about that."

"Not so much now, I should think. Your marriage seems very happy."

"Yes, it is. Now." Cordelia took a sip of tea. "I'm beyond fortunate."

"I'm happy for you. A happy marriage is almost beyond my comprehension, but I've seen the two of you together." Pippa poured milk into her tea. "And even when you were estranged, I never thought you were wholly indifferent to Harry. In fact, I thought you were far from indifferent."

"You always were insightful. You're quite right, but I wouldn't have admitted it myself at the time. Not in so many words."

Pippa settled back amid the sofa cushions. "Easier to see it about someone else."

"I was certainly lacking in self-knowledge. Waterloo threw a lot of things into perspective."

"You chose well when you married."

Cordelia felt herself give an unforced smile. "Yes, I did. It didn't feel so at the time. It felt like an act of desperation."

"I think we're often the last to understand our own actions." Pippa cradled her cup in her hand. "God knows I am. But as an outside observer—at least when it comes to you—I can say you chose far better than I did."

Cordelia set her cup down. "I'm sorry. I know I called after, but it's always so hard to know what to say—"

"Thank you." Pippa gave a quick, tight smile. "You were very kind. You understood better than most. Because of course, the truth is, it wasn't a deathless love." She frowned into her eggshell teacup. "It wasn't even a love. Not properly. Even at my most deluded, I don't think I ever thought it was. To own the truth, I think that's part of why I've withdrawn a bit. Difficult to play the grieving widow role that seems required when one isn't grieving as much as one should be. But of course, one can't help mourning someone one's shared a home with. However unlike a home it often seemed. And it mattered to the girls. Though they were never as attached to him as I'd like to think children should be to their father."

"Harry's a good father," Cordelia said without thinking. "It's one of the reasons I fell in love with him. That is, when I saw him again in Brussels. He was good with Livia from the first. Instinctively. Despite rather horrendous circumstances. You're right, I was already far from indifferent to him, but that helped tip me over the edge."

"I used to envy you," Pippa said. "Not having to answer to anyone else in your household. And I confess a part of me likes that now." Her brows drew together. "I even go out less, because there's nothing at home to escape, and an evening at home is much more agreeable if it means an evening with only the girls. They're amazingly good company. Thank God I never quite let myself lose sight of how much that mattered to me."

A hundred questions sprang to Cordelia's lips, but she bit them back. This wasn't the time.

Pippa watched her for a moment. "Why did you come? I mean, why today? There must have been a reason, especially the day of your ball. I don't mean that we aren't friends. But we haven't seen each other for some time. I didn't write. I take the responsibility. So there must have been something about today. Especially with your ball tonight."

Cordelia cupped her hands round her teacup. It was warm through the porcelain. "James Blayney was killed last night. I'm so sorry."

Shock flared in Pippa's gaze. Cruel, perhaps, to have put it so quickly, but Cordelia had learned the advantage of observing surprise. And bad news was sometimes easier to take all at once.

"Dear God." Pippa put her hand to her throat. "Thank you for letting me know."

"I didn't do it very carefully."

"There's no easy way. But doing it quickly is probably best." Pippa took a quick drink of tea. "How did you even know I knew him?"

"His brother mentioned it."

"You've talked to Edmund."

"Mr. Rannoch did."

Pippa's gaze narrowed. "You said Jamie was killed. That's how you know, isn't it? You and Harry are investigating his death with the Rannochs."

"The Rannochs are assisting Bow Street. And Harry and I've been pulled into it."

"Of course." Pippa tugged at the cameo she wore on a velvet ribbon round her throat. "I told you I envied your adventures. And I do. I just never thought they'd touch me personally. A good lesson, I suppose. Everything touches someone personally." She paused a moment, and Cordelia had the odd sense that Pippa, who never seemed afraid of anything, was afraid of the answer to the question she could not but ask next. "What happened?"

"He was found dead in a tavern. The Chat Gris. In an upstairs room," Cordelia added to avoid the obvious assumption that it had been some sort of brawl.

"Good God, Cordy. Are you telling me Jamie was killed by a woman he'd paid for a tumble?"

"No, it doesn't seem that way. The woman he'd gone upstairs with had already left the room." Out the window and into her husband's arms, but that was another matter.

Pippa reached for her tea but stared into it instead of taking a drink. "It sounds so sordid. I mean, one knows it goes on, but —who on earth did kill him?"

"That's what we're endeavoring to discover. Do you know if he had any enemies?"

"I'd scarcely seen him in years." Pippa took a drink of tea. "It's odd with the people one's known as children. They seem so important somehow. Even years later, when one's gone off in quite different directions. Some of my memories of Jamie are so vivid I'd swear they were yesterday. Whereas I can scarcely recall the color of the eyes of the last man I danced with. Come to think of it, that was a bit ago, but not that long."

"When did you last see Captain Blayney?"

"Last spring, I think." Pippa leaned forwards to refill the tea. "At Somerset House. No, I saw him a bit later in the park. I was driving with the girls and he rode by. He always managed to have good horses. He was a good judge of them too, I'll give him that. And treated them rather better than he treated people. We stopped to exchange greetings but we only said a few words." She set the teapot down. "We hadn't talked properly in years."

"Since he joined the army."

"And I married Haworth. And then, after his father died, there wasn't really any reason for him to go back to Shropshire, and I didn't go back so often either. As I said, one's lives go in different directions."

"But he stayed closer to your sister Sophia."

Pippa's fingers stilled on the handle of her teacup. "You know."

"I don't *know* anything. We've heard rumors."

"From?"

"Captain Blayney's brother."

"Oh, God." Pippa drew back as though the cup had burned her. "I suppose Edmund did know."

"You can't think I'd be shocked by any indiscretion, Pippa. You know my history."

"No, not shocked. I suppose it's just—" Pippa set her cup down. "It's not my story to share."

"No, of course not. But that's the ghastly thing about a murder investigation. Private secrets aren't private anymore. I learned that when I found myself investigating my own sister's murder."

Pippa's gaze locked on Cordelia's own. "I'm so sorry. That's worse than anything I've been through. I should have said—"

"You wrote and said everything anyone could. Julia's not the issue now. It was horrible, and I'll never be over it, but it doesn't haunt me. I've learned to live in the present. What matters now is James Blayney. And your sister's relationship with him could be connected to that."

Pippa's dark brows drew together. "You think Sophia's affair with Jamie is to do with why Jamie was killed?"

"Not necessarily. But anything about his life could be relevant."

Pippa turned her cup by its handle, staring into the milky depths. "I didn't see it when they were young. I'm not even sure there was anything between them when they were young. Oh, Jamie is—was"—her brows drew together—"indecently attractive, so I suppose Sophia couldn't have but noticed, and she did flirt with him. But I never thought they were star-crossed lovers. She seemed quite pleased with herself when she snared Prescott. God, that's a ghastly word, isn't it? Snared. I should be kinder. To my sister. To another woman. But Sophia wanted a secure establishment and a position in society. And she got them. And unlike me, she seemed quite content with her choice. For the first two or three years. I never really noticed she was dissatisfied. Perhaps I was too busy being dissatisfied myself."

"It's easy to be self-involved when it comes to a sister," Cordelia said. "And I speak as someone who regrets the loss of her sister every day. But it's amazing how rivalries and jealousies from the nursery can linger."

Pippa met her gaze, her own weighted with understanding and regret. "Yes. Sophia always struck me as being idiotishly content with life, and so damnably sure she had everything worked out. So perhaps it's no wonder that when I was wretchedly unhappy with my own choices and trying to work out what I'd done wrong and how to sort myself out, I thought Sophia had everything sorted. I remember seeing her come off the dance floor with quite another gentleman and smile at Jamie —just smile—and suddenly all my assumptions about my perfect sister were blown to bits." Pippa frowned. "In one way it was oddly reassuring. If Sophia wasn't happy in this life, the life she'd always wanted, it was no wonder I wasn't. On the other hand, if she couldn't be content in this life we were both supposed to aspire to, how could I ever hope to be so?"

"Did you talk to her about it?" Cordelia asked.

"Not at first. I don't think we were ever as close as you and Julia. We always got along best when we let each other go our own way. But a few weeks later I saw her waltzing with Jamie, and then we happened to be in the retiring room at Lady Cowper's at the same moment, and I asked her if she was quite sure she knew what she was risking. Sophia just seemed to look right through me and said she hadn't the least idea what I was talking about. Which was always Sophia's defense when one accused her of anything, whether it was borrowing Mama's diamonds or sneaking a glass of sherry. Not that I was accusing her, precisely. But even a rebel like me could tell Jamie was a sure path to ruin."

"That can be the attraction."

"Yes, I can quite see that. Though I wouldn't have thought it would be that way with Sophia. She seemed so sure of what she wanted. Why would she risk it?"

"Perhaps once she had it, she was bored."

Pippa's brows knotted again. "Perhaps."

"And then?" Cordelia asked.

"Sophia and I were never confidantes and certainly not at that point in our lives, so I don't know all the details. Papa was suddenly in London at a time when he wasn't expected, and Sophia didn't attend Lady Sefton's musicale the next night. Pen put in an appearance, but he looked grim and wouldn't answer when I asked when he'd last heard from Sophia. Then when I was dancing with Major Willoughby, he asked if I knew why Jamie had gone back to the Peninsula so abruptly. And two nights later, Sophia and Prescott appeared at the theatre looking as though they were attempting to put on a show of marital harmony. I asked Pen straight out if he knew what had happened, but he wouldn't talk about it. I asked Sophia if she wanted to talk, and predictably, she said, 'We talk all the time.'"

"Do you think she saw Captain Blayney again?"

Pippa reached for her cup, twisted the handle, set it back

down. "I saw them meet once at a large party. Dorothea de Lieven's, I think. They were faultlessly polite and only spoke for a moment. As to whether she's seen him or written to him otherwise—as I said, my sister and I aren't ones for confidences. I didn't have the sense he was the love of her life. But then I never saw Sophia as the sort to have a love of her life, which is perhaps unfair of me. I'm not sure I'm the best person to ask."

"What about Captain Blayney?"

"What about him?"

"Have you talked to him about your sister?"

"I've scarcely seen him either, as I said. That was true. Jamie and I may have climbed trees together, but we were hardly confidants either. Certainly not when it came to my sister."

"Do you think *she* was the love of *his* life?"

Pippa choked. "Difficult to imagine Jamie's having a love of his life. But perhaps he liked what we—what she—represented. We were so close when we were children. It wasn't until we were in our teens that it was clear how different our lives were. Edmund didn't want anything to do with us. He writes—rather well—about all the problems we represent. People like us, that is. And he has a point. But Jamie was more like a boy with his face pressed up against the glass." She rubbed her arms. "I wish I'd understood that sooner."

"Do you know of any enemies Jamie Blayney had?"

Pippa frowned as though sifting through the past. "I don't think my father ever forgave him. He loved Jamie. Like a son. He got on better with him than with Pen. And yet for all that, I think Papa might have balked at Sophia's marrying Jamie if she'd wanted to, before she met Prescott. It's an odd world we live in. Edmund's quite right to question it. So I think Jamie broke Papa's heart. But Papa's been gone for years. I don't know much at all about Jamie's life since."

"Did Sophia's husband know about the affair?"

"Lord Prescott?" Pippa said, as though the very mention of his name was startling. "Why—you don't think—"

"Even if a marriage is damaged, husbands aren't necessarily complaisant about that sort of thing. Harry quite lost his temper with George. Understandably." Cordelia was pleased her voice remained steady. It was not easy to speak of George Chase.

"Harry was—is, from what I've seen—madly in love with you. I don't think Prescott was ever any more in love with Sophia than she was with him."

"Jealousy can be as much about possession as about love. I thought that's what it was with Harry. I was wrong. But that doesn't mean it isn't in other cases."

Pippa frowned. "I think Prescott may have known. I don't think Papa would have been so concerned if he hadn't thought Sophia's marriage was in jeopardy. But surely you don't think Prescott, of all people, would have turned violent."

"I was seated next to him at a dinner at the French embassy. He talked about fishing until it was time to switch sides. But if there's one thing I've learned in assisting with investigations, it's that one can never predict who may be capable of violent acts."

Pippa's gaze narrowed. "Does that mean you suspect Sophia as well?"

"Malcolm Rannoch would say that at this point, we suspect everyone." Cordelia watched Pippa. "Do you think Sophia was angry with Captain Blayney?"

"Not so far as I know."

"But as you said, you don't know your sister well."

Pippa reached for her cup and took a sip of tea. "No. I don't."

CHAPTER 12

élanie glanced at Kitty as they ascended the steps to the Prescott house in Upper Grosvenor Street. Her face was carefully set beneath the bronze velvet of her bonnet. "Nervous?"

"Why should I be?" Kitty lifted the skirt of her gown as they climbed the steps. "Sophia Prescott is hardly the most challenging suspect we've interviewed. It's always a bit distasteful to break such news, but though I haven't been doing this as long as you, we're all getting used to it by now. The connection to Edward would have disturbed me a bit a year ago, perhaps. But not now."

"I wasn't thinking of that. I was thinking of James Blayney."

Kitty paused on the top step. "Caught. You are damnably acute, you know. You're right. I can't help feeling responsible."

"You aren't. But I understand."

Kitty fingered a fold of her amber sarcenet gown. "All right, I suppose a part of me feels if I can help find who killed him, it will balance the scales somehow. Or perhaps it's that I want to know that my giving him that drug didn't have to do with his being killed."

Mélanie touched Kitty's arm. "We've all done things we can't forgive ourselves for."

"Perhaps I have more luxury for a conscience now." Kitty's gloved fingers tightened on the shiny sarcenet. "Sophia Prescott loved Jamie Blayney once, or at least was his lover. And I was half undressed in bed with him last night. Which should cause more guilt when it comes to my husband than to Sophia. But somehow doesn't."

"Well, Julien knew what you were doing."

"There is that."

"And offered to do it himself."

"There is that too."

A liveried footman answered their ring, glanced at Kitty's card, and conducted them up the gilt-railed stairs without first ascertaining if his mistress was at home. He opened one of the perfectly proportioned doors on the first-floor landing and announced them.

Sophia Prescott got to her feet at their entrance. She was above average height, with dark hair dressed to accentuate her long throat. She wore a Wedgwood-blue gown a shade darker than the wall hangings in her sitting room. Pearls glowed round her throat and at her ears in the light from pristine wax tapers. All elegant, all understated, all of the best quality.

"Kit—Lady Carfax."

"Please, I'm still not used to Lady Carfax. And we are cousins of a sort. I don't believe you're acquainted with Mrs. Rannoch?"

Sophia's gaze moved to Mélanie with well-bred composure. "We've never met, but I could scarcely fail to be aware of you, Mrs. Rannoch. Your play was the talk of London, as I'm sure you know. I found it charming."

"Thank you." Mélanie couldn't be sure how sincerely meant the words were. Charming was one of those words that could damn with faint praise. And she suspected that being the "talk of

London" for a theatrical venture was not entirely something Sophia Prescott approved of.

Sophia gestured to two chairs covered in pale blue satin that matched the wall hangings and returned to the settee set at a right angle to the chairs.

"I trust you and your husband are comfortably settling into Carfax House," she said when they were seated.

"We're doing our best." Kitty adjusted the folds of her gown. "It's a beautiful house, but not one that lends itself to comfort, I fear."

"You're wonderfully clever. You'd done delightful things with it at your ball. Few hostesses give a first ball that is so talked of."

There it was again, that double-edged comment. Kitty's first ball had been an event few in Mayfair wanted to miss. But the guest list had been decidedly eclectic and surely not what Sophia Prescott was accustomed to.

"We were so pleased you and Prescott could be there," Kitty said. She clasped her hands round her gilt-framed reticule and met Sophia's gaze directly. "Sophia—I fear we've come with bad news."

"Not the children?" Sophia asked with quick concern. "Or your husband?"

"Oh no. Nothing like that. It's about a childhood friend of yours. James Blayney."

"Good heavens." Sophia drew back on the settee and reached for the paisley shawl draped over its back. "I haven't heard that name in years. I hope he hasn't met with some misfortune." Wariness was writ in the way Sophia drew the shawl about her. But no hint she knew of what had actually happened.

"I'm afraid he was found dead last night," Mélanie said.

"James Blayney?" The color drained from Sophia's face.

Kitty got to her feet and put a hand on Sophia's arm. "I'm so very sorry."

"It's the shock. I scarcely knew Captain Blayney in recent

years." Sophia drew away from Kitty's touch and looked between them. "What happened? Was he attacked?"

"He was knifed," Mélanie said. "But it appears he was deliberately targeted."

"How dreadful. He was always a bit wild, but I wouldn't have thought he'd be caught up in anything so unsavory." Sophia's gaze shot between Mélanie and Kitty. "That's why you're here. You and your husband investigate crimes, Mrs. Rannoch."

"We've assisted Bow Street," Mélanie said. "My husband worked in intelligence and we were involved with some intelligence investigations on the Continent."

"And now you're trying to learn who killed Jamie. Captain Blayney."

"We're assisting Bow Street. Because of your connection to Kitty, we thought it might be easier if the two of us called on you rather than a Bow Street runner."

Sophia pulled the blue and black folds of the shawl tight round her. "Without question. Though I don't know how much I can tell you. We played with the Blayney boys as children, but once Jamie joined the army and I married and set up my own household, I saw little of him."

Kitty had returned to her chair. Mélanie sensed Kitty's response, though she didn't risk a look at her. Always so challenging how to confront someone with hard truths without alienating them.

"We understand you had seen him in London more recently," Mélanie said.

Sophia settled the folds of the shawl over her shoulders. "Naturally, one runs into all sorts of people from all different parts of one's life, at the theatre and in the park and at Somerset House and other places that aren't exclusive. Lord Prescott and I have encountered Captain Blayney a handful of times. Of course, one is polite."

"Sophia." Kitty folded her hands in her lap and regarded

Sophia with the look Mélanie had seen her give her children when they were prevaricating. "We know about you and Captain Blayney."

The blood drained from Sophia's well-tended skin, throwing into relief the delicate rouge she applied, so subtly it hadn't been clear she wore it before. "You can't—"

"Of course, we have no wish to spread the story," Kitty said. "But if you won't tell us what happened, we shall have to make further inquiries. Mr. Rannoch will have to make them. I thought you would so much rather talk to us."

Sophia's shoulders shot straight. "You can't expect me to lend credence to this outrageous story, whoever has told it to you."

"In that case, I daresay Malcolm won't find anything to support it. Perhaps you could at least tell us the reason Captain Blayney quarreled with your father," Mélanie said.

Sophia stared at them with mingled fear and rage, glanced away, looked back at them. "Damnation."

"We'll keep anything you tell us in confidence," Kitty said. "As much as we're able."

"As much as you're able." Sophia reached for the shawl again. Her fingers trembled.

"I'm sorry," Mélanie said. "All this must be forcing you to deny your grief at Captain Blayney's death. It must be quite horrible news."

Sophia put a fist to her mouth. The shawl slithered about her again. "Jamie was so alive. The most alive person I've ever met." She shook her head. "We flirted when we were young. The way one does when one is in the country and there are only so many agreeable young men to dance with. I fancied myself in love with him for a time, I suppose, but even then, a part of me knew it couldn't go anywhere."

"I understand Captain Blayney was a favorite of your father," Kitty said.

"Oh, yes. But I don't think Father would have actually

wanted one of his daughters to marry Jamie. And that wasn't the life I saw for myself."

"I can see that," Kitty said.

Sophia sent her a sharp look.

"Most women had few options for shaping their lives," Kitty said. "Marriage locks one into so much. In some ways shaping one's whole life just because one happens to fall in love with a man who is set in a particular course in life himself seems foolish."

"I think my parents would have said much the same," Sophia said.

"Yes, I can see that. Though I doubt we'd agree on the solution. Which to me is to let women carve out lives for themselves, but that doesn't seem to happen often enough."

"Many of us carve out lives for ourselves perfectly well when we marry," Sophia said, a touch of asperity in her voice.

"In any case," Kitty said, "you can't think Mrs. Rannoch and I would be shocked by any revelation of romantic indiscretion. Especially given everything about the king and queen being bandied in Parliament and every drawing room in Mayfair."

"Royalty are different." Sophia's fingers tightened on her shawl. "In any case, I went to London and had my season and forgot all about Jamie Blayney. Or at least, thought I was over my tendre for him. Lord Prescott was an unexceptionable choice. I was quite sure we'd be happy together. I was quite sure being Lady Prescott would give me everything I wanted."

"It can be difficult," Mélanie said. "Thinking any one person can give one everything one wants in life."

"To be honest," Sophia said, in a tone that made Mélanie think she was perhaps being honest for the first time in the whole interview, "I wasn't thinking so much of Lord Prescott's making me happy as of my life as Lady Prescott doing so. He's a very decent man, of course. But after a few years, after the novelty of running one's own household and being able to go about in society without a chaperone wears off—it does seem less than ideal to have a husband who falls asleep after dinner with the *Morning Post* draped over his face and snores. And then one night I saw Jamie. Home on leave in his regimentals. And I realized I hadn't got over my tendre for him after all. After producing three children and faithfully supporting Prescott's career, I thought I deserved some adventure. No, that makes it sound too calculating. And it wasn't." She stared down at her fingers on the folds of her shawl. "I loved him desperately. So much so that for a time I was ready to throw over everything for him." She gripped her arms. "Jamie could be foolish. But he was the most charming man I've met."

"But you decided you weren't ready to throw everything over for him?" Kitty said.

"What on earth does that mean?" Sophia demanded. "It sounds like something out of a novel. I wasn't ready to give up my children and the life I'd built and my connections to my family and friends—no. It's hard to imagine a woman who would be, though I know some do."

"I know what you mean," Kitty said.

Sophia raised her brows.

"I was quite desperately in love once," Kitty said, gaze on Sophia's own, not looking at Mélanie. "I didn't have children yet. But I wasn't prepared to throw over what I had. For a number of reasons."

Sophia's eyes widened. "That's a great admission."

"You made a great admission."

"You forced me to it."

"Perhaps all the more reason for me to do the same."

Sophia inclined her head and a subtle shift took place in the room.

"So you broke it off with Captain Blayney," Kitty said after a moment.

"Not precisely." Sophia's mouth curled. "My sister took him from me."

"Your sister?" Mélanie said.

"Pippa. I'm quite sure she's the one who told Papa about Jamie and me. Because she wanted Jamie for herself. Oh, nothing happened between them until a few years later—at least, not as far as I know. But I'm sure she set it up."

"What makes you think so?" Kitty asked.

Sophia wrapped her shawl about her, with steadier fingers than before. "Do either of you have sisters?"

"No," Kitty said. "Only a cousin who's a bit like a brother."

"No," Mélanie said, as she'd answered for the past eight years whenever anyone asked her about her family. Because her sister Rosie, who had been so much a part of her life, wasn't part of the fictional life she'd been inhabiting since the mission on which she'd met Malcolm and unexpectedly ended up marrying him. Malcolm knew about Rosie. Raoul did. But she hadn't mentioned her to the others. Not even Cordy. And Colin and Jessica didn't know they'd had an aunt on their mother's side.

"Brothers are different," Sophia said. "Brothers can be overprotective at times, but in general they stay out of the way, and they can be quite useful when it comes to bringing agreeable friends home from university and introducing one to dance partners. Sisters are endless rivals. Not Phoebe—my youngest sister—so much. She's a decade my junior. Pippa and I are only a year apart. I can't remember a time we weren't rivals. She was better at lessons than I was, but she was always breaking rules and making a stir and getting in trouble for it. I knew how to play the game from the start. Pippa didn't seem to care. She— Oh, here's the tea at last." In an instant, her voice and posture reverted to Mayfair lady of the house. "Perhaps it's as well."

Sophia sat decorously while the footman arranged the tea service on the polished walnut sofa table. "Thank you, Thomas," she said, in a tone so effortless it would have done credit to the stage at the Tavistock. Even after Thomas withdrew, she poured tea and handed them cups before she continued speaking. Then, unexpectedly, she got to her feet. "Do you mind? I think I require something stronger than tea." She went to a gilded ebony Boulle cabinet, opened the doors, and took out a small flask. She splashed brandy into her tea and raised a brow at Kitty and Mélanie. They both nodded. For a moment, Mélanie remembered their friend Bet Simcox serving brandy-laced tea in chipped mugs and other drinking vessels in her rooms in St. Giles. Bet, who now lived with Sandy Trenor, but was still a world away from being his wife.

Sophia took a sip of brandy-laced tea, then another. "Pippa complained that I followed the rules, I complained that she broke them. I did try not to get her in trouble, but really there were times when I had no choice but to tell the truth, and if she hadn't wanted me to do so, she should have thought before she sneaked out to the village fête, or borrowed Papa's best hunter, or sneaked scandalous books under the covers, or any of the starts she got up to. Often with Edmund."

"Edmund Blayney?" Mélanie said.

"Jamie's elder brother. He publishes some sort of dreadful newspaper now, advocating that aristocrats be murdered in their beds and that sort of thing. I couldn't give you his direction, but I assume your husband will try to talk to him. Unless he has already." Sophia looked from Mélanie to Kitty. "Of course. Is it Edmund who told you about Jamie and me? My God, I should have guessed."

"We can't possibly comment," Kitty said.

"No, I suppose not. Devil take Edmund. He and Pippa used to say the most provoking things. At least Pippa seemed to see sense when she was older and actually managed to have a creditable season and make a creditable marriage. I can't tell you what a relief it was, as it fell to me to oversee her season. The quarrels we had about her wardrobe alone. Only then, of course, she was restless." Sophia took another sip of tea. "I don't know why I'm surprised. I was restless too and I had far more sense of what mattered in the world than Pippa ever did. I don't begrudge her her adventures, assuming Haworth understood. Being Pippa, of course, she was likely to splash the whole about town and make a spectacle of herself like Caroline Lamb, or actually run off with a lover like Cor—" She broke off. "I forget. You're friends with Cordelia Davenport."

"Yes," Mélanie said, "but I wouldn't deny her past. Cordy wouldn't deny her own past."

"Easier perhaps when she's living with her husband again and accepted most places. More fool me, perhaps." Sophia returned her teacup to its gilded saucer. "Pippa and Jamie used to get into scrapes together. Daring each other to exploits, that sort of thing. Edmund would sometimes get them out of it, while I ran the other way. I hadn't thought Pippa had much interest in Jamie as an adult, but she worked it out about Jamie and me somehow. She pretended to show concern for me, but I'm sure she told Papa. Someone did, and scarcely anyone else knew. Papa stormed into London—which he avoided in general —and the next thing I knew, Jamie was back on the Peninsula. While Papa read me a lecture about not throwing away my life and hurting my children." Sophia drew a hard breath. "I'll confess he had a point. If Pippa had told him out of concern for me, I could almost forgive her. But then a few years later, Jamie took up with Pippa. He carefully avoided me, which didn't surprise me. We'd both seen the dangers. But I saw him with Pippa at the theatre. Just standing together, but it was plain to anyone who knew them what was going on." Sophia's fingers whitened round the eggshell handle of her teacup. "What in God's name possessed her? I swear she did it just out of spite against me. I can't believe she really loved Jamie. I can't believe she knows the meaning of the word."

"It's difficult to believe that about anyone who takes a lover away, or even who succeeds one with a lover," Kitty said, quite as though she wasn't sitting next to the woman who had succeeded her with one of her own lovers. Come to that, in a sense, Kitty had succeeded Mélanie with Julien, though Mélanie and Julien could hardly have been said to have a sustained relationship. At least, not a sustained romantic one.

"We had a fearful quarrel about it," Sophia said. "One of the worst we've had, actually. Mostly Pippa and I simply sniped at each other and went about our separate lives. But I couldn't let this pass. I couldn't bear to see Jamie being trifled with. So I called on Pippa and asked her what the devil she was doing. Pippa had the audacity to claim it had nothing to do with me." Sophia frowned. "I've never quite seen her as she was then. She's always been heedless of consequences, but she looked quite cut loose from her moorings."

"As though she was so in love nothing else mattered?" Kitty asked.

"No." Sophia frowned and set down her teacup. "As though she'd stopped caring about anything at all and was wallowing in the depths of depression."

"An odd way to feel in the midst of a love affair," Kitty said. "Even an affair one knew was doomed at the start."

"I suppose so." Sophia's frown deepened. She picked up her cup and tossed down another swallow, then set it down again. "Even when I admitted to myself that things couldn't possibly go anywhere for Jamie and me, I was happy. Despite everything. That's why I couldn't bear for it to end, for all I knew from the start that it had to. But then, that's Pippa. She was always odd. I don't think she really loved Jamie, I think she did it to settle some obscure score with me. She always claimed to disdain the sort of life and success I wanted, yet at the same time she seemed to resent that I had it. So even though what I had didn't make her happy, she took it away from me. When I asked her if she loved Jamie, she refused to answer. She refused to even admit to the love affair, though I knew it must be a reality."

"How long did it last?" Mélanie asked.

Sophia reached for the teapot and refilled their cups, then splashed in more brandy. "I don't know. Not for a certainty. As I said, Pippa wouldn't even admit to it. But Jamie went back to his regiment. The next time he was home on leave—and yes, I did notice, I did scan the casualty lists every day, terrified to see his name—I didn't see him with Pippa."

"He has a wife," Kitty said.

"Yes." Sophia frowned at the silver tea tray. "Apparently it was an unfortunate entanglement during a fortnight's leave at Bath. It was after our affair. He didn't say much about her the few times I saw him in recent years, though he did mention his children. I believe being a father mattered to him. How could it not?"

"It doesn't for a number of men," Kitty said. "And for a number of women as well, for that matter."

"One doesn't need to hover over the nursery to take one's children seriously. You must realize that."

"I'm not sure." Kitty returned her cup to its saucer. "I've always tended to hover."

Kitty was the last person one would use the word "hover" about. On the other hand, she was a very devoted mother who tended to her children herself, so perhaps it was apropos.

"When did you last speak with Captain Blayney in private?" Mélanie asked.

Sophia took another sip of tea, twisted her cup on its saucer, twitched the folds of her skirt straight. "Not for years. I'd have risked it if he had, but he was always oddly protective. Sometimes I thought it was better to live with my memories. Sometimes I desperately wanted to see him. But I'd stopped thinking I ever would again, except for an occasional glimpse or a few words exchanged in public. Across a crowded theatre, in Hyde

Park, in the Burlington Arcade." She turned the handle of her cup again. "Until a fortnight ago."

"What happened?" Kitty asked. "He came to see you?"

"I was shocked," Sophia said. "And oddly overjoyed. Though I knew that wasn't why he'd come."

"He wanted something from you," Mélanie said. "Did he ask for money?"

"No. Jamie was always scraping by, but he'd never have made such a request of me. He wanted me to deliver a parcel for him."

Mélanie exchanged a quick look with Kitty. "A parcel? To whom?"

"Lord Danbury."

Lord Danbury was a prominent Tory politician, very much involved in the case against the queen, among other things. "Are you well acquainted with Lord Danbury?" Mélanie asked.

"Yes, it's not as odd a request as it might seem. Lord Danbury was at school with my father and is my godfather."

"Did you deliver the parcel?" Kitty asked.

"I had one of the footmen take it round. Later, when I saw Lord Danbury at the Esterhazy musicale, I asked if he'd received it. He said yes, and then asked if I knew what it contained. I said no, I'd been asked to deliver it by a friend. He said 'Quite so, my dear,' as though I was were still in the nursery. But later that evening, I caught him looking at me in the oddest way. As though he was re-evaluating everything he thought he knew about me."

"Have you seen him since?" Mélanie asked.

"No. I was rather dreading encountering him at the Sherringtons' the next night, but Lady Danbury told me he was indisposed. He hasn't been at any event I've been at since, and I haven't seen him in the park or at the theatre." She picked up her cup. "I imagine he's much preoccupied with the case against the queen."

"Did you open the parcel?" Kitty asked.

"Of course not. I wanted as little to do with it as possible. I rang for a footman as soon as Jamie left and gave him instructions to deliver it immediately."

"But you must have noted something about it," Kitty said. "Was it a large one?"

"Not very. It was bound up in brown paper and string." She took a drink of tea. "It seemed to contain papers."

"Have you heard from Captain Blayney since?" Mélanie asked.

Sophia took a sip of tea. "He stopped beside my barouche in the park three days after he gave me the parcel. We exchanged greetings, as we might have done at any time. Then he thanked me for my assistance, tipped his hat, and rode away."

"How did he seem?" Kitty asked.

Sophia hesitated. "Excited. As though he was nervous but whatever he had in motion was unfolding as he wanted." She filled half her teacup with brandy and tossed down a long swallow. "I haven't seen him again since." Her fingers stilled on the porcelain. "Which means that was the last time I ever saw him."

CHAPTER 13

*K*itty tugged her glove smooth as she and Mélanie descended the steps of the Prescott house. "Do you believe her?"

"Do you?" Mélanie asked.

"No." Kitty paused on the third step. "That is, I'm quite sure she isn't telling us the whole truth, though I'm not sure where the lies leave off and truth begins. But I do believe she loved him." Kitty tugged at her other glove. "I spent half an hour alone with Jamie Blayney. He paid me some fulsome compliments that sounded as though he'd given them to a dozen women before. Or more. He unlaced my gown and had my corset half off. Nothing I haven't been through before. He was on top of me when he finally passed out. I was a long way from having to go further. It didn't seem important to go into detail last night. Not that Julien wouldn't understand, but I don't know that he actually needed to hear it unless he had to."

"I quite understand," Mélanie said.

Kitty paused on the last step and shot a look at her. "Do you?"

"Julien wouldn't fuss or be jealous, but he'd be worried about you."

"Yes, no point in unnecessary worry." Kitty adjusted the brim of her bonnet. "Would you tell Malcolm?"

"Not unless there was some detail that was relevant to the investigation. For the same reasons. And however matter-of-fact one is, and however much one knows it's all part of a mission, it's never agreeable to hear those details."

"No." Kitty tightened the gold satin ribbons on her bonnet.

"Thank you, by the way," Mélanie said.

"For what?"

"Saying you'd be the one to get the papers from Blayney, so quickly I didn't even have to consider offering."

Kitty met her gaze, a look that contained acknowledgement of a world of things they'd never directly discussed. "We've both been through rather a lot. But I thought it would stir up more memories for you."

Because while they'd both been brutalized, Mélanie had actually worked in a brothel not unlike the Chat Gris. "Yes, I could have managed, but the memories don't go away and places like the Chat Gris tend to bring them back. I'd just as soon Malcolm didn't know how much."

Kitty nodded. "Sometimes worrying about others' concerns makes it harder. I'm sure Malcolm would listen to anything you want to say. Just as Julien would listen to me. But I'm here whenever you need to talk."

Mélanie touched Kitty's gloved hand. A simple touch that bridged a world of differences. "Thank you."

CORDELIA SAT BACK in her chair at Gunter's Tea Shop. "Sophia said Pippa and Jamie Blayney were lovers?"

"Is that surprising?" Mélanie tugged off her second glove. By prior arrangement, she and Kitty had met Cordy at Gunter's following their morning calls on the former Langdon sisters.

"Given how Pippa spoke about Jamie Blayney just now—yes." Cordy frowned. "I don't know whether it's that Pippa's my friend, or that I don't like the idea I could be so thoroughly deceived, or both, but I can't credit that Pippa was lying so convincingly."

"It's possible Sophia made it up to distract us from her own story," Kitty said, "though she was also very convincing. But it's also not something one easily shares, even with a friend. I wouldn't lightly reveal a past love affair, even to someone I trusted. And I'm far less careful of my past than I suspect Mrs. Haworth is. Well, some things in my past."

Mélanie cast a glance round the shop, but they had chosen a table to one side (one the waiters knew they favored) and the others present were busily engaged in their own gossip. Nothing like a buzz of conversation for cover. "It's also possible Sophia thought Pippa and James Blayney were lovers, but they actually weren't," Mélanie said. "Sophia said Pippa denied the affair. But unless Sophia made the whole thing up, Pippa and Jamie Blayney were closer recently than it sounds Pippa admitted to you."

"Yes. If—" Cordelia bit her words back as a waiter approached with the tea and cakes they had ordered.

"Thank you, we'll pour," Kitty said, when he had arranged things decorously on the table top.

"It makes sense, in a way." Cordelia took a sip of tea. "Though I'd hardly think I'm the sort of person one would conceal a love affair from."

"It's not something one shares easily with anyone, as Kitty said." Mélanie reached for her own tea. "On the other hand, while Sophia was in many ways surprisingly frank, both Kitty and I don't think she told us everything. Or that everything she told us was the truth."

"One thing seems clear from both their stories," Kitty said. "Jamie Blayney was obsessed with the Langdon family and what it represented."

"And finding his way into their world," Mélanie said. Her gaze met Kitty's across the table for a moment. They had both married into that world and had mixed feelings about it. Neither quite belonged, but they had an entrée Jamie Blayney hadn't possessed. Worth remembering perhaps.

Cordelia looked between them and gave an ironic smile. "Odd how one can fail to notice the attractions of something one was born to. I think Malcolm feels the same way. Pippa's saying Jamie Blayney had his face pressed up against the glass rather haunted me." She looked from her gold-rimmed cup to the plate of iced cakes, pink, ivory, and chocolate with white icing as delicate as embroidery.

"Yes, it's very affecting." Kitty set down her cup. "But he seems to have seen blackmail as a way to break that glass."

"And if he tried it with Sophia, he may have tried it with Pippa," Cordelia said.

"What he asked Sophia to do doesn't appear to be a motive to murder," Mélanie said.

Kitty reached for her teacup. "Not if Sophia's telling the truth about what he asked her to do. The whole truth." Kitty took a sip of tea and frowned over the rim. "But I'm not at all sure she is."

CHAPTER 14

After dropping Roth in Bow Street, Malcolm drove to the Berkeley Square mews and left his curricle and pair with his groom Giles, then went through the garden and in through the back door to the house. Valentin sprang up from the bench in the hall.

"Mr. Rannoch. Mr. Brougham called for you. Half an hour since. He was most insistent on seeing you and wanted to wait. Mrs. Rannoch isn't back yet and Mrs. O'Roarke's taken the children to the park, so I've shown him into the library."

"Thank you, Valentin." Malcolm relinquished his hat and gloves and greatcoat. Henry Brougham was the queen's attorney-general. He and Malcolm met frequently, so it wasn't unusual for him to call, but it was unusual for him to have a half hour to spend cooling his heels in Berkeley Square.

When Malcolm opened the library door, Brougham came forwards quickly. "Rannoch. Where the devil have you been?"

Malcolm closed the door. "I'm sorry, Henry. I know I wasn't at Brooks's today. We ran into a situation last night. We're in the midst of an investigation."

"Yes, I know." Brougham cast a glance round the empty expanse of the library. "That's why I've come."

Malcolm stared at his friend and colleague. "You knew Jamie Blayney?"

Brougham looked round the room again. "Can we go into your study? It seems more private somehow."

"Of course."

In the study, Brougham watched Malcolm pull the door to, then flung himself into one of the chairs beside the desk. "It's the devil of a mess."

"Henry." Malcolm studied Brougham. They had worked closely together on a number of initiatives from abolition to the current case against the queen. He had seen Brougham's drive and determination. His dedication to winning his point. And his willingness to run risks. "Were you at the Chat Gris last night?"

"The where?" Brougham asked.

Malcolm settled in the chair opposite Brougham. "The tavern where James Blayney was killed."

"Oh. No. I didn't know the name of it." Brougham frowned and settled back in his chair. "I didn't see Blayney last night. I hadn't seen him in a week."

Malcolm scanned his friend's face. He was used to trying to read Brougham in a political discussion. Not in this context. "How long had you known him?"

Brougham drew in and released his breath. "The first I clapped eyes on him was a fortnight ago. When he caught up with me at the King's Arms in Westminster. I'd just finished a challenging meeting with Denman and Grey and wasn't in a mood to be waylaid, but Blayney caught my attention and offered to sell me certain papers."

Malcolm leaned back in his chair, even as he felt tension shoot through his shoulders. "Papers concerning the queen?"

"No." Brougham's gaze fastened on the toe of his boot. "Though it was the queen's case that had me concerned about these papers." He dragged the toe of his boot over the carpet. "The papers could have done damage to me. Difficult at any time, but right now I was concerned someone would try to use them to compel me to act a certain way in conducting the queen's case." He looked at Malcolm, gaze at once armored and entreating. "Don't deny someone might."

"It's quite clear people on all sides would go to great lengths over the queen's case." Malcolm studied his friend and colleague. Brougham did not strike him as a man who would easily give way to blackmail. "What's in these papers?"

Brougham tapped his fingers on the chair arm and stared at a nick in the wood.

"I can't help you if you won't tell me, Henry."

"No. I do realize that." Brougham ran a hand over his disarranged hair. "It was four years ago. When I was on the Continent."

"When you went there with Mrs. Lamb." The former Caroline St. Jules, whom Malcolm had known since she was a little girl in the Devonshire House nursery. Now the wife of George Lamb, known as "Caro George" to distinguish her from the wife of George's brother, William. Caro George was another childhood friend with murky parentage. Nominally the duke's ward, she was almost certainly his daughter with his mistress, Lady Elizabeth Foster, who had lived for years with the duke and duchess and had married the duke after Duchess Georgiana's death. Malcolm could still remember the moment, at a children's ball at Devonshire House, when the pieces had fallen into place for him. He hadn't even been particularly surprised. It was certainly of a piece with his own family. He still wasn't sure if Caro George knew the truth of her parentage herself. Or if her sisters Georgy and Harry-O and her brother Hartington, now the Duke of Devonshire, did.

Caro George had been reluctant to marry George Lamb, and from what Malcolm had seen of the marriage, she hadn't been happy in it, though unlike her sisters-in-law Emily Cowper and Caro William, she had appeared to be a faithful wife. But four years ago, she had gone off to the Continent and joined Brougham. George Lamb's sister Emily Cowper had gone after them. Malcolm and Mélanie had been in Paris at the time, and though Mel and Emily were now good friends, they hadn't known each other well then, so most of Malcolm's knowledge of the events came from letters from his aunt Frances. Eventually, Brougham and Caro George had ended their relationship and Caro had returned to her husband.

"Er—yes," Brougham said. "Caro and I had decided to end things." He grimaced. "Not my finest moment, any of it, though I see little to be gained from making excuses for my personal behavior, and I daresay you don't want to hear about it."

"Not particularly," Malcolm said. "But I will if it's relevant to the case at hand."

"Only tangentially, as it happens. Though that's part of why —" Brougham coughed. "In any case, I was feeling out of sorts and perhaps a bit ashamed of myself after Caro left, so I went to Paris before I came home. You may remember. I saw you and Mélanie at a few events. You were kind enough not to refer to my recent misadventures."

"It was clear you weren't happy." That was before Malcolm had stood for Parliament, so he hadn't known Brougham as well. He'd been preoccupied with the situation with the Ultra Royalists and with the wonder and excitement of Mélanie's second pregnancy and what it meant for their marriage, which had been proving far happier than he had dreamt possible.

Brougham nodded. "You were a happy husband and father reveling in domesticity, so we hardly frequented the same haunts. I was seeking escape and distraction in the Palais Royale and the other places one seeks such things in Paris. I met Danielle at the Salon des Etrangers."

"Danielle?" Malcolm asked.

"Danielle Darnault. An opera singer."

"I saw her on stage a few times in Paris," Malcolm said. "She has a magnificent voice. And she's a beautiful woman."

Brougham grinned. "Even a happy husband married to one of the most enchanting women on the Continent couldn't fail to notice that, could you? Danielle was known for being connected to a number of powerful men."

"Yes. I've heard that as well." She was rumored to have been the mistress of Tsar Alexander, the Duke of Wellington, and possibly Napoleon Bonaparte. Also rumored to perhaps have been an agent. Which stirred a number of suspicions.

Brougham curled his hands round the arms of his chair and frowned at his fingers. "Oddly enough, we were both rather bored at the des Etrangers that night, so we struck up a conversation in an antechamber while debating the merits of some rather naughty paintings. She's a clever woman. She said she wasn't in the mood for flirtation. Neither was I, after the mess I'd been in. One thing led to another, and I escorted her home. Which led to more." He gave a sudden grin. "I was jaded—I wasn't blind. Fascinating woman. And she was—" Brougham frowned for a moment, looking out the window. "Kind. Unexpectedly. She didn't make demands. And so I found myself talking to her. Rather more than I should have done."

"About?" Malcolm asked in a neutral voice.

Brougham shot a look at him.

"You're right that I don't want to hear about your personal behavior," Malcolm said. "But this touches on a murder investigation."

"My relationship with Caro had just gone disastrously wrong. I wanted her. I pursued her. Then, when I had her—she's the sweetest of women, but I confess sweetness can pall a bit. I found myself bored. And though I'm certainly no paragon of virtue, I felt more than a bit guilty at persuading a woman away from her husband and then growing bored with the affair. I was trying to make sense of it. Not the most logical thing to discuss with another mistress, perhaps, but Danielle had a way of listening that made one confide almost without intending to. I revealed things that I'd prefer not be shared with the general public. For my own sake, but even more for Caroline's."

"That's all?" Malcolm asked.

"My God, isn't it enough?" Brougham looked up at Malcolm with an uncharacteristically open gaze. "I may not share your fine-tuned scruples, Rannoch, but I'm not a monster. I wouldn't wish that sort of social slander on anyone, and particularly not on a woman I once loved. Of whom I am still very fond."

Malcolm inclined his head. "What does this have to do with James Blayney?"

"He had papers he wanted me to buy. Papers written by Danielle."

"Letters?"

Brougham sank back in his chair with a grimace. "Memoirs."

Malcolm released his breath. "Well, that explains a lot."

"You don't sound surprised."

"I am, in a way. But it ties in with other things." And raised a number of other questions with far-reaching implications. "How did Blayney get these memoirs?"

"I don't know. I was shocked Danielle would have written them."

"Where is she living?"

"She settled in London. Abruptly. She's been living very quietly."

"Had you seen her in London?"

"No. She wrote to me when she arrived, to say she hoped to remain anonymous and would appreciate my help in doing so, and that of course we both wanted what had been between us to remain in the past. Which I did. Do." He gave a half smile, despite the frown in his eyes. "More or less."

"Was she in want of money?"

"She didn't seem to be when I knew her in Paris. And the tone of her letters from Paris, and later when she arrived in London, certainly didn't imply it."

"Did Blayney say how he got the memoirs?"

"No. He showed me a few pages to prove what he had and named a price."

"And you hadn't had a chance to buy them?"

"Rannoch." Brougham sat forwards, gripping the arms of his chair. "With everything going on, do you think I'd have risked those papers lying about? I paid him what he asked."

"But you hadn't got the papers yet?"

Brougham grimaced in a way Malcolm remembered from discussions of the defeat of a bill that particularly rankled. "I bought them Tuesday last. At a coffeehouse in Clerkenwell. I hoped to never see Blayney again. Which has proved true, though not as I suspected. I was shocked to hear he'd been killed. I went to get the papers out." His fingers bit into the wood of the chair. "They've been stolen."

Christ. "When had you seen them last?"

"The night I brought them home, I locked them in a cabinet in my study. I should have burned them. I suppose I felt there might be something in them I'd need."

"Something about someone else?"

"No. He only offered me the chapter about me." Brougham's hands tightened on the chair arms. "You must have searched Blayney's rooms. Did you find the rest?"

"No. He appears to have been in the act of selling another chapter when he was killed. He only had a few pages on him at the time, like the ones he first showed you. We didn't find the rest or anything else of interest in his rooms."

"Damnation." Brougham's fingers dug into the chair arms. He glanced out the window, then looked back at Malcolm. "I said I didn't see Blayney again. But I'd reached out to him to see if he'd be willing to sell me the rest of the memoirs."

"Because you thought there was more about you in them?" Malcolm asked in a neutral voice.

"No. Though I suppose there might be. But I was more concerned because Danielle had a number of lovers. Not to put too fine a point on it, she was a courtesan."

"Yes, I know."

"And you weren't remotely tempted, because you're besotted with your own wife. Which, knowing Mélanie, isn't surprising."

"I don't know that I'd ever call myself besotted. But it's true I wasn't interested in anyone else. Am not."

"Not using a word doesn't mean it doesn't apply to you, old fellow. I've seen the way you look at your wife. In any case, Danielle had powerful lovers before and after Napoleon fell. A number of them were British."

"Including Wellington, to hear the rumors."

"Yes, I've heard that as well, though Danielle never quite admitted it to me. But she did admit to a number of her lovers, and many of them sit in the Lords and will be voting on the queen's case. I'm sure I don't have to spell out to you what use the memoirs could be put to in the wrong hands."

"Would the threat of your secrets being exposed impact your actions in the queen's case?"

"Of course not." Brougham dived his hand into his hair again. "You said it yourself. I'm committed to winning this case, for a number of reasons. I'm a lot of things, but I don't think I'm a coward. So if the threat of exposure was held over me, I'd have to defy it. Which might well mean the truth would be made public. And that in turn would create no end of distraction and probably earn me new enemies. Caro's father-in-law was excused the trial due to his age, but Hart—the new Duke of Devonshire—is a vote we're counting on. So is Lord Cowper. This is the last moment I want to remind people I ran off with the sister-in-law of a prominent Whig who comes from another powerful Whig family. All of which could damage my ability to defend the queen's case and muster Whig votes."

"Which could well mean that someone with the memoirs who had any sense of who you are would simply make them public rather than attempting to blackmail you."

Brougham frowned. "At least the part about me. Possibly. All the more reason to recover them."

"Do you think Mademoiselle Darnault would let them be used against you?"

Brougham's frown deepened. "I wouldn't have thought so. I liked her. I believed she liked me. We wrote occasionally after I left Paris. I—" He hesitated. "I considered her a friend. Perhaps a fatal mistake. I said things to her I shouldn't have said to anyone but a trusted friend. Perhaps not even to a trusted friend."

"Henry." Malcolm studied Brougham. He understood and honored Brougham's concern for Caro George, but there was an added level of anxiety here. "Is there anything about the queen in the memoirs? Anything you told Danielle Darnault?"

Brougham shifted in his chair. He had been advising Princess, now Queen, Caroline, for years. "I told you I talked to Danielle. I confided things. About my life." He drew in and released his breath. "And about my work. I was concerned about the way the princess—queen—and Bergami were living. I already was strategizing for what might be to come. It was much on my mind. So yes, I did discuss the queen with her."

"You shared information that might help Princess Caroline —the queen—in a legal case."

Brougham crossed his legs. "No comment."

"And information that might hurt her."

"Definitely no comment."

"You don't need to comment to me. But is there information in these pages that you bought and that were then stolen that you're concerned could damage the queen's case?"

Brougham grimaced, drummed his fingers on the chair arm, nodded. "Yes."

"Which is why you didn't burn them—because there's also information that might help."

"Yes."

"Who has access to your rooms?"

"No one. Well, the servants."

"Any deliveries lately?"

"No."

"Henry. You're running a household. Surely food and laundry soap and all sorts of things are delivered."

"Oh, well, yes. Through the area door."

"Which leads to the rest of the house. I can't tell you how many times I've gained access to a home disguised as a tradesman, made my way up the backstairs, changed my appearance, and strolled through the house."

Brougham stared at Malcolm as though he'd transformed into another person. "In Vienna?"

"In Vienna, in Brussels, in Paris. In Lisbon before that. And various parts of Spain. In London, more recently."

Brougham passed a hand over his face. "Christ. I forget who you are, sometimes."

"Being an agent's rather dull in many ways. Trying to blend into the woodwork."

"While sneaking into houses."

"There is that."

Brougham shifted in his chair. "You want to talk to my staff."

"It would help, if you'll let me. I presume you want to recover the papers."

"My God. Of course." Brougham frowned. "Who was Blayney trying to barter papers to the night he was killed?"

"Not anyone directly connected to the queen's case."

"How can you be sure of that?"

"The papers involved were of another type."

"You saw them?"

"I saw the papers he was offering as proof he had more. The rest are gone." Malcolm sat back in his chair. "Did you ask Blayney how he came to have the papers?"

"Yes." Brougham scowled. "Not surprisingly, he wouldn't say. He did say I was a fool if I trusted a woman like Danielle Darnault. He used worse language. I knocked him to the floor of the coffeehouse and spilled a pint of porter on him. That was satisfying. But not very helpful."

"Did you try asking Danielle Darnault?"

It was Brougham's turn to hesitate. "I said she'd asked me to stay away in London. Which she did. And which I did. I hadn't seen her since Paris or attempted to communicate with her. But after Blayney's first visit to me, I stormed over to Danielle's house. I said a lot of things I now regret."

"What did she say?"

Brougham frowned at a knot in the walnut of the chair arm. "She went quite pale. One would have sworn she was shocked. But then she's a very good actress. After a moment, she asked if I really thought she was so heartless as to turn on an old friend. I said I didn't think she was so heartless—or so foolish—as to commit secrets confided to her to paper, let alone paper seemingly meant for publication. She admitted I had a point. Turned away and wrapped herself up in her shawl. One she'd once told me Bonaparte had given her. She said memoirs could be a form of insurance. But she hadn't expected them to see the light of day. I asked her how the devil Blayney got them. She said she couldn't explain, but she had things she had to attend to. She promised to do her best to make it right." Brougham shook his head. "It's odd. In the moment, I found myself believing her. Enough that I left far less concerned than I'd been when I arrived. By the time I returned home, I was less sanguine."

"But you think she was surprised Blayney had the memoirs?"

"I can't swear to it, but—yes."

"And she wanted to recover them."

"Assuming Blayney wasn't working for her, of course she would want to recover them." Brougham stared at Malcolm. "You aren't suggesting Danielle—got rid of Blayney?"

"I'm not suggesting anything. But do you think she'd be capable of it?"

Brougham looked away. "Blayney was a bastard. Danielle was kind, as I said. But she wouldn't have got where she was without being ruthless. I suppose that's true of me as well. Does that make us both suspects?"

"At the moment," Malcolm said, "nearly everyone connected to this is a suspect."

CHAPTER 15

"Good God," Cordelia said. "Captain Blayney somehow had the memoirs of one of the most celebrated opera singers and courtesans in Europe?"

They were all gathered in the Berkeley Square library sharing tea and updates. Mélanie, Cordy, and Kitty, returned from Gunter's, Laura, whom they had met in the square garden with the children, Malcolm, who had returned before them and spoken with Henry Brougham, Harry and Julien, who were both looking distinctly restless at not having had designated missions yet this day.

"It appears that way," Malcolm said. He looked at Mélanie. "Did you ever meet Danielle Darnault?"

She shook her head. "She wasn't in the Peninsula that I know of. She left Vienna before we arrived. In Paris, I was living the life of a diplomatic wife, which has its limitations. Sadly. I only saw her on stage. She has an amazing range. Her Susanna and Vitellia were brilliant." Mélanie could still remember the way Danielle Darnault's burnished voice and magnetic presence had held the theatre in thrall in those very different roles. "Harry?"

"I saw her on stage in Paris as well. Remarkable. She was

pointed out to me at a party in Brussels once. An officers' party at which wives weren't present. But we were never so much as introduced."

"Pity," Cordy said.

Harry looked at her.

"Well, you weren't tied to me then. You might have acquired useful information."

"Define 'tied.' And I doubt she'd have looked twice at me."

"Ha."

"I knew her." Julien's measured voice cut with surprising force in the room. "In several guises. And eventually as myself. That is, as Julien St. Juste."

"So she *was* an agent?" Mélanie said. "I always wondered."

"She was a free lance like me," Julien said. "Perhaps better at it than I was."

"That's hard to believe," Laura said.

Julien's mouth curved in a smile. "You wouldn't say so if you'd met her."

"Had you seen her in London?" Kitty asked.

"Once or twice. She claimed, quite convincingly, to want to retire. Something I could sympathize with at that point." He looked at Kitty. "Sorry, sweetheart."

"No reason for you to have told me," Kitty said.

Julien's gaze met her own for a moment in a simple look that spoke volumes about what was between them. "I'd worked with her on a few missions. She reached out to me when I settled in London, to let me know she was here and living in retirement, and that she'd stay out of my way if I stayed out of hers. I told her I was happy to do so and had no wish to revive my former life myself. Which hasn't entirely been the case." He looked down at his shirt cuff.

"You like her," Kitty said.

Julien met his wife's gaze. "We weren't lovers. Not even briefly." He hesitated just a moment. Mélanie thought she understood. Mostly Julien cheerfully ignored his past, as she did. At least, that part of their past. But it wouldn't quite go away. And understanding as their spouses were, at times it could not but be an issue. At least, Malcolm and Kitty wouldn't be human if it weren't an issue.

"That's not what I meant," Kitty said. "At least, that's not what's relevant. You've slept with all sorts of people. You like far fewer. Though you like a few of those you've slept with." She cast a very brief glance at Mélanie.

"I wouldn't put Danielle in the same category as Mélanie." Leave it to Julien to confront a difficult issue head on, in front of both their spouses and a number of their closest friends. "But she has a keen understanding. And a sense of humor. We shared an appreciation of spycraft and a sense of the foibles of those who employed us. Danielle didn't have any particular beliefs, not that she admitted to. And neither did I—at least, not that I professed to at that point."

"You sound as though you trust her," Laura said. As usual, she was sitting quietly, observing the whole. Seemingly on the edge of the discussion, yet in many ways she had more of a knack for managing missions than any of them.

Julien settled back into the cushions on the settee where he sat beside Kitty. "I wouldn't say I trust anyone. Present company excepted—and I do mean that." He reached for Kitty's hand. "Danielle is a bit capricious. And she could be quite mad. All the most interesting people can be. But she was refreshingly direct."

Kitty smiled. "Coming from you, that's high praise."

"Are you sure she's retired?" Harry asked.

Julien gave a wry smile. "I'm not sure of anything, where it comes to Danielle."

Malcolm sat forwards in his chair. "Whom might she be working for, if she's still working for someone now?"

Julien stared down at his and Kitty's interlaced hands. "Difficult to say. She was always an agent for hire. Like me."

"You've always had a certain code," Mélanie said. "Difficult as it was for some of us to decipher it. Does she?"

Julien's brows drew together. "If so, I may not have deciphered it myself. She was a pragmatist, at least on the surface. But she could be quixotic in her choices. And loyal to friends."

"Who are her friends?" Laura asked.

"I'd have said I was one. Though I wouldn't quite have admitted to having friends in those days. She was kind to the people who worked for her. She was fond of some of her lovers, though she laughed at most of them. Perhaps that's why I never became one of their number."

"Would she try to blackmail Brougham and others?" Laura asked.

Julien frowned. "As Malcolm would say, who can know what anyone might be capable of? Danielle was—is, I presume—hard-headed. But I wouldn't have pegged her for a blackmailer. For one thing, she was too well able to take care of herself. For another—she had morals of a sort. Rather more than I did."

"It sounds as though Mademoiselle Darnault was shocked to find the memoirs were being used," Malcolm said. "Granted she's a good actress, but piecing together what we have, it seems likely Captain Blayney's Grace is Danielle Darnault's lady's maid and she stole the papers, or Blayney used her to steal them. That would account for Mademoiselle Darnault's shock."

"She wouldn't be the first woman recently to find she couldn't trust her maid," Cordelia said. Louise Demont, Queen Caroline's maid, had testified against her, including about stains on the sheets and the queen's leaving Bergami's bechamber clad in only a nightdress.

"So when Mademoiselle Darnault said there was something she had to do," Laura said, "presumably she meant confronting Grace and Blayney."

Julien met the gazes that were turned on him. "You're wondering if Danielle would have killed Blayney to get the papers back? That would surprise me less than her resorting to blackmail in the first place. She's certainly capable of being ruthless. And I don't think she'd take kindly to her words being used by others for their own ends. However foolish she was to have written them down in the first place."

"Practically every politician in London is going to want to get their hands on those papers," Mélanie said.

"And someone has them," Malcolm said. "Which may lead to another whole set of complications." He looked at Julien. "Did Danielle Darnault ever work for Hubert?"

"Not that I know of. But I'm the first to admit I don't know everything. Especially when it comes to Uncle Hubert."

Malcolm nodded. "I should talk to him. Given the possible implications."

"Better you than me, old fellow. Meanwhile, I should try to talk to Danielle," Julien said. "And at least see what she'll be willing to say. I think it would be good if Kitty and Mélanie would come with me."

"Gladly," Mélanie said.

Kitty slid her hand through the crook of Julien's arm. "You always have the best ideas, darling."

DANIELLE DARNAULT LIVED in a terrace house with a shiny yellow door and window boxes that still held the last autumn gold of geraniums. Lace curtains showed at the white-framed sash windows. It looked like the home of a respectable widow, not a former agent, opera singer, and courtesan who had cut a swathe through the major events on the Continent in the past decade.

"There was a time when I'd have found it odd she escaped to this," Kitty said as they climbed the steps. "Now I think I have a glimmering."

Julien shot a look at her. "Carfax House is hardly on this scale. More's the pity."

"Quite. At times, a house like this seems quite appealing. More like our rooms in Carnaby Street."

"I miss our rooms in Lisbon sometimes," Mélanie said. "And our house in Paris." She glanced from one window to another. "No lights showing."

"No." Julien scanned the house. "Everyone could be in the back rooms." He rang the bell. No answer. After a couple of minutes, he rang again.

Kitty put up her hand to better anchor her bonnet. "I suppose she could have gone away and shut up the house. But—"

"That seems a bit odd, just at the time her memoirs are being used. And just after Brougham told her what was happening and she said she'd attend to it." Julien tested the door. It was latched. He glanced round the street. A nurse was walking, holding a toddler girl by the hand, while a boy a few years older followed, pushing a wagon. A manservant bounded up the area steps of a house across the street and trotted down the pavement carrying a parcel. A newsboy ran by shouting a headline that promised new details about the queen's domestic arrangements.

They exchanged glances, and then of one accord went down the area steps of Danielle Darnault's house. No light shone below stairs either. Julien rapped on the door, then tried the latch. It too was locked. They exchanged glances again. Mélanie reached for her picklocks and lifted a brow.

"By all means," Julien said.

It was the work of a few minutes to unlatch the lock on the area door. They stepped into a tile-floored kitchen. Even in the shadows Mélanie could make out copper pans on the walls, a deal table, tins beside the range. No whiff of recent cooking hung in the air.

Kitty touched her finger to the table and held her gloved hand up to the light from the windows. "No dust."

Julien picked up a lamp on the table and lit it, and they went into the passage. A small bedchamber for a cook or kitchen maid opened off it to one side. A narrow bed with a flowered quilt was made up. Kitty opened the wardrobe to reveal clothes hanging on pegs and a pair of shoes at the bottom.

"They look like best shoes," Mélanie said, noting the shiny black leather.

"Yes," Kitty agreed. "She's probably wearing her other pair. Wherever she is."

They climbed the pine stairs to the ground floor and went through a door into the entry hall. It had a fanlight over the door as in Berkeley Square, but was narrower. A console table held a basket probably intended for calling cards but now empty. No sound broke the stillness save muffled traffic from the street.

A book room at the front of the house was painted in a warm peach and filled floor to ceiling with bookshelves. A book bound in red leather lay open on the arm of a petit-point chair pulled close the fire. Mélanie glanced at the spine. "*Sense and Sensibility*. She has good taste in books." A Norwich shawl was tossed over the back of the chair, as though discarded by a wearer who intended to come back shortly and continue reading.

Julien examined the grate. "The fire was banked but the ashes haven't been swept up."

A parlor across the hall was also empty and looked less used than the book room. The walls were papered in blue, the chintz-covered chairs and sofa stood at precise angles, no personal possessions lay about. But the roses in a vase on the table were still fresh. They returned to the hall and climbed the graceful mahogany railed stairs. The doors at the landing were all closed. But a faint sound came from behind the central one. They exchanged quick glances again. Mélanie and Kitty flattened themselves on either side of the door. Julien flung the door open.

A man in a dun-colored coat was in the process of going through a chest of drawers with the efficiency of a professional. Julien hurled himself at the man. His quarry sprang back at the last instant. Julien stumbled and caught him round the knees. The man pulled away, lurched towards the window, which had the sash up, and sprang into the street. Julien sprang after.

itty and Mélanie ran to the window in time to see Julien racing down the street after the escaping intruder in the dun-colored coat.

"He gets to have all the fun," Kitty murmured. "No, I know, no sense in our running after." She turned back and glanced round the room. "Best get to work ourselves."

The room was not overly large, but the furnishings were of polished walnut. Clothes were scattered over the pale blue Turkey rug. The drawers were pulled out and the wardrobe doors gaped open. Mélanie picked up a pale blue sarcenet gown, cut on stylish lines but with long sleeves and a relatively demure neckline, and then a chemise threaded with pale blue ribbon, also with a demure neckline. "She has a good modiste, but she dresses to fit this house, not her old life."

"She has some nice jewels, but nothing like the fortune one would expect." Kitty was looking through Danielle Darnault's jewel box.

Mélanie opened another door onto a small room hung with yellow-flowered paper and stopped short. The room contained a narrow iron bedstead with a cheerful yellow-and-blue quilt, a chintz armchair, a low shelf with books, wooden blocks, a slate and pastels. She glanced at Kitty. "Did Julien say anything about Danielle Darnault's having a child?"

"No." Kitty came up behind Mélanie and glanced round the nursery. "I wonder if he knew himself."

Mélanie moved into the nursery. A small nightdress, linen threaded with pink ribbon, was tucked beneath the pillow. "A little girl a bit older than Jessica by the look of it." She lifted the lid of a chest. "There are quite a few clothes here, but it's possible some were taken."

"This room doesn't appear to have been searched," Kitty said. "He must have started with Danielle Darnault's room. And he doesn't appear to have found anything." She started across the room, then went still as they both caught a faint sound from the floor below. Mélanie reached for a sturdy candlestick.

An owl's call sounded, and Kitty released her breath. "Julien."

Julien came into the room with quick footsteps a few moments later. His coat was rumpled and there were patches of dirt on the knees of his pantaloons. Kitty scanned his face. "Lost him?"

"In the alleys round Portland Place." Julien paused and took in the room.

"Did you know?" Kitty asked.

Julien hesitated. "I knew she was with child about six years ago. She went off to have the child. That's why she left Vienna before the Congress properly began. I heard rumors she had the baby with her in Brussels, but she never mentioned the child to me. Danielle did mention her daughter in London, but she didn't seem to want to talk about her a great deal."

"Toys and books, a chair for reading, the nursery adjoining her own bedchamber. She appears to be quite a devoted mother," Kitty said.

"And to have taken the child with her and packed their things," Mélanie said.

"How do you know?" Julien asked.

"Look at the toys." Mélanie gestured towards the shelf that held the toys and books. "All the sorts of things a child would want, but there's something obvious missing."

Julien and Kitty looked from the shelves to the bed. Kitty seemed to get it first. "A favorite stuffed toy."

Mélanie nodded. "It's a bit difficult to tell with the jumble in the other room, but Danielle seems to have taken lip rouge and eyeblacking, and I think one nightdress and some clothes. I think they ran quickly but were able to pack."

"If she was planning something, she might have feared people would come looking for her," Kitty said. "She might have shut up her house and set up an operation elsewhere. Or she might have run to protect herself, if she knew someone else was trying to use her."

"Quite." Julien frowned at the shelf of toys as though it were an elaborate code. "The question being what she or someone else might be planning."

"To get the memoirs back, presumably," Kitty said. "Unless she lied to Brougham and she was behind the blackmail. In which case you'd think she'd have had more time to pack. But it's obvious someone thinks she left something of value behind."

"Could she still be an active agent?" Mélanie asked.

"Couldn't any of us?" Julien said with a wry smile.

"So the question is who could she be working for or running from?" Kitty said.

"Her staff appear to have gone with her," Mélanie said. "Or else they all ran."

"You think Danielle Darnault is behind whatever plot Captain Blayney was involved in?" Kitty asked.

"It's possible," Mélanie said. "But it's also possible Mademoiselle Darnault ran because she'd discovered what her maid and Captain Blayney were involved in, and it put her at risk. Or that she and Grace both ran because of Captain Blayney's plan.

Although from what she said to Brougham, it sounded more as though she was going to deal with the situation than run from it. She might have thought she could deal with it better from somewhere else."

"Or whatever she did to deal with it could have made her run," Julien said. "Including if she was behind Blayney's death." He looked between Mélanie and Kitty. "I don't want her to have been, but there's no sense in avoiding an obvious possibility just because I don't want it to be true."

Mélanie looked at Julien. There was a time when she wouldn't have been able to imagine his admitting he didn't want someone to be guilty of a crime on personal grounds. "Do you know who the father of Danielle's child is?" she asked.

"No. We were hardly confidants on that level. And given her life, she may well not have known herself. I don't think many of her relationships were exclusive. As was true of me, until recently." He cast a quick smile at his wife. But something lingered in the air, unsaid.

"Julien?" Kitty asked, watching her husband. "If you aren't sure, what do you suspect?"

Julien drew in and released his breath. "I can't say I suspect it. I don't have enough data to even add up to suspicion. But around the time Danielle admitted she was pregnant, she was involved with Napoleon Bonaparte."

"Oh good." Lady Frances Davenport paused in the doorway of the Berkeley Square library. "I was hoping we'd find you all here. Well, almost all." Her gaze swept the room. "I assume Mélanie, Julien, and Kitty are off investigating."

"Why would you think they're investigating?" Malcolm crossed to his aunt's side. Frances always knew all the news in

London—or at least Mayfair and Westminster—but this was quick even for her.

"Darling." Frances held her cheek out for his kiss. "Michael is seeing one of our maids. Surely you knew."

"No, actually." Malcolm kissed his aunt's cheek. "Michael is creditably discreet. And we'd never pry."

"Nor would we, but Lottie told Maggie, who told Nell, who told Jem, who couldn't resist mentioning it when he brought up Archie's boots this morning. He seemed to think we already knew, while at the same time hoping he could add to the news." Frances drew back and tugged at one of her gloves. "I must say I'm rather hurt we didn't know. Not about Michael and Lottie, about the investigation."

"Don't be difficult, Fanny," Archie said with a grin. "Unless we're misinformed, it all just began last night."

"A world of time in Mayfair." Fanny moved to the sofa and sank down in a swirl of lavender skirts stitched in violet. "Do pour me a glass of something. And don't worry about the time of day. An investigation throws all of that out the window."

Archie seated himself beside his wife. He was a former agent himself, both against the Elsinore League and in the war. During which he had worked for the French. It was a measure of how far they had all come that that now seemed the least of their concerns. Malcolm moved to the drinks trolly and poured sherry for his aunt and Harry's uncle. "It's as well you're here. We wanted to update you. But things have unfolded rather rapidly. If it's any comfort, Raoul doesn't know any of it yet."

"Only because he's gone from town." Frances took the glass Malcolm was holding out to her.

"Well, if you'd happened to be here last night, we'd have told you as well." Malcolm gave a glass to Archie. "I'm on my way to see Carfax—Hubert—but first—what do you know about Danielle Darnault?"

Frances took a drink of sherry. "Who?"

"I might have known. Your knowledge is formidable, aunt, but unless you happened to see Mademoiselle Darnault on the opera stage on the Continent, you'd likely not have met. She didn't move in respectable circles."

"If you're calling me respectable, Malcolm, that's rather insulting."

"I wouldn't dream of it, Aunt Frances. But Mademoiselle Darnault doesn't mingle with certain portions of society. And you wouldn't have had balls in Berkeley Square or at Carfax House at which to meet her."

"Oh, the secrets gentlemen will keep from ladies. What has this opera singer or courtesan become involved in?"

"Apparently she's written her memoirs."

"And she's making them public?" Archie asked.

"The man who was killed last night is trying to sell them." Malcolm updated Archie and Frances on the events of the previous night and the morning, assisted by Harry, Cordelia, and Laura.

"Good God," Frances said. "I must say I should quite like to have seen Julien masquerading as a cyprian

"He looked aggravatingly exquisite," Cordelia said. "Harry was quite enchanted."

"Never let it be said I don't put all my energies into the verisimilitude of a mission," Harry said.

Archie was frowning, sitting forwards in his chair. "Danielle Darnault knows who Alexander Radford is?"

"Apparently." Malcolm had returned to his chair. "She had a number of illustrious lovers, but most of those we've been able to identify so far were on the Continent. So far, Brougham's the only Englishman we know for a certainty is in the memoirs, though Blayney appears to have tried to blackmail Lord Danbury with them."

"I'm not surprised Henry Brougham found himself in the midst of this," Frances said. "He has a way of positioning himself where he can get the most notice possible. But from what you say, I certainly doubt he's the only Englishman in the pages of these memoirs."

"Yes." Archie stretched out his bad leg. "There undoubtedly are others. I suspect I'm in the memoirs."

Frances shot a look at him. "I should have guessed. Paris?"

"Like Brougham, I met her at the Salon des Etrangers. Not surprising, it's a haunt of Englishmen in Paris. I used to avoid it for that reason, but I went on occasion, and she caught my eye. She had a way of catching the eye."

"I don't doubt it," Fanny said.

"It wasn't a particularly long affair, and I don't think I gave her anything of particular interest to report."

"Did you know she was an agent?" Harry asked.

"I'd heard rumors. That wasn't the reason for the affair. At least, not on my side. At least, not entirely. But still…"

It was Fanny who put it into words first. "Did she know you were working for the French?"

"I never told her," Archie said. "I'm certainly capable of foolery, but I wasn't a fool in that way. And I wasn't working with her. Truth be told, as I said, I got close to her partly because I'd heard the rumors and wanted to find out whom she was currently working for. I wasn't able to determine anything for a certainty. But it's possible she had similar thoughts when it came to getting close to me. She was—is—a very astute woman."

"Well." Frances folded her hands together. "We've always known this is a risk. We wouldn't be the first in the family to flee to Italy, and I expect Malcolm would let us have the use of the villa."

Malcolm looked at his aunt. They owed their present safety to her. She had got the regent, now the king, almost certainly one of her legion of former lovers, to pardon Mélanie and Raoul for unspecified former actions. They were both foreign, so it had been possible to make a case for their divided loyalties. She hadn't been able to secure a pardon for Archie without revealing his own past in the process. "It hasn't come to that yet," Malcolm said. "But of course."

Archie looked from Malcolm to his nephew Harry, to Cordelia, and then to Laura, the wife of his friend Raoul. "It puts all of you in an awkward situation. To say I'm sorry doesn't really seem adequate."

"We've all put the whole group in an awkward situation, one way or another, at some point," Malcolm said.

"And some of us are only safe because of Fanny," Laura said. "Or at least some of our loved ones." She looked at Archie. "Does Raoul know Danielle Darnault?"

"Not that I know of," Archie said, with a quick frankness that suggested he was telling the truth. "But that isn't to say she never worked for him. Apparently, she was a free lance."

"That's what Julien told us," Malcolm said.

"One would think she'd be a risk to the League." Harry leaned forwards. "Do we know if she numbered League members among her lovers? Other League members. Besides Alexander Radford, whoever he is. And you. I keep forgetting technically you're a League member," he added, looking at Archie.

"Beverston, briefly, in Paris," Archie said. "And possibly Glenister, not long after. And—" He hesitated. "I can't be sure, but I think she was involved with Alistair in Paris in '17. Not long before his death." He glanced sideways at Fanny.

"Do you think Alistair told me about other women he was involved with?" Fanny asked. Her affair with Alistair Rannoch, her sister's husband and Malcolm's putative father, had been one of the few love affairs she'd held secret for a long time, but now she was frank about it. "We may not have been exclusive, but even Alistair had a modicum of tact and taste in such matters."

"He told you about some of them," Archie said in an easy voice. "And he may have let some things slip inadvertently."

"A point." Fanny smoothed her hands over her lap. "But he never mentioned anyone called Danielle Darnault, to my recollection. I don't wish to appear a slave to social class or to offend anyone's Republican sensibilities, but the lovers of Alistair's I knew about were generally members of the beau monde. Gentlemen who will seduce their friends' wives on a bet and take all sorts of liberties in the shrubbery or an anteroom during a ball can still decide some women need to be protected from knowing about others. It's quite idiotic, and yes, the world does need to change. But that's the reality we're living in now."

"So besides the information about Alexander Radford, the League could want the papers for information to use against Beverston or Glenister," Cordelia said. "Or potentially to cover up information about them or some of her other lovers. Or one faction could want to use them to blackmail the other, and the other faction could want to cover it up."

"Or they could both want to blackmail the other, or to blackmail votes in the queen's trial, or to blackmail powerful men in general," Laura said. "Blackmail has always been one of the League's main tools. This is the sort of thing they could make capital of for years."

"But it's of particular interest to others because of the trial," Harry said. "And though I doubt the League care about the trial in and of itself, they might well care about the power they could reap from influencing the outcome."

"Hubert Mallinson would give a great deal to get his hands on those memoirs, I imagine," Malcolm said. "To protect some, and to use against others."

"You think he's dealing with the League again?" Laura said.

"I don't think he'd hesitate to do so if he had a chance to get the memoirs," Malcolm said. "He made it clear in June that being allies with us in one thing doesn't make us allies in everything.

Whether or not the League would sell him memoirs that contain information about some of their own is a different question. Even if the League members named are in a different faction, it might be an issue. Turning on their own is one thing. Turning them over to Hubert might be something else entirely."

"You may be crediting the League with too much fraternal feeling," Archie said. "But they've always been insular and protected their own, despite disagreements. I'm not sure about the current struggle, but it may hold true—out of self-preservation as much as anything else."

"The stage community often interact," Cordelia said. "Did she know Manon in Paris? Or Jennifer Mansfield? That is, Geneviève Manet, at that point?" Manon Caret and Jennifer Mansfield, formerly Geneviève Manet, now leading ladies at the Tavistock Theatre, had once reigned over the Comédie Française.

"I don't know," Archie said. "I'm quite sure Danielle didn't come to prominence until after Jennifer left Paris. That doesn't necessarily mean she couldn't have crossed paths with Jennifer. Which is interesting, because of Smytheton."

Jennifer Mansfield's longtime lover and now husband, Sir Horace Smytheton, had been an Elsinore League member and a Royalist agent. He had left the League and intelligence and devoted his energies to being an active patron of the Tavistock Theatre, where Jennifer performed. But last January, the League had attempted to have Sir Horace assassinated at the opening of Mélanie's play at the Tavistock. Though they had foiled the attempt, they still hadn't been able to discover the reasons for it.

"This seems excessively off, given his devotion to Jennifer for more than two decades, but Smytheton wasn't involved with Danielle Darnault, was he?" Cordelia asked.

"Certainly not that I ever heard of," Archie said. "But they definitely knew each other. Smytheton used to pop over to Paris well after he and Jennifer settled in London. I distinctly remember being out with Danielle one night in the Palais Royale when Smytheton was there. Smytheton was losing heavily at roulette, and I was doing rather well. Danielle was encouraging me."

"Hanging over your shoulder and whispering encouragement?" Fanny said.

"Er—yes." Archie sent her an apologetic smile. "Sorry, my love."

"No need to apologize. Anything before we met is quite your own affair. That is, anything in the days when I was so foolish as not to see you as anything more than an acquaintance."

Archie lifted her hand to his lips.

"Someone could be in the memoirs without having been Danielle Darnault's lover," Laura said. "There could be a passing comment that revealed information she wasn't even aware she was conveying. If Danielle Darnault was involved with Alistair Rannoch, it could even be something generally to do with the League."

"A good point," Archie said.

"Not to mention, if she was a spy, the memoirs could contain all sorts of secrets," Harry said.

"There's one other League member she was involved with," Archie said. He hesitated for a moment, gaze on his sherry glass. "The late Duke of Trenchard."

"Without knowing anything else about her, I pity her," Laura said. Trenchard, one of the more powerful League members, had been Laura's lover and later compelled her to spy for him. "When?"

"In Paris, in 1817."

"Just about the time he was blackmailing me into working for Mélanie and Malcolm and spying on them. Funny. I confess I didn't have the least interest in who was sharing his bed then."

"No reason you should have done," Archie said with an easy smile. "But Trenchard was at the heart of the League then. And focused on Malcolm and Mélanie enough he set you to spy on them. Which rather makes one wonder what he may have revealed to Danielle Darnault."

"Even if he told them about both Mélanie and Raoul, the truth can't hurt them now," Frances said.

"It can't lead to their arrest," Malcolm said. "It could still make life complicated."

"We've dealt with complicated," Laura said. "We rather thrive on it."

"Did Trenchard know about you?" Frances asked Archie.

"I don't think so. I'm going on the assumption that the League in general don't know. Partly because I like to think I've concealed it, but mostly because I assume if they knew, they'd use it against me."

"Still," Frances said. "I'd like to know what's in these memoirs of hers."

"So would a number of people," Malcolm said. "And as I said I imagine Hubert is in their number."

"Unless he happens to have the memoirs," Harry said.

"There is that," Malcolm agreed.

CHAPTER 17

"Malcolm." Hubert Mallinson looked up from his papers. "I was wondering when I'd see you."

It was amazing how visiting Hubert felt the same as it had in all the years he'd been Malcolm's spymaster, even in a smaller study, in a smaller house, with a simpler desk. Though Malcolm had no doubt Hubert had fitted the desk out with as many secret compartments and hiding places as the more elaborate desk in Carfax House that now belonged to Julien.

Hubert was a bit more inclined to actually look up from his work and look Malcolm in the eye these days. Malcolm wasn't sure if that was due to a change in Hubert or to the fact that he needed Malcolm as an ally at present.

Malcolm hooked a chair with his foot and dragged it over to the desk, just as he'd have done in the old days in Carfax House. "Danielle Darnault."

"Who?"

"Don't pretend you don't know."

Hubert sat back in his chair. "How did you learn about her?"

"James Blayney was apparently trying to sell her memoirs."

Hubert started at him. "My God. Do you—"

"No, I don't have them. Except for the few pages Kitty took off Blayney last night. Blayney appears to have been selling them chapter by chapter."

"At Darnault's behest?"

"We're not sure. It seems more likely he stole them from her." Malcolm wasn't prepared to share Brougham's story yet. "I can quite understand why you'd want to keep them away from me. The question is who else wants them. Who else may have bought chapters. Which goes to the question of who precisely is named within the pages."

Hubert adjusted his spectacles. "I'd say people who commit foolish indiscretions deserve what they get. Except that you'd rightly throw my past in my face."

"That depends. Are you named in Mademoiselle Darnault's memoirs?"

"I wasn't quite so foolish. And it would have taken more than the level of information she seemed to have to offer to convince me to make the attempt."

"Did she ever work for you?"

"She's French."

"So's Sylvie St. Ives."

Hubert moved a paper from one pile to the other and set his pen on top. "Danielle Darnault was a very capable operative. I say was because I do believe she's retired. Though I can't be certain. Agents who work for whoever pays best can be a risk for obvious reasons. But there's also something to be said for those who treat it like a business and don't let causes and emotions get in the way." He tugged his right earpiece into place. "I used to think that was Julien's greatest strength."

"St. Juste was a very able agent."

"Oh yes. And still is. I have no illusions he's retired. But he cares about far more than I realized at the time. There are certain advantages to his having commitments, for all we disagree. But it also makes him inclined to tilt at windmills. Like someone else I could name."

Malcolm sat back in his chair and folded his arms across his chest. "I can't imagine whom."

"Don't be cheeky, Malcolm. You're a bad influence on Julien."

"I'll take that as a compliment. Did Danielle Darnault work for you? Julien says he isn't sure."

"Julien knows her?"

"Surely you know the answer to that."

"My dear Malcolm. Whatever my dealings with Danielle Darnault, surely you realize there's a great deal about Julien I don't know." Hubert tented his fingers together and frowned. "Are you saying he's in her memoirs?"

"He says he wasn't her lover, if that's what you mean, and since I see no particular reason for Julien to lie about that, I'm inclined to believe him."

"Was he working with her now?"

"If he was, he'd know a deal more."

"Assuming Julien would tell you. Assuming you'd tell me, if he did."

"Always worth questioning. So you can decide what to believe when I tell you Julien wasn't working with Danielle Darnault and hadn't seen her in some time." Malcolm sat back in his chair. "Did she ever work for you?"

Hubert raised a brow. "You're better at seeing through prevarication than you used to be." He rubbed at a smudge on his cuff. "Yes, she did work for me. In Paris, after Waterloo. She was an able agent, though I never entirely trusted her. But I think by then she was sensible enough to know the British offered the most stability."

"From what I heard about her, I imagine she did. Whom did you have her spying on?"

"Tsar Alexander."

"She was his mistress?"

"She said she was. I can't swear to what actually passed between them, but one way and another she acquired excellent intelligence."

"Do you think she was sharing it with anyone else?"

"I wouldn't be surprised, but things played out to our advantage. I doubt anyone was paying her as much as I was at that point. It helps to have a generous purse to fund one's agents. She also got me some quite good intelligence on the League."

"Did you know she may have been Alistair's mistress?" Malcolm asked.

Hubert took off his spectacles, folded them, put them back on. "Oh yes." He settled the sidepieces over his ears. "I asked her to get close to him."

"You—" Malcolm stared at his former spymaster.

"Don't turn prudish, Malcolm. It's not as though you've never set an agent to seduce someone. And Alistair wasn't your father. Or loyal to your mother."

"No." Malcolm sat back in his chair. "I'm not surprised you did it. I am a bit surprised Alistair didn't tumble to it."

"Yes, so am I." Hubert's brows drew together. "I don't know for a certainty that he didn't, of course, though Danielle told me she was certain he hadn't. She'd have been difficult to deceive, yet Alistair might have pulled it off. But Alistair never blocked any of the information I got from her."

Malcolm folded his arms across his chest. "Why did you do it?"

"Why? Good God, Malcolm, surely that's obvious. You're the League's enemy as much as I am."

"The League have targeted my family. Set a spy in my house, tried to blackmail my wife and stepmother, tried to kill my father. You were running British intelligence. Just after Bonaparte had fallen. When the Continent was being remade. Surely you had more important concerns than the Elsinore League."

Hubert capped his pen. "And surely you realize the number

of agents and missions I run. Just because I set Danielle to spy on Alistair didn't mean I didn't have many other agents conducting other missions."

"No, but even granted the League are a threat—certainly not a threat I'd discount—I've never quite understood your level of interest in them. Especially given that their interests and yours often align."

"They'd stab anyone in the back. Or anything."

Malcolm sat back in his chair. "That sounds like someone else I know."

Hubert adjusted his spectacles. "It's not the people they attack that concern me as much as the institutions. They may not be Radicals, but in pursuit of their interests they don't care what they smash. They don't see that those very institutions are what keeps the world from the chaos they themselves fear."

Malcolm folded his arms across his chest. "At another time, I might make a case for chaos. Or argue how resistance to change is more likely to produce it. But instead—what particular chaos were you concerned about Alistair causing when you set Danielle Darnault to seduce him?"

Carfax swung his feet up onto the desktop. "Two and a half years ago, Trenchard was angling to be made prime minister."

"Did Alistair support him?" Malcolm realized he'd never been clear on that. Alistair had been killed before they had uncovered Trenchard's plot to become prime minister—by which point Trenchard himself had been murdered. It had been a chaotic few months, to say the least, both personally and polit- ically. Malcolm had learned the truth about Mélanie and Raoul just before. And Malcolm hadn't been sharing information with Hubert—quite the reverse—because he hadn't known Hubert knew the truth about Mélanie, and had been desperately afraid of the consequences if Hubert had learned. A fear which had proved well founded. Funny how they had in a sense got past that. To the point where they were sitting strategizing across

Hubert's desk. Save that it was a different desk, in a different house.

"That's part of what I wanted to discover," Hubert said. "In point of fact, when I set Danielle Darnault to try to get close to Alistair, I didn't know quite what he and Trenchard were planning. Only that it was something significant and close to home. Danielle managed to intercept some correspondence between Alistair and Trenchard. Their plot was in the very early stages then. But there definitely was a plot, and becoming prime minister was Trenchard's goal. And according to Danielle Darnault, Alistair was very much working in support of Trenchard's actions. In fact, I think Alistair saw himself as being a significant power behind the scenes."

"Trenchard was no puppet."

"No, but Alistair could run rings round even him. Alistair was a lot of things, but he was no fool. If they'd succeeded, I suspect they'd have fallen out, but they were allies at the time. Easier to make alliances in taking power than in keeping it, as many have found, including Napoleon Bonaparte."

Malcolm drummed his fingers on the chair arm. "Danielle Darnault was involved with Trenchard as well."

"Yes." Hubert turned to a console table that held a set of decanters, poured two glasses of sherry, and pushed one across the desk to Malcolm.

"You were behind that as well?" Malcolm asked.

"Given the League's activities, seduction was an obvious way to gather intelligence on them." Hubert took a drink of sherry.

"The League must have known she was an agent."

"Oh, yes. They thought she was working for them. But I flatter myself I paid better."

Malcolm picked up his glass but didn't drink. "All of this is round the time Trenchard got Laura established in our household."

"Yes." Hubert took another drink of sherry. "It was."

Laura, now Malcolm's stepmother and one of the people he loved and trusted best, had spied on them in their household for over a year. The first year of their daughter Jessica's life. "Alistair was behind that?"

"Surely you know the answer," Hubert said.

"Only that Laura was reporting to Trenchard." Laura's past association with Trenchard, her first husband's father, was not something Malcolm had any intention of sharing, no matter how much they might at present be allies.

"You know as much as I do," Hubert said. "Alistair and Trenchard are both dead. And I didn't know Laura had been working for the League until after you did."

Malcolm held his former spymaster's gaze. "That isn't one of the secrets Danielle Darnault ferreted out?"

"My dear Malcolm. I'd have told you."

"Would you? We weren't precisely allies."

"You were still working for me. At least officially, and I flatter myself you hadn't gone completely rogue."

"No." Malcolm tossed down a drink of sherry. "I didn't have the guts to, more's the pity."

"Well, then. It would have been a risk to me for you to have had a League agent in your house. Was a risk to me."

Malcolm looked into the pale depths of the sherry. "I've always wondered why Trenchard went to such lengths to spy on us. I suppose there's a certain logic to Alistair's having been behind it, but given the entire lack of interest he showed in me, I find that a bit puzzling as well."

Hubert twisted the stem of his glass in his fingers. "Far be it from me to claim to understand Alistair, but I believe he appreciated your understanding."

Malcolm stared across the desk at Hubert, his own glass clutched in his fingers. "But I didn't even know about the League at that point."

"He may have wanted to be sure he'd know if you did find out. And he knew Mélanie was the Raven."

Malcolm shifted in his chair. Even now, with Mel pardoned and their new alliance with Hubert, his skin crawled a bit when it came to discussing Mélanie's past with his former spymaster. "Supposedly, a lot of the League weren't happy with Trenchard's trying to become prime minister."

"So I've heard."

Malcolm took a drink of sherry. He'd have preferred whisky, but it supplied a welcome jolt. "Was that the beginning of the schism in the League?"

"I don't know." Hubert's brows drew together in seemingly genuine puzzlement. "Though it makes a certain sense. According to Danielle Darnault, Alistair and Trenchard were very secretive about their plans."

Malcolm took another drink of sherry. "Had Alexander Radford appeared then?"

"Not that I've been able to tell. But it's possible Radford took advantage of a schism that had already developed within the League. From my knowledge of the League, they've had disagreements before, but nothing as serious as the one over Trenchard's plans to become prime minister or the one that exists now."

"And then Trenchard went on with his plans—seemingly on his own—after Alistair was killed." Malcolm took another drink of sherry. It had a surprising bite. "Did Trenchard have anything to do with Alistair's death?"

Hubert reached for the decanter and refilled both their glasses. His hand appeared steady. "As you ably proved, Dewhurst had Alistair and Harleton killed. To protect the fact that they'd learned he wasn't the rightful earl."

"Funny how far people will go to protect titles."

Hubert set the decanter back on the console table. The cut glass flashed in the lamplight. "I never went that far."

"No, even I'd say you're better than Dewhurst. And I know that's the story of why Alistair and Harleton were killed. The one we've all been following."

Hubert's fingers froze on the stopper of the decanter for a moment. "You don't believe it?"

"I've always wondered if there was more to it. If Alistair would really have brought down Dewhurst. If Dewhurst was really able to outwit Alistair. I can see Dewhurst's killing Harleton. Alistair would be more difficult to outwit."

Hubert took a drink of sherry. "Dewhurst is a lot of things, most of them despicable, but he's no fool. And even clever people can miscalculate."

Malcolm turned his glass in his fingers. "So Danielle Darnault may not just know who Alexander Radford is. She may know how he's entangled with the League and what other members of the League are plotting."

"Possibly."

"And then later—or presumably later—Danielle Darnault became involved with Alexander Radford."

"Yes. That's interesting."

"It's not clear from the papers we saw when she met him. He could well have sought her out because of her past with Alistair and Trenchard. But what if Radford's been about far longer than we thought? What if he wanted her to get close to Alistair and Trenchard?"

"I told you I was behind that."

"That doesn't mean Alexander Radford couldn't be taking advantage of it." Malcolm watched the lamplight warm the sherry. "All these months we've been wondering who was trying to take over the League. And then who Alexander Radford is. And a woman may have been sitting in a house in Marylebone with all the answers."

"Possibly. Though there's no guarantee she'll share them with us."

"You never thought to ask her?"

"I thought I knew what she knew about the League. I thought her interactions with them were in the past." Hubert tossed down the last of his sherry. "Not for the first time, I was wrong." He reached for the decanter. "What does Gisèle know about this?"

Malcolm's fingers tightened round the stem of his glass. His sister Gisèle, who was undercover with the League, was Hubert's daughter, though Gisèle and Hubert had only learned the truth less than two years ago. "She told us the exchange was happening tonight," Malcolm said. "She didn't know what the League were trying to buy, let alone anything about Danielle Darnault."

"You mean she said she didn't." Hubert refilled their glasses.

Malcolm took a drink of sherry. "A point. But I don't see why Gelly would lie about that. She's not quite so byzantine as you."

Hubert grimaced. "These memoirs of Danielle's make Blayney's death and your investigation far more dangerous. You must see that. Particularly now. Whoever has the memoirs could attempt to impact the outcome of the case against the queen."

"You have a high opinion of the integrity of the House of Lords."

"Don't be clever, Malcolm. It wouldn't take that many. My God, if this farce of a trial is proof of anything it's proof of the embarrassment that can come from dirty linen being aired in public." Hubert frowned. "Literally dirty linen, in the case of some of the testimony. All it would take is a few men not willing to put themselves through that to swing the case either way."

"I take your point." Malcolm moved back to his chair. "Given that we're on opposite sides, I fail to see why that should make me inclined to assist you."

"My dear Malcolm. Are you telling me you want to win

based on blackmail? Perhaps my character reading of you has been wrong all these years."

"My dear Hubert." It was still hard to say the name, yet Malcolm found a certain satisfaction in doing so. "Are you telling me you wouldn't stoop to using the memoirs to win influence for your side if you came into possession of them?"

"Blackmail's a messy business. It's inclined to spawn unintended consequences. You know what I think of those."

Malcolm sank further back into his chair. "Tell me you've never employed it."

"That would be foolish, given that you know perfectly well I have. It doesn't mean I would do so on this occasion." Hubert pushed his spectacles up. "I'm hardly enamored of the king's case."

"You're enamored of stability, and you don't want to aid the Radicals."

"Do you think the queen's success would lead to victory for the Radicals?"

"The question seems to be whether you think it would. I've seen the lengths to which you're willing to go. I didn't want you to have the papers the League were dealing last June, and I don't want you to have these."

"And I'd understand, if it were just a question of the queen's case." Hubert sat back in his chair. "But the League aren't selling these particular papers. Quite the opposite, they're one of the possible buyers."

"The League have always dealt in blackmail. I imagine they could do a great deal with the memoirs."

"Possibly. But most of those being asked to buy them are subjects in the memoirs. Which raises the question of whether the memoirs reveal damaging information about the League."

"Are you saying I should deliver the memoirs to you to strike a blow at the League?" Malcolm asked.

"I'm saying we have a common interest in seeing what's in them."

"And once we examine them?"

"If they reveal something about the League, we make use of it."

"Blackmail them in turn?"

"My dear Malcolm. Would you be above blackmailing the League?"

"That would depend on the information. And the collateral damage."

"To Danielle Darnault?" Hubert said. "She's behind the whole thing."

"To anyone caught up in the story. And we don't know Danielle Darnault's role."

"You can't think she's an innocent." Hubert shook his head. "But then you've always had protective instincts when it comes to female agents."

"Most of the women agents I know don't need protecting and wouldn't thank me for it. But they have helped me see that there's often more than one side to a question."

"Among other things, those papers reveal who Alexander Radford is. That could be the key to unraveling what's going on in the League now."

"Don't imagine I'm not well aware of that." Malcolm scraped back his chair.

"Malcolm." They might be in a different room with a different desk, and Hubert might no longer be Lord Carfax, but that was the voice of the spymaster Malcolm had known since childhood and worked with for over a decade. "You'll find these memoirs."

"I'll make every effort to do so."

"And you'll share them with me."

Malcolm turned back, one hand gripping the chair back. "Surely you realize that depends, sir."

"On what?" Hubert's voice was taut. "These aren't a lady's private love letters. You can't return them to their rightful owner. Danielle Darnault clearly isn't to be trusted with them."

"That has yet to be seen. We don't know Danielle Darnault's role in this. But I agree the memoirs aren't the same as private correspondence. And that they pose a danger in a number of hands. Including yours."

Hubert sat back in his chair and gripped his hands together. "So what do you intend to do with them if—when—you recover them?"

Malcolm permitted himself a small smile. "I haven't yet decided. I'll keep you apprised as seems appropriate. Good day, sir."

CHAPTER 18

Malcolm returned to the Berkeley Square house to see a familiar beaver hat and pair of doeskin gloves on the console table in the hall. The library door was ajar and lamplight spilled through. Relief shot through Malcolm for more than one reason. He went into the library to see Raoul by the library table, scanning a note.

"Father." Malcolm pulled the door to behind him. "Thank God."

Raoul looked up with a quick smile, the note still in his hands. "That's quite a greeting." His gaze shifted over Malcolm's face. "Is it something specific?"

"I'm always glad when you return, but yes." Malcolm moved to the table. "Laura took the children to the park, and Mel's out with Julien and Kitty. Cordy and Harry and Archie and Frances were here, but they've gone because of Cordy's ball tonight. We're in the midst of a new investigation."

"Laura says so in her note"—Raoul indicated the paper in his hand—"though she doesn't offer details."

They moved to the fire. Valentin brought in coffee, and

while Raoul poured, Malcolm explained about their expedition to the Chat Gris and James Blayney.

"Good God." Raoul put a coffee in Malcolm's hand. "I picked the wrong time to be gone."

"We've been managing, but it's good to have you back." Malcolm took a drink of coffee. "What do you know about Danielle Darnault?"

"I know of her. I never worked with her. I was in Spain much of the time she was active, and then I was preoccupied with saving my agents after Waterloo, so an agent for hire seemed risky to employ. They might be paid more to betray you to the opposite side. I saw her on stage—she has a magnificent voice—and once or twice at the Salon des Etrangers and other places in Paris. I may have crossed paths with her other times when she was so well in disguise I didn't recognize her."

"Hubert just admitted she worked for him."

"That's not surprising."

"And that he set her to seduce Alistair and Trenchard."

Raoul raised his brows. "That shouldn't be surprising. But—"

"Yes." Malcolm said. "I was shocked too, and then wondered at my own reaction." He reached for his cup and felt his fingers tighten round the handle. "So much has changed in the past three years. I forget sometimes that it hasn't really been that long since Alistair left us—since Alistair was killed." He looked at Raoul. "Do you believe Dewhurst killed him?"

"Dewhurst hasn't denied it."

"Dewhurst has refused to say anything at all, one way or the other." Malcolm took a drink of coffee. "Alistair went to Devonshire with Aunt Frances not long before he was killed."

Raoul gave a wry smile. "Alistair went away with Fanny a number of times. You know that now."

"Yes, but on this occasion, Fanny says he was oddly keyed up and thanked her for their time together. It almost sounds as though he was saying goodbye. Or knew it might be goodbye."

"He was involved in a very dangerous game with Dewhurst. Not to mention that he and Trenchard were trying to bring down Liverpool."

"Yes, but if he thought he might be saying goodbye to Fanny, he'd have sensed things were coming to a head in the near future. And while I can barely imagine Dewhurst's taking Alistair by surprise and managing to kill him, it strains belief to imagine Dewhurst's getting the better of Alistair if Alistair was on his guard. I certainly can't claim to have known Alistair well, but I think I understand him to that degree."

Raoul turned his cup on its saucer. "What are you suggesting, Malcolm?"

"I don't know, precisely. Save that we now know just how obsessed Carfax—Hubert—has been with bringing down the League—and for how long. We know how Hubert prizes stability. Trenchard and Alistair were trying to bring down the prime minister. And they both ended up dead."

"Carfax—Hubert—didn't kill Trenchard."

"No." Malcolm heard the hesitancy in his own voice.

"And I think enough of him as a father to think he'd have stopped Louisa if he'd had the least notion of what she was doing, when it came to Trenchard." Raoul sat forwards in his chair.

"So do I. I think." Malcolm stared into his cup. The Duke of Trenchard's death and the role of Louisa Craven, Hubert's second daughter, whom Malcolm had known since they were children, was still a raw wound, buried amid the numerous wounds of the past few years. "Although Louisa's husband was killed by one of Hubert's usual assassins."

"Craven was, but not Trenchard. And don't think I haven't wondered if Tommy went to Carfax—Hubert—before he shot Craven. Save that if he had, I think Hubert would have intervened before Louisa killed herself."

Malcolm dragged hand through his hair. "It was a damnable

time. Laura was arrested for killing Trenchard. She could have gone to trial."

"Don't think I'm not keenly aware of it. But we'd have broken her out first. And I'd have taken her somewhere we could disappear."

"Even then?" Malcolm asked. Raoul played his cards close. When he'd come to feel what he felt for Laura wasn't something Malcolm fully understood.

"Even then." Raoul tossed down a drink of coffee. "Mind you, I'm damned glad it didn't come to that. Getting the truth from Laura and extracting Emily would have been a challenge." He sat back in his chair. "And I'd be unhappy, to say the least, to be away from you."

Malcolm folded his hands round his cup. "Likewise." He met his father's gaze for a moment, then realized they had strayed quite far from the point of the conversation. "Which doesn't account for Dewhurst's getting the better of Alistair. Especially if Alistair was on his guard."

"No." Raoul settled the cup on its saucer. "Mind you, I've seen often enough how the most seemingly clever people can be caught unawares, when all sense would scream they should know better. Alistair was clever—brilliant—in many respects. But he could have made a mistake. Even if he was on his guard."

"And if he didn't—if Hubert had him killed?"

"Would that change how you feel about Hubert?"

"I—" Malcolm swallowed his instinctive rejoinder. "I know Hubert's had people killed. I know while we're allies at present, while I can sit across his desk talking rationally about strategy with him, I don't agree with him on much. Christ, I knew that was true when I worked with him, and I still worked with him, and I'll never forgive myself for that, but that's another story." He drew a hard breath. "Alistair wasn't my father. In any sense of the word. I don't feel I owe anything to him. But—it would cut close to home."

Raoul nodded. "I can see that."

"Can you?"

"My dear Malcolm. He was the first person you called father. Whatever's between you and me—for which I am more grateful than I can say—doesn't change that."

"He didn't raise me. You did. More than he did, more than Arabella did, though you had to go to great lengths to do so. But I do have—a connection of sorts with him—that goes back a long way."

"Of course you do." Raoul stretched his legs out with an ease that inspired confidences. "I'm sure your memories of him are older than your memories of me."

"Not really. Truly. I remember you at the villa in Italy. When I couldn't have been more than two. Maybe one and a half. I can't date any memory of Alistair back that far. But he is part of the fabric of my childhood. Which isn't to say I'd make different decisions right now if I knew Hubert had had him killed. We're rather stuck with Hubert as an ally, at the moment."

"So we are." Raoul took a drink of coffee.

"And we need him in this investigation." Malcolm sat back in his chair. "It seems to be tangled with a lot of our lives. It's hit Julien and Kitty the hardest so far. Kitty's blaming herself for Blayney's death. Which is foolish, but which we'd all be doing in her shoes. And Julien has a past with Pendarves. A rather close past. From a mission at the time of the tsar's visit in '14."

Raoul frowned. "Yes, I've heard about that. He was working for Talleyrand. How well documented is it?"

"Julien says there's nothing in writing. You know how careful he is. And he was in disguise at the time. Though when he saw Pendarves last night, Pendarves admitted to recognizing him."

Raoul's fingers froze on his cup. "Julien's already seen Pendarves?"

"He thought he should, as soon as we knew Blayney was a

blackmailer and that his things had been ransacked. It was possible he had something on Pendarves."

"Did he?"

"Not in writing, according to Pendarves. Though Pendarves admitted Blayney had been subtly using his past to get Pendarves to lend him money for years."

Raoul grimaced.

"But Pendarves said he had no reason to think Blayney or anyone else knew about his involvement with Julien."

"But Pendarves at least knows."

Malcolm shot a look at his father. "You seem awfully concerned."

"My dear Malcolm. It's still a hanging offense. Regrettably. Horribly. But it's a threat we live with."

"Yes. I suppose—" Malcolm frowned into his own glass. "I'm used to seeing Julien as invulnerable."

Raoul gave a faint smile. "So am I, to a degree."

"You're sounding very paternal."

"Well, I am the senior generation." Raoul frowned into his coffee cup. "Julien was always frighteningly intelligent and self-possessed. I saw him carry out an assassination the night we met. While scarcely breaking his stride as we walked through the Palais Royale. The skill and the sangfroid were impressive to say the least. And bone chilling. I knew then what I was dealing with."

"And yet," Malcolm said.

Raoul gave a wry smile. "There were moments, perhaps, when I glimpsed something beneath the surface. Perhaps more moments than I acknowledged to myself at the time. The uncertainty of a very young man. Scarcely more than a boy. Of a person picking his way through intrigues that could set governments toppling, and where human life could be viewed as collateral damage. And perhaps on occasion the concern of one who wasn't as deaf to ideals as he let on."

"And you think like a parent."

Raoul refilled their cups. "I try to do so. I can't claim to be an expert—certainly not then. But I was concerned."

"I think it's always been your instinct. Does Julien know?"

"That I've always had a glimmering of his ideals?"

"And that you have parental twinges where he's concerned."

Raoul set the coffeepot down. "How dreadfully embarrassing."

"Sentiment can be embarrassing. That doesn't make it unnecessary. Or unwanted. Knowing Julien's history, I rather think he could do with all the affection he can get." Malcolm took a drink of coffee and regarded his father for a moment. "This explains why you weren't more concerned sending Mel on that first mission against him."

"I was petrified." Raoul's gaze went hard. And bleak. "It was a dangerous decision. That I'm not sure I'd make again."

"I wouldn't have made it," Malcolm said. "I don't think. But I can understand why you did."

Raoul reached for his cup. "Julien's life is dangerous. This is an added measure of risk. Not as much so for him as for David, but still enough to worry those who love him."

"You said that awfully easily."

Raoul tossed down a sip of coffee. "I said it to you, not him. Though little sense in hiding it now."

"No." Malcolm reached for his coffee. "In fact, it might help, I would think. We're all getting better at dropping our masks." He took a drink. "Risks aside, I think Julien liked Pendarves. That gets complicated in a murder investigation."

"So it does."

"Speaking of which, I liked Edmund Blayney."

"He's a good man," Raoul said. "And an interesting one. When I first met him, I thought I'd find an earnest young Radical stuffed with principles but afraid to get his hands dirty. Or a young lout more interested in shocking his parents than changing the world. He's neither. He's not afraid to get his hands dirty and he seems to have no concern for his reputation or appearance in the world."

"Yes, comparing him with Pendarves, it's hard to believe they grew up together. Though they're both committed to reform, in their way. Just in different ways and to different degrees."

"Story of our lives."

"Did Edmund Blayney ever mention his brother to you?"

"I don't think so. Not in so many words. He mentioned his father's having had a living in Shropshire. He mentioned growing up with Pendarves once, but only because Pendarves had come to notice over the Corn Laws. I gave him information. He asked me to look over articles about Spain and Ireland. I'd say we're friends of a sort, but not on a personal level. He hasn't met Laura. Or you, or Mélanie, or any of the children."

"And you haven't met any one of his personal connections."

"If you're asking if he has a mistress, he hasn't mentioned one. And he wouldn't have done, necessarily. He seems to live a quite focused life. But he doesn't strike me as a monk. I certainly imagine he has friends. And very likely more."

"It would help to learn whatever more about him we can."

"I'll do my best. But I don't know how successful I can be."

"I have every faith in you, Father."

Raoul smiled. But for some reason, the smile looked more twisted than usual.

LAURA O'ROARKE OPENED the front door for the children to tumble into the hall, followed them into the house, and then went still at the strains of a familiar voice from the library. Emily, her almost seven-year-old daughter, cast an excited look at her over her shoulder and then hurtled into the library, followed by the other children. Laura followed, carrying her toddler, Clara.

"Daddy!" Emily launched herself at Raoul. "You're back early."

"Sweetheart." Raoul got to his feet and swung her up in the air. A few seconds later, Colin and Jessica and the Davenport girls also flung themselves on Raoul. The Ashford boys hung back, then rushed in when the rest of the children knocked Raoul back into his chair.

Laura stood smiling in the doorway. "Da." Clara wriggled to be put down, then ran to the join the other children.

Malcolm poured Laura a cup of coffee and left the children to their questions and exclamations for a time, but when they started demanding food, he pushed himself to his feet. "Let's see what Mrs. Erskine can find in the kitchen. That will give Laura and Raoul a bit of time to catch up."

He swung his little sister Clara up in his arms, grinned at Laura, and led the children out of the room.

"Darling." Laura walked over to her husband and put her face up for his kiss.

He kissed her and let his fingers linger in her hair. "My timing appears to be atrocious."

"We've managed."

"I have no doubt." He tucked an errant strand of hair behind her ear. "I just hate to miss the action."

Laura scanned her husband's face. Sometimes it was so hard to know when to ask questions, what questions to ask if one did, when to let things alone. And yet finding that balance, in so many ways, was the secret to making their marriage work.

"You needed to go away." She made it not quite a question. He hadn't told her where he was going. He didn't always, and he'd been more secretive about his work in Spain of late. Which she understood, especially as it would be difficult for her to keep information from Malcolm and Mélanie. But in this case, she knew he hadn't gone to Spain, and yet he'd been gone long enough that he wasn't meeting a contact in London. It was possible he'd gone to the coast to meet someone coming over from Spain or France. But she had an odd sense that this trip hadn't been about Spain at all.

Raoul glanced out the window at the tawny leaves on the Berkeley Square plane trees. In the light from the window, his face seemed sharpened, the hollows deeper, lines of strain about his eyes. Not that the strain wasn't always there, but these days it was tempered by the joy of his children, the excitement of his work in Spain, sometimes even by flashes of contentment. Now he looked more like the man she had first met in Paris after Waterloo. Haunted by failures, navigating a landscape in which no choice was good and the best he could do was try to mitigate damage.

"Sweetheart?" Laura reached for his hand. "Do you want to talk about it?"

Raoul turned his head and his smile reminded her of the first time he had smiled at her in Malcolm and Mélanie's salon in Paris, almost four years ago—sweet and lit with life, yet unable to banish the ghosts he lived with. "I don't know that I can, beloved. Not yet. But we may be in for an even more challenging time than I suspected."

Laura leaned her head against his shoulder. "Are you leaving for Spain?"

"No. Not for some time, I think." He lifted her hand to his lips and kissed her knuckles. "Which I suppose is an advantage in all this."

He'd said much the same when he'd had to stay in Italy because of their fears about Carfax—Hubert Mallinson—and the Elsinore League. But he'd smiled more as he'd said it. He was worried. More worried, perhaps, than she'd ever seen him. And considering what they'd faced, that was saying a lot. Whatever he was worried about, it was something he couldn't share with her, likely because he couldn't share it with Malcolm and Mélanie.

And that meant it was a secret that didn't just threaten their fragile life and family from the outside, like so many others. It threatened them from within.

CHAPTER 19

"So we have a down-on-his-luck schemer bartering memoirs that may reveal the identity of the man trying to take over the Elsinore League, memoirs that Brougham claims could influence the case against the queen, memoirs written by a former agent involved with key figures on all sides all over the Continent, who may have a child by Napoleon Bonaparte." Malcolm cast a glance round the library, where the team were now all gathered. Harry and Cordy had come back for an update shortly after Mélanie, Kitty, and Julien returned from Danielle Darnault's.

"It's difficult to see what Danielle Darnault's child could have to do with Queen Caroline's trial," Mélanie said. "It's a shock, but why would the child's being Napoleon's be so very impor-tant at all? Bonaparte has other illegitimate children. Hortense's legitimate children would be more likely to be a rallying point for a Bonapartist revival."

"Any Bonaparte descendant is a potential focus for some sort of plot," Raoul said. He'd been frowning at his hands. "But as you say, an illegitimate child would seem to be less of a rallying point than other options. And certainly not connected to the king and queen. Unless there's a great deal we're missing."

"Who else could the father be?" Laura asked.

Everyone looked at her.

"It's a reasonable question," she said. "Danielle Darnault had a number of powerful lovers. Julien said he wasn't sure she knows who the child's father is."

"True enough," Julien said.

"And those are secrets one holds close." Malcolm met Julien's gaze. "My own sister didn't confide in me in similar circumstances."

"Even so," Cordelia said, "unless the regent—the king—is the father"—she looked round at the surprised faces—"well, it's possible, he had one child—it's difficult to see how it could impact the queen's case." She frowned. "In fact, even if the king were the father, I don't see how it would impact the case. Unless the child's existence could be used as leverage against the king, which I suppose is possible. But kings don't tend to hide their bastards."

"Very true." Julien dropped down on the sofa beside Kitty and stretched out his legs. "But a child might prove a bargaining chip with someone else involved in the queen's trial."

Kitty frowned. "You think someone would go to such lengths to blackmail over just one vote?"

"I can imagine stranger things, if one vote seemed important enough," Malcolm said. "I think it's more likely they'd target someone they thought could influence other votes. The Whigs need a lot more votes, but each one is important." At the last division, the Whigs had had forty-one votes to rescind the bill against the queen and the government's majority had stood at one hundred and sixty-five. "But again, having a child with a mistress is hardly a secret most members of the House of Lords would go to great lengths to keep. In fact, they'd be more likely to boast about it over the port."

"I don't know much about Danielle's life in Britain," Julien said. "But there are some people I can ask." He looked at Raoul. "I suspect some of our contacts are the same."

Raoul gave a slow smile. "There was a time when I'd have been petrified at sharing information with you, Julien. But by all means, let's make inquiries together."

"I should update Roth," Malcolm said. "Who wants to come with me?"

"Thought you'd never ask." Harry glanced at his wife. "Unless—"

"Oh, by all means, stay and have fun," Cordelia said. "I need to go back home and make sure the champagne is delivered and start seeing to the flowers. What an inconvenient time to have chosen to give a ball."

"On the contrary," Malcolm said. "Just what we need for investigating tonight. Your timing couldn't be more impeccable."

"Well, that's some comfort. I'd much rather be interviewing suspects than arranging flowers."

"I could arrange the flowers," Harry said.

"Thank you, darling. It's a truly heroic offer, but I won't take you up on it." Cordelia grinned. "This time."

HENRIETTE VARON REGARDED Raoul and Julien across the sofa table in the sitting room of the rooms she shared with her two daughters. So different from the garden at Malmaison, or various salons where Raoul had been accustomed to speak with her. The coffee was the same, though, strong and dark, brewed to perfection. Served in cups of white and dark blue with small gold bees that had been a gift from the Empress Josephine. Whom Henriette had served as seamstress for many years. And whom her daughter Lisette had served as an agent. Raoul still wasn't sure Henriette would ever forgive him for recruiting Lisette.

Henriette and Lisette now exchanged quick glances. "Madame was aware of La Darnault," Henriette said. "But we didn't know a great deal. It was after the divorce."

"Funny," Lisette said. "It used to seem so distinctive that the emperor and empress had been divorced. And now the king and queen may be." She looked at her mother. "There were rumors, though. Just before Danielle Darnault left Paris."

"Yes." Henriette took a careful sip of coffee. "I know even the thought of Bonaparte's fathering another child hurt the empress. She never got over the fact that she hadn't been able to have a child with him herself."

"Did she give any indication Bonaparte had told her as much?" Julien sat forwards in his chair, face unusually intent and free of irony. "She still saw him. He confided in her until the end."

"If he confided in her about Darnault's child, she never told me," Henriette said. "Not that she necessarily would have done."

"I think—" Lisette frowned and set down her coffee. "From something Hortense said, I think it's possible the emperor wasn't sure about the child's parentage himself."

Henriette nodded. "That could be. I do know that at about that time, Bonaparte and Darnault had a falling out. Josephine said a part of her could not but be pleased, because she was still jealous where he was concerned. But at the same time, she pitied Danielle Darnault, because Bonaparte would never trust her again."

"She left Paris for Vienna," Lisette said. "And then she disappeared for a time. Perhaps because she was with child. But Hortense said Bonaparte had admitted he was afraid she was selling information to the British."

Raoul looked at Julien. "Well, that would be just like Uncle Hubert," Julien said. "To admit to Malcolm that he had Danielle spying on Alistair Rannoch, but quite neglect to mention that she was also reporting to him on Napoleon Bonaparte. Assuming she was."

"If she was spying on Bonaparte, and he was the father of her child, that makes for a particularly fraught situation," Henriette said.

"Yes, it could have been why she was particularly secretive about the child." Julien turned his coffee cup in his hand. "Then by the time the child was born, Bonaparte was on Elba and Josephine was dead."

One had to know Julien well to catch the note of grief in his voice. Henriette reached across the table and touched Julien's hand. "Josephine would be glad to see you now. She said once that if you ever married, you'd make a good husband."

Julien gave a whoop of laughter. "I very much doubt she said anything of the sort. Or if she did, it was only because she thought it was so unlikely I'd ever marry that I'd have changed into quite a different person."

"I don't think she thought that at all." Henriette sat back and refilled the coffee. "And I don't believe you've changed so very much."

élanie darted out from behind a plane tree as Colin hurtled towards her in a game of tag-go-seek. Her jaconet flounce caught on a tree branch. She detached it, just in time to avoid a tear, only to have Emily seize the back of her spencer. "Caught you!"

Mélanie grinned. Laura and Kitty had gone to help Cordy with preparations for the ball. She had remained in Berkeley Square and taken the children to the square garden for some exercise, but in truth, the romping in the fresh air cleared her head as well. If the pieces of the investigation hadn't fallen into place, at least she felt better able to approach it.

She shook out her skirt and tugged her rose velvet spencer smooth. "All right, shall we—"

"Someone's coming," Livia Davenport said.

Livia was near the garden gate with Leo Ashford. A tall dark-haired woman in green was approaching the square. Mélanie stepped out of the shade of the trees and put up a hand against the sun. "I think it's Mrs. Haworth."

Pippa Haworth hesitated, her gloved hand on the black metal rail of the Berkeley Square garden gate. She wore a high-crowned green velvet bonnet and a sage green pelisse trimmed in the same velvet and fastened with the frogged clasps that had been so in vogue since the military fervor of the war had reached a crescendo with Waterloo. She had a good modiste, but the ribbons on her bonnet were tied a bit carelessly and the skirt of her pelisse was crushed. She either had the freedom not to be too concerned with her dress—or the wisdom to know that such unconcern only made one more stylish.

"Mrs. Rannoch? I'm sorry, I know this isn't a conventional way to call."

"Do come in." Mélanie scooped up Jessica, who had hurtled into her knees. "You've saved me as I was caught ingloriously."

She introduced the children, who greeted Pippa Haworth with grown-up courtesy, though Timothy Ashford and Drusilla Davenport were dancing on their tiptoes with eagerness to return to the game.

"I need to talk to Mrs. Haworth for bit," Mélanie said. "Livia can score keep."

"New game," Livia said.

Pippa Haworth smiled. "Your children have a wonderful freedom."

"I hope so." Mélanie smoothed her own crushed skirt and moved towards Pippa. "It's one of the things I've tried to give them."

"You're an unusual mother, Mrs. Rannoch. But I think I knew that already."

"I'll take that as a compliment." Mélanie moved to one of the black metal benches.

"It was meant as one."

Pippa dropped down beside Mélanie on the bench. "I'm sorry to interrupt the game."

"I do need a break every now and then." Mélanie tightened the ribbons on her bonnet, which were slipping. "I think you're no stranger to romping with children yourself."

"What makes you say that?"

Mélanie glanced at the moss green sarcenet skirt of Pippa's pelisse. "I've known small hands to crush the fabric of my gowns and pelisses in just that way."

Pippa laughed. "Caught. My sisters would be scandalized. At least, Sophia would. But we were romping in the nursery before I left. Now my husband's gone, there's no one to look askance at it. And in truth, even when he was alive I paid less heed to his opinions than a good wife perhaps should."

"I'm not sure I have the least idea what being a good wife is. But I don't think it means doing everything one's husband approves of. And certainly not if it goes against one's children's welfare."

"Perhaps not." Pippa watched the children a moment longer. "I'm quite in sympathy with the queen. But I own at times I think, 'How can she fight so hard against divorce? It sounds like freedom.'" She cast a sidelong look at Mélanie. "I'm talking quite scandalously. But then I came here to discuss a scandalous topic. As you must suspect."

"I don't know that I'd have used the word scandalous. But I suspect you came here to discuss James Blayney."

Pippa's gaze narrowed. Perhaps, Mélanie thought, in an effort to keep emotion at bay. "I talked to Cordy this morning. But that was a civil chat between friends. Oh, Cordy was frank about the investigation, but in the sense that she was gathering background information from someone on its fringe. But I know you and Lady Carfax called on Sophia today as well."

"Your sister told you?" That would change Mélanie's view of the relationship between the elder Langdon sisters.

Pippa's mouth curled. "Hardly. That would indeed be a sign of a world turned upside down. But my underhousemaid is the sister of her second footman. Their father was the gamekeeper at Pendarves Chase. You know how fast news travels in Mayfair."

"Many of our investigations are built on it."

"Well, then. Knowing my sister, I imagine she told you a number of things. Including that my relationship with Jamie Blayney was more complicated than I admitted to Cordy."

"She did." Mélanie regarded Pippa while the children's carefree shouts carried on the breeze. "We've been debating if she was telling the truth."

"You have a keen understanding, Mrs. Rannoch. So does Lady Carfax, from what I've seen of her. And Cordy, who I imagine is struggling with my having lied to her and her having not seen it. I appreciate that you weighed Sophia's words with a grain of salt. But she was telling the truth. Or at least, some of the truth, assuming she said what I think she did. I was Jamie Blayney's lover. Though I certainly never intended to take him from my sister. As I suspect Sophia claimed."

"She made an allusion of the sort."

Pippa gave a rueful smile. "I suppose it's not surprising. Given our relationship. Given how Sophia seems to feel—to have felt about Jamie. In truth, I think we were both too caught up in our own view of the situation to see the other's very clearly. I know I've never felt Sophia saw me clearly, and I daresay I'm not very clear-eyed when it comes to her. And it's difficult when it comes to Jamie, because we're both so tangled up with him, going back to childhood." She looked across the square garden at the children as they darted between the gnarled plane trees in their game of tag. "I remember all of us playing together when we were your children's age. Jamie and Edmund and the four of us. Jamie was the sort who'd scramble up a tree and step right off into space without any fear of falling. Sometimes he pulled it off with some crazy move. But he fell on his head more than once. As a child, I admired his daring. As a mother, I'm grateful that my children have a bit more common sense."

"Yes," Mélanie said. "It's much easier to give them their freedom knowing they have a bit of common sense."

"Even as a girl, I knew Jamie didn't have any of that. Not that I did myself. But somehow, I had the wit to recognize Jamie as the braggart he was. He was amusing to flirt with—mostly to scandalize my parents, and because he's—he was"—she paused for a moment, the reality of Jamie's loss seeming to sink into her gaze—"a capital dancer. But I never wanted it to become more. Not then. And it was clear if he had a favorite, it was Sophia." She looked at Mélanie again. "How much did Sophia tell you about their relationship?"

"She admitted to the affair. We already knew. From Jamie's brother."

"Oh." Pippa drew a sharp breath. "Yes, Cordy said you'd talked to Edmund. I didn't realize quite how much he knew. Is he—how has he taken Jamie's death?"

"I didn't speak with him, my husband and Inspector Roth did. I understand he was shaken, though he and his brother had not been close of late."

"I'm not sure they ever were." Pippa gripped her elbows. "It's funny. Sophia's always been much more decorous I am, but she was the one Jamie dazzled."

"It's often that way, I think."

"Yes, perhaps. I was never decorous. As Cordy may have told you, even when I made my debut, I had a hard time taking the whole thing seriously. It seemed absurd that one's future depended on dancing, and driving, and paying and receiving calls, and attaching the right gentleman. And yet I couldn't really see a different future. So I went along with it, because what else was I to do? When I married, I found marriage was—I wouldn't say a mistake, because I didn't have high hopes going in. Though I didn't think it would be quite so—dull, I suppose."

"I'm sorry." For all the challenges Mélanie had found in marriage, it had never been dull.

"I really only have myself to blame. I didn't have a great many choices. Funny to say that, considering all the young men at the average ball. Perhaps I mean I didn't have a great many interesting choices." Her mouth twisted. "Any interesting choices. In any case, several years after my marriage, when Jamie was home on leave, I was restless enough to be less impervious to risk. What did Sophia tell you about us?"

"She mentioned you and Captain Blayney had been close."

Pippa snorted. "I think Sophia got it in her head I was a rival. But I wasn't, really. What transpired between Jamie and me wasn't serious enough for that. It was a moment's mad diversion from my general dissatisfaction with my life." She gripped her hands together. "I'm talking quite recklessly. But then, just now I have a feeling secrets are more dangerous than truth."

"In an investigation, that's very true," Mélanie said.

Pippa shot a look at her. "Jamie wasn't my only diversion in the course of my marriage, but he was the most dangerous. I think half of me was so unhappy with my marriage I wanted to push things and take a risk. I'm exceedingly fortunate my husband never found out." Her gaze moved to Colin, swinging Jessica in a circle round him as she giggled with glee. "If my marriage never meant a great deal to me, my children do. I don't know how I could have been so mad as to risk it."

"Despair can make one run risks one wouldn't when sane." After the battle of Waterloo, Mélanie had been particularly prone to risk. Only Colin had kept her anchored. And Malcolm, though her feelings about Malcolm had been tangled with a guilt that was part of her despair.

"Do you think so?" Pippa watched Colin lift Jessica to pick a leaf off a tree. "I wouldn't have said I was in despair, but looking back—I certainly didn't know what to do with myself. I should have found a more constructive solution. And I confess the fact that Jamie had been my sister's was probably part of the allure. Sophia accused me of taking him from her, and it wasn't that—

they'd ended things years before. But I can't say I was free of sisterly rivalry."

"And Captain Blayney was apparently fascinated by your family."

"More fool he." Pippa shook her head, stirring the green ribbons on her bonnet.

"I imagine growing up you represented everything he aspired to."

"Yes, I can see that. It never occurred to me at the time. Jamie seemed so much more assured than any of us. Though it's true he didn't have a lot of things that we did. But at that age, those things didn't seem so important to me." She smiled as Colin and Jessica ran over to Emily, who had Berowne on his lead. "I suppose it's easy for things like good china, and wax candles in the school room, and pin money, and a new wardrobe every year not to seem important when one's never had to do without them." She frowned at an overhanging leaf, green turning to gold. "It never seemed to bother Edmund. That is, it did, but in a different way. It made him want to change things for everyone."

"My husband wants to change things too. Though he'd be the first to acknowledge he's always had plenty of creature comforts."

Pippa picked up a fallen leaf and turned it between her fingers. "Edmund would say that for all he and Jamie didn't have what we did, he had more than most people in Britain. And that's the really intolerable thing. Edmund's put his dissatisfaction to much more use than I did mine."

"You've followed his career closely."

Pippa shrugged. "Difficult not to be intrigued, when someone one's grown up with makes such a stir. Edmund and I were friends as children. We were both dissatisfied. But I rather think Edmund's more satisfied with his life now than I am." She loosed her fingers and let the leaf drift to the ground. "In any case, I managed to call it off fairly quickly with Jamie. I saw the risks and I wasn't in love enough to run them. I wasn't in love at all. And Jamie's feelings weren't engaged enough for him to make more than a gallant protest. We parted as friends. I didn't see him again for years, except for the occasional meeting in public that one can't avoid in London society. Until he called on me, making threats." Her jaw tightened, shaking the ribbons of her bonnet.

"Over what?" Mélanie asked.

Pippa's gaze shot to Mélanie's face. "Isn't that obvious, given what had transpired between us?"

"With many women it would be. But your husband is dead. You don't seem overly concerned with your reputation. I can see how scandal would be a concern for your children, but if anyone would stand up to Captain Blayney's threats, I could see you doing it."

Pippa gave a wry smile. "Perhaps I'm less of a rebel than I let on. Easy enough to be a rebel sitting home in Mayfair, I imagine Edmund would say. Until one's threatened with losing something. Even if it just means not having vouchers for Almack's or being cut in the park."

"We don't have vouchers for Almack's anymore. Because of Mr. O'Roarke's divorce. I confess I find it quite liberating."

"Well, yes, I do think that would be liberating. But I found I had an instinctive aversion to the other comforts in my life being threatened. I'm not proud of it, but there it is."

"What did Jamie ask of you?"

"You'd think it would be money, wouldn't you?"

"You would. But that isn't what he's asked of others."

"He was blackmailing others?"

"A number of them."

"That's—interesting. He wanted me to deliver a parcel to someone. Is that what he asked of others?"

"Yes. Whom did he want you to deliver the parcel to?"

"Lord Beverston."

Not surprising, given that they knew Danielle had been involved with Beverston, but interesting in that Beverston was a League member and opposed to Alexander Radford's faction. "Did you deliver it?" Mélanie asked.

"I had my footman take it round. Beverston sent back a polite note of thanks. He was a friend of my father's, though I haven't seen him much of late."

"Did you examine the parcel?"

"I didn't open it. But I think it contained papers. I don't much like that Jamie blackmailed me into being a party to blackmailing someone else."

"If it's any comfort, Beverston is well able to take care of himself. And Captain Blayney would have found another way of getting the papers to him if you hadn't delivered them."

"That's kinder of you than I deserve." Pippa tugged at her gloves. "I didn't see Jamie again after that. Which means that was the last time I'll ever see him. I can't help but—" She looked at the children, who had resumed their game of tag, with Colin holding Berowne. "We were friends. Once."

"And there's a particular strength to one's bonds with childhood friends." At least, so it seemed from what Mélanie had observed. She wasn't connected to anyone from her childhood.

Pippa nodded, as though she didn't trust herself to speak, then got to her feet. "Thank you, Mrs. Rannoch. I know you can't promise to keep this in confidence."

"No." Mélanie stood as well. "But I'll do my best to respect your privacy."

"That's also more than I deserve. I imagine Cordy will despise me for lying to her."

"I wouldn't think so. Cordy understands how complicated personal secrets can be, for a number of reasons."

"Lack of confidence can be hard on a friendship, though. Cordy's and my friendship rather suffered in recent years. I should like to get it back. Though I don't know if that's possible."

Jessica hurtled into Mélanie's knees. "No more tag now. Snuggles."

Mélanie scooped her daughter up and held her against her. Jessica looped her arms round Mélanie's neck and buried her face in the muslin frill spilling over Mélanie's spencer.

Pippa smiled at the two of them. "It's good to be reminded of what's important, Mrs. Rannoch. Good day."

CHAPTER 21

"It's interesting," Julien said, as he and Raoul left the house where the Varon family lodged. "But it doesn't get us much further. If Danielle was spying on Bonaparte for Uncle Hubert, that's hardly a secret that would shock people today."

They turned down Berwick Street, filled with a midday crowd of tradesmen, errand boys, mothers and nursemaids with children, hawkers pushing barrows, many of them wearing the white cockades that had become a symbol of the queen. Julien caught snatches of French and Greek and Russian in the babble of cries. Soho, once a haunt of the fashionable, was now popular with immigrants. He and Kitty had lived not far from here, on Carnaby Street near Golden Square, for several months before and after they married. He'd felt at home there in some ways he never would in Carfax House.

"No," Raoul agreed. "But if your uncle knows or suspects her child is Bonaparte's, he could be concerned about the uses the child could be put to."

Julien skirted a puddle from last night's rain. "You think he'd try to get rid of Danielle's daughter, like the supposed dauphin?"

Even Julien had been a bit surprised at the lengths his uncle had gone to on that occasion, which included having a sniper shoot into the Berkeley Square library.

"I wouldn't think so. But Mademoiselle Darnault might be worried about what he'd do. It could be one more reason for her to have run."

"Danielle was always loyal, after a fashion." Julien dodged round an apple barrow. "But she was good at reading the changing winds. But by the time she was involved with Bonaparte, the winds were changing against him. Uncle Hubert might have seemed a much more promising employer." He paused to toss a handful of coins to a trio of boys roasting potatoes on a fire in a charcoal brazier at the crossing. "Odd to remember the days when most intimate relationships were a matter of work."

Raoul shot a look at him. "Quite."

Julien could feel Raoul's gaze upon him, but they walked on in silence to the next crossing. A stall across the street offered prints about the trial. One depicted the queen and Bergami in the bath together in a position that looked as awkward as it was compromising. Julien didn't know the queen well, but he was sure she was too sensible to have taken her pleasure in such an uncomfortable manner. Another showed Majocchi, the queen's former manservant and a witness against her, reaching out to snatch bags of gold from Liverpool, the prime minister. Majocchi may well have been paid for his testimony, but there was no denying the British could be savage to outsiders.

"Julien," Raoul said.

Julien turned with a raised brow.

Raoul's gaze locked on his own in the shadows of an overhanging upper story. "We need to talk."

Simple words delivered in a soft, even, friendly tone that nevertheless sent a chill through Julien. "In this family, we talk all the time."

"That's not what I meant."

Julien adjusted the brim of his hat. It had been worth at least pretending that this did not mean what he feared. What he had feared ever since Raoul had gone off on his recent trip. It was not worth it any longer. Julien regarded the man he had worked with and for and against for a quarter century. The man who was more of a role model to him than he would ever admit. "Christ. I've been expecting and fearing you'd work it out for almost two years now."

"I've been extraordinarily slow."

"You must see why we've kept quiet."

"I do. I'd have been tempted to do the same. But you're—we're—running out of time. This is going to come to a crisis before you can head it off. And Malcolm may work it out for himself at just the worst time."

Julien felt his jaw tighten. "I've been telling Gelly that for months. But I'm still not sure of our next move."

"Sometimes there is no good move to make. Malcolm halfway put the pieces together with me just now."

Cold dread coiled in the pit of Julien's stomach. "And?"

"I headed him off. For the moment. I have no illusions it will last long. Or that it was the right move to make. Part of me was sorely tempted to tell him the truth then and there."

"But you didn't."

"Our world would have tipped upside down if I had. It probably means I'm a coward."

"You're the last person I'd call coward, O'Roarke." Julien looked at Raoul for a long moment. "I understand better now that I'm a parent."

"What?" Raoul's gaze was more hooded than usual.

"What it's like to want desperately to protect one's children and know there's no way you can."

Raoul grimaced. "I never envisioned this. Failure of imagination."

"It would take even more imagination than storytellers like Mélanie, and Laura, and Tanner possess to have foreseen this. What's that Shakespeare line? 'If this were played upon a stage now, I could condemn it as an improbable fiction.'"

"Yes, no decent dramatist would attempt it. Which is why it took me so long to accept that it was true. Even after I had my first suspicions. But sometimes one has to accept that there's no explanation beyond the improbable. And so the improbable must be true."

Julien nodded. He had come to much the same conclusion. Which didn't make the situation any easier. "And of course, this is all happening while we're in the midst of a case."

They turned and began walking down the street. "Speaking of improbable connections," Raoul said. "Pendarves."

Julien felt himself draw inwards. "What about him?"

"I suspected Talleyrand had tasked you to get information on the Russian delegation six years ago. And I suspected Pendarves was part of the mission."

"You mean that I seduced him in the course of it."

"Your methods are your own business. But yes, I suspected something of the sort."

Raoul was good at seeing things. Still—"Had you heard rumors about Pendarves?" Julien asked.

"I try to avoid those sorts of rumors. But I saw him looking at you one night at Emily Cowper's."

"That's concerning. Though it's the sort of thing you see better than others." Julien stepped into the street to avoid the contents of a chamber pot dumped onto the pavement. "Were you thinking you could make use of it?"

"No. I have some limits. But I was concerned about you."

"I didn't think either of us admitted to concern in those days."

"Admitting to it is different from experiencing it. I'd say Pendarves's feelings were more engaged than yours."

"Probably."

"Is there any proof?"

"That I took papers?" Julien's voice came out more mocking than he intended.

"That you had an affair."

Julien raised a brow with great care. "I know we're friends now, but surely that's a bit personal. I don't ask you about proof of your past affairs."

"You'd be entitled to if they impinged on an investigation." Raoul paused in the archway as they turned into Portland Mews. "We're talking about a hanging offense." He was watching Julien with the same sort of closely veiled concern he often accorded Malcolm. "*Is* there any proof?"

"There's rarely—if ever—proof of anything I do."

"You're very good at covering your tracks. But you don't have the ability to fade into the background that you used to have."

"Oh, believe me, Kitty and the children and I are prepared to disappear should it prove necessary. But I don't want it to—largely because of the people I care about here—and I don't think it will come to that."

"I'd like to help make sure it doesn't."

"I don't think this will precipitate a crisis. But I—appreciate your concern."

"A lot of knives are out in the beau mode, Julien. For all sorts of reasons. And not just directed at matchmaking mamas and hopeful debutantes."

"I take your meaning. I have few illusions about this world, despite having grown up in it. Because of having grown up in it." Julien stared into the shadows of the mews. "It's odd, if my grandfather hadn't freed and married my grandmother, I could have been born a slave, despite being the son of Earl Carfax. But because there's an official seal on my birth, I'm a Mallinson, which apparently covers a multitude of sins. If I went to trial, it would be in the House of Lords, like the queen. Yet I could face the hangman's noose for whom I choose to go to bed with."

"I recognized long since that the world is intolerable. I hope I never accept it so much that I cease trying to change it. But laws being unjust doesn't mean we can ignore their existence." Raoul's gaze shifted over Julien's face. "You have enemies. From your days as Julien St. Juste. And from your work now as Lord Carfax."

"I hardly think I've drawn much notice as Carfax."

"Don't underestimate your abolition work," Raoul said as they crossed the mews. "The planter interest, and quite a few Tories, and some Whigs who don't want the issue interfering with their immediate agenda, however much they deplore it, aren't happy with you. And then there's the League."

Julien nodded. "I don't take it lightly. And—thank you."

Raoul nodded as well. There were still some things—quite a few things—neither of them could put into words.

"I shouldn't be your main concern now," Julien said.

"One concern doesn't drive out another."

They moved into the alley on the far side of the mews. "Malcolm will cope," Julien said.

Raoul gave a twisted smile. "I'm not sure what coping means. Or how he can manage it."

Julien reached out and touched Raoul on the shoulder. A simple gesture, but he wasn't sure he had done it before. He'd shaken Raoul's hand. He'd embraced him. But he hadn't offered that sort of comfort, friend to friend. "I wouldn't underrate him. After all, he's your son."

Raoul smiled and then went still, because Julien had gone still. A man had lunged out of a doorway and had a pistol pressed to Julien's back.

"Don't move, either of you," he said. "Or I put a bullet through him. I've been sent with a warning. Stop meddling, or the next time it won't just be a warning. For you or your families."

Julien spun away, grabbed the man's wrist, and knocked the pistol loose before the man could do more than start to pull the trigger. Raoul retrieved the pistol. "Whoever engaged your services doesn't know me—or O'Roarke—well if they thought such shoddy tactics would work. Was your employer stupid enough to reveal their name? No, I thought not." Julien released the man and took a step back. "I advise you to make yourself scarce. The last man who attacked us and bungled it was knifed by one of his compatriots."

The man stared at Julien for a moment, then took off down the alley.

Raoul pocked the pistol. "Things change."

"There wasn't any point in killing him. I never killed people without a point. I never *liked* killing people. You of all people should appreciate the value of cultivating a persona."

"It wasn't all a persona."

"No. There's a bit of truth in everything we do," Julien said. "Just as there's a bit of truth in the charming fairy tale that I've become a sober and responsible citizen."

CHAPTER 22

*J*eremy Roth frowned at the greasy waters of the Thames as he and Malcolm and Harry walked along the terrace by Somerset House. The day was fine, though the wind was a bit sharp, and sometimes outside was the best place for private conversation. "How many people know about these memoirs?"

Malcolm and Harry exchanged glances. "Certainly all the people who've been sent pages in an attempt to get them to buy sections of the memoirs," Malcolm said.

"A list that is growing by the minute," Harry added. "And as word spreads, I imagine a number of others will want to get their hands on the memoirs."

"Including a number in the government." Malcolm turned his collar up against a gust of wind.

Roth shot a look at him, eyes narrowed against the sunlight. "Such as the home secretary?"

"Certainly the government would find the memoirs of inter-est. At the very least, to stop their being used to influence the trial in the queen's direction. It's difficult to imagine it wouldn't occur to at least some to consider using them to further their own cause. And that's quite without the possibility that some in their number are named in the memoirs."

"In other words, I should be prepared for pressure from high places," Roth said.

"Aren't you always?" Harry asked.

Roth grinned. "We've had some developments ourselves. Thanks to Hopkins, one of my more enterprising patrols. He's been questioning the staffs of those we've connected to Blayney. Apparently, Blayney called on Lord Prescott four days ago."

"Interesting," Malcolm said. "I suppose Blayney could have threatened to make his affair with Sophia public."

"That was my first thought," Roth said. "But the timing surprised me. Especially given that the story doesn't favor Blayney either. In light of your new information, I can't help but wonder if Prescott is in Danielle Darnault's memoirs."

"Prescott's a dull fellow," Harry said. "But he goes over to Paris regularly. And we already have evidence that his marriage isn't ideal."

"An interesting possibility." Malcolm frowned. "Prescott's usually to be found at White's. It sounds as though I'm going to have to find someone to take me into the Tory sanctum."

"Harry," Mélanie said to Harry Palmerston, not Harry Davenport, as he approached the Berkeley Square garden gate. "Are you looking for Malcolm?" Though Palmerston, the secretary at war, was a Tory, he and Malcolm frequently worked together, or at least discussed politics. But the queen's trial had made it more difficult for even casual conversations to take place across party lines.

"Yes, as it happens." Palmerston smiled at her over the gate. "Is he in the house?"

"No, he's out. With Harry and Jeremy Roth. We're in the

midst of an investigation. Scarcely seeing each other, as often happens."

"Yes, I heard. About the investigation. That's partly why—" Palmerston hesitated, his hand on the gate latch. "It's connected to why I wanted to talk to Malcolm. But in many ways, perhaps it's better if I talk to you." He lifted the latch, but still hesitated. "May I?"

"Of course."

Palmerston came into the garden, paused, waved to the children, who waved back, then continued with their game.

"It's all right," Mélanie said, as Palmerston joined her on the bench. "They have spy instincts, but playing at being princesses and pirates is still much more absorbing than practicing spycraft."

Palmerston gave a faint smile. "For a beautiful woman, you're a remarkably good fellow, Mélanie."

"I'll take that as a compliment."

"It was meant as one."

"But I see no reason why a man can't view a woman as a confidante. I'm perfectly comfortable confiding in men."

Palmerston laughed, though it didn't quite reach his eyes. "You're remarkably easy to talk to. Don't know why I didn't seek you out in the first place, rather than Malcolm." He stretched his legs out on the gravel and stared at the toes of his boots. "Danielle Darnault."

Mélanie had suspected as much, but she still released her breath. "What have you heard?"

Palmerston kept his gaze on his polished boot toes. "There are rumors that the man who was killed last night had papers of hers."

"Rumors spread quickly in Mayfair and Westminster. And yes. He did."

Palmerston's gaze shot to her face.

"But we believe she had more papers, which are missing.

Memoirs, to be exact. I take it you have reason to believe you might be named in them?"

Palmerston's fingers froze on the bench. "I—"

"Harry." Mélanie covered his hand where it lay on the bench between them. "I detest meddling in my friends' personal lives. But one of the sad results of investigations is that sometimes one has to. And really, given that Emily makes no pretense of being faithful, why should I be surprised if you aren't? Whatever might suit me, I'd hardly suggest others need to subscribe to it."

Palmerston colored, but gave a shout of laughter. "The world would be a better place if more people had your tolerance. It was when I went to the Continent after Emily. When she went after Mrs. Lamb and Brougham."

Mélanie hadn't been close friends with Emily Cowper at the time, but she'd heard the story in bits and pieces from Emily since.

"I was concerned," Palmerston said. "About what Emily was going through. But also about whom she might encounter."

"Giuliano." Count Giuliano had followed Emily back to Britain, and though Emily had not been the only English lady he pursued, she had perhaps been the most serious of them. Mélanie vividly recalled Palmerston's burning gaze fixed on Emily and Giuliano one night at the theatre. It was the closest she had come to seeing the bond between Emily and Palmerston, remarkably steady if not exclusive, frayed to the breaking point.

Palmerston grimaced. "Even before I left for the Continent, I wasn't in the best humor. I'd been harassed in Parliament all spring about the army estimates, with Brougham leading the charge."

"And then he led to the breakup of George and Caro Lamb's household, which contributed to your own domestic upheaval."

"Only you would call my relationship with Emily domestic."

"Well, it is, even if you have to keep it in the shadows. Which makes it all the harder to preserve." Something she knew more than a bit about, in various ways.

Palmerston gave a wry smile. "Emily led me the devil of a dance across Switzerland and northern Italy. I had an easier time finding Brougham and Caro than her. When I caught up with them in Milan, it was clear the affair was waning. I finally managed three days with Emily in Geneva. But she made it clear she needed to focus on Caro George, and that our movements couldn't shadow each other all over the Continent. She and the family spent months traveling round Italy. Where she met Giuliano and God knows whom else. I didn't know the half of it when I started on my own way home. But I knew—or suspected—enough to be out of sorts. I stopped in St. Omer to see a review of British cavalry. I met Danielle at the review. She was riding a splendid bay instead of sheltering in a carriage. She rides like the devil. She was—sympathetic. I needed a sympathetic ear. And I needed to prove my independence."

"I can understand that."

"Can you?" His gaze shot to her. "I know few women as devoted to their husbands as you are to Malcolm."

"Malcolm makes it easy to be devoted. But sometimes one feels the need to show one's happiness isn't wholly dependent on another person. All the more so, I should think, if one doesn't feel one can be entirely sure of that person."

"Yes, perhaps. Though I rather think you're letting me off the hook." Palmerston flexed his fingers and stared at them. "Remarkable how you can be such a good friend to Emily and to me."

"Why not? You and Emily are very good friends to each other. And you're a good friend to Malcolm and also to me."

"Touché." Palmerston gave a faint smile. "In any case, Danielle Darnault was a diversion when I very much needed one." His gaze fastened on a green-gold leaf. "I've known many beautiful and brilliant women. I count many as friends, regardless of what other relationship we do or don't have. You included. But Danielle had a way of listening that made it seem she really understood. And it wasn't an act, because then she'd suddenly make a comment or ask a question that showed she really was listening. And I needed to talk. More than I needed— other things." He slumped his shoulders against the back of the bench and tented his fingers together. "This may sound a bit laughable, given how open Em and I are in many ways with our friends, but it can be a challenge loving someone one can't love openly. Em has a family. A household. I—fit my life in round her schedule in many ways."

"As many women do with their lovers."

Palmerston raised his brows.

"Women who are mistresses."

Palmerston gave a shout of laughter. "Leave it to you, Mélanie, to suggest I'm like a kept woman. I'm fortunate to have a comfortable fortune and some quite tolerable properties. But it's true in our relationship I'm the one in the shadows. Don't get me wrong, I have a very agreeable life. Emily is central to my agreeable life." He dragged a boot toe through the gravel. "But sometimes I do feel I spend rather a lot of time dancing atten- dance on Emily. And I perhaps felt that particularly after traipsing across the Continent after her and then being packed off home like a lapdog." Bitterness cut through his voice like a too-strong squeeze of lemon in a civilized cup of tea.

"So you talked to Danielle about how you felt about Emily?"

"I said I needed to prove my independence. Which is how it felt. Part of it was—loving—Danielle. Part of it was talking to her. Pouring out my frustrations. And because I was unhappy. Because I trusted her. I said things I've never shared with anyone else. Things I would not want shared with the world in general."

"Things you'd pay to keep secret?"

Palmerston shot a look at her.

"Did anyone ask you to purchase the memoirs?"

Palmerston drew a long, rough breath. Mélanie could imagine him with the same breath and expression as he debated the wisdom of making a tricky political concession. "Last week. That man, Blayney—I'd never met him before, though I now know he grew up with Pendarves. He showed me a few pages. He told me what was in the others he had."

"Did you buy them?" Mélanie asked, in the same tone she'd use to ask one of her children if they'd told an untruth.

Palmerston dug his boot toe into the gravel. "I was considering." The breeze stirred the leaves overhead, casting shadows over his face. "I told you I'm comfortably situated, which I am. But I have my sisters and brothers to see to."

"Blayney asked for a lot."

"Blayney asked for a bloody fortune."

"Did you think about defying him?"

"Of course. It's not as though I don't live with gossip. It's not as though Emily doesn't. But you know how Mayfair works. There's gossip, and then there's gossip. One can live with the subtle kind that everyone knows but no one really admits to knowing. That everyone—or at least, everyone who matters— can turn a blind eye to. That sort of scandal seems to take place behind one of those pretty half-see-through curtains they drop before the main action of a play begins."

"A scrim."

"Yes. Very different when that curtain gets pulled up and the dirty business is in full view of the footlights. Em has a secure life. But she thrives on being a political hostess. She thrives on Almack's and being an arbiter of the ton. I'm not sure how she'd fare if she lost that." He hesitated, fingers working on the arm of the bench. "I'm not sure how we'd fare."

"You could talk to Emily."

"What she'd say, and how she'd actually feel if the truth came out, especially if it came out due to me, are different things.

Even Em couldn't say for a certainty how she'd react until—unless—the events came to pass."

Jessica shouted to Colin in their game of tag round the trees. Colin raced after her and caught her as she skidded, just before she fell headlong on the gravel. Palmerston watched them. "And then, whatever Em could put up with, there are the children."

Mélanie was quite certain at least two of Emily's children, supposedly fathered by Lord Cowper, were in fact Palmerston's, including the baby girl Emily had given birth to the previous winter. And she strongly suspected Emily's elder daughter might be Palmerston's as well.

"You told Danielle about the children," Mélanie said.

Palmerston's mouth twisted. "I know, I was a fool. I was unhappy, as I said. Feeling like a lapdog at Emily's beck and call, feeling I had no control over anything in my life. Including my children." He cast a quick glance about the garden. "Whom of course I can't possibly claim as my children." He watched Colin, and Jessica, and Emily, who now had Berowne, and the Davenport girls and Ashford boys as they resumed their race. "It's one thing what the children may be able to understand when they're older and we explain it to them. If we explain it to them."

Mélanie bit her tongue. They had told Colin the truth of his parentage, and he had taken it far better than she had dared hope. But even with a good friend like Palmerston, she couldn't share those secrets. Even though she knew, at least implicitly, about the parentage of Palmerston and Emily's children, she couldn't share the truth about her own son's parentage. Not for Colin's sake. Or Malcolm's. Or Raoul's. There was no reason to think Palmerston suspected. And even if he did, no reason for her to put it into words.

Palmerston smiled as Jessica dangled a twig for Berowne while Emily held his lead. "Whatever the children may understand when they're older, having truths—or accusations that aren't even true—bandied about in the papers would be very different. It could damage the children's prospects. It could damage their relationships with their parents. Meaning Emily. And Cowper. And me."

"I understand that," Mélanie said, and then wondered if she'd admitted too much.

Palmerston met her gaze for a moment, his own quizzical. "You're always a marvel of understanding. So you must understand why I couldn't put the children through that."

"So you were going to buy the part of the memoirs about you?"

Palmerston shifted on the bench. "I was still making up my mind. When I heard Blayney had been killed." He turned his head to hold her with his gaze, at once rueful and armored. "Which I realize gives me an excellent motive."

"You're hardly the only one."

His gaze stayed steady. "Do you know who has Danielle's memoirs now?"

"No. We don't have them. I'm sorry, Harry."

Palmerston nodded. "I was afraid of that. They could do a lot of damage. Especially given those no doubt included in their pages, and the climate now."

"Could they be used to sway your position?"

"On our esteemed king's efforts to disentangle himself from a wife he's treated abominably? I'm an Irish peer. I don't have a vote, thank God. But others—I can only imagine how it would scramble an already fraught choice."

"Precisely."

Mélanie put up a hand to her bonnet as the wind whipped up. "Brougham apparently succeeded you with Danielle Darnault. Or preceded you, but from the timing I'd suspect you were first."

Palmerston's eyes widened. "Good God. I suppose it's not surprising, in a way. I know he went to Paris after he and Caro George separated. Damn the man. Whether in politics or my personal life, he always seems to be underfoot. He was being blackmailed as well?"

"He bought the papers concerning him. Then those papers were stolen."

"By the same person who killed Blayney? The same person who has the rest of the memoirs?"

"We aren't sure. If it's the same person who has the rest of the memoirs or if that person killed Blayney. I'm telling you this to get across how serious the situation is, Harry. There are other actors involved besides Blayney."

"Christ. Though not surprising." Palmerston drew in his breath as though to say more, then went still at the sound of footsteps. Malcolm was approaching along the Berkeley Street side of the square. He paused by the gate and took in Palmerston's presence. He smiled, but his gaze narrowed, and Mélanie suspected he had already surmised much of what had transpired between her and Palmerston.

"Harry." Malcolm closed the garden gate and walked over to the bench after waving to the children. "Just the man I'm looking for. I need to get into White's."

CHAPTER 23

*P*almerston looked at Malcolm. Malcolm could see the pieces falling together in his friend's gaze. Just as pieces had fallen together for him when he saw Palmerston talking with Mélanie.

"Let me guess," Palmerston said. "Part of your investigation? I can't imagine why else you'd want entrée to White's. Especially now with Whigs and Tories so set against each other."

"I need to talk to Lord Prescott."

Palmerston raised a brow. "Interesting. Westminster seems to be about to be even more shaken than it already was this autumn. I'd find it rather fascinating if I weren't in the middle of it myself." He pushed himself to his feet. "I'll take you to White's now. And I can update you on what I've told Mélanie."

Malcolm listened to Palmerston's account of his relationship with Danielle Darnault as they made their way to St. James's.

"Why did you come to us with this?" Malcolm asked as they reached the club.

Palmerston stopped on the pavement, a few steps away from White's famous bow window. "Surely you want the information."

"We want a great deal of information people aren't willing to share readily."

Palmerston gave an abashed smile. "Partly because I hoped you might know where the memoirs were. Partly because I suspected you'd tumble to the truth eventually, and I'm enough of a tactician to have realized it was better to confess first. And partly, I like to think, because I thought the information might help you."

Malcolm touched his friend's arm. "You're a good fellow, Harry."

Palmerston grinned. "I said the same thing to Mélanie just now. Your wife's one in a million, Rannoch."

"Don't think I don't know it."

They went up the steps and through the door. Even in the entry hall, the buzz in the air was palpably different from usual times, just as it was across the street at the Whig Brooks's these days. The coming confrontation in Westminster hummed in the air. Malcolm was aware of several surprised looks shot in his direction, when generally his presence at White's wouldn't elicit more than some good-natured ribbing about his Whig sensibilities tainting the air.

"The cardroom's my best guess," Palmerston said, relinquishing his hat and gloves to the porter. "I'll go up with you." They made their way through the crowd, Palmerston cheerfully deflecting the looks of inquiry. Prescott was at a game of whist in the cardroom, a glass of port at his elbow. "Supposedly doing parliamentary work over cards," Palmerston murmured. "Prescott." He strolled up to the table. "Rannoch wants to have a word with you. Prevailed upon me to bring him into this Tory sanctum."

"What?" Prescott looked up from his cards with a frown. He was a portly man with a florid face and blue eyes that were surprisingly hard. "What's important enough to interrupt a hand of whist, Rannoch?"

"I'll wait," Malcolm said in an easy voice.

"No, we can talk now." Prescott pushed back his chair and nodded to his whist companions. "But if it's to do with the case against the queen, I warn you I'll have nothing to say. Saving all that for the Lords. Isn't even properly your business."

"The king's rather made it everyone's business," Palmerston murmured.

"You can fuss about it all you want, but you don't have a vote. Either of you." Prescott conducted Malcolm into an adjoining anteroom, glass of port in hand. He moved to a set of decanters by the window and topped off the glass. "What's this about?"

"Surely by now you've heard James Blayney was murdered last night."

"Looking into that, are you?" Prescott took a drink of port. "Suppose I shouldn't be surprised. You seem to look into every murder in Mayfair, and some that are God knows where else in the city. But that's nothing to do with me." He held up the decanter and raised a brow.

Malcolm shook his head. "I understand Blayney was a friend of your family's."

"Hardly. I scarcely knew the man."

"Your wife grew up with him."

Blayney took another drink of port. "His father was the vicar or something. Long before I married Sophia. And Blayney's father pegged off before my father-in-law. Captain Blayney was long gone from Shropshire before I married Sophia."

"And yet Blayney called on you only four days ago."

Prescott's hand froze, the glass of port midway to his lips. "Oh, yes." He gave a rough laugh. *"Non mi ricordo."* The phrase had been the persistent response of Theodore Majocchi, the first witness for the prosecution, under Brougham's cross-examination. Majocchi, the former manservant of Queen Caroline's supposed lover Bergami, had left the queen's service and given evidence to the Milan commission, which the king had

had set up to gather evidence of her infidelity. But his inability to remember anything under Brougham's cross examination had seriously damaged his credibility. *Non mi ricordo* had become a popular catchphrase throughout London, and the king's witnesses became known as *non mi ricordos*.

Malcolm moved into the room and dropped into a chair. "Odd. I would have thought the news of Captain Blayney's murder would have brought it to mind."

Prescott moved to a chair across from Malcolm. "Blayney had a proposal for a trade venture. Tobacco from America. Foolish thing, wanted way too much. I put it aside for my man of business to look at, but whatever he said, Blayney's the last man I'd have trusted with my money."

"That's a good story," Malcolm said. "It fits with what we've learned about Blayney. But somehow, I doubt that was it. Or at least, not all of it. Given that the other people Blayney had communicated with recently are people he attempted to blackmail."

"Here now, Rannoch." Prescott clunked his glass down on a table beside his chair. "What the devil would Blayney have blackmailed me about? As I said, I scarcely knew him. Not that even those I know well would have cause to blackmail me. Much too dull a life for all that."

"You go to France regularly, don't you?"

"From time to time." Prescott picked up his glass and tossed down a gulp of port. "Surely that's not a subject for blackmail."

"Did you ever encounter a woman named Danielle Darnault?"

Prescott was better at bluster than Malcolm had expected, but for a moment fear shot through his gaze. "What? No, never heard of her."

"Never even heard of her? Surely not. Do you frequent the Salon des Etrangers?"

"Of course. Every Englishman in Paris does."

"I understand Danielle Darnault was frequently to be found there. I imagine she was acquainted with a number of your colleagues who are at White's at this very moment."

"Can't speak for them."

Malcolm settled back against the well-worn velvet of the chair. "We know Blayney was selling Danielle Darnault's memoirs, Prescott."

"Was he? Sounds like the sort of thing Blayney might have done, though difficult to connect him to a high-flyer such as this Danielle Darnault seems to be. That doesn't prove that's why he called on me."

"No, it doesn't." Malcolm rested his hands on the chair arms. "Not conclusively. It could also be to do with his past with Lady Prescott."

Prescott's hand jerked, spattering port on his blue-striped waistcoat and biscuit-colored pantaloons. "What the devil—"

"Believe me, I have no wish to create scandal," Malcolm said. "And I honor you for standing by your wife." That was a bit of a stretch, but it was certainly true Prescott's behavior could have been far worse. "Lady Prescott and her brother have both acknowledged that Lady Prescott was close to Captain Blayney some years ago and that it caused a rift with her father."

"By God, Rannoch, I won't have you making filthy accusations, to me or to anyone else." Prescott tugged out his handkerchief and wiped at the spilled port. "Whatever you may have bamboozled Sophia into saying—"

"Lady Prescott spoke to my wife and Lady Carfax, but she doesn't strike me as a woman who could be easily bamboozled."

"You set your wife and Lady Carfax to ask my wife—"

"I don't set my wife or our friends to do anything. And would you rather I'd spoken to her myself? Or sent a Bow Street runner?"

"This is too much." Prescott pushed himself to his feet, knocking his chair over on the Turkey rug. "I've tried to be polite, given that you're a gentleman, but I have no need to answer your impertinence, and I will say the same to my wife when it comes to your wife or Lady Carfax or anyone else you may send. Should you make baseless allegations to Bow Street or anyone else, you will hear from my seconds." He strode towards the door, his exit marred when he slipped on the spilled port, tangled his foot in the fallen chair, and thudded to the rug.

Malcolm sprang to his feet to help Prescott. Prescott pushed himself to his knees and knocked away Malcolm's proffered hand. "You've done enough, Rannoch. I won't say good day, given that I wish you at the very devil."

"Malcolm." A familiar voice stopped Malcolm on the first-floor landing. "What are you doing at White's?"

Malcolm turned to see his godfather, Lord Glenister. One of the founding members of the Elsinore League along with Alistair Rannoch, though of late Malcolm and Glenister had been cautious allies. "Palmerston brought me in. I had some inquiries to make for an investigation we're in the midst of."

"Yes, I've heard." Glenister ran a hand over his sleek dark hair, barely touched by gray. "It's a lucky thing I found you. I was about to call on you in Berkeley Square. I need your help."

That was interesting. But in some ways, not surprising. "Sir—"

"Not here." Glenister glanced round the landing and opened a white-painted door onto another sitting room, smaller than the one in which Malcolm had spoken with Prescott.

"This feels like a repeat of a year ago." Malcolm followed his godfather and closed the door behind them.

"It's not. It's a whole new mess. I thought it was over. And then all of a sudden, I'm facing a completely different threat."

"From whom?"

"From someone who wants me to pay an obscene amount to recover papers that may contain a pack of lies."

Malcolm moved to where he could see Glenister's face. "Or may contain some hard truths?"

Glenister banged his boot toe against the fender. "Possibly."

"Just what did you reveal to Danielle Darnault?"

Glenister's head shot up from contemplation of the fire. "What do you know about Danielle Darnault?"

"Apparently her memoirs are being bartered all over London among interested parties."

"Oh, Christ."

"It is certainly causing a good deal of consternation."

"I thought she liked me." Glenister gave a wry smile. "I suppose that sounds idiotic."

"No, I've heard the same about her from others."

Glenister stared at him. "How many people have come to you about the memoirs?"

"A surprising number. And I doubt you're the last."

Glenister looked into the fire again, as though seeing scenes from the past. "It was in Paris in late '16. The boys were causing trouble—it was before Quen married Aspasia—and I had just had a difficult breakup with—well, never mind about that. I went over to Paris for a fortnight to get away. Met her at the Salon des Etrangers."

"That seems to have been a favorite haunt of hers."

"The thing is, I wasn't even looking for a mistress. She was easy to talk to. And diverting."

"And you found yourself confiding in her."

"Well, yes." Glenister ran a hand over his hair. "It was a time when I needed a sympathetic ear."

"What did you confide in her about?"

Glenister hesitated.

"I presume you sought me out because you want my help."

Malcolm's godfather released a breath that grated like nails on iron. "My frustrations with the boys. Val's tendency to ape my habits, which I was starting to think I had looked on with too much indulgence —both when it came to Val's behavior and when it came to my own. Quen's public dissolution and complete lack of respect for me. Which led to the story of Quen's birth." Glenister looked up from the grate to meet Malcolm's gaze. "She's the only person I'd told it to until I told you."

"That speaks volumes about what she meant to you," Malcolm said in a quiet voice. A year ago, in the midst of an investigation, Malcolm had uncovered papers that revealed that Glenister's eldest son, Viscount Quentin, known as Quen, had in fact been fathered by Alistair Rannoch, Malcolm's own putative father. Only then had Glenister admitted to Malcolm that Alistair had seduced Lady Glenister after a bet with Glenister that a gentleman couldn't seduce a wife who had not yet given her husband an heir. A revelation that had cast in a whole new light the relationship between Alistair and Glenister, supposed best friends since their days at Harrow, and co-founders of the Elsinore League.

Glenister gave a wry grimace. "It speaks volumes about how she could get a man to talk. But yes, she meant more to me than any woman had for a long time. Than any woman has since. And so I confided not just about Quen, but about Annabel. And about Cathy."

The revelations about Quen had unraveled as part of an investigation into the attempted murder of Annabel Larimer. Whereas Glenister had not, in the biological sense, fathered Quen, his putative eldest son and heir, he was Annabel Larimer's biological father, unbeknownst at that point to Annabel. Glenister's amorous adventures, like those of most of his set, read like a somewhat less focused version of *Les Liaisons Dangereuses*, but Malcolm had been shocked, in the course of the investigation, to discover that Glenister had apparently been deeply in love with Cathy Collingwood, Annabel's mother. Who had herself been married and had given the baby to her cousin to raise, to preserve her relationship with her husband and custody of her legitimate children. "That was a great admission," Malcolm said.

"And you see what the devil of a fix it puts me in now." Glenister spun away from the fireplace and strode the width of the hearth rug to the sofa, like a caged lion. "Can you imagine what the revelation of the truth would do to my children? To all my children?"

"Annabel knows the truth now," Malcolm said. Annabel, herself a former agent, was now happily married to Raimundo O'Roarke, Malcolm's own cousin.

"For which I'm endlessly grateful. But can you imagine the talk it would cause? She doesn't need that. Her husband's work in Spain—which I assume you support—doesn't need that. Not to mention what it would do to her children and half siblings. And Collingwood."

Cathy's husband, who knew the truth, but had made a great effort to pretend not to. Who was himself a member of the Elsinore League.

"Collingwood's on your side in the fight in the League, isn't he?" Malcolm said.

"So far. To the extent he's chosen a side at all." Glenister gripped the back of one of the Queen Anne chairs. "This could send him to the other side. And he's respected. Within the League and outside of it. He could give this—insurgency—legitimacy."

"I wasn't aware the League were concerned with legitimacy."

"Legitimacy always matters. From one's children to one's position. At least, the appearance of legitimacy. Why do you think the League are so careful about our membership?"

"So you can keep your secrets and wield power."

"And who wields power? Those whose bloodlines—or putative bloodlines—give them that power legitimately. Look at Carfax. Arthur Mallinson. Julien St. Juste. Whatever he calls himself. His grandmother was born a slave, and the story of his past five-and-twenty-years raises all sorts of questions, but at least everyone accepts he's a Mallinson." Glenister spun away, staring at a hunting print on the wall. "And then there's Quen. He's happy with Aspasia. Young Will is growing up happy. Quen and Val are getting on better than they have in years. I'd give a great deal to avoid seeing that smashed to bits."

"Quen's sensible enough not to give way to gossip."

Glenister stared at Malcolm as though he'd lost track of the truth. "You grew up in Mayfair, Malcolm. You know what gossip can do. Even when one has the best will in the world to look beyond it."

"Does Quen know the truth?"

Glenister jaw tightened. "Quen knows. He's got past it. We told Val as well. Quen insisted on it. He said he couldn't live with Val's not knowing. Val's handled it better than I'd have thought. A sign, perhaps, of his starting to grow up a bit. But it's one thing for all of us to know it. Quite another for the world to. If the truth becomes public, the world will see Val as the rightful heir. Quen will be seen as an imposter and Val will get sympathy and veiled comments, and everyone will stare at them. My sons are piecing their lives and relationship together. But that would put an unbearable strain on things."

"Yes, I can imagine." Malcolm swallowed, bitterness welling on his tongue like blood from a knife cut. A knife cut his own brother might have delivered.

Glenister met his gaze. "You should understand."

"None better. Although, though Val has driven me to distraction, I can't see his ever trying to kill Quen. He's more mature than Edgar. Which I never thought I'd find myself saying."

Glenister grimaced. "Your father—Alistair—was a fool. If

he'd seen what he had in both of you, he could have had a decent relationship with both his sons. And Edgar wouldn't have come to grief."

"Possibly. Edgar was very angry, and Alistair can't take all the blame for that. And Alistair wasn't ever my father."

"He could have been if he'd chosen differently."

That was something Malcolm wasn't prepared to contemplate. Impossible to think of anyone but Raoul as his father. Even if at one point he'd been desperate for any sign of acceptance from Alistair. "I know who my father is," Malcolm said. "I always did, in a way."

Glenister met Malcolm's gaze. For a moment, he was the godfather of Malcolm's childhood, in one of his moments of careless warmth. And at the same time, the tempered Glenister of recent years, whom Malcolm recalled playing on a blanket with his grandson. "A child can have two fathers, Malcolm. I'd have thought you'd realize that."

Malcolm swallowed and tasted something raw. The conversation had suddenly stripped him to the bone, rather than Glenister. It was true he was comfortable thinking of both Raoul and himself as Colin's fathers. Easier perhaps because Raoul was also Colin's grandfather. But it was impossible to think of anyone else as his own father.

"Not Alistair," Glenister said. "I'm not sure, as I've grown rather inexpertly closer to my own children and seen Quen with his son, that Alistair was capable of being anyone's father."

"He was a father to Gisèle, more than to either Edgar or me."

"Yes." Glenister frowned. "He seemed easier with her. Perhaps because she couldn't be an heir. I don't think Alistair was capable of navigating the situation with you and Edgar. But a different man could have handled the situation differently."

"You did," Malcolm said. "You're to be credited for that."

"That's good of you. I don't believe I deserve much credit for anything. But I would like to spare my sons and my grandson and Aspasia the pain of a public scandal."

"Just how far would you go to spare them?"

"What's that supposed to mean?"

"Has anyone tried to use the memoirs to influence your vote over the queen?"

"What? No, nothing like that. Just asked me to make an offer for them. But I gather the seller is looking for the highest bidder."

"And if the highest bidder tries to influence your vote?"

"On which side?"

"It could be either."

Glenister grimaced. "I never had much care for our current sovereign. He and the queen have made this mess."

"And what it might do to the balance of power in Parliament?"

"That's the concern of those who run both parties. So if it came down to that or protecting my family—"

"Quite," Malcolm said. "That's precisely why the memoirs represent such a risk. To everyone. As well as to Alexander Radford."

Glenister's head jerked up. "Who?"

"The man trying to take over the League. He was Danielle Darnault's lover as well. Apparently, the memoirs reveal his identity."

Glenister went still. "You're sure?"

"As sure as can be. The League—Radford's faction in the League—were trying to buy them."

"You saw them?" Glenister's voice was taut.

"I saw a teaser from the memoirs. It didn't reveal anything. But apparently, others in the League were involved with Danielle Darnault. Including Alistair."

"Good God."

"You didn't know?"

"My dear Malcolm, at this point you must realize Alistair and I were not quite the friends and confidants we appeared to the world."

"Trenchard was her lover too. At the time, Alistair and Trenchard were plotting to make Trenchard prime minister."

"I can't say I'm entirely surprised. She had an influential list of lovers."

Malcolm folded his arms over his chest. "Do you believe Dewhurst killed Alistair?"

"Who else would have done?"

"A number of people had cause."

"You're not suggesting Danielle Darnault did?"

"It's an interesting thought, though she wasn't in England at the time, that we know of. But I can't help feeling there's a piece I'm missing. Did Alistair tell you he suspected Dewhurst?"

"No. But Alistair didn't confide a great deal in me. Especially by that point. I didn't even know directly about his plan with Trenchard." Glenister gave a curt nod. "I know you'll do your best to recover the memoirs." He turned to go.

"Uncle Frederick?" Malcolm hadn't called Glenister that since he was fifteen.

Glenister turned back, as though compelled against his better instincts.

"So you don't know who Radford is?" Malcolm asked.

Glenister drew a hard breath, like a man winded in a race he was losing. "Radford's dangerous, Malcolm. And he needs to be stopped."

"I am endeavoring to do so. So are a number of others. It would help if we knew who he was."

"I can't claim to know that. Not with a certainty. But if you did know, I'm not sure it would help."

"What's that supposed to mean?"

"The truth can be paralyzing, Malcolm. Go on with your work—if anyone can win this battle, you can."

CHAPTER 24

"Seems like an age since we've done this." Blanca Mendoza Addison, Mélanie's companion, twined a length of Mélanie's hair round the curling tongs and clamped them closed.

"It is an age." Mélanie met Blanca's gaze in the looking glass and resisted the urge to swivel her head round. "I'm sorry you have to fuss with it." In the early days of Mélanie's marriage, Blanca, an accomplished agent herself, had learned to be very proficient as a lady's maid, caring for Mélanie's gowns and creating elaborate hairstyles and toilettes in Vienna and Brussels and Paris and London. But since their time in Italy and the somewhat quieter and more bohemian life they were leading in London, Mélanie mostly dressed herself and did her own hair, frequently leaving it down, pulled back with combs or a bandeau. Tonight called for something more, though. In general, Mélanie would dress herself for an entertainment at Cordy's. But tonight, they weren't merely enjoying an evening out at a ball hosted by friends. They were, in a sense, going undercover.

"I don't mind." Blanca adjusted the curl and wound another.

"It's rather fun, for a change. Reminds me of old times. Not that I want to go back to then."

"Quite and quite."

"It's a good thing, all in all." Blanca stuck a hairpin into the Psyche knot at the back of Mélanie's head. "That this business of the king and queen is happening now. If it had to happen at all."

Mélanie swiveled her head round to look up at her friend. "What on earth's that to say to anything?"

"Hold still. I won't forgive myself if I burn your neck, and you won't like it either." Blanca took Mélanie's head between her hands and turned it back towards the looking glass. "A marriage is falling apart in front of all London. Better you and Malcolm sorted things out before it happened. Better Addison and I did too."

"Well, yes. Better, in general, for all sorts of reasons. But as to the royal marriage, I'm not sure anything can be said to be falling apart that was never properly together."

"That's a point. Poor Princess Charlotte was born almost nine months to the day after their wedding night, you know. One rather wonders if they ever again—"

"Yes, one would wonder. Assuming one dwelled on the unhappy couple at all."

"One can hardly do otherwise. It's all over London. Including in Edmund Blayney's papers." Blanca adjusted another ringlet with a pin so it wouldn't fall into Mélanie's face. "Malcolm asked me to go through them looking for anything that might impact on the case. I'd rather be undercover, but it was good to have something to do. And I could have Pedro with me." She set down the curling tongs, stepped back, and frowned at Mélanie's image in the looking glass, then added another pin to anchor the curls on one side. "In any case, everyone's talking about marriage just now. Better to feel confident in one's own."

"Which makes the appearance of Danielle Darnault's

memoirs and the influence they could wield particularly fraught." Mélanie got to her feet.

"Precisely." Malcolm appeared in the doorway. "Prescott wouldn't say much, though the temper tantrum he threw suggests he's concerned about more than his wife's scandal. And then Glenister buttonholed me. Apparently, he's in the memoirs as well."

"That's a new wrinkle." Mélanie unfastened her seafoam silk dressing gown and slipped it off her shoulders. "Did he know about Danielle Darnault and Alistair?"

"He says not. Quite convincingly. Though with Glenister I'm never sure I'm convinced. He mostly seemed worried about the impact on his children and grandchildren. All of them."

"I can see that." Mélanie gave the dressing gown to Blanca and stood watching her husband in her pomegranate silk slip. Sometimes at home she wore the slip to dinner on its own. She'd even worn it out with a silver belt. "Glenister certainly has enough secrets to fear being exposed. Though as to why he'd share them across the pillow—"

"Danielle Darnault seems to have been singularly adept at getting people to confide. I've heard more than once how easy she was to talk to, how people trusted her," Malcolm said.

"It's an art." Blanca set the dressing gown down on the bed and held out Mélanie's blush-colored lace overdress. "Not getting someone into bed. That's easy enough, after all. But putting them at ease. Getting them to talk."

"Yes." Malcolm strolled into the room. "And some of us have been known to reveal all sorts of things. Good thing you never wrote your memoirs, darling."

"They wouldn't have been nearly as interesting as Danielle Darnault's. Well, not on that account." Mélanie slid her arms into the overdress and did up the silk strings that fastened it on the side.

Malcolm paused, arms folded across his chest. "You look beautiful. And quite different."

"I used to dress like this all the time. In Vienna, this would have seemed positively simple."

"Yes, but it's been a while. It's rather like seeing you in costume."

Mélanie glanced in the looking glass and adjusted one of her garnet and antique gold earrings. "Oh, going out in the beau monde always means playing a role. We're just more aware of it these days."

"That's what domesticity does to you." Blanca picked up the curling tongs and moved to the door.

"Are you accusing us of getting rusty?" Malcolm asked.

"Heaven forfend. Addison has your things laid out in the dressing room. But you'd best let him help you with your cravat. He still cares about his reputation as valet."

"Don't worry. I won't let him down." Malcolm grinned and shrugged out of his coat.

"Go get ready yourself," Mélanie told Blanca.

"Don't worry, I have plenty of time. People won't be looking at me nearly as closely as you."

Malcolm studied Mélanie. "You aren't wearing a corset, are you?"

"Is it that obvious?"

"Only to someone who's used to helping you lace it."

"I need to find some way to be subversive."

"It's the darts in the dress," Blanca said, at the door. "They do wonders."

"And I'm much better suited to action this way," Mélanie said. "Yet another difference from Vienna. I rarely went without a corset. I was too worried about fitting in. And probably too afraid you'd notice."

"Why on earth would I have minded your not wearing a corset?"

"It might have shaken your opinion of who I was."

"A sensible woman who isn't afraid to be practical? And comfortable? Or who realizes a woman's natural shape is much more appealing?"

"I love you, Malcolm."

Malcolm grinned and strolled across the room, tugging his cravat loose. Mélanie followed him to the dressing room and leaned in the doorway while he whipped the shaving soap into a lather, reached for the razor, and told her about his interviews with Prescott and Glenister.

"Prescott seems to have lost his temper more over the mention of Sophia than over your suggestion he'd known Danielle Darnault," Mélanie said.

"Yes." Malcolm angled the razor over a bit he'd missed on his jaw. "But then he could legitimately take offense at the insult to his wife's honor. He couldn't take offense over Danielle Darnault without admitting he'd known her. But I rather had the sense his bluster over Lady Prescott was an attempt to turn my attention away from whatever happened between him and Danielle Darnault."

"It has to be more than an affair. An affair with a famous courtesan sounds like the sort of thing a man like Prescott would boast about. I doubt he's worried about unsettling his marriage, given what we know about it. Given the way Sophia spoke of him."

"No." Malcolm set down the razor and wiped his face with the towel Addison had laid out. "With all of them, it doesn't seem to be the fact of the affair they're worried about, but the things Danielle Darnault got them to confide. A far greater talent, as Blanca pointed out."

"Which she employed as an agent. But then, she was willing to barter those secrets."

"She wrote them down as insurance."

Mélanie moved to her husband's side and wiped a bit of

lather he'd missed at the corner of his mouth. "She sounds like me."

"Not really." Malcolm caught her hand and kissed it. "She wasn't loyal to any cause."

"There is that. And she had a far more exalted string of lovers than I did."

"You got married young. Not that that stops some people."

Mélanie pulled a face at him.

Malcolm began to undo his shirt cuffs. "She sounds more like Tania."

Mélanie studied her husband. The loss of his sister Tatiana was still a raw wound, she knew. "She sounds intelligent and clever like Tatiana." Funny to be calling her by her given name, which Mélanie would never have done in Tatiana's lifetime—when she had believed the other woman was her husband's mistress. Even now, it didn't seem right to call her Tania. "And as though she was loyal to those she cared about, like Tatiana."

"Tania was that." Malcolm started on the second cuff. "She was also Napoleon's Bonaparte's mistress at much the same time Danielle Darnault was. Perhaps at the same time. And we know Tania was fully capable of indulging in blackmail. Which was hard for me to face, and which I was therefore slow to admit."

"And you think Julien's having the same problem?"

Malcolm gave a wry smile. "A year ago, even nine months ago, if you'd told me I'd be saying Julien could blinded by his feelings—But yes. I think it's possible."

"And even Julien admits Danielle Darnault might have been capable of having Jamie Blayney killed."

Malcolm dragged his shirt over his head. "Yes, well, I'd have admitted Tania could be capable of murder in the same circumstances. And I'd have had the devil of a time if I'd been investigating."

Mélanie handed him the fresh shirt Addison had laid out. "I

don't think Danielle Darnault quite means to Julien what Tatiana meant to you."

"No. But I'm coming more and more to realize that a number of people and things mean far more to Julien than he would ever admit. Even to himself."

"I think he'd be the first to admit he's biased."

"Yes, I agree." Malcolm pulled on the fresh shirt. "He's not short on self-knowledge. Poor devil."

Mélanie looked at her husband in inquiry.

"He's not close to a lot of people. And two of those he is close to are tangled in this mess."

"I know. It's still odd to be working with Julien."

"Is it?" Malcolm asked with a crooked smile.

Mélanie folded her arms. In their months traveling with Hortense Bonaparte, she had relied on Julien, as he had seemed to rely on her. "Perhaps not entirely. We were allies. Comrades."

Malcolm began to do up the cuffs on the clean shirt. "When we first met—that is, when I first met him as Julien St. Juste— you talked to him like—"

"Don't say an ex-lover."

"Not really. Though I already knew he was that. More like a provoking brother of whom you were fond, despite his challenges."

Mélanie felt herself frown, then laughed. "Damn it, Malcolm, as usual, you're far too insightful." She adjusted the strings on her gown. "Perhaps I sensed Julien was looking for something, without admitting it. Perhaps because I was looking for it myself, without admitting it. I do think, even then, I realized Julien could be hurt, despite all appearances to the contrary." She met her husband's gaze, countless moments from their eight years together flashing between them. "And yes, I do think both Danielle Darnault and Lord Pendarves could end up hurting Julien."

ADDISON MADE a last adjustment to Malcolm's cravat. "It's rather refreshing to be doing this again, sir."

"I thought you'd finally got round to calling me Malcolm."

Addison gave the faintest of smiles and reached for the black cassimere coat he had laid out. "Only on occasion. Sir."

"So I don't only have to squeeze my arms into a coat that's uncomfortably tight, I have to lose free discourse with one of my best friends."

"Your coats have never been cut tightly enough to be considered truly fashionable. And you always spoke quite freely with me long before it occurred to either of us to use given names."

Malcolm grinned as he slid his arms into the coat. "It certainly feels cut tightly enough."

"That's because half the time at home you don't wear one at all."

"Mmn. The things I learned in Italy. Speaking of which, I think it would be a good thing if you could strike up an acquaintance with Lord Prescott's valet. Also Lord Danbury's."

"Gladly, sir." Addison brushed the shoulders of the coat.

"Thank you. Miles." Malcolm picked up his gloves and moved to the door. Mélanie had already gone into the nursery, and Raoul and Laura would be there as well. They were taking the children with them to Harry and Cordy's to spend the evening with the Davenport girls, and then they were all staying the night.

"Malcolm," Addison said.

Malcolm turned back from the door and met his friend's gaze. "Yes?"

"Alexander Radford sounds like a very dangerous man."

"I believe he is." Malcolm twitched his shirt cuff straight beneath his coat. "We've dealt with dangerous men before."

"I know. But there's something different about this one."

"That sounds unusually dramatic from you."

Addison frowned into the bowl of shaving water. "You can tell it from the way everyone talks about him. Mostly from what they don't say."

"I'm always careful."

"I know." Addison lifted his gaze to Malcolm, his own unusually intent. "But in this case, I'm asking you to be more so. As a friend."

Malcolm clapped Addison on the shoulder. "I can hardly fail to take a request from a friend seriously. I'll be on my guard. You have my word."

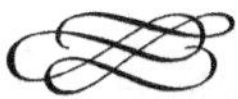

"I like Pippa Haworth," Mélanie said. "But I'm not sure she was telling the truth."

"About the affair, or about what Captain Blayney asked of her?" Kitty said. They were in Cordy's drawing room, turned into a ballroom for the evening, with Cordy and Laura, making last minute adjustments, though they'd been talking of nothing but the investigation. It was a good thing entertaining was like a memory ingrained in the muscles for all of them now. When she'd first married Malcolm, it had taken all Mélanie's concentration to get through an evening like this.

"About why she agreed to his blackmail demand," Mélanie said. "I do understand the threat to one's peace can shake a person. But having spoken with her, I can't help but think it would have taken something more to make her succumb to his threats."

Cordelia adjusted her aquamarine bandeau. "Scandal can sometimes seem more of a threat when one's been born inside society."

"Yes, I do see that. But what would you do if someone threatened to reveal information about your past?"

Cordelia frowned. "Tell Harry to be prepared for more scandal. Possibly leave London. No, I don't think I'd leave. I'd brazen it out."

"Precisely. Pippa reminds me of you. I can see why you're friends. And since I see no reason why she'd lie about agreeing to Captain Blayney's blackmail, I think he was holding something else over her."

"Perhaps he threatened Sophia Prescott," Laura said. "Sisters can be protective even when they don't get on."

"Perhaps." Mélanie tugged one of the autumn roses in a vase on a pier table by the door so it showed to better advantage. "I do have the sense she was protecting someone else, rather than herself. But we haven't seen much to indicate either sister would protect the other. Of course, Pippa might feel guilty about having had an affair with Sophia's former lover, for all she denies it. That might make her want to make amends."

"Pippa has more of a conscience than she lets on." Cordelia inched a chair further back from the space cleared for dancing. "I can't help feeling there's something about her affair with James Blayney that we're not seeing. Or that Pippa isn't telling us." She glanced at the mantelpiece clock, which she had bought in Switzerland on her way to Italy. "Poison, the guests could be here any minute. I should go to the head of the stairs. I know just how you felt at your ball last summer, Kitty. Hostess duty is like being sidelined."

"Take comfort in the fact that you'll be greeting a number of the suspects," Kitty said. "Goodness knows how many of whom are in Danielle Darnault's memoirs. I can only hope we'll know more at the end of tonight."

"We'll undoubtedly know more," Mélanie said. "Whether or not it will make sense is another question."

"It's odd." Cordelia cast another glance round the ballroom and righted a taper tilting in one of the candelabra. "When one is first out, the entire story of a ball seems to be who dances with whom, who might be on the verge of a proposal, who might be going another season without a proposal. People our age seem hopelessly dull. Then a decade later one can scarcely keep track of the doings of the younger set." She pushed the candelabrum to the center of the polished walnut table. "I suppose we'll have to pay attention again when the girls are old enough."

"The girls are too sensible." Harry appeared in the doorway, followed by Malcolm, Raoul, and Julien. "They'll fall in love with someone entirely unsuitable, like a writer, or a journalist, or a painter, or an actor."

"Or a classical scholar." Cordelia smiled at her husband. "But if I hadn't gone to the Devonshire House ball, I'd never have met you."

"For that matter, if I hadn't gone, which is far more surprising, I'd never have met you. Don't imagine I don't thank my lucky stars every night that I let Archie drag me to that party."

"I met Julien at a ball." Kitty tucked her hand through her husband's arm.

"On the dance floor?" Laura asked.

"No, he was masquerading as a woman. He was wearing the most beautiful mantilla and silver comb. I wanted both before I had the wit to want Julien."

"I gave you the comb and mantilla, as I recall," Julien said.

"You did, darling. Long before you gave me yourself."

"Did you see through his disguise?" Malcolm asked.

"Yes, but only after I spotted him lifting papers and realized he was on a mission."

"I don't know which part of what you saw through shows a more shocking lapse of judgment on my part," Julien said.

"Well, in fairness, no one else saw through you that night." Kitty said.

"Very true." He lifted her gloved hand to his lips. "Your skills caught me. I've been a lost man ever since."

"How did we ever do this, night after night, when we didn't have an investigation to divert us?" Cordelia asked.

"Don't ask me," Julien said. "I ran away from home to avoid it. Well that and to avoid being arrested."

"Take it from one who was once a governess," Laura said. "There's something to be said for not being on the sidelines."

Mélanie surveyed her friend. Laura's gown of ivory silk net over satin, adorned with blonde lace and gold embroidery that caught the candlelight, was anything but designed to blend into the shadows. Very different from the sober dark blue and gray she'd worn in her days as their governess. "I'm sorry. I don't think I properly appreciated how beastly it must have been."

"Don't be. You included me far more than most governesses. I'm the one who was trying to hide. And I met Raoul on the sidelines."

"For which I could not be more grateful," Raoul said.

Malcolm glanced round the group. "Is everyone clear on the mission?"

"As clear as can be," Julien said. "I imagine tonight is going to take improvisation. Because just about anyone here could be a subject in the investigation."

"I've warned the footmen to pay extra attention to the guests, and we have someone watching the garden gate," Harry said. "Just in case whoever was behind the attacks on Mélanie and me and Julien and Raoul tries anything. Though a part of me rather wishes they would. It might give us some answers."

"And it would certainly ensure the ball was talked of." Cordelia moved to the door to the landing. "Time to go to work."

~

As THE BALLROOM filled with guests, Malcolm made his way downstairs, pausing to flash a sympathetic smile at Cordy, who was looking radiant in gauzy azure draperies over white satin at the head of the stairs and giving an excellent impression of thinking of nothing but greeting her guests. He slipped down the stairs, nodding at arriving guests, and made his way to the library. There was a time when he'd escaped to the library whenever he could at balls. He'd met Kitty in the British minister's library in Lisbon, and in the early days of their marriage Mélanie had frequently gone in search of him there and pulled him out into the crowd.

But now he was bent on investigation, not escape. Not that the library would have been a good place to escape to tonight. It was already quite full, with political groups seeking a quiet place to discuss the trial, and classicists poring over Harry and Cordy's books. Malcolm grinned at Edith Simmons, a young classicist and former governess who now lived with Harry and Cordy, then strolled over to the fireplace where Fitzroy Somerset was talking with the current Duke of Trenchard. They both greeted him as a friend, but Malcolm caught the quick way their talk silenced at his approach.

"Difficult to share chitchat across party lines these days," Malcolm said.

"It's always good to see you." Fitzroy, who had excellent diplomatic skills, gave a quick smile. He had been Wellington's secretary in the Peninsula and Waterloo and was now in Wellington's new role as master-general of the ordnance. He had also been elected a Tory MP in 1818 but had lost his seat in the recent general election. "Away from Westminster. Though these days, what's happening in Westminster seems to follow us everywhere."

Malcolm returned Fitzroy's smile. They had been friends and colleagues since the Peninsula. "Sorry to interrupt your conversation."

"On the contrary," Trenchard said. Like Fitzroy, he was a Tory, but he could not be more different from his late father, the

Elsinore League member who had schemed with Alistair Rannoch to be made prime minister. "We've spent enough time on politics. I promised my wife at least two dances." He touched Malcolm on the arm, nodded to Fitzroy, and made his way off.

"I heard there was an unfortunate incident last night," Fitzroy said. "I'm glad you're safe and able to be here tonight."

"Only a minor scuffle," Malcolm said. "But speaking of the investigation, I was hoping for a word with you. Perhaps we could go into the garden?"

"Excellent." Fitzroy's brief start of surprise was quickly masked by a smile. "I could use some fresh air."

They made their way out of the library and down the passage through a door to the garden. Cordy had strung colored-glass lanterns overhead that danced in a gust of wind, sending brilliant washes of shadow over the shrubs and stone benches. The light of a cigarillo glowed in the dark, and jewels flashed in the lamplight. Faint murmurs of conversation and gusts of laughter carried on the breeze, but in the shadows of a topiary hedge, round which Malcolm had often played hide and seek with the children, he and Fitzroy had relative privacy.

"Tell me what you know about Danielle Darnault's memoirs," Malcolm said.

Fitzroy's eyes blazed at him in the shadows. "Damn it, Malcolm, you don't think I'm in the blasted memoirs, do you?"

Fitzroy had been happily married to Wellington's niece since before Waterloo. "At least you don't deny knowing about them."

"I know you too well. There'd be no point. But if you think I'm in them—"

"I don't. But I'm quite sure the duke is."

Fitzroy's mouth twisted, a hard line in the shadows.

"It's hardly a secret he was one of her lovers. And hardly a shock, given that I know his marriage is very different from yours. Did Blayney approach the duke?"

Fitzroy drew in and released a breath that frosted in the autumn night. "A parcel was delivered to me five days ago."

"Sample pages?"

"Yes. I wanted to find Blayney and thrash him, but I told the duke. I expect you can imagine his reaction."

"That anyone could publish anything they liked about him?"

"Precisely. With a few choice words thrown in."

"So that was the end of it?"

Fitzroy shifted his weight from one foot to another. "Not quite. I felt compelled to learn more. We didn't know precisely what was in these pages about the duke. It's not so much that he had a mistress, but—you must have heard talk that Danielle Darnault may have been an agent."

"I have. And she was."

"Christ. The duke says he didn't admit anything to her. But God knows what she might have made up." Fitzroy drew a hard breath. "So I met Blayney. In a coffeehouse in Westminster." His gloved hands curled into fists at his sides. "I can't tell you how hard it was not to plant him a facer. To think that that blackguard fought for Britain. That he served under the duke in any way. It's monstrous."

"Like a number of former soldiers, he was struggling to make a living after Waterloo."

"Are you making excuses for him, Rannoch?"

"Hardly. Blackmail's an ugly business. And he doesn't seem to have cared whom he hurt. What happened when you met him?"

Fitzroy's jaw tightened. "He named an extravagant sum."

"Did you pay it?"

"I was considering." Fitzroy folded his arms across his chest. "And yes, I know damned well Wellington would have my head for even considering it. But while he's Britain's greatest hero, he's not invincible. My God, five years after Waterloo he's got a mob hurling insults at his carriage when he goes to Parliament for the queen's trial. I won't apologize for having concern for his reputation. Think of what he can do for our country."

"I'm likely to disagree with much—if not all—of what he may try to do. But I wouldn't argue with your instinct to protect him. I can imagine doing the same to protect someone I loved."

"Yes, well, I'm damned sure Wellington wouldn't see it that way. Which is why I didn't come to you, when I heard Blayney had been killed. As I have no doubt you are about to ask me. I'm less afraid of the repercussions from your and Bow Street's knowing I had dealings with Blayney than I am of the duke's response to knowing I went behind his back."

"I won't tell him unless I have to."

"You're a good fellow, Malcolm. But we both know you may have to."

"We've both seen battle, Fitzroy. You more than me. But we both know the hell it can lead to."

Fitzroy's usually open gaze fastened on Malcolm's face, as armored as fortifications. "Quite."

CHAPTER 26

*R*aoul made his way round the edge of the ballroom and into the salon given over for conversation. He'd been attending Mayfair balls since he was in his late teens. He'd met Malcolm's mother at one. Arabella had been in the act of stealing papers from Lord Glenister. Searching for information at a ball was nothing new to him. Perhaps more often on his own than with colleagues, though investigating with colleagues was not an alien experience. But investigating with his family was. Having a family was. Which seemed particularly precious tonight. And particularly precarious.

He spotted his quarry crossing the salon, unattached as he moved from one conversational group to another. "O'Roarke," Rupert Caruthers said. "I hear you're in the midst of an investigation."

"Yes. I came home in the middle of it today. Rather a lot's happened in the past twenty-four hours, or I imagine Malcolm would have updated you already."

They moved to an empty corner of the room, and Raoul went on to update Rupert on the incident at the Chat Gris, Jamie Blayney's death, and Danielle Darnault's memoirs. "Did you know Blayney?" he asked. Rupert had been a soldier in the Peninsula and at Waterloo and in military intelligence and was part of many of Malcolm and Mélanie's investigations.

"I've heard his name, but no. I knew the Langdons a bit growing up." Rupert flushed, then said in an even voice, "My mother had her heart set on my marrying Sophia Langdon for a while. One of many girls she tried to throw may way."

Rupert had resisted marriage for years until the man he loved, Bertrand Laclos, had been presumed dead. It occurred to Raoul to wonder if Rupert knew about Pendarves, but asking seemed an intrusion. They could talk with relative discretion in this quiet corner, but this was no place to discuss the affairs of the Langdon sisters or of their brother.

"I found it easier to talk to Pippa Langdon," Rupert added. "I thought she deserved better than Haworth."

"Did you ever meet Danielle Darnault?"

"I saw her on stage in Paris a few times, but we never met. You must have better sources of information about her."

"I'm endeavoring. I was hoping Bertrand knows her."

"He may. But he's not here. He went off on one of his missions last week."

Bertrand Laclos, with whom Rupert now lived a happy if secret life, put his formidable intelligence skills to use rescuing those who fell afoul of the French authorities. He had saved a number of Bonapartists Raoul knew.

"I hope he'll be back in a day or two," Rupert added.

Raoul nodded. "There's something else I need to ask you about." He hesitated, because stepping forwards was committing himself even more irrevocably to a course that could not have a happy ending. "I've been to see your father."

Rupert's expression hardened. "I can't imagine what that has to do with me."

Rupert hadn't been on speaking terms with his father, Lord

Dewhurst, since he'd learned Dewhurst had attempted to have Bertrand killed and caused Bertrand to disappear for years.

"It answered some questions," Raoul said. "But left me with more." He hesitated a moment, then stepped over the precipice. "I need your help."

∼

"FUNNY," Manon Caret Harleton said, surveying the ballroom. "I still feel more on stage at a Mayfair ball—even one given by one of my best friends—than I do on the boards of the Tavistock."

"Oh, I certainly do," Mélanie said. "I imagine I always will."

Manon, who had once reigned over the Comédie Française and was now a leading lady at the Tavistock Theatre, as well the wife of Viscount Harleton, smiled and unfurled a painted silk fan that matched her pomona green gros-de-Naples gown. "I hope you're going to ask me about Danielle Darnault. I shall be quite disappointed if you don't."

"Did you ever meet her?" Mélanie asked.

"Oh yes. I know her. Or, knew her would be more precise. Not well. But I saw her at some parties. I remember seeing her with one of Napoleon's marshals. Rumor has it she may have moved on to Napoleon himself."

"Julien says the rumors are true. You never worked with her?"

"No. Or even talked with her about being an agent, though she must have known I was, just as I knew she was. In any case, she ran off with an Austrian grand duke just in time to be safely in Austria when the emperor fell. Then she disappeared for a time."

"Apparently she was with child," Mélanie said.

Manon shot a look at her. "I didn't know. And the father—"

"We aren't sure. She may not be either."

Manon raised her brows. "Interesting. So the father could be—"

"The timing's right. We don't know more."

"She was the mistress of a Prussian general by Waterloo. She didn't go back to Napoleon's side when he escaped from Elba, from anything I've heard. And then, like a number of us, she went on to Paris after Waterloo. I heard she'd taken up with Wellington, and then Tsar Alexander for a time. It's a wonder she found time to sing as well as she did."

"Did you know she'd settled in London?"

"I heard rumors, but I never encountered her. I could understand wanting to retire from espionage, though it's harder to imagine wanting to retire from the stage with her talents."

"Did you know she had a child?"

"No. Though that's hardly a bar to performing."

"No. But perhaps protecting the child made her want to live a retired life."

"That makes sense." Manon took a sip of champagne. "Especially if the father is who you suspect."

"*R*annoch."

Malcolm turned at the sound of his name as he walked down the ground floor passage past the library after his talk with Fitzroy. Lord Pendarves stood just outside the library door, regarding Malcolm with the look of one who wanted to talk. Which was interesting, as Malcolm might have expected Pendarves to be avoiding him just now. "I was hoping we could have a word."

"Certainly." Malcolm inclined his head towards the door of Harry's study. Harry wouldn't mind lending it to them, and they could count on being private.

"I know you're in the midst of an investigation," Pendarves said, when he followed Malcolm into the room.

"Julien told you last night."

Pendarves cast a quick glance at him. He was a tall man with curly hair the color of late autumn leaves and an air of carrying the responsibilities he had been born to tight within him.

"We none of us share personal details lightly," Malcolm said. "But unfortunately in an investigation all sorts of details become relevant. You have my sympathies."

Pendarves drew a breath. "I knew Carfax would have to tell you. I just didn't—I'm still realizing the consequences of every-thing that's happened. That is happening."

"You'd best come in and sit down." Malcolm gestured to the chairs by Harry's desk. The desk was piled with scribbled-over drafts of Harry's latest monograph and several research books. The carved walnut chairs were scratched and nicked but very comfortable.

Pendarves sat with care, as though uncertain about what he was opening himself up to. He was always formal and serious in meetings, but he had some sound ideas and he wasn't afraid to work.

"We have no reason to think Blayney had any papers that betray you," Malcolm said. "Unless there's more we aren't aware of."

"No. That is, yes, there is more. That's why I've wanted to talk with you. But it's not to do with papers. That is, not papers relating to me. To my relationships. I didn't say this to Carfax last night, but I saw Blayney a week before his death."

"He'd been pressuring you to give him money."

"Yes. For years. But this visit wasn't to do with that either. I thought it was, at first. But Jamie could still surprise me." Pendarves gripped the arms of his chair. "I've known him my whole life."

"You were friends."

Pendarves' mouth tightened. "'Were' being the operative word."

"I heard his father was a clergyman. Your father—"

"Gave his father his living. We all played together, Jamie and his brother Edmund, my sisters and me." Pendarves drew a breath. "Jamie was an engaging boy. Much more so than I was myself. My father paid for him to go to Eton. He helped settle his debts and bought him a commission."

"Your father was a generous man."

"He was fond of Jamie. Fonder than he was of me, I think."

"That can't have been easy."

"Relationships between fathers and sons often aren't easy. I'm trying to do better with my own sons, though I don't know how well I'm managing. My father liked riding to hounds and sport of all types. Jamie was always better at that than I was. Father couldn't understand my interest in Parliament." Pendarves's hands closed on the carved chair arms. "Father died a few years after Jamie went off to the Peninsula."

"But before that, they quarreled over your sister Sophia."

Pendarves drew a sharp breath. "We spoke with Edmund Blayney last night," Malcolm said. "And my wife and Lady Carfax spoke with Lady Prescott this afternoon."

"Did Julien know this last night?"

"We wanted to get your sister's version of events first."

"And Mrs. Rannoch and Lady Carfax know—"

"We're all involved in the investigation. We all take secrecy very seriously. My wife and Lady Carfax have both been agents. They're as careful with confidential information as anyone I know."

"I understand. I knew our secrets were being spilled in the open. I just didn't expect—"

"We thought it would be easier for Lady Prescott to speak with two other women. Lady Carfax and she are connected through Lady Carfax's first husband."

"Yes." Pendarves ran a hand over his hair. "I remember that now. And yes, I'm sure it was easier. Sophia must have—I imagine it was hard for her to hear."

"She was still fond of Blayney?"

"I believe so. It is hardly something we could speak of." Pendarves shifted in his chair. "My father told me about the entanglement. He wanted me to understand that he was cutting his ties with Jamie, and why, and that I should follow his course in future as head of the family. I still remember the look on Sophia's face that night."

"What did she say?"

"You can't imagine I talked to her about it, Rannoch. Would you discuss such a thing with your sister?"

Malcolm considered his two sisters, Tatiana, who had been dead six years now, and Gisèle, who was undercover with the League. He had plotted missions with both. Broken codes. Shared risks. Tania had told him more than he wanted to know about some of her affairs, and kept others entirely secret. Including one that had produced her child. Gelly had confided in him about her love for Andrew Thirle. But not about anyone else. He didn't think there'd been anyone else. But as with so much about Gisèle, he couldn't be sure. "That would depend on a number of things. Including if my sister confided in me."

"We've never been much for confiding." Pendarves's hands tightened on the carved wood. "Whatever Father wanted, we couldn't entirely cut Jamie without drawing attention to the unfortunate episode. But it's certainly true that in yielding to Jamie's—persuasion—I went against my father's wishes."

"I hardly think your father would have wanted your secrets exposed either."

"My father," Pendarves said, in a ruthlessly flat tone, "would be horrified by who and what I am, Rannoch. I have to live with that."

"Which is damnable."

"As I said, I'm endeavoring to do better with my own sons. In any case, I was resigned to my uncomfortable connection with Jamie. Until he tried to seduce another of my sisters."

"Jamie was involved with Mrs. Haworth?" Malcolm hadn't been sure if Pendarves knew about that.

"With Philippa?" Pendarves said, with a surprise that made Malcolm realize he almost certainly did not know. "No. With Phoebe. My youngest sister."

"Lady Molyneux?" Like her sister, Sophia Prescott, Phoebe Molyneux was married to a prominent politician, though Molyneux, like Pendarves, was a Whig. Malcolm had seen him at Brooks's the day before yesterday—God, was it really only two days? Brougham had asked for Malcolm's help securing Molyneux's vote.

"Yes, she's Lady Molyneux now." Pendarves gave a strained smile. Then he drew a hard breath. "When Father died, Sophia and Pippa were already married, but Phoebe was only fifteen. She became my ward. She was at school in Bath, and it seemed least disruptive to her life for her to stay there until she was ready to make her debut. My wife was adjusting to becoming Lady Pendarves, and our children were very young. We thought Phoebe would be happy among friends her own age. It seems a tragic mistake now. Even more ironic, I thought about asking Sophia to take her, but hesitated because of her entanglement with Blayney. But if there's one person I could have counted on to keep Phoebe away from Blayney, it was probably Sophia."

"I'm sorry," Malcolm said. "I have a younger sister myself. Our mother died when she was eight. Our father"—damned odd to use that word for Alistair—"was still alive, but she lived with our aunt. Which was a good place for her. But looking back, there's a great deal I wish I'd done differently. I wasn't there for her nearly as much as it sounds like you were for Phoebe. It can be a difficult relationship, especially when one loses one's parents. One takes on some of the burdens of a parent, while still having the tensions inherent in many relationships between siblings."

Pendarves looked up quickly and met Malcolm's gaze. "Yes." It was only a word, but for a moment his careful reserve broke. "I said I was trying to be a better parent to my children. Better than our father was to us. And better than I was with Phoebe. I don't know that I've been a good brother to Phoebe. Or perhaps, more important, a good guardian. I certainly wasn't in those early months." He stared at his signet ring. "Phoebe was scarcely out of the nursery when Jamie went into the army. She wasn't his playfellow the way the rest of us were. It never occurred to me he'd seek her out. As far as I knew, he was on the Peninsula. The first I knew of anything between him and Phoebe was when the headmistress wrote to tell me they'd eloped." He stared at his hands and looked up at Malcolm. "I don't speak lightly of my sister's misfortune. I know you are a man of honor and will not reveal this unless you have to."

"Of course not. As I said, I'm a brother myself. And a father. It must have been a horrible shock."

"Apparently Blayney contrived to speak with her when she was out walking with other girls from the school. As he was a friend of the family, and spoke well, and was in regimentals, the teachers thought it harmless for them to speak in public. Which I understand. To a degree, at least. But then apparently they began to correspond. And Phoebe began slipping out of the school to meet him. She—at this point, it seemed to me she had only recently left off playing with dolls."

"I know the feeling. And the truth is, both girls and boys grow very quickly from children to young adults." Of course, at sixteen his own wife had been a seasoned agent, but at sixteen Mélanie had been through things he hoped his own children would never face. Things he hoped no one else would ever face.

Pendarves gave a bleak smile. "Phoebe left a note with one of her school friends to forward to me. Thankfully, the other girl had the wit to give it to the headmistress before she was supposed to. More fortuitously, I was already on my way to Bath to visit her. Though I think my impending arrival also pushed them to the elopement. They knew—or at least Jamie knew—that I would put an end to any association between them." He glanced to the side, profile stark against the lamplight, and scraped a hand over his hair. "I set off at once. I could afford the best teams and they'd had trouble with their carriage. I intercepted them on the road to Scotland. Jamie tried to convince me that marriage was the only alternative to scandal, but I was determined not to have Phoebe locked in a marriage that I was convinced would only make her life a misery. Phoebe fancied herself in love, but I was able to persuade her this was no way to begin married life."

"She agreed to call it off?" Malcolm's own experience with his younger sister made him doubt this.

Pendarves grimaced. "I said I'd agree to the marriage if Jamie would accept that she had no dowry. It was a risk, but as I anticipated, Jamie made himself scarce. I took Phoebe home. Needless to say, she was devastated. But eventually she saw him for what he was. It was a hard lesson, but she's married herself now and seems happy."

"Perhaps the most important thing, to a brother or parent or guardian."

"Perhaps." Pendarves's brows drew together for a moment, as though he was playing over past decisions. "I didn't see or hear from Jamie for some time after that night I intercepted him and Phoebe. Then I had the occasional request for a loan. Which I found it easier to grant, before he could make more threats against me or Phoebe. So I could preserve the illusion that I wasn't giving way to blackmail. I avoided actually seeing him as much as I could. But a week ago, he sent me a message. Asked me to meet him. I came very close to refusing. But old ties die hard. And I was afraid of what he might do." Pendarves shifted in his chair. "How he might threaten Phoebe's peace. Or Sophia's. Or my own. So I went to see him." He met Malcolm's gaze. "I should have told Carfax last night, but I was still sorting out how much I could admit." He drew a hard breath. "My fears were right. Jamie said he had letters from Phoebe. He threatened to reveal them."

"Did he ask for money again?"

"No." Pendarves's brows tightened. "He wanted me to deliver a parcel to Lord Hartlebury."

"What did you say?"

"What the devil do you think? We may not always agree, Rannoch, but we both take our duties with the same seriousness, I think. My services aren't to be bought with any currency. Including my sister's honor."

"I don't think honest expressions of affection could taint anyone's honor. Though my wife would quarrel with the very word."

"Mrs. Rannoch's views are—interesting. I have the greatest respect for her. But the fact remains, these letters could do damage to Phoebe. As I said, I couldn't let that taint my actions. But I did agree to deliver the message in an attempt to hold off Jamie and at least buy some time."

"Do you know what the parcel contained?"

Langdon uncrossed and recrossed his legs. "I'm not a fool. I know the currency of information. And while I may believe in honor, I'm willing to stretch it in dealing with a scoundrel. I looked at the papers. I couldn't make sense of them, truth to tell. But I hesitated to deliver them. I was still mulling it over when I heard about Jamie." He reached inside his coat. "And so I have them here to give to you."

Malcolm took the papers and tucked them into his own coat. "Both your sister and Captain Blayney's brother Edmund have suggested Jamie Blayney was fascinated by your family."

Pendarves grimaced. "He certainly got as much as he could out of us."

"They suggested it was a bit more than that. Their stories paint a picture of a man who wanted to be part of your world. Had done since childhood."

Pendarves frowned. "I suppose—when we were children, we all seemed on a more or less equal footing. But by the time we were all at school—Edmund and Jamie and I—I realized I had a great deal they didn't. And certainly, I was aware their prospects in life were less. Edmund went a very different way. I don't agree with him, but I can respect his having the courage of his convictions. But to dress Jamie's despicable actions up as pining for a world he didn't belong to seems to me to be making excuses for him."

"Just because he was pining for a world he didn't belong to doesn't mean his actions weren't despicable."

"No." Pendarves frown deepened.

"It does account a bit for his fascination with both your sisters." With all three of them, apparently.

Pendarves's expression hardened. "It may account for it. I'm inclined to think we were merely easy marks. He certainly had little consideration for the happiness of either of my sisters. Whatever motivated him, I don't have the dispassion to determine. But I am quite sure Jamie Blayney was a monster."

CHAPTER 28

"Good heavens," Mélanie said. "And yet, how unsurprising, in a way. Given Captain Blayney's fascination with the Langdon family."

"I wonder if all three sisters knew about each other," Kitty said.

They were gathered together on the balcony near the railing. A gust of wind had driven all but a few couples indoors.

"As a motive?" Laura asked.

Kitty looked into her champagne glass. "I can't imagine being so wound up as to kill over a lover. I mean, one would have to care a great deal first, and then even if one did"—she cast a glance at Julien—"one would have to care enough to take action over a lover who didn't want one. Instead of saying more fool them. But jealousy is certainly a motive. And not just on the stage."

"Succinctly put as usual sweetheart." Julien reached for her hand.

"Mind you, I'd be desperately unhappy if you left me for a lover. But I think I'd blame you, not the other woman. Or other man."

"Molyneux hasn't committed to voting on the queen's side," Malcolm said. "He says he means to weigh all the evidence, and he's one of the few peers who may actually mean it. Prescott's pretty clearly a government vote. Leaving aside potential blackmail."

"What about the papers Blayney gave Pendarves for Lord Hartlebury?" Mélanie asked.

"Another teaser. They don't reveal much save that he was Danielle Darnault's lover. But his vote could be in play as well."

"Everything in London seems to circle back to the trial one way and another now," Raoul said.

"Whatever their connection to the trial, Molyneux and Prescott clearly had a reason to resent Jamie Blayney," Harry said. "Speaking as one well aware of the effects of jealousy." He looked at Cordelia, who had only recently left her position greeting guests at the head of the stairs. "Sorry."

She squeezed his hand. "Understood."

"Mind you, it didn't drive even me to murder," Harry said. "But one never knows."

"And Pendarves now has more than one reason to have wanted to get rid of Blayney." Julien regarded his nails in the torchlight as though looking at something at the end of a telescope.

"That doesn't mean he did," Kitty said.

Julien shot a smile at her. "No. But it makes it more likely. It means we can't ignore the possibility."

"You haven't ignored the possibility from the first," Malcolm said. "That's what's bothering you."

Julien flicked a bit of lint from his cuff. "I'm probably not the best judge in this case. But I could see Pendarves killing more to protect his sisters than to protect himself. He's very proud. But he's protective of those he loves. And a younger sister can bring that out especially. He didn't talk about her much, but I remember his concern for her."

"Yes," Malcolm said. "I can understand it. Though she might not thank him for it. Gelly certainly wouldn't thank me."

"That doesn't stop you from worrying," Julien said.

"Well, no. Don't tell Gelly."

"My dear fellow. You can't fool her that much."

"I remember Phoebe Langdon dragging a doll about," Cordelia said. "I've been to her house. I just greeted her and Molyneux on the stairs tonight. It would never have occurred to me—"

"They may not know anything's amiss," Harry said.

"Do you really think that?" Cordelia asked. "Captain Blayney seems to have been blackmailing anyone he could. Especially the Langdons. I can't believe he hasn't approached Phoebe and Molyneux. I know we always find people we know in the midst of investigations. But this one seems to be exposing so many secrets."

The French windows opened to admit three laughing girls in white frocks, clutching shawls round them.

"How intrepid of you to brave the wind," Cordelia said with a brilliant smile. "I so admire young women willing to take risks."

KITTY MADE her way down the narrow spiral stairs at one end of the balcony to the garden. It appeared empty at the moment, but it was quicker to go into the library this way than going through the ballroom, and the library offered the promise of interesting conversation. She reached the flagstones and sensed a presence behind her, but as she started to turn round, sharp steel pressed against her back.

"Don't turn round, Lady Carfax. I only want information, but I'm not afraid to use this knife should it prove necessary."

Kitty modulated her voice. "What do you want to know?"

"What did you do with the papers you took off Blayney?"

Kitty whirled round, seized the man's knife hand, and gave a sharp twist. "Tommy, honestly, do you think I don't recognize your voice?"

Tommy Belmont's blue gaze had just the glint it had held in a ballroom in Lisbon when she first saw him. "I wasn't sure you remembered."

Kitty grabbed the knife hilt. "I remember a lot of things."

"Then I'm surprised you were convinced I wouldn't use that knife."

"My corset is remarkably sturdy. And I'm very quick." She clasped her hands behind her back, holding the knife.

"Blayney."

"Why on earth should I tell you anything?"

Tommy's gaze settled on her own, cobalt dark. "Believe me, fair Katelina, it would be better for everyone for Danielle Darnault's memoirs to become the League's. Especially better for Malcolm. For whom I believe you still care."

"You can't imagine I'd take your advice on what's good for Malcolm." And yet, for some reason, a tremor of fear shot through her.

"Surely you can imagine there are some secrets that might hurt Malcolm and the League."

"I think Malcolm would say he's far better off knowing the secrets. And one could certainly argue that at this point he's prepared to handle anything."

"Even Malcolm can be mistaken."

"What makes you think I know any more about James Blayney than anyone else present tonight? Wouldn't one of his blackmail victims be more likely to have his papers?"

"Because you were with him just before he died."

Kitty's fingers tightened on the knife.

"No," Tommy said. "I didn't kill him. If I had, I might know more."

"And if I'd recovered more of his papers, I might know why the League are so determined to get them. I might know who Alexander Radford is."

Tommy's gaze shot over her face. With calculation, but also with relief.

"Speaking of which," Kitty continued, "did you hire the man who tried a technique similar to the one you tried on me just now on my husband this afternoon?"

Tommy's eyes widened. "Good God. What did St. Ju—Carfax do with the body?"

"He let the man go, quite alive."

Tommy whistled. "I can't imagine who thought such tactics would be effective on Julien. At least I knew I could talk to you if you recognized me." He regarded her for a moment. "It's lasting longer than I'd have thought."

"What? Julien's feelings for me? Or his ability to live as Lord Carfax?" Kitty was used to such questions by now.

"Your ability to live a domestic life."

"My dear Tommy. I was married when I met you."

"Marriage doesn't necessarily mean domesticity. Much as I've avoided it."

"Precisely."

"Yes, but this new one of yours—" He watched her for a moment in the colored lamplight, as though seeking secrets beneath the wash of violet and gold and crimson. "It looks remarkably earnest."

"Don't tell Julien that. It sounds gag-inducing. But if you mean we take it seriously, you're closer to the mark than you often are."

He shook his head. "You'll get bored. You aren't made for a settled life."

Kitty drew the folds of her shawl about her, concealing the knife within them. "I don't think you can have the least idea what I'm made for. Tommy."

"My darling Kitty. I know better than you think."

CHAPTER 29

*K*itty fell into step beside her husband in the passage outside the library and slid her hand through the crook of his arm. "I've just had an interesting encounter."

Julien drew to the side beside a bust of a Roman lady, which knowing the Davenports was probably genuine and someone one or both of them had written about.

"Easier to pretend to flirt with someone one isn't married to," Kitty said, as he bent his head to hers.

"People are used to our being unfashionably demonstrative." Julien snagged two glasses of champagne from a passing waiter and put one in her hand. "Whom did you encounter?"

"Tommy Belmont." Kitty took a sip of champagne. "He tried something similar to the man who attacked you and Raoul. Only with a knife, not a pistol."

"Did he?" Julien took a drink of champagne. "I should have quite liked to see you disarm him."

"It was silly of him to try, because I know his voice perfectly well. We were rather close once. Well, a few more times than once. In Lisbon." Kitty scanned her husband's face. "I'm not sure if you knew."

"No, actually."

"And I'm quite sure Malcolm doesn't. He and Tommy never got on as attachés, long before we knew Tommy was working for the League. I don't object to telling him precisely if we need to, but—"

"No particular reason to as I see it. At this point."

"Tommy thought I might have more of Blayney's papers. He—and the League—know I was with Blayney before he was killed. Then he tried to convince me that we'd be better off turning the memoirs over to the League."

"Well, that's not surprising. Tommy seems to work for Alexander Radford."

"No, it's not surprising. But he also tried to convince me it would be better for Malcolm for the League to have the memoirs."

"Well, that was brazen of him." Julien nuzzled her ear.

"So brazen, I wonder why he tried it." Kitty took another sip of champagne. "He seemed oddly serious."

"Probably couldn't think of any other way to try to make his case." Julien's lips slid to her jaw.

It was a good show for anyone passing by and wondering at what they were discussing. But it also might be an attempt to distract her. Kitty studied her husband. "Julien? Do you know any reason the memoirs would be particularly damaging to Malcolm?"

Julien was a master at deflection, but in this case he didn't even try. His gaze settled on her face. "Kitkat—"

"Fair enough," Kitty said. "We both knew we'd always have secrets. But surely Malcolm needs to know whatever this secret is."

Julien drew in and released his breath. "Let's get through tonight. But, yes. A number of us are playing with fire."

Kitty drew back a little and held her husband with her gaze. "I trust that you have your reasons. But for God's sake, you know how betrayal can cut Malcolm, of all people."

"That," Julien said, fingers white round the stem of his glass, "is precisely why this is such a conundrum."

~

"CORDY." Pippa came forwards with her usual forthrightness. "It's a splendid party."

"Thank you for coming."

"I almost didn't." Pippa's gaze flashed over Cordy's face. "I'm sure this is the last thing you want to talk about now. But I assume Mrs. Rannoch told you I went to see her today."

"Yes. And I'd much rather talk about the investigation than the ball. In any case, the ball will take care of itself right now."

"I should have told you the truth when you called on me," Pippa said. "I was in shock. Trying to work out what to say— that sounds dreadful, doesn't it. As though I'm scheming."

"It's not easy to confess secrets," Cordy said. "One's natural instinct is to hold them close."

"You're very generous. The truth is, I think my entanglement with Jamie is part of why I didn't write to you much, for a time. It's difficult to keep secrets from a friend, and I was embarrassed by it."

"Pippa. Darling. Embarrassed to admit a foolish affair to me, of all people?"

"To you now, happily married and a pattern card of how one can create blissful married life?"

"Well, I'd never have thought you could create blissful married life with Haworth. And I'd hardly blame you for seeking consolation elsewhere. Even with an unworthy object. Especially with an unworthy object." Cordy watched her friend for a moment. "I'm sorry. You must have cared for him."

"Not as much as I should have done, given what passed between us. But—yes. It's hard to believe he's gone. Though I was telling the truth when I said I keep seeing him as a boy. More than when we were together."

"I can understand that." Cordelia studied her friend. "I'd be a bad friend if I expected confidences as some sort of proof of friendship, Pippa. I hope you know I'm still your friend, and sorrier than I can say for what you've been through. But given that you know—knew—Jamie Blayney better than I thought—do you have any idea of who may have killed him?"

Pippa drew a sharp breath. "I can't point to any specific enemies. I hadn't spoken to Jamie in months. But I can say—he didn't care whom he hurt."

CHAPTER 30

"Mrs. Rannoch."

Mélanie turned and met a direct blue gaze set beneath a fringe of glossy dark hair. "Lady Molyneux."

Phoebe Molyneux had her sisters' clear skin and thick, dark hair, though she was not quite as tall as either. She had Sophia's assurance and a touch of Pippa's directness. "I trust you and your adorable children are well, Mrs. Rannoch. But I know you aren't the sort to waste time on conventions, which I've always appreciated about you. I was hoping we might speak."

"Of course." Mélanie gestured towards a settee Cordelia had arranged between two classical busts. At this point in the evening, the buzz from the music and conversation and patter of feet on polished boards was loud enough to drown out any confidences.

"I'm sure you realize what this is about." Phoebe smoothed the figured bronze satin of her gown. "At least—I suppose that depends on how much you know. I knew James Blayney." She looked up. "Rather well."

"Yes," Mélanie said. "Your brother spoke with Malcolm."

Phoebe grimaced. "I thought he had. And I thought your husband would have told you."

"It's difficult," Mélanie said. "First love can be very challenging. Even when no one is trying to take advantage of one."

Phoebe's head shot up. "Is that what Pen said? Yes, I suppose he would. He saw everything through a warped glass. Jamie didn't take advantage of me. I knew who he was from the first. I wouldn't precisely say I loved him for it—though, to an extent, I did. But I also loved him despite it." She drew in a breath and folded her hands round her black lace fan in her lap. "I suppose one could say, when I was a little girl, I worshipped Jamie. He was older and dashing—so much more so than my brother, or Jamie's brother Edmund, who said he wanted to turn the world upside down, but mostly seemed to try to do it by reading books and scribbling papers. Which he still seems to do, only now he publishes the papers. Which I admit are quite well written, and my husband actually reads them and appreciates them. But it was hardly the sort of thing to quicken a young girl's pulse. Yet at the same time, by the time I was eleven or twelve, I could see how reckless and foolish in some ways Jamie was. I knew he was a gamester. I knew he was a spendthrift. But he took risks. Everyone about me was so cautious. So careful of the forms. Even Edmund, with his writing and editing, and basing everything off John Locke, and Thomas Paine, and Rousseau, and a lot of fusty books, so far as I could tell. Jamie knew how to live." She drew a sharp breath.

"It's hard to believe someone is gone," Mélanie said. "Especially when they seem so vibrant."

Phoebe hunched her shoulders, crunching the ruched bodice of her gown. "Pen probably said Jamie took advantage of me. But the truth is, I had the devil of a time making Jamie see I'd grown up. It can be quite challenging when a gentleman remembers one with scraped knees. When he turned up in Bath and tipped his hat, and then stopped to talk with us on Pulteney

Bridge, I had a lowering feeling he still saw me as Sophia's little sister." Phoebe's gaze jerked up to meet Mélanie's. "I knew about Jamie and Sophia. Everyone thought I didn't and was at great pains to keep things from me, as though somehow, because I was an unmarried girl still at school, I'd never heard of such things. And that I couldn't listen to gossip. As though children aren't better at listening to gossip than anyone."

Mélanie thought of her own children, and put up a wish as a bulwark against the future.

"I assume you know about Sophia by now," Phoebe said.

"Yes. I talked to her this morning."

Phoebe's mouth twisted with equal parts irony and regret. "I should be grateful I haven't betrayed her secrets. But honestly, for all her façade of being the purest matron in Mayfair, Sophia wasn't very good at keeping them herself." Her fingers tightened on the fan. "I suppose Sophia painted herself as the great love of Jamie's life."

"I wouldn't say she painted herself as anything. Save regretful over the past, and regretful over Captain Blayney's death."

"She could have had Jamie if she'd really wanted him. If she'd paid more attention to him when she was younger, and if she'd known how to push Father. But she wanted to be a great lady then, only when she was, that wasn't enough to make her happy. Not that she'd ever have been happy as a soldier's wife." Phoebe stared at her gloved fingers. "I couldn't tell Jamie that. I was afraid bringing up Sophia would only make him pine for her. I was terribly relieved when he didn't ask me to pass a letter to her or anything of the sort. But I knew it would take more to make him see I was no longer a child. So I pulled him behind a pillar and I kissed him. That seemed to get the point across. Even then, he apologized. I had to tell him not to be an idiot and push a note into his hand. Thank goodness he at least showed up on our walk again. Not the next day, but the day after. I had another note ready, with directions to my room."

"You were ready to risk a lot." Mélanie was torn between seeing herself as Phoebe and seeing herself as Phoebe's mother. Amazing how different the story looked from those perspectives.

"Oh, I didn't expect him to climb up into my room." Phoebe frowned. "Mind you, I might have done, if I hadn't shared it with three other girls. But I climbed out and met him in the garden. He didn't need much persuading to go further then. Or to come back the next night. And the next. But he was still careful. It was my idea to elope. I know Pen probably said Jamie was after my fortune, and I'm sure that was part of the appeal. But I had to persuade him to the risk."

"Your brother told Malcolm that he offered to agree to your marriage with Captain Blayney if you gave up your dowry."

"And Jamie said he wouldn't marry me without my dowry, thus proving himself a fortune hunter?" Phoebe shook her head, whipping her side curls round her face and loosening a citrine pin. "Yes, I suppose Pen would put it that way. I suppose in Pen's mind, he thought he was protecting me, and perhaps, after a fashion, he was. He let me talk with Jamie alone after he made his offer about my dowry." She jammed the pin back into her hair. "I hate saying 'let,' but from Pen's view of his responsibilities as my guardian, that was quite a concession." She folded her hands in her lap again. "I told Jamie I'd risk it. And I would have done. I wanted to. In truth, living in an attic with Jamie seemed paradise to me, at that point. Jamie said he couldn't drag me into poverty. That love wouldn't outlast privation. And even at sixteen, a part of me knew he was right. In some ways, I'm tougher than Jamie. I might have handled it better. But I grew up with silver and china and pin money. I could imagine life without them. Jamie wanted them his whole life. And even then,

I knew that while fortune doesn't guarantee happiness, lack of fortune can cause unhappiness."

"A good point." Mélanie certainly couldn't argue with that. Malcolm's fortune had cushioned them through a number of crises. In perhaps their most frightening moment, it had allowed them to escape to Italy and seek shelter in a beautiful place. If at times it had felt like a cage, it had certainly been a gilded one. And one that had allowed them a great deal of latitude.

Phoebe gripped her hands together. "So I don't see Jamie's not wanting to marry me as selfishness or a sign that he didn't love me enough to risk it. I think it was that he loved me *too* well to risk it."

Beneath Phoebe's veneer of sophistication, the yearning of a sixteen-year-old girl shone through. "I can see that," Mélanie said.

"But you don't agree."

"I don't know Captain Blayney or you well enough to agree."

Phoebe drew a sharp breath that shattered the smooth elegance of cropped curls and Parisian-cut satin and carefully plucked brows. "Pen thinks he saved me. I'm not scraping by in poverty. I haven't fallen out with my husband or quarreled with him over drink or cards or women—yes, I knew even at sixteen there was a risk all that would happen with Jamie. I'm comfortable. My husband is a good man. But he doesn't love me. I'm not sure that sort of love is something he's capable of."

Lord Molyneux's face shot into Mélanie's mind. He was a serious man with a kind smile. He discussed politics with her more seriously than some of Malcolm's colleagues did and seemed genuinely interested when he asked after the children. But he did not appear a man for whom emotion came easily. "There are different types of love," she said. "I've understood that more and more as time has gone by. My own husband doesn't share his feelings easily."

"Mr. Rannoch clearly loves you, Mrs. Rannoch. I understand emotions enough to understand that. My husband has what he wants from me. A hostess, and a mother for his children, and someone who can run the house tolerably well, or at least direct the servants to do so. It's a trade-off most of the couples in this ballroom have made. He has all that and I have a comfortable home, and position in society, and plenty of pin money. So my brother sees me as settled well. The problem is what I got in the bargain isn't what I wanted from life at all."

"All too often people don't ask women that."

"Yes."

"Did you see Captain Blayney after the elopement?"

"Not for a long time. He went back to the Peninsula. I heard he'd married. It caused me a qualm, though by then I was married myself. A part of me hoped he was happy, and I confess the less generous part hoped he still pined for me. Then a few months later, I was driving in the park with Sophia and we saw him. He tipped his hat. We stopped and exchanged greetings. It was particularly awkward because Sophia was there."

"She doesn't know about you and Captain Blayney?"

"Good God, no! We aren't the sort for confidences at the best of times, and certainly not over a man we both loved. And I can't imagine Pen's telling her. It was painful seeing Jamie again, but I knew it was bound to happen. Easier, perhaps, that we were constrained from speaking. After that, I saw him occasionally—once, at Drury Lane, we spoke briefly and he said he was glad I was happy. I said I hoped he was happy, and he merely smiled." She swallowed. "I called on him once about a year ago. I went veiled. I wanted to assure myself he was all right. Or perhaps I was seeking escape. He was kind but sent me on my way. I'd have risked a lot for Jamie, as my sister once did, but somehow we both knew the time for that had passed."

"When was the last time you saw him?"

Phoebe smoothed her hands over her lap, as though she was

reconsidering a decision. Or perhaps making a decision she hadn't settled on until now. "A week since, he called on me. For the first time since the elopement. The first time ever. He never properly called on me in Bath. He apologized for disturbing my peace. He made it clear he had no intention of importuning me. Which I confess I found a bit disappointing. But he said he had a favor to ask of me."

"Did he ask to borrow money?"

"No, I thought that was it. I even started to say I'd be glad to lend him what he needed. But he said that wasn't it. He just wanted me to deliver a parcel to someone. He said he couldn't explain, but it could be vital to his future prospects."

"Whom did he want you to give the parcel to?"

Phoebe's fingers tightened on her gloves. "Lord Prescott. Sophia's husband."

"And did you agree?"

"Jamie said it was important. I saw no reason not to agree. I took the parcel. Jamie thanked me fervently. If perhaps not as fervently as I'd have liked. I took the parcel with me the next night when we dined with Sophia and Prescott. I hid it under my cloak and contrived to put it in his study. Then I told him I'd left something there that I'd been asked to deliver to him. Prescott looked surprised, but not concerned. But then he must have gone down to the study and opened it, because when the gentlemen came into the drawing room after dinner, he came over to me while Sophia was playing the piano and asked if I knew what was in the parcel. He was calm, but quite white about the mouth. I said I didn't know, though from the way it felt, I assumed it was papers. He asked me not to speak of it to anyone, and I assured him I would not. Which I meant, until now. But then, a murder changes everything."

"Yes, it does. What do you think was in the papers?"

"I haven't the least idea. But—do you think Jamie was black-mailing Prescott?"

"Is that what you think?"

"I couldn't but wonder. Though if it was something to do with Sophia, I should have thought he'd go to Pen. From the look on his face that night, Prescott was frightened. And angry. His hand gripped the sofa arm as he talked to me. And when he got up, there were marks on the velvet. Such deep marks it had torn." She looked at Mélanie, gaze wide with fear. "Do you think Prescott could have killed Jamie?"

"A number of people had motives to have killed Captain Blayney," Mélanie said. "But this is helpful information. I know it can't have been easy to share. Thank you."

Phoebe nodded. "I need to know who killed Jamie. And I need them brought to justice. Even if it means destroying my family."

~

"Malcolm. I'm so glad to see you." Emily Cowper stopped beside Malcolm on the edge of the dance floor. Her gaze was bright, her color high, and not, Malcolm thought, just because of rouge and the exertion of dancing. Her gloved fingers closed on his wrist, unwontedly tight. "I need to talk to you. I was afraid, between the investigation and the trial, I was going to have to don a footman's garb and hunt you down in Brooks's. I'm not sure even the Lamb name would be enough to protect me."

"You can always send word to me, Em." Malcolm took her hand and kissed her cheek. "Which is it, the trial or the investigation?"

"The trial is endlessly fascinating, but I remain a detached observer. Mostly. It's difficult not to be a bit alarmed when we have mobs in the street outside Parliament—yes, I know you're all on the side of the people, Malcolm, but William was ordered to be in readiness with his yeomanry—he sent to Cowper to ask for four horses should he need them. And with all the shouting one hears in the streets, I found myself rather wishing the royal crown was off the arms on my carriage. On the other hand, now many of the more disgusting details have been proved false, it really comes down to the queen's having taken a courier for her lover. If Bergami were a gentleman no one would have a right to object."

"No one?" Malcolm asked.

Emily wrinkled her nose. "Well, no one but the lover." She tucked her hand through Malcolm's arm. "I'm babbling because now I've found you, I'm afraid to come to the point. There's a little parlor through that door, I believe. It should be empty, and no one will accuse us of dalliance. Or if they do, it will only add to my consequence for having engaged the most faithful husband in the beau mode."

"I can name you at least ten such."

"Yes, I suppose so. It's positively an epidemic among your set." Emily drew him into an anteroom papered in a rose trellis pattern, empty but lit by the glow of three gilt branches of candles. She sank down on a settee covered in a darker rose than the walls, where the Davenport girls sometimes napped downstairs. "It's Harry. My Harry, not your Harry. That is, Cordelia's Harry, but you know what I mean." She tossed down a sip from her glass of champagne.

Malcolm pulled a lyre-back chair up close to the settee. "Did you know Jamie Blayney, Em?"

CHAPTER 31

$\mathcal{E}$mily frowned. "I think I met James Blayney at a party once, in Sophia Langdon's first season. I even danced with him. He grew up with the Langdons. I suppose you know that by now."

"Yes. That's one of the few things we've been able to establish with clarity."

"Not that I'd have remembered him," Emily said. "Not that I could distinguish him from all sorts of other agreeable young men I danced with that season." She frowned. "Except I did rather think he caught Sophia's eye. I remember watching them dance together, and the way they looked at each other. Especially the way Sophia looked at him. I remember thinking when she became betrothed to Prescott at the end of the season that he wasn't nearly so good-looking as Captain Blayney, and she was bound to be disappointed. Not that good looks are a guarantee of much of anything, but Prescott—well, one can't pretend he has much to offer."

Malcolm considered his conversation with Prescott that afternoon. "He's a reasonably effective politician."

"That's not the sort of thing that was going to make Sophia

happy. Not that she didn't want to be a political wife, but she was nineteen. She wasn't a rebel like her sister, but at that age one tends to want a bit of dash. Or at least one tends to be drawn to it, even if one knows it doesn't make for the best husbands. In any case, I shouldn't cast aspersions. I can hardly claim—well, that's not the point." She touched her jade beads, perhaps a gift from her husband, perhaps from Palmerston, then took another sip of sherry. "I'm prevaricating. Harry. He's always been rather more inclined to jealousy than I am. I hope I'm not shocking you."

"In my family?" Malcolm said. His mother and aunt gave him cover for that without any need to mention his wife and father.

"And in mine." Emily's mother, Lady Melbourne, had been known to be the mistress of the Prince of Wales—now the king —among others, and it was common knowledge that Emily's brother William, the second son but now the heir on the death of his elder brother, was not Lord Melbourne's son. "Which is why Harry would be much more embarrassed to talk about this than I am. Not that I'm precisely pleased by it, but one learns to accept these things. Or at least to get past them. And really, reconciliations are so delightful it would be rather a shame not to quarrel, wouldn't it?" Emily smoothed a fold of her gauze overdress. "Though I suppose you don't know about that."

"My dear Emily. You're far too wise to think any marriage— any relationship—immune to quarreling."

"Well, no, but not this sort of quarreling. You can't tell me you've looked at another woman since Mélanie. It's actually terribly romantic. Even I can recognize that."

"Most people think I'm too phlegmatic to have the appropriate emotions for anyone, including my wife."

"Yes, and most people are very foolish. I may not be a scholar or a spy or an investigator, but I have the wit to see what's in front of me. Still, different things work for different people, and I wouldn't want Harry to be any different from the man I love. I do tease him at times and I don't really know why." Emily spread her fan in her lap. "Because I'm afraid I'll get complacent, or he'll get complacent, or because I don't want to dwindle into anything too comfortable. But this wasn't really that. I was preoccupied. I couldn't be focused on my own relationship when I was trying to preserve my brother's. His marriage, that is." She looked at Malcolm. "Oh, I haven't explained properly, have I? This was four years ago, when Caro George ran off with Brougham and I had to go to the Continent after them. Well, that, and to economize; there's no denying it's handy to escape to the Continent every now and then. Harry followed me, which was sweet, and I was dreadfully happy to see him in Geneva. But however much people may be aware of my relationship with Harry, it would be a bit much to flaunt it in front of Caro George when I was trying to convince her of all the benefits of matrimony. Not that I'd ever run off to the Continent or anywhere else with Harry. Well, not without a good cover story. Really, I think so many fewer marriages would come to grief if people knew how to play the game better."

"I imagine a number of people would agree with you."

She gave a crooked smile. "But you wouldn't?"

"I think fewer people would come to grief if more couples could agree on what the marriage was supposed to mean. Which can be a number of different things."

Emily wrinkled her nose. "Yes, I suppose so. That's a rather less cynical way of saying what I just said. In any case, I was trying to be a good sister and preserve my brother's domestic tranquility—or what passes for it. And Cowper and the children were with me. So I had to tell Harry I'd see him back in London. He said he understood, but I think he was a bit jealous. I think he had questions about what I was really doing. Which is absurd, of course. Betraying my lover with another lover, while persuading my sister-in-law to leave her lover and return to her husband is a bit complicated, even for me. A part of me knew he'd likely seek consolation on the way home, which wasn't something I wanted to dwell on." She swallowed the last of her champagne. "Harry had a liaison with a lady named Danielle Darnault. I understand she wrote papers—memoirs—and that James Blayney had come into possession of at least some of them."

"News travels fast."

"It certainly does, but I confess I knew before yesterday." Emily's fingers tightened round her fan.

"Em? Palmerston is in the memoirs?"

She hesitated.

"Actually, we already know he is," Malcolm said.

Emily's gaze shot to his face. "He told you?"

Malcolm returned to his chair. "He told Mel."

She gave a faint smile. "I can see that. Mélanie's easy to confide in. And Harry's good at talking to women. I didn't know about the affair at the time. I was busy with Caro George, and the gossip didn't get across the Channel. We had a lovely reunion when I returned, and that was that. I was caught up in trying to save the other Caro from her folly, and grateful to have Harry beside me. With a few challenges. Yes. I admit I rather tried him with Count Giuliano, but that's nothing to do with this. I didn't know anything more about what he'd got up to on his way home from the Continent until Captain Blayney approached me at Gunter's, of all places, and asked me to buy the memoirs a week since."

"And did you buy them?"

Emily looked into her empty champagne glass. "Captain Blayney hadn't aged well. Facing him over tea and cakes at Gunter's, I couldn't believe I'd ever thought him dashing. But he was frank, I'll give him that. He told me he'd offered the papers to Harry, but Harry was prevaricating, and in the event Harry couldn't buy them, he wanted me to have the next opportunity, before anyone else. He made it sound as though he were doing me a favor—the impertinence!"

"I don't know how clever he was, but he seems to have been brazen."

"He showed me some pages," Emily said. "Just enough to prove what he had was genuine. Which it quite certainly seems to have been. Honestly, whatever Harry chose to do in bed, that he actually talked about—"

"I know," Malcolm said. "It can seem a worse betrayal. But sometimes one needs to talk."

"That's what I told myself. After I got over my first anger. I told Captain Blayney I had to think about it, but really I knew from the start I didn't have a choice. I know Harry's circumstances. Even if he managed to come up with the money, I knew what it would cost him. Literally. I didn't want him to go through that. And letting Blayney give the papers to someone else was unthinkable. Oh, I could probably weather the scandal, though I certainly wouldn't like it. But I was actually more concerned what it might do to Harry. If he'd have to leave the war office or lose his chance of preferment." She frowned. "I sometimes think I have more faith in his future than he does."

"It can be hard to have faith in one's own future."

"You and Harry should both believe in yourselves enough to do so. Scandal right now would be hard on William too, and he has enough to contend with. And it would be a challenge for Cowper, whom I already put through quite enough." She folded her hands round her fan. "But Harry and I and Cowper and William and George and the Caros could get through it. It's the children that really concern me." She glanced down at her hands, then met Malcolm's gaze, her own still and fragile as glass. As much as was understood and alluded to among all of them, there were certain things no one ever put into words. Such as children's parentage. Malcolm understood, probably better than most. "Caro George has always been a bit naive," Emily said. "She didn't realize who her parents really were until years after the rest of us did. Harry-O and Georgy and Hart, and even me and my brothers. Poor girl, she's quite gullible, which may account for the mess with Mr. Brougham. But in any case, thinking of her, I've always known we'd have to explain matters to the children at some point, before they heard gossip or were so grown up when they found out that they felt betrayed because we hadn't told them sooner. So difficult to judge the right moment. But I know now isn't the right moment. They're far too young. And even if they did know, it's all very well to know privately, and quite different to have the gossip bandied about the ton. To hear remarks on the playing field at school, in the park when they're out driving with me, to endure sidelong looks. I couldn't put them through that. You must see that."

"See the need to protect one's children? I'd hope most parents would."

Emily regarded him for a moment. "Would you buy letters to protect your children in the circumstances?"

That was perhaps a more apropos question than Emily realized. "It would depend on exactly what the letters contained, and exactly what my children knew. And what was likely to come out anyway. But I'd be tempted." Malcolm sat back in his chair. "So you bought the letters from Blayney?"

Emily shifted her position on the settee. "Yes. I sent my maid to sell a pair of earrings to raise the required funds. And then Blayney told me he'd had a lot of interest, so the price had gone up."

"That must have been galling."

"It was." Her gaze shot to Malcolm's face. "Not enough that I'd have killed him, but I can understand your wondering that."

"Em—I have to wonder things about everyone. Even people a part of me knows would never do certain things. I can't let my own judgments and friendships stop me from asking the right questions."

"It sounds ghastly, but I do understand that. I was supposed
to buy the papers the night after Blayney was killed. Do you
know what became of the memoirs?"

"Unfortunately, no. Either someone stole them the night of
the murder, or Blayney hid them where no one's been able to
find them yet."

Emily shivered. "I realize there are a number of implications.
For a number of people. For the government and the queen's
trial. Set beside that, worrying about my children probably feels
foolish."

"Not in the least. You're a good parent." He leaned forwards.
"I'll do what I can, Em."

Emily smiled in a way that took him right back to the girl
she'd been. "Thank you, Malcolm."

"JULIETTE. PAUL." Harry stopped beside Juliette Dubretton and
Paul St. Gilles. "I'm glad you could make it."

"We wouldn't have missed it," Paul said. "Though, given the
rumors, we were wondering if perhaps you were going to miss
your own party."

"On the contrary," Juliette said as Harry kissed her cheek, "a
ball must be the perfect place to investigate. As a writer, I can
quite see the possibilities for bringing key characters together."

Juliette was a novelist and political writer, and Paul a
painter. Neither had ever been an agent, but they had crossed
paths with agents before they fled Paris during the White
Terror. And in Paris, as now in London, they had been at the
heart of literary and artistic society. "By any chance, do you
know Danielle Darnault?" Harry asked.

Paul and Juliette exchanged a look. "Not well," Juliette said,
"but we were at some of the same parties in Paris."

"Did you know she was an agent?" Harry asked.

"We heard the rumors," Paul said. "From Tania. Who, not surprisingly, didn't trust her."

Malcolm's half-sister, Tatiana Kirsanova, had been Paul's friend and, briefly, his lover. She had also been an extremely skilled agent.

"They had a certain amount in common," Juliette said. "Though Danielle never moved in high society. At least, not at the sort of events ladies attend. We got to know her more towards the end of Bonaparte's time in power, and after Waterloo. She seemed to have more of a reason to mingle with the artistic set."

Paul shot a look at her. "I'm still not convinced you were right about that. He wasn't nearly dashing enough for her."

"For a hopeless romantic who can capture love beautifully on canvas, you sometimes fail to see what's in front of you, *mon cher*." Juliette smiled at her husband, then turned to Harry. "Pierre Ducroix."

"The journalist?"

"You've heard of him?"

"I read him closely when I was in Paris. I admired his writing and his courage. He was flirting with arrest speaking out against the Bourbon government. Are you saying he was also flirting with Danielle Darnault?"

"I don't know if one would call it flirting," Juliette said. "They weren't even openly lovers. But I'm quite sure Danielle was in love with him."

Paul frowned. "I'll own I tried to watch them when you suggested it years ago, but I rarely even saw them speaking together."

"I know," Juliette said. "They went to great lengths to make it appear they had no interest in each other. That was part of what convinced me."

"By that logic, I could suspect you were madly in love with Lord Cowper," Paul said. "You show no interest in him."

"That, and the way I caught them looking at each other in unguarded moments," Juliette said. "It's my trade to observe. One night I went out into Louise Sevigny's garden and saw them conversing together."

"And that was enough to convince you?" Paul said.

"Barring evidence to the contrary. Yes."

"Ducroix was arrested in the White Terror, wasn't he?" Harry asked.

"Actually, no one's quite sure what happened to him," Paul said. "He vanished from sight two years ago. After we fled Paris, but from the letters we have from friends and the stories in what's left of the Radical French press, there are rumors the Comte d'Artois's people had him killed."

"Did he disappear before or after Danielle Darnault left Paris?" Harry said.

Juliette and Paul exchanged a look. "I'm not sure," Juliette said. "But it was about the same time. You think there's a connection?"

"Something made her decide to leave France for a life of seeming retirement. If her lover was killed, it's possible she feared the same people who killed him."

"Are the rumors she'd written her memoirs true?" Juliette asked.

"They are," Harry said. "Which means it's also possible there's something about whatever happened to Pierre Ducroix in the memoirs."

CHAPTER 32

"All in all, "Kitty murmured, stopping beside Mélanie on the edge of the ballroom in a stir of almond-colored barège silk, "it's easier to gather information disguised as a footman."

"Oh, prodigiously. One can listen without having to make conversation. On the other hand, I do enjoy wearing a ball gown."

Kitty grinned. "So do I, I'll confess. I've just never been adept at the small talk with dowagers."

"You seem like you are."

"Practice. But I'm still an outsider. Which makes it easy to draw attention, but far more difficult to get people to open up." Kitty regarded Mélanie for a moment. "I saw you talking to Lady Molyneux."

"She sought me out. She claims to have loved Blayney. And she's the one who gave Blayney's papers to Prescott." Mélanie turned to smile at Cordelia, who had just joined them. "It's going splendidly, Cordy."

"The ball or the investigation?" Cordelia asked.

"The ball. Though we are managing to talk to people."

"It's going better than I expected, by far." Cordelia surveyed the crowd, a faint frown between her finely arched brows. "I'm used to entertaining Whigs and Tories, but all the normal rules about politeness between the parties seem to have gone out the window. The tension in the air is thicker than the icing on a cake from Gunter's."

"It will only make your ball more talked of," Kitty said.

"There's a fine line between being talked of for the wrong and right reason. And sometimes even I can't discern the line until it's crossed. By way Sally Jersey just told me she thinks your gown is the color the French are calling *chagrin de la reine d'Angleterre*, Mélanie. I told her I didn't think the queen was embarrassed in the least."

"I can quite see her ordering a dozen gowns in the color herself if she hadn't taken to wearing white," Mélanie said.

"Nothing like a sense of humor for facing down scandal." Cordelia looked between Kitty and Mélanie. "Go off and investigate. I may even manage to learn a bit as I circulate."

Mélanie moved past the French windows to the balcony. A lone figure at the rail outside caught her eye. A young woman in a gauzy violet gown caught by the torchlight against the night sky. Nerezza Russo, Mélanie realized. The young woman Benedict Smythe, Lord Beverston's youngest son, was madly in love with. The young woman the Elsinore League had tried to have killed the previous winter because she knew Alexander Radford.

"All right?" Mélanie stepped onto the terrace and closed the French window from the ballroom.

"Just got a bit overheated." Nerezza turned from the gilded railing. Her smile was bright, but in the light of the torches, her eyes looked bruised in her pale face. "You're in the midst of another investigation."

"Yes. It just started last night. There hasn't been time to update people."

"You have enough to worry about without giving updates. But is it to do with the League?"

"Among other things." Mélanie leaned against the railing beside Nerezza. "In fact, one of my missions tonight was to talk to you. The man who was killed was selling papers to a number of people. Including members of the League. The memoirs of a woman named Danielle Darnault. Have you heard of her?"

"She's an opera singer."

"And an agent, though she seemingly retired from the game about two years ago. But apparently her memoirs mention Alexander Radford."

Nerezza's gaze quickened. "And reveal his identity?"

"We think so."

"So we shared a lover, but she knows more than I do."

"So it seems."

"Have you talked to her?" Nerezza asked.

"She's disappeared."

"By choice?"

"We aren't sure." Mélanie touched Nerezza's arm. "There's no reason to think this should put you more in danger. The League have apparently decided you aren't a risk—we have inside information to confirm that—and I don't see that the threat Danielle Darnault poses should make you more of a threat. But we'll be careful."

Nerezza grimaced. "Meaning Rupert and Bertrand and Gaby will be more watchful than ever." Nerezza had been staying with Rupert and Gabrielle Caruthers and Rupert's lover Bertrand Laclos since she'd come to Britain. She shook her head. "No, I don't mean that. They're amazing and so kind. They make me feel like I really am the distant cousin we all pretend I am, and in truth it's rather splendid to have people fussing about my safety."

"Yes, I know the feeling. Frustrating at times, but also a sign of affection. Benedict fusses about your safety as well."

Nerezza gave a wry smile. "I never thought I'd put up with a man's doing it so much. Though in fairness to Ben, he's become quite sensible about understanding what I need to do. And what I'm capable of. And the wonder of it is he's still—fond of me."

"I wouldn't call that a wonder. Ben sees you for who you are."

"You don't think that's a wonder? Lov—caring for a man who sees one for who one is?"

"In some ways, it's such a wonder it still takes my breath away. Yet I can't imagine loving a man who didn't do so. And judging by my friends' lives, it's not as rare as I once would have thought."

"I still can't get over it. Though my case is a bit different." Nerezza hugged her arms round herself. "It's not true that I came outside because I was overheated. I still find it hard to imagine getting overheated in England. I was standing round the punch bowl with the Greville sisters and thinking that they actually feel almost like friends. I mean, not the way Sofia and Bet do. Not the way you do. But more than I'd have dreamed possible. Then Horatia said how delightfully adventurous my life had been, and I nearly spilled my champagne thinking how they wouldn't so much as speak to me if they knew what my life has really been."

It was something Mélanie thought nearly every time she went into a Mayfair ballroom. Or it had been. Somewhere in between navigating the Congress of Vienna and the battle of Waterloo and the Bourbon restoration, having two children, spying on her husband and working with him, she'd grown comfortable with the pretense of a life that would always be, at its heart, a lie. "There's no reason they ever should know," she said to Nerezza.

"You really think so? That one can step into a fairy story and close the book and just go on living in its gilded pages forever? That sounds like something out of one of your plays. No, I take that back, your plays are much more realistic."

"Plays also need conflict. Life doesn't always. Sometimes the path to happiness is remarkably simple."

"My life's never been simple." Nerezza pulled her spangled scarf about her shoulders. "Though it's certainly been easier than I ever expected, these past months."

"Sweetheart. Someone tried to kill you."

"Well, yes. After we got past that part." Nerezza glanced into the ballroom. "It's almost been easier of late precisely *because* we have to pretend. I have to pretend I'm someone I'm not. Ben has to pretend I'm someone he knows I'm not, even if he won't let himself quite admit it. At least, not out loud. Our friends are doing everything they can to protect us, and of course I love you all for it." She shot a quick smile at Mélanie. "Funny, I'm saying that after how difficult I was that night we first met at the Tavistock. You were wonderful putting up with me."

"I wouldn't have trusted anyone in your situation either." And in point of fact, thinking back to her own life before she married Malcolm, she hadn't. "It's rather amazing you trusted us as much as you did. As quickly as you did."

"It was that or get myself killed. I've always been rather good at knowing what I needed to do to take care of myself." Nerezza gripped her elbows through the gauze of the scarf. "But we've all had to playact since then. I'd be a fool to protest it. Ben would be ungallant to do anything but go along with the fairy tale charade."

"I'm quite sure Ben doesn't see anything to do with you as a charade."

Nerezza's mouth twisted. Her gaze went to the French windows, as though perhaps she was looking for a glimpse of Ben amid the swirl of pale gowns and glossy ringlets and dark coats on the dance floor. "Ben's too honorable for that. Whatever honorable means. I'm not sure I understand it, but I do appreciate it in Ben. But the point is we've been acting out a story for almost a year now. A story in which we're a much happier couple than we could possibly be in real life."

Mélanie's fingers tightened on the cold metal of the gilded rail. She'd accepted Malcolm's proposal on a balcony in Lisbon, during a ball. Acting out a story was something she knew well. She also knew how the lines could blur until one wasn't sure where the story left off and real life began. Whatever "real" life was. And yet she had learned there were some things one could hold fast to amid the shifting reality. "I've seen you and Ben together. I don't think there's anything manufactured about it."

"Not about parts of it, perhaps. But there's no denying we're playing parts. And that to do anything else—to think about the future at all—would risk breaking the fairy tale, which would risk danger. Which gives us license to indulge the fairy tale. Which I confess is distinctly agreeable." Nerezza hunched her shoulders.

"Perhaps the fairy tale is much more real than you think," Mélanie said.

"It's not a life we can live in forever. Whatever sort of dress I put on"—Nerezza touched the skirt of the silver spangled violet gauze Mélanie had taken her to order—"I'm never going to belong in this world, and we both know it. Ben would know it, if he'd stop and consider for two minutes together."

"Ben doesn't think about it, because he doesn't give a scrap for this world. It's simply the life he's always known. Malcolm's the same, in many ways. Just a bit more clear-eyed, a decade further on."

"But it will always be the world they belong in. I don't want to pull Ben away from that world. From his world. And I can't be something I'm not." Nerezza frowned. "I don't want to be something I'm not."

"I'm quite sure Ben wouldn't want you to be."

"But I don't want him to be something he isn't either!" Nerezza drew a breath and pulled the sheer folds of her scarf tight round her throat. "I don't want to drag him into a life that will be a misery. I have to be practical. Because much as I love Ben—and I can admit to you that I do—he isn't practical in the least. And when you love someone, you don't want them to make a mistake."

"That depends on how you define a mistake," Mélanie said.

Nerezza fingered the end of her scarf. "I'd be bored, living the life of Horatia and her sisters. I can see how they might be happy with it, but my life's been too different. I've seen too much."

"I'd be bored too," Mélanie said, aware that she might have admitted too much. Nerezza's gaze flew to her face. "But I've seen Ben change a lot this year as well. I think he'd be bored with a girl like Horatia Greville." Precisely the sort of girl she'd once worried would have made Malcolm happy. Which was funny, given that before her, the closest he'd come to a commitment was Kitty.

Nerezza's eyes opened wide. For a moment, she looked as young as she in fact was. "Ben wouldn't be happy away from his world. You can't think he could be."

"I don't think, seeing you together, that Ben would be happy away from you."

"There are different ways of being happy. I think I have a sense now of how you feel about Mr. Rannoch. Would you want to be with him if it meant he'd be cut off from the life he knows, and the people he loves?"

Mélanie bit back a desperate laugh. "My instinct is always to protect Malcolm. Perhaps to a fault. Because, in the end, what matters is not what I think would make him happy, but what would actually make him happy."

"How on earth do you know what that is?" Nerezza demanded.

"I'm still working it out."

Nerezza grimaced. "Ben's young. I'm older. In experience, at least. It's up to me to be responsible. His parents have their challenges, but he loves them. And his brother and family."

"I'm quite sure Roger and Dorinda wouldn't turn their backs on Ben, no matter what."

"And Lord Beverston? Can you imagine me as his daughter-in-law?"

"I can imagine stranger things." Arguably, her being Raoul's daughter-in-law was stranger.

"And Lady Beverston? She doesn't approve of me as it is, and that's without her knowing a fraction of the truth."

Barbara Beverston was a challenge, Mélanie had to admit. "Lady Beverston is a woman of the world."

"She's a woman of her world. I can imagine her accepting a daughter-in-law who took lovers, like Lady Cowper, and even gave her grandchildren who might not strictly speaking be her grandchildren. Yes, I've learned to listen to gossip, and I quite like Lady Cowper. But she's a viscount's daughter. Lady Beverston would probably tolerate a lot in a viscount's daughter with impeccable bloodlines. No matter what such a woman did to Ben."

"Which rather says she doesn't know what will make Ben happy." Mélanie touched Nerezza's arm through the fragile gauze of the shawl. "I think you do."

"Yes." Nerezza's smile was sweet and filled with understanding. And sadness. "And it isn't me."

CHAPTER 33

"Malcolm."

"Kit." Malcolm grinned at his young friend Kit Montagu. Even if the ball was about investigation, it was good to see friends. "Enjoying yourself? I hope you've had a number of chances to dance with Sofia."

Kit, who had married Sofia Vincenzo the previous spring after a long betrothal and time apart on two continents, gave a grin, though his gaze remained serious. "Yes, still enjoying the fact that we can dance more than two dances together without a scandal. But tonight seems to be more about politics."

"Parties with this set are always as much about Westminster as Mayfair. But tonight the battle lines seem a bit more out in the open."

"My God, Malcolm." Kit's gaze turned molten. "We're dancing and drinking champagne and London's about to explode."

"London's had a lot of reasons to explode for years. Decades."

"You've seen what's happening, Malcolm. The craft guilds sending the queen addresses. The gifts they've made for her. The demonstrations. The crowds in the streets."

"Emily Cowper would agree with you. She was telling me she regrets having a crown on her carriage. And Fitzroy Somerset's worried about the duke."

"Wellington deserves to be heckled for a lot more than his vote over the queen. Sorry, I know you're fond of him."

"I am. And I could scarcely be further from his politics."

"The government's used the same tactics against the queen they've used on anyone who wants change. Agents provocateurs, spies, bribed witnesses. This has been brewing for years. Spa Fields. Peterloo."

"That's undeniable. And the grievances are real. But I don't know that I agree the marital difficulties of our sovereign and his wife are going to be what finally set tinder to them."

"You read history at Oxford. You must know it's not always the logical thing that strikes the spark to rebellion."

"Touché. I'm still not sure that's what we're dealing with. But it wouldn't be the first time I've been wrong. And I'm certainly committed to the queen's case. For a number of reasons."

Kit cast a glance about. "I'm sorry to bother you. I know you're in the midst of an investigation."

"It's all right. Are you saying you want to talk?"

"Er—yes."

Malcolm turned, leaning against a column, so his back was to the ballroom. "What is it?"

Kit turned as well and shifted his weight from one foot to the other. "I scarcely know where to begin."

"Let me guess," Malcolm said. "Someone wants to sell you papers that you could use to wield influence in favor of the queen's case."

Kit stared at him. "How—"

"Surely you don't think you're the only possible buyer."

"No, that is—" Kit scraped a hand over his hair. "Christ, who else?"

Malcolm cast a sideways glance at the crowd. "Who not

might be easier to answer. Whoever has the papers has been making offers to interested parties all over London. Just about anyone named in the memoirs. Or anyone who could make use of them. Many of whom are probably in Cordy's ballroom tonight."

"Has anyone bought them?"

"Not yet, as far as I know. Though one person bought a chapter and had it stolen."

"Good God." Kit frowned at the silver buckle on his shoe. "Who?"

"We're in the midst of an investigation, Kit. I can't share that."

."Of course. I forget—Do you mean this has to do with the man who was killed?"

"He was the one trying to sell the memoirs."

"Good God. I didn't know—the offer was sent to the Levellers anonymously. Two days ago. We've been trying to decide what to do."

"Were you sent sample pages?"

"No. The writer said he'd show us pages if we went to the meeting. Which was supposed to be tomorrow." Kit's blue gaze shot to Malcolm's face. "So you have them now?"

"No. Someone else does, apparently. We're endeavoring to discover who."

"And you can't talk about it."

"Investigations can challenge friendships. I appreciate your understanding."

"I still can't make sense of the whole thing." Kit dropped his hand to the wall behind him. "Do you really think these memoirs could make a great difference in the trial?"

Malcolm regarded his young friend. Who, in so many ways, reminded him of his younger self. "If someone was willing to use blackmail—yes."

Kit scraped the toe of his shoe over the polished floor. "Someone's going to end up with them."

"Perhaps. Unless we can recover them first."

"And if you can't?" Kit's head shot up and he fixed Malcolm with a gaze that was at once hard and entreating. "Someone else will have them and use the information to influence the outcome of the trial."

"Kit—" Scenes from his own past played out in Malcolm's head. Debates across scarred tables in coffeehouses, walking across Oxford courtyards, lounging on the banks of the Cherwell. "Do you really think someone else's doing wrong is an excuse to do it yourself?"

Kit's gaze clashed with his own, like a sword wielded by an apprentice who has learned his craft. "That depends on whether doing so prevents another wrong."

"Two—"

"Don't say two wrongs don't make a right."

"I wouldn't. Not precisely. But playing the game to the lowest level degrades everyone."

"And if one doesn't? What good is standing on principles if the others win?"

"It's not a match that ends. It's a constant, evolving struggle. What you do now has implications, thirty, fifty years, who knows how far in the future."

Kit frowned in a seemingly genuine effort to puzzle it out. "And when we get to that future? What do we say to the people who are in slavery now—some of them literally. How do we justify not doing everything in our power to create change as fast as we can?"

Conversations with Mélanie echoed in Malcolm's head. "And if we act now and the country dissolves into something worse because of it?"

"You're so damnably sure."

"Oh, my God, Kit." Malcolm stepped forwards and touched his friend's shoulder. "I'm not sure of anything. I play past and future decisions over in my head on more sleepless nights than I can count. I debate things with Mélanie. With O'Roarke. With myself. I can't tell you what's right. All I can tell you is what I'd do in your shoes."

"And you're sure you wouldn't use these memoirs to gain advantage?"

Malcolm drew a breath. It scraped against his throat. "I can't even tell you I'm sure of that."

"KITTY'S BEEN HELD at knifepoint. How is everyone else's evening going?" Julien pulled out a chair for Kitty at a supper table where Mélanie and Malcolm were sitting with Laura and Raoul.

"Julien's exaggerating." Kitty set down her reticule and champagne glass. "Or rather there was a knife, but it was Tommy Belmont, who is not a serious threat."

"Oh Christ," Malcolm said. He was, Mélanie realized, far calmer than he would have been if she'd made a similar comment early in their marriage. But then he'd recognized Kitty as an able fellow agent long before he'd recognized her as one. "How did he get past the footmen?"

"I suspect he scaled the garden gate when the grooms weren't looking." Kitty let her spangled scarf slither over the chair back. "Anyway, Cordy and Harry wouldn't have wanted to keep him out. He might have had something interesting to reveal."

"Did he?" Raoul handed them a plate of leek-and-onion tarts.

"Only that his faction in the League desperately want the memoirs." Kitty tugged off her second glove. "Which we already knew. He thought I might have the memoirs. And they know I was with Blayney right before he died."

"That's interesting." Mélanie took a sip of champagne. "I

wonder if they had another agent inside the Chat Gris, or if his information came from whoever was supposed to meet with Blayney."

"Yes." Julien slid into a chair beside Kitty. "It could still mean that the League's agent killed Blayney either way. Whoever killed him didn't find any papers on him. Not unless Kitty missed them."

Malcolm refilled the champagne glasses from the bottle on the table. "Did Belmont say anything else?"

"Just some tiresome comments about my lack of ability to be a conformable wife." Kitty took a bite of leek-and-onion tart.

"Your husband would run screaming in the other direction if you ever tried to be anything of the sort," Julien said. "And I suspect what he actually said was that your husband would bore you to tears."

"Tommy," Kitty said, "has never been known for his insights. What's everyone else learned?"

"Rupert knew the Langdons growing up," Raoul said. "But doesn't know Danielle Darnault. Bertrand's away on a mission. I'm hoping he'll be able to help when he's back."

Malcolm cut a slice of stilton. "Blayney tried to interest Kit Montagu in the memoirs."

"He isn't in them, is he?" Laura asked.

"No." Malcolm added the stilton to a slice of pear. "But he realizes the impact they could have politically."

"Interesting." Raoul sat back in his chair.

Malcolm's gaze locked on his father's. "Would you use them?"

"Not in this case. I think there's a reasonable chance the queen will prevail. And blackmail's an ugly business. But in other circumstances—Say after Waterloo when we were looking for any leverage to save people from the White Terror —" He picked up a walnut and cracked it. "I might be tempted."

Malcolm nodded. "I tried to convince Kit of the folly of using such methods. But I admitted I wasn't sure what I'd do myself."

"James Blayney did his research," Mélanie said. "He didn't just know who was in the memoirs, he knew what they could mean politically."

"Or someone else working with him did," Kitty said. "We still don't know how he pulled this off."

"Or where the papers are," Malcolm said.

Raoul handed round the walnut pieces. "The night is young."

"You look as though you're enjoying yourselves, so I assume you're discussing the investigation." Harry pulled up a chair between Malcolm and Laura.

"Don't worry, there will still be plenty to resolve when you're finished playing host," Malcolm said.

"Actually, I've learned something." Harry topped off his glass from the bottle on the table. "Paul and Juliette knew Danielle Darnault. Juliette thinks Mademoiselle Darnault was involved with the journalist Pierre Ducroix. Paul claims not to see it, but Juliette's quite convinced. The affair—if there was one—seems to have been secret."

"Didn't Ducroix disappear?" Laura said.

"He did indeed," Raoul said. "Just about the time Danielle Darnault abruptly retired to Britain."

"Do you know what happened to him?" Malcolm asked.

Raoul shook his head. "I tried hard to find out. He was a lost voice that needed to be heard. And also a very good man."

"Did you hear anything about his being involved with Danielle Darnault?" Mélanie asked.

"No, but though I met him a few times, that's hardly something he'd have confided in me about. Especially if the affair was secret."

"I wonder—" Kitty's fingers slid along the stem of her champagne glass. "Well, she was working for Hubert at the time."

"If you're asking if Ducroix was the sort of person my uncle would have thought it expedient to get rid of, then the answer is yes," Julien said. "That doesn't mean this supposed affair was part of a mission."

"No," Mélanie said. "But for spies, affairs often are."

CHAPTER 34

"Are you all right, Nerezza?" Malcolm stopped beside Nerezza Russo near the door from the supper room to the ballroom. She was standing on her own, gaze fixed on a Chinese vase filled with roses.

"Of course." Nerezza shot a quick smile at him. "Just thinking. With everything going on, there isn't much time to think about the future."

"I don't think most people here can think beyond the queen's trial."

"That's understandable. Winning must seem like everything."

"Yes. But while it will impact the king and queen's lives, the rest of our lives will go on. And I'm not sure how much they'll be changed."

"You can never know, can you? How certain choices will change your life?"

"No. One can only make the best determination based on what one knows at the moment."

Nerezza looked up, gaze fastened on his face. "You mean do what seems right at the moment?"

"Do what seems best for everyone involved. Including yourself."

"Hard to know what's best, isn't it? And sometimes one has to weigh the needs of different people."

"Always a challenge. But don't ignore yourself."

Nerezza gave a laugh sharp as smashed crystal. "When I first met you, I thought what was best for me was running and hiding. If I'd succeeded, I'd have got myself killed. And perhaps others as well."

"But within the space of a few hours—less, minutes—you reassessed the situation and accepted our help. You have good instincts, Nerezza."

"That's kind of you."

"It's the truth."

"I don't know about that. But—" Nerezza straightened her shoulders, making her gauze scarf slither down round her elbows. "In this case, I think I do know what the right thing to do is. I've just been putting it off. Because the right thing isn't always the easy thing, is it?"

"No. Far from it."

"Yes, I expect you know about that." She pulled the ends of the scarf together with quiet determination. "Thank you, Malcolm."

"Nerezza," Malcolm said, as she turned to go.

Nerezza looked at him.

"It's a challenge, making any relationship work. That doesn't mean it isn't worth it."

Nerezza frowned. "I know you honor your commitments, Mr. Ran—Malcolm. But you wouldn't be happy cut off from your life, would you?"

"That depends on how you define my life. Mélanie and the children are the most important things in my life."

"And the rest of your life—your home, the people you grew up with, your work in Parliament? All this"—she gestured round the room. "Not the dancing and flirting and conventions—the buzz of politics. You can feel it in the air. Whatever you think of society, I know that quickens your blood."

"I'd be lying if I said it didn't," Malcolm said. "Or that I didn't love my home or countless people in my life. And no one should have to give anything up. But if it were a choice between Mel and anything else in my life—except the children—the choice would be clear."

Nerezza gave a twisted smile. "Of course you'd say that, Malcolm. You'd never turn your back on your responsibilities."

"I hope that's true. But that's not why I'm saying it. I'm saying it because it's true. And I'd certainly not want anyone to choose for me. Especially the woman I loved." There'd been moments, especially right before they ran to Italy, when he'd been afraid Mel would do just that. For a self-proclaimed pragmatic realist, she could be extraordinarily hard on herself.

"But the woman you loved might feel differently," Nerezza said. "Especially if the choice wasn't a hypothetical."

"MELLY." Simon Tanner came forwards through the throng on the edge of the dance floor as he caught sight of Mélanie. "Haven't seen you all evening."

"I know." Mélanie leaned forwards as he kissed her cheek. "It sometimes seems one sees one's friends least in a crowd."

"And you're investigating."

"That too." Mélanie scanned her friend's face. "You didn't know James Blayney, did you?"

"No. Not precisely. I know his brother Edmund. I've written things for Edmund's paper. I certainly support the things Edmund has to say. Edmund never talked about his brother though, save once to say they were estranged. But—" He cast a glance round the ballroom. "We should talk. Waltz with me? It's good for cover."

"You're learning." Mélanie stepped into his arms.

"I didn't have the least idea who James Blayney was," Simon said as they moved into the dance. "What he looked like. Until Letty talked to me today."

Letty was a talented young actress at the Tavistock who had been in Mélanie's recent play. "Letty knew him?"

"She said he came round to the green room on occasion and was one of the crowd who gave her flowers and flirted with her. She said she didn't know him well, and I don't think she did. These days she has eyes for no one but Will. But she knew who he was when she heard he'd been killed. The talk was all round the theatre by the time rehearsal started this morning. Probably more so because of the murder at the Tavistock last winter. I had a hard time getting them to focus. Letty took me aside when we had a tea break. She was quite concerned. Apparently, she saw Blayney at the theatre five days ago."

"He came to see her in the green room?" Mélanie kept her gaze on Simon's face as he twirled her to the side.

"No." Simon spun her under his arm. "She didn't speak with him at all. She saw him talking with Jack."

"Jack Tarrington?" Jack was a young actor who had joined the Tavistock Company the previous spring.

"Yes." Simon's dance steps didn't falter,, but his brows drew together.

"In the green room?"

"In one of the dressing rooms. When she went to fetch her things at the end of the evening." Simon hesitated as he twirled Mélanie forwards and then back to face him. "She said she heard raised voices."

"Saying what?"

"She wasn't sure. Apparently they stopped talking when they

saw her. Letty said she went on and didn't think much of it, as it wasn't any business of hers. But when she heard Blayney had been killed, she decided she should tell me. She knew I'd be seeing you tonight. We're all on edge since Lewis Thornsby's murder."

None more so, perhaps, than Letty. Thornsby had been killed, at least in part, because he wanted to marry her.

Jack Tarrington was a talented actor of little more than five-and-twenty. He seemed an unlikely candidate for Danielle Darnault's memoirs, but one never knew. "Has Jack spent time in Paris?" Mélanie asked.

"Not that I know of. He was acting in the provinces before he came to London."

"Blayney dealt in blackmail. He'd been making a number of threats lately. Have you heard of Danielle Darnault?"

"Oh, yes. I heard her sing once in Paris. Exquisite voice. Is she connected to James Blayney?"

"He was trying to sell her memoirs."

Simon whistled.

"He was also using people to send blackmail demands to others. Could Jack be connected to anyone powerful who might be a subject in the memoirs?"

Simon hesitated for two measures of music.

"James Blayney grew up in Shropshire. His father had the living on the Pendarves estate. Could Jack have a connection?"

Simon drew in and released his breath. "Damn." He spun her away from him. "I was afraid of this."

Mélanie turned, their hands linked overhead. "Simon, is Jack involved with Lord Pendarves?"

Simon's fingers tightened on her own. "My God, that's quick even for you. Or has there been gossip?"

"Not about Jack. But I had reason to believe Lord Pendarves might be involved with a man."

Simon grimaced. "They've been very discreet. I don't know anything for a certainty. But Pendarves has taken to coming to the green room. He talks to Jack more than to anyone. No more than talking. But I'm rather good at reading the looks in two people's eyes."

"You saw what was between Rupert and Bertrand before anyone else did." Mélanie spun to face him. "I'll talk to Jack. We don't know that it means anything."

"No." Simon forced a smile to his face that did not reach his eyes. "I don't like to talk about friends. Even when it's to a friend. But Jack's seemed unsettled of late. Forgot his lines in rehearsal twice. Can't remember his blocking. I hadn't thought it might be the relationship with Pendarves. But I didn't think— Is Pendarves a suspect?"

"Right now, everyone's a suspect."

CHAPTER 35

"Rannoch." Beverston seized Malcolm's arm in the passage outside the ballroom. "Walk with me. Pretend we're going into the cardroom."

"No one who knows me would believe that. For that matter, I haven't seen you in the cardroom much of late."

"Pretend. Isn't that what you spies do?" Beverston tugged open a door onto a small parlor beside the cardroom. "Empty. Good." He strode into the room. "We're in the devil of a mess."

"Interesting to hear you use the word 'we.' I wasn't aware it applied to us about anything."

"Shut the door, Malcolm." Beverston strode to the fireplace. "We haven't time for verbal fencing. How much do you know about Danielle Darnault?"

"Considerably more than I did yesterday." Malcolm shut the door. "Are you in her memoirs too?"

Beverston spun round to stare at him. "Who else has asked you to retrieve the memoirs?"

"You can scarcely expect me to answer that."

"Would it help if I told you I may be in them, but that that's not my chief concern?"

"The League want the memoirs."

"My rivals in the League want them. And will go to considerable lengths to get them."

"Yes, they've already held a knife to Kitty's throat. At least, I think the man was their agent."

Beverston frowned. "Lady Carfax is all right?"

"Lady Carfax is well able to take care of herself." Malcolm crossed to stand beside Beverston at the fireplace. "The League want the memoirs because they reveal Alexander Radford's identity."

"Have you seen the papers that reveal this?"

"Only a few pages that don't reveal much except that Danielle Darnault knew him. But I assume that's why the League are so invested. Unless they want to use the papers to influence the queen's case. But I tend to think that's a side issue."

Beverston frowned at the andirons. "Yes, so do I."

"And so Danielle Darnault herself is at risk. Did the League get rid of her?"

Beverston's brows drew closer together. "I don't know."

"But you don't deny they might have. They tried to get rid of Nerezza."

"And stopped."

"So you've assured me."

"My dear Rannoch. Surely by now you at least realize I don't want Nerezza hurt."

"I think so. I also think they stopped going after Nerezza because they realized that though she knew Alexander Radford, she didn't know who he really was. So as long as he remains hidden, she isn't a risk. Which I assume means whoever Alexander Radford is, he isn't showing himself in Britain. And that if he chooses to do so, Nerezza will be at risk again."

"Possibly." Beverston's gaze showed calm resolution. "And in that case, we'll have to take action."

"But Danielle Darnault is an international agent. She'd know the major players."

"You think Alexander Radford is a major player?"

"You tell me."

Beverston bit his lip, as though aware he'd made a mistake. "She'd be good at seeing through disguises. You're right, she might know who he is."

"And then, of course, there's always the possibility that you or one of the others in the League who may have been her lover told her."

"What sort of fool do you think I am, Rannoch?"

"It rather depends on how you felt about Radford. And when you turned against him."

"Who says I ever wasn't against him?"

"Just a hunch. Alliances have a way of changing in the League." Malcolm regarded Beverston. "Alistair was her lover. So was Trenchard."

"Yes, I know."

"Let me guess. You got close to her to get information about them."

"Not entirely."

"Danielle Darnault also has a child. She's missing too."

Shock flared in Beverston's gaze, though Malcolm wasn't sure at which statement.

"Did you know she had a child?"

"No. She didn't when I knew her." He frowned again. "At least if she did she didn't tell me. Do you know who the father is?"

"No. The child is about four. But she seems to have been at pains to keep her daughter secret."

"If the child is four, it's not mine. I wasn't thinking of me."

"You think Alexander Radford could be the father? Would he care?"

Beverston's brows knotted tighter. "Most men would care if they had a child."

"On the contrary. A number of men are quite indifferent to it. Women too."

"I didn't say be a good father. But it's a point. Some men seem quite uninterested. I rather think Radford wouldn't be, for a number of reasons."

"Do you think he'd try to get control of the child?"

"What makes you say that?"

"Something made Danielle Darnault disappear. We've been assuming she ran because she wanted to use the memoirs. Or because someone else had them, and it threatened her. But it's possible she ran to protect her child. Or herself. Or both."

Beverston frowned into the cold grate for a long moment. "If you're asking me if Radford is dangerous—of course he is. That's apparent, even if he wasn't a League member. If you're asking me if he'd harm a woman he'd been intimate with—we know he tried to harm Nerezza, so yes." Beverston's mouth turned grim. "As to a child—I can imagine his wanting to control a child. If he'd hurt it—I don't know. I don't much care to find out. And I speak as one with little more faith in my own morals than I imagine you have." He jerked his head up and fixed Malcom with a hard gaze. "If Radford gets the memoirs, he'll destroy the parts about himself, but he won't hesitate to use the rest."

"To get control of the League?"

"That's his aim. And to impact the queen's case, if he cares enough."

"Some of your own allies in the League might do the same."

"So might a number of people. Including a number of your allies. I doubt your friend Brougham would hesitate for a moment. He wants to win, after all."

"And you?"

"Do I want to win?"

"Would you use the memoirs?"

"The king's divorce isn't my fight. And if it topples Liverpool, he deserves it. I don't think it will, mind you. Perhaps I'd be more concerned if I did. But if they could get me something I cared about—do you really need to ask that, Malcolm?"

"When you put it that way—perhaps not."

"Well, then. If you recover the papers, we won't have to explore the question further."

"That rather evades the question of what I might do with the papers if I recover them."

"You'll destroy them, as should be done."

"Is that what you'd do?"

"You're leading the investigation, and I freely admit you have talents I don't. And I know I can count on your instinct to do what's right."

"You seem very sure of what's right."

"What I think is right—not that that's something I ponder a great deal—isn't the question. It's what you do."

"I'm not in the least sure what's right in this case. One would think it would be to return the papers to Mademoiselle Darnault."

"Who got us into this in the first place."

"We have no reason to think that. It seems far more likely they were taken from her."

"So you'd give them back to her and risk her doing this again? Or the papers' being taken again? She was fool enough to write it all down."

"Or clever enough. It was perhaps the one currency she had to protect herself."

"You think she's in danger?" Beverston asked.

"I don't know. She's missing. Which is of concern."

"Yes." Beverston's brows drew together.

"And then, of course, there are my own feelings when it comes to the outcome of the trial."

"You don't want to win through blackmail, Malcolm. That's no sort of victory."

"No, it isn't. But it's damned hard to act with conscience when the other side fails to display it."

"You're never going to win by being more ruthless than your opponents, Malcolm. Though it's not a strategy I've favored myself, there are advantages to being more principled."

"Thank you for your advice, sir." Malcolm did not try to keep the irony from his voice.

Beverston grunted. "I don't expect you'll believe this, but it's sincerely meant. The truth is, of late, I wonder more often than you'd think if your way isn't the more sensible."

"That is hard to credit, sir."

"Yes, well, whatever else I am, I hope I'm capable of learning. And risking losing certain things, one sometimes realizes they don't matter as much as one credited. And other things seem more valuable. Things one's practically let slip through one's fingers." He hesitated, tapping his fingers against the mantel-piece. "Speaking of which, there's something else I want to talk to you about, Malcolm. I need to ask for your help."

"Sir?" Malcolm kept his voice even.

"It's not going to be easy for Ben and Nerezza. It's not even going to be particularly safe. I want to see them married as soon as possible."

Malcolm stared at one of the leaders of the Elsinore League. Who had used his own eldest son for the League's ends. Whom Malcolm was used to viewing through the lens of an enemy even if they were occasional allies. "You want—"

"I assume they're tending that way. I rather thought they might be secretly engaged already. Perhaps they are, and you don't want to betray their confidence?"

"Assuming I was in their confidence, I would scarcely betray it."

"Because you thought I'd protest? I should have pushed for it sooner. Ben's feelings are remarkably steady. As are Nerezza's, which is a bit more surprising. But she seems to be genuinely fond of my son."

"She does. I think just now she was trying to tell me she feels she should give him up, for his own good."

"Damnation. I thought she was more hard-headed."

"So did I. It's a sign though of how deeply she cares."

"Yes." Beverston's brows knotted. "I trust Ben will be able to talk her out of it."

"The fact that marriage won't mean he'll be cut off from his family should certainly help. And I'd say Ben has more than proven himself worthy of her regard. He's grown up amazingly in the past year."

Beverston's mouth twisted in a wry smile. "Children have a way of doing that when one isn't looking, as no doubt you will see. Benedict's priorities seem clearly fixed, and I imagine he'll continue to grow, especially as circumstances demand it. And Nerezza is certainly well able to take care of herself. But I'd like your word you'll protect them."

"They're my friends," Malcolm said. "Of course I will."

"Roger will stand up for his brother, but he doesn't have your skills. Though he isn't doing badly for himself. And it seems it was a good thing for him to marry Dorinda."

"Yes, I would say very much so."

Beverston frowned at a framed watercolor of Lake Como that Cordelia had done in Italy, as though deciphering secrets in the washes of blue and green. "Odd to find oneself wanting one's children to be happy with their marriage partners. It was never much of a concern for me. But perhaps it should have been. It seems to have worked well for you."

"You can't tell me you take me as an example to follow in anything, sir."

Beverston looked up with a brief smile. "We may not agree,

but I have a lot of respect for you, Malcolm. I don't doubt your father is very proud of you."

"My father is very different from you, sir."

"Undoubtedly. But there's a certain commonality in being a parent. God knows Roger and Benedict haven't followed the path I'd have chosen for them. But I'm rather proud of both of them. And I'd like to see them settled as comfortably as possible." He held Malcolm's gaze for a moment.

Malcolm studied Beverston. He was used to seeing the other man as unassailable. A force to be worked round, if anything. Certainly not a subject of concern. And yet— "Sir—"

"We don't know where we're headed, Malcolm. But we're clearly in a crisis, and a crisis has a way of crystalizing the mind. As I said, I find certain things matter to me far more than I thought. What's clear to me is that my children's happiness matters rather more than anything else I can think of at present."

"If there are things you know, that you haven't told me—"

"I've told you what I can, Malcolm." Beverston's moved to the door. His signet ring caught the flare of the candlelight as he reached for the handle. "I have no doubt you'll do the best possible. There are parts of this I need to handle on my own."

MÉLANIE FOUND Julien in one of the side salons talking to Emily Cowper and Granville and Harriet Leveson-Gower.

"All of this endless talk about how far apart the queen's and Bergami's beds were and whether or not they slept in the beds," Emily was saying. Her color was high and her voice a shade more brittle than usual. "As if they couldn't contrive to do whatever they liked in or out of bed and actually sleeping has nothing to do with it. To be sure, the queen has shown a sad want of discretion—"

"Oh, if she wanted to be really discreet she should have chosen a lover who was absent—or better yet dead," Harriet said. She turned to smile at her husband. "If I didn't adore Granville so much, I'd adopt a dead lover at once. There's nothing like absence and death to make a romance really respectable."

"If rather dull," Mélanie said.

"Which is why a sensible man knows the best love affair is with his own wife. Or learns it eventually." Granville kissed his wife's hand, then looked at Mélanie. "And no, I never saw Danielle Darnault except on stage. I was married to Harriet by then."

Granville had had a very active romantic career before his marriage, including a long affair with Harriet's aunt. The affair had produced two children whom Granville and Harriet were now raising. Not to mention that "Caro George" was Harriet's illegitimate half-sister. As Malcolm had pointed out to Mélanie, their own situation was far from the most unusual in Mayfair. "I never thought you had," she said.

"I wonder how many men in the ballroom can say as much." Emily wielded her fan. From the look in her eyes, Mélanie suspected she was quite aware of Palmerston's involvement with Danielle.

"I imagine even a number who can are not unaware of the meaning of loyalty." Julien said. "It comes in different forms."

"Well said." Emily gave a smile that was less arch. "You have the makings of a diplomat."

"But he's quite forgot he promised me a waltz." Mélanie slid her arm through Julien's own.

"Then by all means, you mustn't disappoint her, Carfax," Granville said.

"Do you really want to dance?" Julien asked Mélanie as they moved off.

"It's always agreeable to dance with you, Julien. But I have information about your friend Pendarves."

Julien's brows drew together.

"It doesn't necessarily mean anything." Mélanie drew him to the side as they stepped into the ballroom. "But it seems he's involved with Jack Tarrington. He's—"

"A very talented young actor. I know."

"Letty heard Jack quarreling with James Blayney five nights ago. She didn't hear what about. I'll talk to Jack."

"And I obviously need to talk to Pendarves again. I suspected there might be someone now. But Pen's lover's quarreling with Blayney is certainly a wrinkle."

That note of worry in Julien's voice was something new. Or perhaps she simply hadn't been keyed to notice it before. "You couldn't have guessed this, Julien."

"I don't make guesses. But you're right, I couldn't have deduced it. I still feel I missed things."

Mélanie hesitated, then decided to venture it. "It's not surprising there are echoes. When you talk to Pendarves. I feel that with—people I've got information from."

He gave a quick smile. "Including me."

"I failed woefully with you, Julien." It had been her first mission, and it still rankled.

"Not really. I almost didn't wake up." This time he watched her for a moment. "It's different," he said. "When you've used intimacy for information, it means something else. Even when you aren't using it for anything."

"We aren't the only ones who've done that," Mélanie said.

"No. But we've done it more than anyone in our group. I'm not sure the others can quite understand the echoes. Not even Kitty. And I'm quite sure Malcolm can't, remarkable as he is."

"God, I hope not. I wouldn't want him to."

A faint smile pulled at Julien's mouth. "I used to think everything could be sold. But intimacy—real intimacy—can't be. It's difficult, drawing the line." He squeezed her hand. "Save a dance for me later. I need to talk to Pendarves."

FRANCES STEPPED out into the cool air of Cordelia and Harry's garden. Cordy's parties were always diverting, and certainly the trial made for refreshing gossip instead of the usual on-dits. But she found herself wanting to escape the crowds more than she once had. A little of this life went a long way. Odd to think it had once been the hub of her existence. But then, she hadn't had other things to fill her days. And she was at an age where the heat was likely to overwhelm her more. She stepped further into the garden, wielding her fan.

A few others were wandering along the garden paths, beneath the dancing light from the colored glass lanterns. There was a time when she'd have escaped into the garden at a ball in a gentleman's company for something more than fresh air. Though amorous encounters in the shrubbery were generally more alluring in theory than in fact. Cold stones and prickly shrubbery were no match for a featherbed. And none of the men she'd dallied with then was a match for Archie.

"Fanny."

She gripped the stone wall behind her, scrabbling to hold on to her sanity. The disembodied voice deluged her senses with memory. Surely she was dreaming?

"I'm quite real," he said. "I never knew you to believe in ghosts."

"Not in the literal sense."

"Surely you've wondered, through the years."

"No. Yes. Sometimes."

"I sent you violets. More than once."

"I couldn't be sure that was you."

"Well, no, I couldn't be more explicit. But I'm being so now. I'm very real. And I need your help."

Myriad conflicting emotions tore at her throat. "I'm not the same woman I was."

"You'll always be the same woman, Fanny. We both know that."

She gave a low laugh, though her pulse was hammering in her throat. "When it comes to me, I wouldn't assume you know anything at all. I love my husband."

"Love's a complicated thing, Fanny. We've both always known that too."

"I never thought you knew the meaning of the word."

"One can know the meaning of a word without using that word. We both always knew what was between us."

"Yes. And the word for it isn't love."

"Fanny, I need your help." His voice was low and oddly serious.

"Why in God's name would I help you?"

"Because whatever you feel for Davenport, I don't think you want to see me destroyed."

Her nails dug into the stone through the kid of her gloves. "You must know I'll never forgive you."

"My love." His voice stroked over her nerve endings. "When has forgiveness had anything to do with it?"

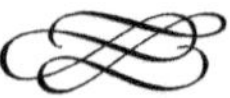

CHAPTER 36

Julien found Pendarves in the room that was given over to cards, not sitting at one of the baize-covered tables but standing to the side, an almost-empty glass of port in one hand. He didn't drink much in general. At least, he hadn't when Julien had known him. Julien moved to stand beside him. "Davenport has some excellent whisky in the adjoining room. If you're not in the mood for a game of cards, I'll pour you a glass."

Pendarves met Julien's gaze for a moment. Julien could see the calculation. Further talk was unlikely to be comfortable. On the other hand, if Julien wanted to talk, Pen would know he'd seek him out sooner or later, perhaps in more challenging surroundings. Pendarves inclined his head and they opened the door in the bookshelves onto the adjoining sitting room. They'd been known to slip into anterooms in the past. Julien would have taken more care that no one was watching in those days. Perhaps he ought to be more concerned now, although he didn't think there was gossip about either of them.

The sitting room was where Harry or Cordelia sometimes worked upstairs. It had a bust of the Emperor Claudius and shelves of well-born books, an overflow from the library and study downstairs, very much Harry's mark. But the mahogany desk set with a gilded blotter, a silver pen set, a bronze paper-weight, crested stationery, and gilt-embossed ledgers were the accoutrements of an English gentleman. Of the world both he and Pen had grown up in. Into which neither of them quite fit. The decanters on a tray beside the desk did indeed hold some excellent whisky from near Dunmykel, the Rannochs' Scottish estate. Julien poured two glasses.

"You're better at deception than I credited," Julien said, as he put a glass in Pendarves's hand. "I knew you were hiding something the first time we spoke. Oddly, I didn't think it was a lover."

Pendarves's fingers tightened round the cut glass. "You must see why I kept quiet."

Julien took a sip from his own glass. "Odd world we live in. Keeping a pretty actress who's the toast of the London stage is the sort of thing a gentleman would boast about at his club. And it would probably lend her credit as well and draw crowds to the theatre. Having a liaison with one of London's most admired young actors is instead something for both to keep secret."

"I'm not—I'm not keeping him," Pendarves said, gaze on the glass in his hand.

"No. It wouldn't be that way with you." Julien surveyed his former lover. "I'm glad."

Pendarves's gaze flew to his face. "About what, for God's sake? What is there in this sorry mess to be glad of?"

"That you've found someone to care for."

"How can you possibly know this—liaison—is that?"

Julien dug his shoulder into the paneling. "Because I think I know you that well. I don't think you do anything lightly. You aren't the sort to keep an actress. You take vows seriously. You're not going to be intimate with someone you don't care for. You even cared for me, I flatter myself, though I gave you little enough reason to. But I think this is more."

"It—" Pendarves's gaze fastened on the depths of his glass. "He means a great deal to me."

"It's damnable," Julien said. "To have found someone, even if you have to keep it secret, only to have it caught up in this whole sordid business. It should just be between the two of you. You shouldn't have to answer questions from me or anyone. Perhaps particularly not from me. I'm the man who got you into bed and took information from you."

Pendarves's gaze clashed with Julien's own. "And information is what you want now."

"We need to learn who killed Jamie Blayney. Because everyone deserves justice, as Malcolm Rannoch would say, and as I am coming to find I agree. And because Blayney's death is part of something larger, and information he had is being used against a number of people."

Pendarves's gaze remained trained on Julien's face. Odd how different such focus could be. There was a time when it would have indicated romantic intensity. There was nothing soft or romantic about it now. "You said 'we' need to learn who killed Jamie. You mean Carfax. Hubert Mallinson, that is. Your uncle."

Julien swallowed. His work for Uncle Hubert had been convenient cover when he last spoke to Pendarves. Now it was in the way. Pendarves was astute enough to know Hubert Mallinson for the man he was. Or close to it. "I don't work for my uncle any longer. Though we're allies on occasion, I disagree with him about a number of things." He bit back the impulse to tell Pendarves precisely whom he'd been working for six years ago. Where did this damnable impulse to tell the truth come from? How did Malcolm, with his infernally fine-tuned conscience, survive for five minutes in intelligence?

Julien bit back the words he knew he couldn't say. Out of loyalty to all sorts of other people. Loyalty was another damnable thing. So much easier, in so many ways, not to give a damn about anyone or anything. "I'm working with the Rannochs." He chose his words with care. "And Jeremy Roth from Bow Street. We're trying to discover who killed Blayney and what use they are trying to make of the information he had."

"And Rannoch works with your uncle."

"Like me, Rannoch used to work with my uncle. We both make our own choices now about where our loyalties lie." Julien hesitated, weighing what he could and couldn't say. "I wouldn't tell Uncle Hubert about you. And us. About you and Jack."

"You can't promise that. I understand intelligence enough to realize that. Louis. Or whatever I'm supposed to call you. Carfax? Arthur?"

"I still cringe at Carfax, and Arthur seems like another person." He hesitated a moment. "The people who know me— the people who love me—call me Julien."

"Julien, then."

Julien took a step forwards. "I know you want to protect Jack. As I'd want to protect Kitty—little though she'd thank me. But knowing the truth gives us our best chance of resolving things and making everyone safer."

"And that's why you want to resolve things?"

"That's part of it."

Pendarves gave a wry smile. "You're honest, I'll give you that." He glanced to the side. "I hadn't—there hadn't been anyone in some time. I thought I could live without that part of my life. I appreciate my work. I appreciate my children. Then one night I saw Jack onstage. I was struck. He's a remarkable actor. And yes, I felt more, but I didn't expect it to lead to anything. But I was at the Tavistock with Tinsbury, with whom I was working on a debt relief bill, and he wanted to go to the green room to see Letty Blanchard, so I went along with him. And I found myself standing beside Jack. So I complimented him on his performance. Simple enough to do. I was sure everyone he met said the same, but he seemed genuinely happy to hear it."

"I don't know that one can ever hear it too much."

"Perhaps. Yes." Pendarves scraped a hand over his hair. "In any case, we began to talk. I ended up going along to a coffee-house with Tinsbury and Miss Blanchard and some others of the company, and Jack and I sat beside each other. We talked. We share an interest in politics." Pendarves drew a breath, as though not sure how much more to say.

"He's one of the Levellers," Julien said. "I know. You must realize I'm in sympathy with them. More than you are, I would have said from what I know of your positions."

Pendarves's brows drew together. "I certainly recognize the ills the Levellers point out. I fear some of their solutions might cause more harm than good. But there are many of their proposals I agree with too. I'm not always sure about their tactics for getting there."

"A discussion I hear a great deal of with my new-found friends." Julien almost referred to David and Simon, but then, though surely Pendarves understood their relationship, it wasn't something to put into words outside their immediate circle. What a damnable world they lived in. "A discussion I join in, I should say."

Pendarves regarded him. "I never thought of you as political. I suppose as an agent, you can't be."

"You can, to a degree, if you pick and choose the assignments you'll undertake, and for whom." It was the closest he'd come to admitting to Pendarves he'd worked for anyone other than the British. "But it's true, I'm freer now." What an odd thought, that his new life was freer than his old one. He was used to thinking of it as happier, but mostly he thought he was happy despite being Lord Carfax, rather than because of his new position.

"You have a knack for speaking," Pendarves said. "So does Jack. I admire that in him. I admire a lot of things in him beyond—Suffice it to say we found a great deal to talk about. Jack said I should come to the green room again the next time I was at the Tavistock. Which I did." Pendarves colored. "Two nights later. And the night after that. Eventually there was a night Jack suggested we go to a different coffeehouse, where it would be quieter, so we could talk more easily. One thing led to another." Pendarves's face closed, but not before revealing a flash of memory that could only be called joy.

Pendarves took a quick drink of whisky. "I knew the risks. I knew—all the things my father said to Sophia about the way she was threatening her family. From the moment I married, I've been determined to shield my wife from injury or distress. I'm sure you understand."

"I'm familiar with the occasional twinge, but Kitty would plant me a facer if I tried to put it into practice."

"My wife is not like Lady Carfax. And I don't—share myself with her. I thought so long as she didn't know, she wouldn't be hurt. I thought Jack and I could have what was between us and keep it to ourselves." He drew a hard breath. "I was a fool."

"Not really. A lot of people manage to make it work with lovers in much that way. It depends on the expectations of all involved. And on one's ability to maintain the secret."

"You wouldn't do the same with your wife."

"Well, no. But we made it clear when we decided to marry that it was to be exclusive. In our situation, there wasn't much point in marrying otherwise. That doesn't mean other arrangements can't work for other couples."

Pendarves grimaced.

"Did Blayney find out?"

"I told you—"

"I know what you told me," Julien said in a hard voice. "Did he find out?"

Pendarves swallowed, glanced to the side, forced his gaze back to Julien. "A week since. I was honest about that. But in addition to asking me to go to Hartlebury, he mentioned that I'd been seeing a lot of Jack. Just that. But it was enough to make me go cold."

"How much did you give him?"

"He didn't want money. Not this time, to my horror." Pendarves's hands clenched together. "He wanted any notes I'd kept from when I was attached to the Russian delegation six years ago."

Julien leaned back, gaze steady on the gaze of his ex-lover. "Did he say why?"

"No. And asking seemed to risk drawing attention to things I preferred not to draw attention to. But no, there's nothing explicitly about us in the notes."

"And unexplicitly?"

"Mentions of our meeting. He might use them to trace who the man I called Louis Duplais really was. He couldn't use them to prove what passed between us. But the fact that he wanted them at all still concerns me."

"Assuming that's why he wanted them. What else is in them?"

"Accounts of the negotiations. Nothing to cause scandal or give fodder for blackmail. I wasn't aware of a great many secrets."

"Don't underrate yourself. I got useful information from you."

"Yes. I'm rather surprised I was considered so important. The most sensitive thing I was party to in those days was secret talks Castlereagh and Metternich were having behind the tsar's back. Speaking of which—did you take the letter?"

"Letter?" Julien asked in genuine puzzlement.

"A draft of a letter from Castlereagh to Metternich that I had. It went missing. We were quite concerned lest it fall into the wrong hands, but it never surfaced. Once I learned you were an agent—"

"I've taken my share of papers. But not that one." He had

gone through and copied plenty of other papers of Pen's, but there was no need to dwell on that now.

"Odd. I thought perhaps I'd solved an old mystery. In any case, there's nothing about the talks with Metternich in the notes Blayney wanted."

"Did you give the notes to Blayney?"

"Need you ask that?"

"In the midst of what we're going through—yes."

"I'm not so lost to honor. I told him I needed to think. To buy myself time. Which gives me yet another excellent reason to have killed him."

"Do you trust me enough to let me look at the notes?"

"Need you ask that?"

Julien smiled. "Thank you."

❀

"THE BALL WAS A TRIUMPH, MY DEAR." Frances smiled at Cordelia over the rim of her champagne glass.

"You're very kind, Fanny. But I'm much more interested in the investigation than the ball."

"The ball was a great help with the investigation." Malcolm stretched his legs out in front of him. "I'd forgot how invaluable these events are for talking to people."

"That's my Malcolm." Mélanie dropped down on the arm of his chair, caught his hand, and kissed it.

"We have more suspects." Julien frowned at his whisky glass. "Pen has an even stronger motive than we thought. As does his lover. Jack Tarrington." He looked at Kitty, who was seated beside him on the library sofa. "Sorry, sweetheart. I haven't had a chance to update you. Or anyone. Save Mélanie, who told me about Jack and Pen."

"Which I got from Simon." Mélanie looked at Simon and David, who were catching up on the investigation. They were sitting by, with the quiet wariness of civilians at a talk among professionals, but Simon's brows were drawn.

"I don't like sharing information about friends," Simon said. "But in the circumstances—"

"Yes," Julien said. "We needed to know. And I don't like sharing information about friends either. That's why it was easier before I admitted I had them." He took a drink of whisky. "Apparently Blayney tried to use Pen's relationship with Tarrington to get Pen to give him notes he'd kept from his time working with the Russian delegation six years ago." He told them more. Including the fact that Pendarves had assured him there was nothing specifically incriminating about the two of them in the notes.

"But Blayney was interested in your relationship with Pendarves," Kitty said. She was watching her husband carefully.

"Possibly. Or he was on to something else about Pen's dealings with the Russians six years ago."

"It's not as though Captain Blayney was a diplomat or a politician or in intelligence," Cordelia said. "How much of the inner workings of negotiations with the Russians six years ago would he even know to be curious about?"

"He was still in the army then." Harry picked up a champagne bottle and refilled Mélanie's glass, then Kitty's. "He might have heard something. Or someone could have hired him to try to discover more. Possibly someone he'd been trying to sell the memoirs to."

"Do you mean the League?" Laura asked, as Harry refilled her glass.

"It's possible," Julien said.

"And the League might want proof about you and Pendarves," Kitty said.

"They might. If they knew about my relationship with Pen, which we have no reason to think they did. And Pen didn't give

Blayney the notes. When I take a look at the notes, we may have a better sense of why they'd be valuable."

David turned his glass in his hand. "You really think these memoirs could impact the outcome of the trial?"

"An attempt to blackmail powerful men about the outcome of a case over which a number don't feel a great deal of personal conviction? In which the government currently have a majority but public opinion is firmly on the other side?" Malcolm said. "What do you think?"

"Put like that—Are you sure Father doesn't have the memoirs?"

"I'm never sure of anything when it comes to Hubert," Malcolm said. "He's certainly acting as though he doesn't have them. Which could be cover. But I'd think he'd be trying to influence some of the people we've heard from, if he had them."

"And he might know who Alexander Radford is if he had the memoirs," Kitty said.

"Beverston and Glenister do, I think," Malcolm said. "But they're not willing to share it. Playing both sides? I'm not sure."

"What about Kit Montagu?" David looked at Simon.

"What about him?" Simon asked. Kit was part of the Levellers, an organization of Radicals agitating for change that Simon had helped found.

"Do you think he'd buy the papers to use them?"

"I wouldn't have thought so. But I can understand why he's thinking of it."

"My God." David stared at his lover. "Surely we have better standards—"

"We should stand on our principles and let the other side trample on us?"

"Do you really think—"

"Not necessarily. But I think Kit may."

"Kit's young," Malcolm said. "Issues can seem simpler when one's young."

"Or some of us simply avoided them," Julien said. "Which I wouldn't advocate."

"Some of us sought refuge in other things. Which I still do," Harry said.

Julien turned his head to look at Harry as Harry refilled his glass. "You're writing a monograph about slave women in the Roman empire. Which let me, for the first time, see my mother's family in the classical world as well as my father's. That's a long way from nothing."

Harry righted the decanter and met Julien's gaze for a moment. "Thank you. That means rather a lot. Though I can still hardly claim to have been doing what O'Roarke did at twenty."

"Believe me, I was quite intolerant at twenty," Raoul said. "Fanny remembers."

"Oh, I was fifteen." Frances had been looking a bit abstracted, but she gave a quick smile. "I thought it was dashing."

"You were in the midst of a revolution," Julien said. "Moderation doesn't exist."

"One doesn't necessarily know one is in the midst of a revolution except in retrospect," Raoul said. "At least, not at the start."

"I doubt Kit can afford the memoirs," Malcolm said.

"He and Sofia might try to steal them." Harry paused in the midst of refilling drinks. "They've proved themselves quite good at that."

Malcolm frowned. "Something to watch for. I'd like to think I got through to Kit tonight. But I can't be sure. Of that or of anything else. I wonder—"

He broke off as the door opened to admit Roth. He paused on the threshold, but not with as much reticence as he'd once have shown. "I was hoping I'd find you all still here."

"Is there news?" Harry walked forwards and offered him a glass of whisky.

"Yes." Roth moved to a chair and took an appreciative sip. "Nothing conclusive, but it's interesting. We've been trying to trace the movements of Danielle Darnault's staff. We still haven't been able to locate any of them. But her kitchen maid called on Edmund Blayney twice last week."

CHAPTER 37

*P*ippa had driven by the print shop several times over the years. She'd walked by more than once. Twice she'd stood across the street and watched through the window as he moved type and hung sheets of newsprint. But for a host of reasons, she'd known she couldn't approach the door. Odd how Jamie's death had in a sense freed her. Though only to step into an abyss.

She curled her gloved fingers inwards, drew a breath, and approached the door, heart quickened. With fear. But also anticipation.

She rapped at the door. "Come in," a rough but familiar voice called.

She hesitated a moment longer, then opened the door.

Edmund was at a long table beside a metal rack of type. He spun round, then went still.

Pippa hesitated inside the print shop doorway. "I wasn't sure you'd let me in."

Edmund came forwards, the light from the lamp on his work table gilding his hair. A smear of ink showed against the golden stubble on his jaw. There were lines round his eyes and mouth she didn't remember. Her breath caught, the way it had done in his presence long before she'd been old enough to quite understand the cause.

"I thought you were Tim, who helps me set type."

"Do you want me to go?"

Something unreadable flickered in his gaze, and for a moment she thought he was going to ask her to do just that. But then he said, "I'd be a poor creature to deny a friend.

"Is that what we are?"

"Isn't that what we've always been, in addition to anything else? In fact, being anything else may have got in the way of being friends." He wiped his hands on his printer's apron and glanced round the shop. "I don't have anywhere proper for you to sit down."

"It doesn't matter."

"Still." He moved a stack of books from a ladder-back chair to the floor and dusted the chair off with a rag, after examining the rag for ink. "Odd you've never come here. Not even when—"

"When we were lovers. I didn't think you wanted me to."

"I didn't. I was afraid you'd be seen."

"I'm beyond caring about that now. And we need to talk." She sank down in the chair and set down her fan and reticule. In truth, it helped to have solid wood at her back.

He ran his gaze over her gown of silver net over seafoam satin and her black velvet cloak. "You look very fine."

"I've been to a ball."

"Of course."

"There's no of course about it these days. I don't go out as much as I once did. But this was Cordy Davenport."

"She's a friend."

"Yes. And more to the point just now, she's involved in the investigation into Jamie's death." Pippa met Edmund's gaze, once so familiar, now so armored. "They don't know about us, but I'm afraid they'll find out."

Edmund leaned against the work table, arms folded across his chest. "Who's they?"

"The Rannochs and Inspector Roth of Bow Street."

"Yes, well, we were fools to think someone wouldn't learn. Though obviously we couldn't have expected my brother to be murdered."

She realized her hands were clenched round her reticule. "I hate that what was just between us has become something sordid. Whatever else it was, I thought it belonged to us."

Edmund leaned against the work table, hand braced behind him. "Always difficult to think one can own a part of one's life. As journalist, I should be well aware of that. And I should have been more aware of what I was leaving us both open to."

"I'm not sorry." She blurted it out without planning, then bit her lip. "Are you?" she asked, and then wished she hadn't.

He glanced to the side. A muscle tightened along his jaw. "I am immeasurably sorry for what I put you through and exposed you to. But I'll always be more grateful than I can say for the memories."

For a moment, she wasn't sure she could breathe. "You didn't have to say that."

His gaze swung round to meet her own, as burning as ever. "No, I didn't. I said it because to say anything else would be to deny who I am. But now we have to deal with the consequences." He watched her for a moment, and she felt at once that he wanted to step closer and scour her face, and that he was looking at her from the wrong end of a telescope. "I understand they know about you and Jamie."

She drew a sharp breath. "How long have you known?"

"Only a matter of hours. Sophia told me."

"Oh, my God."

"She said she was giving me a warning."

"She was paying me back."

"Or me. Which I probably deserved after telling Rannoch

and Roth about her and Jamie. I was trying to divert their attention from you." He regarded her with that same detached look. "Did Jamie know about us?"

She swallowed, and thought of Portia swallowing hot coals. "I didn't tell him. Not in so many words. He said, though, that he was surprised I looked at him when I'd always wanted you."

Edmund gave a short laugh. "I'm surprised he noticed."

"Jamie noticed a lot, I think. It's one reason he was good at manipulating people. He just didn't always admit what he noticed or act on it if it didn't help him."

Edmund gave a short laugh. "Excellent description of my brother."

"I had a long time to study him." She looked into Edmund's familiar, unreadable gaze. For a moment, he was her childhood friend, not her former lover, or her former lover's brother, or the man whose heart she might have broken and who might have broken her heart. "I can't believe he's gone."

"Nor can I, half the time." Edmund loosed his hands from across his chest and braced them on the table behind him. "Whatever he was, my brother was a presence—even when I didn't see him for years and tried my best not to think about him."

"It wasn't like us." Again, Pippa found herself blurting out the words without thinking. It was not what she had come here to say, but she couldn't bear for it not to be said. "What was between Jamie and me."

Edmund's mouth hardened again. "You don't owe me any explanation. We'd said goodbye. Whom you took to your bed was your own affair."

"You can't think it was that simple."

"Pippa—" He stretched out a hand, then let it fall to his side. "There's nothing simple about any of it. But I do know I have no claims on you. I don't know that I ever did, but I certainly gave any pretense to them up when we separated. I'll own to worrying about what you might have got yourself into, but you were entitled to find joy any way you chose."

"It wasn't anything to do with joy. I was miserable and sick with myself. I was wallowing." She drew a hard breath that pushed against her corset laces. "I don't even know why I did it. Perhaps I was looking for some way to prove I was alive. Perhaps I was trying to make things so bad I'd force a confrontation with Haworth. Perhaps I was trying to find some connection to you." She hesitated, fingers tight on her gloved wrists. "Perhaps I was trying to get your attention."

His fingers whitened against the deal table. "Don't you think I wasn't trying as hard as I could not to react to anything you did? Damn it, Pippa. As I said, it's not my business, but after we ended things, how could you have run such a risk?"

"I told you I wasn't thinking. Not then. I've never claimed to be rational, or even as considerate as I might be."

"Christ, you were—" He spun away and swallowed the words.

"I was carrying our child. And after we'd separated to protect her, I ran an unforgivable risk with Jamie."

"We'd decided she couldn't be my child," he said in a rough voice. "Though you're damned right about the risks."

"If it's any consolation, that's what got me to pull myself together and end it with Jamie."

He gave a curt nod. "I don't suppose it matters now. Except that the investigation is going to bring all of this into the present."

"That's why I came. I wouldn't have bothered you otherwise."

He nodded, crisp, contained, a professional, no longer her ex-lover or her childhood friend. "Scandal's not such a problem for a journalist. As we're seeing with the king and queen, it helps sell papers. But I'd give anything to keep you out of it. I confess I told them about Jamie and Sophia because I felt I had to give them something. Not my finest moment."

"They'd have learned, one way or another. They'd have learned all of it, one way or another."

He watched for a moment, with that look he'd worn since they were children when she was about to go into danger—climb a tree or skate across the frozen pond or borrow her father's curricle without permission. "Pippa—"

"I'm not worried about myself. Scandal's not as much of a concern with Haworth gone. I don't have to worry about losing the children. That was always the worst. No one can cut off my funds. I don't mind losing vouchers to Almack's."

"Cynthia and Katie might, when they're old enough." Edmund didn't talk about the girls much. His voice was low and rough.

Pippa met his gaze. "I'd rather they knew not to care for such foolish things. And that they saw their mother for who she is, faults and all."

Edmund gave a faint smile, the way one might smile at a dear memory. "You've always had the courage of your convictions, Pippa." He hesitated a moment. "How are they?"

She found herself staring at him. "They're well. Growing, much too fast, it sometimes seems to me. They get along, most of the time. Better than I did with either of my sisters. Cynthia paints. Katie makes up excellent stories." *She reminds me of you,* she almost said, but that seemed to be crossing a line.

"I'm glad," he said. "That's the most important thing, that they're happy." He hesitated again. "Losing their father can't have been easy. They were very young to go through that."

"Yes." She tugged at one of her gloves. "But they never saw him a great deal. In some ways, I think they miss the idea of him more than him, if that makes sense. I kept being afraid it would leave them frightened, afraid of what else might happen. But it doesn't seem to have done. At least, not yet." *Do you want to see them?* She almost asked. But that seemed to be to step over a line. And he'd made it clear in the past that he didn't want to.

"They have you," he said. "You've made them secure. But the last thing I want is for their lives to be shaken further. And I don't want you to close off your options in life."

"What sort of options? I'm hardly going to stand for Parliament or be sent on a diplomatic mission."

"No, more's the pity. But—"

"What? Oh, good God. I assure you, I have no desire to marry again."

He held her gaze and gave another twisted smile. "People can change their minds."

"Little sense wasting time on such a remote option." She leaned forwards, hands gripped round her reticule. "But I am worried about what the authorities could do to you."

"I told you, scandal's good for business."

"And if the authorities try to shut you down?" she asked. "You're skirting prosecution as it is half the time."

"I'm not sure whether to be flattered or insulted."

"You say things that need to be said, Edmund. But the law wouldn't be on your side."

"How do you know what I say?" He sounded genuinely interested.

"I do read the *Clarion*."

"I'm impressed."

She sat back. "I wasn't only interested because of what was between the two of us."

His gaze lingered on her for a moment. She couldn't have put a name on what she saw in it, save that at once it warmed her like a draught of whisky and made her feel a pang, as though a beloved cloak had been wrenched from her shoulders. "I know your understanding, Pippa. I hope I've never underestimated it."

"I know you must see me as a selfish creature, Edmund. I know I am in many ways. But it's not that I don't care. Not just for other people, for the world in general." Again, this wasn't what she had come to say. Again, it seemed deeply important that she say it.

His brows drew together in that way she had seen when he was analyzing a piece of evidence, a new fact, trying to piece it into his understanding of the world. Which he was always eager to expand on. One of the things she loved about him. "I know. Or perhaps, didn't. Not enough."

"You've done something important with your life, Edmund. I haven't done much with mine. I'm proud of my children, and I'm trying not to mess that up. But I couldn't bear it if our past stopped you from doing good in the world."

"Don't make me into some sort of hero, Pippa. You're too sensible for that."

"I'm too sensible not to see you for who you are."

"You've always been kind, sweetheart."

"I'm nothing of the sort. And you haven't called me that in a long time."

"Old habits die hard." He pushed away from the table, crossed to a chest of drawers, and pulled out a flask and two glasses. He peered at the glasses in the light of the lamp on the work table, dusted them off on his shirt sleeve, then poured whisky into both and gave her one. "We aren't the only ones who are going to have to face uncomfortable questions." He took a sip from his glass and leaned against the table again. "Have you talked to Pendarves?"

"No." She took a quick sip. It was the same Highland whisky they'd drunk on furtive meetings in the old days. Warmth and the ache of nostalgia spread through her. "You think the Rannochs and Inspector Roth and the others will talk to him?"

"He knew Jamie from childhood, Pippa." Edmund turned his glass in his hand. "He's part of the past. And God knows what interactions Jamie might have had with him more recently." Edmund took another drink. "What he may have tried to use against him."

Pippa met her friend's gaze. They'd never really talked about her brother. Not in so many words. "You think Jamie knows—knew about Pen?"

"Jamie had good insights into people, as you said. And he didn't scruple to use those for his own ends." Edmund's gaze settled on her face. "Do you know of anything he could have used against Pendarves lately?"

"No! I mean"—she stared into the golden depths of her drink—"I've never actually talked to him about it. Any more than I've talked to him about you. I've just—known. And I suppose a part of me hopes to God he has someone."

"So do I. But it would have given Jamie an opening for no end of mischief."

Pippa met Edmund's gaze. Dust motes danced in the light between them. "We haven't really addressed it, have we? Any of it. I suppose you always knew about Pen?"

"It took me a while to work it out. I suppose it didn't really seem relevant one way or another. Then, when it occurred to me, I felt a fool not to have seen it sooner."

"Yes, so did I. We're a bit of a mess, aren't we? All the Langdons. Not really satisfied in the life we were born into or chose. Sophia seemed to be, but she couldn't have been, not really, or she'd never have risked it with Jamie. And I don't think Phoebe is."

"It's difficult to be satisfied with life." Edmund turned his glass in his hand. "Jamie had a way of preying on that. And it may have got him killed."

Pippa felt her fingers grow numb round her glass. She tightened her grip, not leaving her gaze on Edmund's. "You mean, one of us may have killed him."

Edmund tossed down the last of his whisky, gaze steady on her own. "Someone killed him. And it seems likeliest it was someone who knew him well."

She pushed herself to her feet and took a step forwards. "Edmund—"

He set his glass down. "Is your carriage outside? You should leave while the street is empty."

"I'm not worried about talk," Pippa said, as Edmund scanned the street through the window. Then she noticed the tension in his shoulders. "You want me out of the way."

He looked over his shoulder. "I never said that."

"You didn't need to." For the first time, Pippa realized her childhood friend had his own secrets. And that those secrets might be more dangerous than any she was keeping.

"It doesn't prove Edmund Blayney is working with Danielle Darnault," Mélanie said, as she settled back against the pillows in the room she and Malcolm were sharing at Harry and Cordy's. The children had spent the evening in the nursery with the Davenport girls, and she and Malcolm and Laura and Raoul and the children were spending the night. Blanca and Addison had come to the ball but had gone home fairly early to their young son.

"No." Malcolm drew the covers over them and blew out the candle on the night table. "It's possible she had a wholly separate reason to call there, though it strains coincidence. Or the kitchen maid could be working with James Blayney and Grace Arbuthnot. In which case, Edmund Blayney is probably involved in the blackmail over the memoirs."

"Which surprises you." Mélanie turned her head to look at her husband's profile in the shadows.

"I like Edmund. I like his writing, and I liked what I saw of him. That's no guarantee of anything."

"If Danielle suspected James and Grace had taken the memoirs after Brougham talked to her, she might have reached out to Edmund for information about his brother. She could have sent the kitchen maid."

"It feels like a bit of a reach, sweetheart. But it's possible." Malcolm stretched out an arm and pulled her against him. "We'll have to wait until Roth and I can call on him tomorrow. Not that that will necessarily yield answers."

"No, but you may be able to decipher from what he doesn't say. I wonder if the memoirs could be in the print shop after all."

"James Blayney hid them with his brother? Or Edmund killed him and took them? Both are possible. If—"

A rap on the bedchamber door echoed through the room. They grabbed their dressing gowns and stumbled to the door. Harry stood in the doorway, wrapped in a dressing gown, a candle in his hand, hair on end. "Ben and Nerezza are downstairs. They have a message from Bertrand."

Neither Mélanie nor Malcolm hesitated before fastening their own dressing gowns. By the time they were heading down the stairs, Raoul had joined them. Which wasn't really surprising. His hearing was uncanny. He didn't ask for explanations, which either meant he'd heard Harry as well or he was piecing it together as he went along.

Nerezza and Ben were in the library with Cordy, who'd given them whisky. Neither was sitting.

"Bertrand sent us," Nerezza said. "He just got back from his trip to the Continent. He has someone with him who's wounded. He wants to know if Mélanie can come."

"Of course," Mélanie said, "but I'll need my medical supply box. Cordy, if you can give me what you have—"

"Of course." Cordelia was already halfway to the door.

"I'll go to Berkeley Square and get your things," Malcolm said. "Ben, perhaps you could come with me and then take me to Bertrand, and Raoul and Harry can go with Mel and Nerezza."

Within five minutes—agents learned the art of dressing quickly—they were all on their way. Cordy and Laura, who emerged to help with coats, saw them off with mock expressions of resignation at being left behind.

Nerezza said little on the short drive, other than to apologize for disturbing them. The carriage pulled up in a dark street. When Raoul handed her from the carriage, Mélanie had an impression of a narrow, dark street and a tall building with no glow of light.

Rupert came out the front door, holding a lantern. "O'Roarke. Harry. Thank God. I need to cover Bertrand's tracks and lay a false trail. Can you help?"

"Need you ask?" Raoul said.

While Raoul and Harry went off with Rupert, Nerezza took Mélanie into the house and up a narrow flight of stairs. Mélanie caught a pungent whiff. Ink. Printer's ink. Odd. Before she could think more, they emerged onto a landing and Bertrand was before them.

"Thank you. We ran afoul of a smuggler's gang. He took a bullet to the shoulder. But I got the bleeding to stop."

Mélanie nodded. "Malcolm's bringing the rest of my things."

The wounded man was lying in a narrow bed in a room off the landing. Another man stood beside him, tall with disordered dark blond hair, in his shirtsleeves. He stepped back at Mélanie's approach, merely murmuring, "He's feverish."

The man in the bed had sweat-dampened hair and a thin, sharp-boned face. Partly his bone structure. But not entirely. This was someone who had not been fed well in a very long time. To put it mildly. Despite the comfort of her life in recent years, the war had left Mélanie familiar with the appearance of someone suffering from hunger.

He opened his eyes and stared up at her with fever-tinged eyes from blue-shadowed lids. "Sorry to be a nuisance." His English was clear, but his accent was unmistakably French.

"Nonsense. I'm glad to be of help." Mélanie sat on the edge of the bed. "We need to get the bullet out of you, but I'm afraid this is going to hurt. Bertrand, do you have brandy? We'll need hot water."

"I'll get it," the man in shirtsleeves said.

Bertrand moved to the bed, a flask and glass in his hand.

"I think you've been imprisoned?" Mélanie said to the wounded man.

He nodded. "For almost three years. My family and I owe Laclos an inestimable debt."

"It's what I do." Bertrand slid his arm beneath the man's shoulders and held up a glass of brandy.

By the time Malcolm and Ben arrived with her medical supply box, the man in the bed was half unconscious. The man in shirtsleeves had just returned with a bowl of steaming water. Malcolm leaned across the bed to hand Mélanie her medical supply box and met the man in shirtsleeves's gaze. "Good evening, Blayney."

Mélanie cast a quick glance at the man in shirtsleeves. "Edmund Blayney. I should have guessed."

"I'm sorry, Mrs. Rannoch," Edmund Blayney said. "Explanations, by all means, but my friend needs your assistance first."

Malcolm and Edmund held the wounded man while Bertrand handed her items from her supply box, Ben held the bowl of hot water, and Nerezza cut lint. The wounded man jerked once and cried out twice, but she got the bullet out without doing further damage and got a fresh dressing on the wound before he could lose too much more blood.

He fell back against the pillows.

"Thank you." Bertrand's voice was level but intense.

"He should pull through," Mélanie said. "You did a good job cleaning the wound, so I'm hopeful we can keep fever at bay."

"You have my fervent thanks as well, Mrs. Rannoch," Edmund Blayney said. "Rannoch—"

The door burst open. A dark-haired woman in a dark blue

cloak, a curly-haired child in her arms, ran into the room and flung herself down beside the bed. "*Chéri!* Thank God."

The wounded man had seemed to be unconscious, but at that he turned his head on the pillow. He stretched out a hand and curled his fingers round her own. His gaze went to the child cuddled in her arms, head buried in her shoulder. The child turned her head. The man stretched out his hand and brushed the child's curly hair before his hand fell back to the pillow.

The woman turned to Bertrand. "Is he—"

"Your husband was wounded," Mélanie said, "but he should recover."

"Thank you, madame." The woman had a resonant, melodious voice. "Is—"

The door broke open again. They all spun round. The woman addressed the new arrival before any of them could. "Julien, what are you doing here?"

"Following you." Julien closed the door and stepped into the room. "I had all my contacts watching for you. I got a message that you'd been spotted and picked up your trail. But it seems my friends were ahead of me." He looked round.

The woman surveyed the group, seeming to see them for the first time.

"Danielle Darnault?" Malcolm said.

CHAPTER 38

Danielle Darnault met Malcolm's gaze. "You're Malcolm Rannoch. And you must be Mélanie Rannoch."

"And I believe your wounded friend is Pierre Ducroix," Mélanie said. She had only seen Danielle Darnault on stage, but now Malcolm had identified her, the resemblance was obvious.

Danielle's eyes widened.

"No, no one's betrayed that he's in Britain," Mélanie said. "But we met someone tonight who suspected you'd been lovers."

"Who?"

"Juliette Dubretton."

Danielle's mouth curved in an unexpected smile. "I always knew Juliette was too clever for other people's good."

"Mrs. Rannoch saved Pierre's life," Bertrand said.

"You have my undying gratitude, Mrs. Rannoch." Danielle glanced at Pierre, who had lapsed back into unconsciousness. "And our daughter's." She cupped her hand round the head of the little girl in her arms. Her gaze went to Edmund Blayney. "It's been a long time, Mr. Blayney. You've risked a lot."

"Far less than you and Pierre."

"We all need to talk." Bertrand said. "But perhaps we could sit down. I know you don't want to leave Pierre, Danielle. We'll pull chairs round."

Danielle removed her cloak and sat on the edge of the bed, her little girl asleep in her lap, Pierre's hand folded between her own. Her thick dark hair was pinned in a simple knot and her gray gown, though beautifully cut, had a demure neckline and seemed designed not to be noticed. But her strong bones, vivid blue eyes, and dramatic brows showed traces of the woman who could hold an audience from behind the footlights to the highest balcony.

Edmund supplied coffee and whisky. Bertrand, Malcolm, Julien, and Ben brought chairs in from the adjoining room.

"You can trust them," Bertrand said. "I was going to ask for their help when we got here in any case."

"I think that includes me," Julien said.

Danielle gave a quick smile. "I already do trust you, Julien. More or less. And I've learned I had to reach out for help in some cases." She glanced at Bertrand.

Bertrand gave a faint smile.

Danielle's gaze swept the others. "Have you read my memoirs?"

"We haven't been able to find them," Malcolm said.

"That's—concerning." She glanced at Pierre. "But Pierre isn't in them. I wrote them to protect him. To protect us. Because I thought I might need leverage." Her gaze lingered on Pierre, as though to assure herself he was there. "We met in Paris seven years ago. I went to a party with some of the other singers one night. A blessed escape from the Salon des Etrangers and cafés in the Palais Royale. I met Pierre in the garden. We were both looking for a moment alone. Instead, we found each other." She looked down at her lover, the memories in her gaze. "We kept it secret because we were each concerned about our enemies hurting the other. It was the first relationship I'd had in a long time that was for me. Keeping it secret protected that, in a way. And there were—complications."

"You were Bonaparte's mistress." Julien was never afraid to be blunt.

"Yes. He actually found out about Pierre. He wasn't pleased. To put it mildly. He accused me of spying on him for various people."

"Were you?" Malcolm asked.

Danielle met his gaze. "Some information I got from Bonaparte I passed to Carfax." She glanced at Julien. "Your uncle. The former Lord Carfax. But not all. And I never shared information about Bonaparte or anyone else with Pierre. That would have violated what we had. But when I saw Bonaparte's anger, I realized I was putting Pierre at risk. I ended our relationship. Which led to a quarrel every bit as intense in its way as my quarrel with the emperor. And in the midst of it all, Bonaparte was sent to Elba. I went off to Vienna in advance of the Congress. It was there that I realized I was with child."

She glanced at the company, all of whom had gone still. "Ilia is Pierre's. I know how to be careful. And I know the timing. But I knew Bonaparte wasn't sure. I knew others would wonder. It seemed safest to keep my pregnancy secret."

"Did you tell Monsieur Ducroix?" Mélanie asked.

Danielle glanced at her lover, then her child, and drew a hard breath. "Not then. I told myself I couldn't burden him. That our lives were too complicated. Which they were. By the time Ilia was born, Bonaparte had escaped from Elba. The world seemed to be falling apart or putting itself back together, and it felt as though both Pierre and I had to be part of it, but we couldn't do so together. I went to Brussels, and then back to Paris after almost a year." Her fingers trembled for a moment over her daughter's hair. "It was a very different city. You were gone." She looked at Julien.

"It seemed a good time to make myself scarce, for a lot of reasons," Julien said.

"It was a dangerous time. Pierre didn't seek me out, and I was too proud or too worried for him or too afraid of the consequences to seek him out. Then I went to a café one night after a performance, not thinking I might see him—or perhaps knowing all too well I might." She drew a breath that tightened her gown across the shoulders. "A lot had changed. For both of us. But at the core what had drawn us together was still there. Only of course now there was Ilia. Pierre—wasn't happy that I'd kept her secret. And he wanted us to marry." She frowned. "When he asked me, I burst into laughter, which wasn't the best response. Then I accused him of wanting to put me in a cage, which was worse, because of course he'd never do anything of the sort. Eventually we settled it that for the time he'd see Ilia and we'd go on as before. Having our relationship in secret but going on with our separate lives. Only—I found I was less and less satisfied with that life. In truth, I'd been dissatisfied with it for a long time. I found myself imagining things that had never seemed possible." She glanced at Julien. "From what I've heard about your life of late, I think you may know what I'm talking about."

Julien leaned back and crossed his legs at the ankle. "A bit, perhaps."

She nodded. "And then, just when I was at the point of committing myself to the unthinkable, Pierre disappeared." Her fingers tightened round Pierre's. Her gaze went to Edmund. "Edmund was in Paris then. He and Pierre were friends. I went to him for news and he helped me search for information."

"I'm not an agent," Edmund said, "but in some ways being a journalist is similar."

"And then I went to Bertrand," Danielle said. "We'd been friends for some time."

"Danielle was very helpful in getting a number of people out of Paris after Waterloo," Bertrand said.

"It was little enough. I knew I was absurdly fortunate at the time. We were terrified Pierre had been killed, but finally we learned the Comte d'Artois was holding him secretly. Pierre managed to get a message to me. He wanted me to leave France. He said my connection to him only put him more in danger."

"Which was undoubtedly true," Julien said.

"So I allowed myself to be persuaded. I came here. Bertrand helped me. I settled in Marylebone with Ilia and lived quietly. While Bertrand tried to work out how he could get Pierre out of prison. I tried entreaties. I tried what leverage I could."

"The memoirs," Mélanie said.

"I wrote them as insurance. To keep us safe once we got Pierre out. It was too dangerous to use those secrets with him still in prison. I never meant for them to actually be published. Then Henry Brougham came to see me."

"Did you realize James Blayney had them?"

"He'd been seeing my maid, Grace Arbuthnot. I think they met first because I sent Grace to Edmund to deliver a message and James happened to be there. Later I sent Becky, my kitchen maid, with messages."

"Did you confront Blayney?" Malcolm asked.

"And kill him?" Her mouth curved with hard-edged irony. "I was furious. I trusted Grace, but I was mostly furious with myself, because I was stupid to trust her, stupid not to see her flashy lover was a risk, stupid to let them get anywhere near the memoirs. Stupid perhaps to have written the memoirs in the first place." She glanced from her child to Pierre. "Though we needed a line of defense."

"And you use the weapons at your disposal," Julien said.

"Yes."

"The instincts of a good agent," Malcolm said.

Danielle looked at him for a moment. "I've heard of you, Mr.

Rannoch. And of Mrs. Rannoch. I know how good you both are."

"Their reputations aren't exaggerated," Julien murmured.

"We've heard a great deal about you, Mademoiselle Darnault," Malcolm said. "I understand you know Alexander Radford."

Nerezza tensed. Ben reached for her hand.

Danielle continued to stroke her child's hair. "Yes, he's in the memoirs. Not the most sensational chapter."

"Do you know who he is?" Malcolm's voice was masterfully level.

Danielle raised her brows. "Alexander Radford. An English gentleman abroad. If he's more than that, he didn't reveal it to me."

"The people after the memoirs—some of them, at least— seem to feel differently." Malcolm watched her for a moment. "Have you heard of the Elsinore League?"

Danielle's fingers stilled on her daughter's hair. "They're a group of powerful men. Some of whom I've been involved with. Including your late father."

"My putative late father. My actual, very much alive father is off with Rupert Caruthers and Harry Davenport covering Pierre's tracks."

She gave a faint smile. "I wasn't sure how much you knew."

"We're in the same predicament." Malcolm sat back in his chair. "Alexander Radford is trying to take over the League."

"I didn't know that."

"The League—or his people in the League—think you know a great deal more than you're admitting to. They're desperate to recover the part of the memoirs where you mention Radford."

"They tried to have me killed," Nerezza said, "and I don't know who he really is."

Danielle turned to look at her. "You were entangled with

him as well? He's a challenging man. Though not particularly noteworthy. Not from what I saw."

"Nor I," Nerezza said. "And they do seem to have decided I don't pose a threat."

"Seem," Ben said.

"It might be enough that you'd both recognize Radford if he appeared now," Julien said.

"That would mean Radford is getting ready to become more public," Malcolm said.

"He's hardly of great concern to me now," Danielle said. "I've had many more important things to focus on. But we need to recover my memoirs as soon as possible. For a number of reasons. I'll do everything I can to assist you."

"Julien." Danielle caught up with him in the upstairs passage. Raoul, Harry, and Rupert had returned, and the others were all talking to Bertrand before dispersing to their various houses. Danielle was going to stay with Pierre for the present. This was the first moment Julien and Danielle had had alone. She gripped his arm. "I'm holding off for now. I assume that's what you want me to do."

Julien grimaced. "For now. We can't tell him tonight."

"But you're going to have to tell him. Surely you realize that."

"Only too well." The weight of what was coming settled more firmly on Julien's shoulders. "It's the when, and persuading others, that are challenging."

Danielle nodded. "It's good to see you."

He smiled, despite everything. "You as well."

"I could scarcely credit the stories I heard about you until I saw you."

"I'm not so very changed."

"Not at the core, I don't think. But then, I think your core was quite different from what a lot of people imagined. You've always been a good friend."

He squeezed her fingers. "I only hope when this is over, I manage to keep my friends."

~

"WILL they be safe at Blayney's?" Ben asked as Rupert poured brandy for him and Nerezza and Bertrand in the Caruthers library. "Rannoch said the print shop's already been searched once."

"Which may make it less likely to be searched again." Rupert put a brandy into Ben's hand. "But O'Roarke and Harry and I arranged for guards. It's a quieter place for them now than here. Then we'll figure out where to move them."

Ben nodded. He'd become so matter-of-fact about missions, Nerezza realized, taking a sip of brandy. Hard to believe he was the same man who'd been so shocked by the events the night she arrived in Britain. Save that, fundamentally, Ben would always be Ben.

"If Alexander Radford means to emerge from the shadows, Nerezza's in more danger, isn't she?" Ben said.

Bertrand exchanged a look with Rupert. "Not necessarily. If Radford's decided to emerge, he may not find Nerezza a threat anymore."

"The League gave up on me almost a year ago." Nerezza tossed down half her brandy. "I'm old news."

"None of this will ever be old news," Ben said. "Not until Radford is vanquished, at the very least."

"I'll be all right, Ben." Nerezza reached for his hand, then released it. "We have more important things to worry about."

Ben kissed her hand. "Nothing's more important."

"I agree," Rupert said. "But we've kept Nerezza safe. We'll manage to do so while we confront other things."

Bertrand cast a sharp look at Rupert.

"Sorry," Rupert said. "It's been a long day. We should go up."

"Can you stay a minute, Nerezza?" Ben asked.

"Of course." Nerezza hid a smile at a memory of the days when he'd still been aware that it would be considered improper for them to be alone together. Not that they ever did anything that might be considered improper. Well, not very. But even now, Ben would never knock at her bedchamber door or talk alone with her anywhere but in the public rooms of the house.

"Ben?" Nerezza studied him when Rupert and Bertrand had said goodnight and gone up. "Is something wrong?"

"On the contrary." Ben moved to her side and stopped a foot or so away, face uncharacteristically serious. "I should have said this months ago. In Italy and certainly since we've been back. But we were so focused on the immediate danger, it was hard to think beyond. Tonight proves we can't wait."

Wariness shot through her. Thinking beyond the present forced a reckoning she knew they would have to confront but couldn't bear to face. Really, she was a shocking coward. "Ben—"

"I love you, Nerezza." Ben closed the distance between them and took her face between his hands. "Marry me."

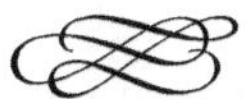

CHAPTER 39

*N*ow the words were spoken, dizziness rushed through Ben. And fear. He felt his fingers trembling against Nerezza's cheeks.

Nerezza stared at him. Her eyes went wide with shock and for an instant something Ben thought might have been wonder. Then her gaze closed. "I can't, Ben. You know what it would do to you."

"Make me happy. What else have we been doing these past months?"

"Enjoying the time we had." She put up a hand to cover one of his own. "Making memories we'll always have."

Disquiet coiled within him. He twined his fingers round her own and gripped her hand hard. "How did you think this would end up? You can't—"

"Go back to what I was before?" She tilted her head to one side. "I could. I can take care of myself."

"I wasn't questioning that." Not that he wouldn't worry about her, but he'd never win that way.

"I'd have freedom. I might even manage to be rather happy.

At least as happy as I was before. Except—" Her brows drew together. "It's difficult to imagine being happy without you."

Relief shot through him. He caught her other hand so he was gripping both her hands in his own. "Well, then."

"Ben. Sweetheart." She gave a husky laugh. "You make it sound so easy. We've been living in an idyll. We're never going to live in the same world."

"We've been living in the same world for almost a year."

"Not really. We've been pretending, and hiding from the League, and able to ignore society. Or we've been with people like the Rannochs, and Bertrand and Rupert and Gaby, and Kitty and Julien, and the Davenports, who don't care."

"That's what I mean. We already have plenty of friends who'll be happy for us. We don't need the rest of them."

"Ben, the rest of them include your parents."

Ben let himself smile. "Father's always been fond of you."

"Ben—" Nerezza hesitated, as though struggling with a truth she couldn't quite put into words. "Your father and I—I knew him in Italy."

Ben looked steadily into her wonderful green eyes. "I know that."

"I didn't just encounter him. I knew him in all sorts of ways." Nerezza swallowed and he saw fear flash in her gaze, followed by determination. "I was his mistress. Assuming one can even dignify it with that."

"I know that." Ben pulled her closer, gently.

Nerezza's gaze flew to his face. "You what?"

He felt himself color, but didn't let himself look away. "I may not be the quickest at piecing things together, but it was fairly obvious some time ago. Not long after you came to England."

"You never said."

"Well, it's not the sort of thing one wants to put into words. And it didn't really impact me. It didn't impact us."

Nerezza eyes widened. "Ben—"

"It was over before you met me. I knew there were others. I mean—" He swallowed, feeling his cheeks go warmer. "I was fairly sure there were. The fact that one of them was my father didn't really make a difference. Not to what was between us. Not if it was over." He almost managed to keep the question from his voice.

"Yes, of course it was over. But—" She looked at him, as though seeking traces of a familiar person beneath a disguise. "You've always been so—You treated me as if—"

"I treated you as I would any lady."

"That's just it. You saw me as—"

"What you were. A remarkable woman deserving of my respect."

"But you knew—"

"Nerezza, I may be a bit slow, but it was fairly obvious you hadn't had the same life as my sisters."

"But if you knew I—You never asked—"

"Well, no. That's not what I wanted from you. That is"—for a moment his voice went unsteady—"of course I want it, but not like that. That's not how I think of you."

"What isn't?"

"I always knew what I felt for you wasn't something temporary. I never wanted a liaison with you"—leaving aside that he'd never had one with anyone, but he wasn't quite ready to put that into words—"I wanted you to be my wife."

"Ben—" Nerezza squeezed his hands. "You don't know how much that means to me. But I'm not really cut out to be anyone's wife."

"What does that mean? You don't"—he hesitated, but it had to be said—"you don't want to be with one person? Only?" Perhaps that should have occurred to him. It was going to be a challenge.

She shook her head. "No. I'd have once said so, perhaps, but you must know it's hard to think of anyone but you now."

"Well, then. Is it children? Seeing you with Stephen, and the Rannochs' children, and the others, I thought—But we could—"

"Oh, God. I hadn't thought—I like children. I mean, I've mostly been worried about not having them, but if—That's not what this is about."

"What, then?"

"I'm not your mother."

"Thank God. I love Mama, but I certainly wouldn't want to marry her. Or anyone like her."

Nerezza choked. "You know what I mean. I'm not even Dorinda or Gaby or any beau monde wife."

"Who said I wanted a beau monde wife? And I'm not sure what a beau monde wife is anyway. Mélanie? Kitty? Cordelia? Laura? Gaby? Lady Frances?"

"They're not typical, but they can afford not to be. And I'm not them either."

"No, you're you. You're unique. And we don't have to live in the beau monde. Not that you aren't navigating it very well."

"That's different. We've had friends about us and we've had a good cover story."

"No reason that has to change."

"Ben. Do you want to live that way forever? Pretending?"

Ben regarded the woman he loved, caught up short for the first time. "Not if it would make it harder for you. I don't mind if we never set foot in a Mayfair drawing room again. Are you worried about being without fortune?"

"Ben." Unexpected laughter gurgled from Nerezza's lips. "I'm far more used to being poor than you are."

He put a hand under her chin and tilted it up. "I know there's a lot I don't have to offer, Nerezza. But I'll spend the rest of my life doing everything I can to make you happy. And I know I won't be happy without you."

"Oh, Ben." She clutched his coat and gave a sound between a laugh and a sob. "I've always been damnably selfish."

He stared down at her, fears and hopes racing though his mind. "What does that mean?"

She leaned into him and kissed him. "That I'll marry you."

MALCOLM DUG his latchkey out of his greatcoat pocket in the portico of the Berkeley Square house and unlocked the door. How many hours was it since Nerezza and Ben had fetched them? Mélanie wondered as she stepped into the hall. So much had shifted. Including something she hadn't mentioned to Malcolm and Raoul yet. A silk fan she'd glimpsed on a chair in the print shop on her way out. Which she was quite sure she'd seen Pippa Haworth carrying at the ball earlier in the evening.

"This shouldn't take long," she murmured. They had just returned for clean clothes, as they were all wearing the change of clothes they'd brought to Harry and Cordy's.

Then, as they took another step, she sensed it. Not a specific sound or sight or smell so much as a general feeling. The house was not as they had left it. Surely the library door hadn't been ajar.

Without looking at them, she knew Malcolm and Raoul had sensed it too. Someone else was in the house. She cast a glance at the stairs to the first floor and then the second floor and the nursery. No sign anyone had gone up. And the children weren't there. Still.

She and Raoul flattened themselves against the wall on either side of the library doorway. Malcolm flung open the door. He took a step forwards and went absolutely still.

"We need to talk," said a voice from deep within the library.

Mélanie went still herself. Because she knew that voice, though less well than Malcolm or Raoul. It belonged to a man reputed to have been dead for over three years. Malcolm's putative father, Alistair Rannoch.

CHAPTER 40

For an interval they could not have counted, they all stood completely immobile.

"I apologize for breaking in," Alistair said. "But in the circumstances, I couldn't precisely call in the conventional way. I'm rather relieved that evidently neither Gisèle nor Julien has told you the truth. At least, not unless you're all even better actors than I know you to be. I thought I could trust them both, but one can never be sure. Especially with Julien. Do you mind if we sit down?"

"By all means." Malcolm's voice was rough but even. "This is your house, after all."

"Not precisely, but that's something we can discuss." Alistair dropped into one of the Queen Anne chairs.

Malcolm lit the tapers on the mantel, the brace of candles on the library table, and two lamps.

Mélanie moved into the room. Raoul lingered by the doorway.

"Don't play coy, O'Roarke," Alistair said. "We can hardly pretend you aren't part of this family at this point." He settled back in his chair. "Pour us some whisky, Malcolm. I assume you still have the Rannoch malt. You always had the sense to appreciate it. One of the few things we agreed on."

"Quite." Malcolm moved to the decanters. "The odd thing is," he said, putting a glass in Alistair's hand, "I've always wondered about your death. I was questioning how it could have happened only today. How you could have been surprised. But it never occurred to me that the answer was that you weren't dead at all."

Alistair turned his glass in his hand and took an appreciative sip. "Death can be a convenient way to escape a situation. Supposed death, that is. As Julien should appreciate."

"Yes, there is a certain sense of a repeat about this." Malcolm sat beside Mélanie.

"Though I imagine it's not quite as happy an experience as learning the truth about Julien."

"Knowing me, can you imagine I'd think learning anyone was alive rather than dead would be an unhappy experience?"

"Really? Not even Trenchard?"

"I'd be quite satisfied if Trenchard were alive." Raoul spoke for the first time. "It would allow me to throttle him."

Alistair turned an impassive gaze on Raoul. "Amazing how much has changed since my—disappearance. So many things are out in the open that we once only alluded to. Better, perhaps." His gaze shifted to Mélanie. "I assume everyone knows about you."

"Surely you know that, sir." Mélanie kept her gaze steady on Alistair's own. "It sounds as though you have excellent sources of information."

"Perhaps." Alistair sat back in his chair and crossed his legs. "There's no reason we can't all be civilized about this. Really, Arabella was at the heart of so much of this, and what's the point in wasting time discussing a woman who after all was little more than a common—"

Malcolm was on his feet, fist drawn back, but Raoul sprang to his feet and slammed his fist into Alistair's jaw first.

"Sorry," he said to Malcolm as Alistair's chair tipped over and Alistair thudded to the carpet. "Prior claim."

"Stop it, both of you," Mélanie said. "No one is going to turn my library into a battlefield." She knelt down and extended a hand to Alistair. "Sit down, Mr. Rannoch." She gave him her handkerchief. "Hold this to your nose and lean your head forwards. That actually stops a nosebleed faster. Yes, I know it seems contradictory, but trust me, I know. I have two children. That teaches one more about nosebleeds and assorted damage than being a field agent." She looked up at Malcolm and Raoul. "Pick up, Mr. Rannoch's chair."

"I suppose you'd like us all to leave," Malcolm said, as he and Raoul righted the chair. "If you'll give us until the morning to pack up the children, it would be much appreciated."

"Don't be foolish, Malcolm." Alistair settled back in his chair, the handkerchief held to his nose. "Do I look as though I were in a position to retake my properties? That's not the goal I have in mind. Thank you, Mélanie."

Mélanie regarded her father-in-law. Her titular father-in-law. "I don't care to see anyone needlessly hurt."

"No?" Alistair looked up at her round the handkerchief. "I'd have thought otherwise."

"I was always opposed to needless violence. But my husband has certainly taught me more compassion."

"An interesting way of putting it."

Malcolm hooked a chair with his foot and dropped into it, at eye level with Alistair. "What do you want, Alistair?"

Alistair pulled the handkerchief from his face and regarded his putative son. "I think that's the first time you've called me that."

"What else am I supposed to call you? 'Sir' seems rather inappropriate now, and I won't make us both laugh with 'Father.'"

"I suppose you call him that." Alistair shot a glance at Raoul.

"Sometimes," Malcolm said in an equable voice.

"I used to wonder if you knew."

"I think I did on some level. Though I didn't acknowledge it until much later."

A drop of blood fell on the handkerchief. Alistair pressed it back to his nose. "I can understand. I didn't much want to acknowledge it either."

"For what it's worth, I'm sorry," Raoul said in a quiet voice.

Alistair stared at him over the blood-flecked handkerchief.

"Not sorry for what happened, but for what it put you through." Raoul perched on the edge of the table.

"Changed your mind now you have a wife of your own?" Alistair asked. "No, I forget you've had a wife for a couple of decades, one way and another. Changed your mind now you have a new wife?"

"It always bothered me, to a degree. But one could say time has given me more appreciation of the feelings involved. On all sides."

Alistair held Raoul's gaze for a moment, then gave a light laugh. "What have we come to, talking about personal reactions when we should be dealing in cold facts?"

"Emotions can be a fact," Raoul said.

Alistair gave a short laugh. "My God, what's happened to you?"

"I could ask you the same thing. I don't imagine you left Britain lightly."

Alistair twisted his glass, watching the play of the candlelight off the cut glass. "It has its compensations, as I'm sure all of you have discovered. But then, one does find oneself wanting to come back. As I suspect you'll all appreciate. Even you, O'Roarke, who did your best to bring the country down."

"I'll own to having a number of goals, most of which I've failed at, but bringing Britain down was never one of them."

"You underrate yourself, O'Roarke. I always thought I was the one who did that. I made the mistake at the start of thinking Arabella would tire of you, as she did of all her other lovers."

"One could make a good case that she did."

"No." Alistair's gaze fastened on Raoul's own. "Infidelity isn't the same as growing tired. I think we both know that by now, even if the younger generation don't." His gaze dragged briefly to Malcolm and Mélanie before settling back on Raoul.

"The past doesn't seem particularly important now beside the present," Raoul said. "Perhaps—"

"What do you want, Alistair?" Malcolm asked.

Alistair sat back in his chair and took a drink of whisky. "Surely that's obvious. I want the memoirs."

"You and half of London. We don't have them."

"But in all London, you're the likeliest to recover them. I've learned not to discount your abilities."

Malcolm kept his gaze steady on Alistair's face. "What on earth makes you think we'd give them to you of all people?"

"Because I've come to offer a deal. You give me the memoirs. I leave you with this house—which Mélanie has redone with, I admit, exquisite taste—and Dunmykel, which I know you love, and the rest of what one might—rather inaccurately—call your inheritance."

For a moment, Malcolm regarded his putative father in complete silence, while Mélanie and Malcolm's actual father looked on without betraying a response by so much as an obvious breath. "I realize we don't know each other well," Malcolm said at last. "But do you seriously imagine that would matter to me?"

Alistair raised a brow. "As you say, we don't know each other well. But I don't think I've failed to understand what Dunmykel means to you. And I imagine this house, at least, means a great deal to your wife. And your wife means a great deal to you. So does O'Roarke, apparently. And I don't think he wants his charming new family threatened by scandal."

"And do you seriously imagine any of that would cause me to make a deal with you?"

"You're a politician, Malcolm. A quite able one, from what I hear. We all make deals, for all sort of reasons."

"And we all have our limits. If mine weren't clear before, they should be now."

"Fair enough. But what if it were a question of protecting your wife?"

Mélanie drew in her breath but held herself immobile. She could feel Raoul's tension, but also his stillness. Malcolm's hands curved round the arms of his chair. "Mélanie has been pardoned by the regent. The king now."

"So I understand. But though I may not move in society, I understand that her past is not generally known. Nor is O'Roarke's. It would be quite a change in all your lives should they become public knowledge."

"I don't know what Malcolm will say," Mélanie said, "but for myself, I've been quite prepared to face the truth since we returned to Britain."

"As have I," Raoul said.

"You'll need to discuss it," Alistair said. "I understand. You'll be searching for the memoirs regardless. When you find them, I ask you to remember my offer."

CHAPTER 41

Mélanie stared at her husband. "Darling—"

Malcolm closed the library door. "No sense in giving him an ultimatum before we have to. This buys us some time. I'm more eager than ever to find the memoirs. To find out why the devil they matter so much to Alistair."

He paused a moment after he said the name. It hung in the air, reverberating among the three of them.

"I still can't quite believe it," Mélanie said.

"I don't think any of us can." Malcolm dropped a hand on her shoulder. "No doubt with a bit of time we'll get used to it."

"Malcolm—"

"We'll have to." Malcolm's gaze shifted to Raoul.

Mélanie squeezed Malcolm's hand and got to her feet. "I'll get clothes for all of us. We have to get back to Cordy and Harry's for the children, and we all still need clean clothes for tomorrow. Which we're going to have to face, somehow."

Malcolm caught her hand and kissed it. "Have I mentioned I love you?"

"I think the subject's come up." Mélanie looked between her husband and Raoul. She couldn't read exactly what they had to say to each other. But she knew they had to talk. And that it would not be a comfortable conversation.

MALCOLM LOOKED at his father as the door clicked shut behind Mélanie. "You knew."

"No."

"You suspected."

Raoul drew a breath. "Yes."

"For how long?"

Raoul hesitated. "I think I started wondering when we first heard about Antonio Barosa."

"Nine months ago. When you asked Hubert if Barosa could have been in disguise." Malcolm returned to his chair. He was shaking. "You were wondering then?"

"In a sense. I couldn't quite admit it to myself. And when I first considered it, it was only an impossible theory that I was sure couldn't be true. It was only recently that I faced the fact I had to investigate further. When I went away a few days ago, I went to see Dewhurst. After I talked to him, it didn't seem so odd that Alistair had faked his death. I talked to Rupert tonight. You know how he feels about his father, but what he said supports Dewhurst's claims of innocence."

Malcolm sat, every muscle armored against collapse. "Were you going to tell me?"

"I was trying to work out how. And when."

"You must have known you didn't have unlimited time."

"And obviously I waited too long. I wanted more information first."

"Christ, O'Roarke." Malcolm's voice came out raw and uneven. "I wasn't asking you to fix it, I was asking you to trust me."

"You know damn well I trust you, Malcolm. But I'm always

going to want to protect you. Can you tell me you ever won't want to protect Colin or Jessica, no matter what accomplished agents they may become?"

"That's a rather terrifying thought. And a fair point." Malcolm scraped a hand over his hair. "All right. But in all fairness—and I respect you more than almost anyone I could name—I don't see how you can protect me from this, Father. Or that I even want to be protected. Alistair is alive. We have to accept that."

"We also have to confront him."

"Obviously. Though if he wants his property back, he can just take it."

"If that was all it was, he'd have taken it long since. There's more that made him go away, and more he wants. More the League want."

"We've known we had to fight the League for years."

"But Alistair complicates it." Raoul watched him for a moment. "You know I wasn't close to my father. That I rebelled against him. And I'd say by now I consider myself more or less free of him. But if he walked back through the door, I can't deny it would shake me. And I imagine all sorts of issues and feelings I thought long settled would come welling to the fore."

"Alistair's not my father. You are."

Raoul gave a faint smile, but his gaze remained serious. "You grew up calling him father. Thinking of him as your father."

"By the time I was twelve I was fairly sure he wasn't. I think I suspected long before. Just as I think on some level, I knew you were."

"For which I'm grateful. But you know it can't be reduced to that. Anyone who occupies such a position in our lives growing up, in whose home we grow up—however absent he may have been—is going to have a certain place in our minds. Simply telling oneself he isn't one's father doesn't make that go away. Not entirely."

"He never acted like a father either. To any of us. Except maybe Gisèle. I'll be all right, O'Roarke. I'll admit Alistair used to be able to slice under my guard far better than most opponents, but I'm a better fencer than I was. And while I agree one can't simply ignore the past, he doesn't have the power over me he once did. I'm rather annoyed with myself for letting him have such power at all."

"He's still bound up in your past. Our past."

Malcolm shot a look at his father.

"He was Arabella's husband. He was the injured party in one of the most important relationships in my life. I'll admit at the time, given the state of their marriage, I didn't let it trouble me much. I've come lately to have more appreciation of what Bella meant to him. Which rather changes things."

"You're saying you feel guilty when it comes to Alistair?"

Raoul hesitated. "I don't regret what I shared with your mother. I can't imagine my life without it. Without her. She brought me an immeasurable amount of joy. And difficult as I find it to understand Arabella, I think perhaps at times I brought her a certain amount of happiness as well."

"I know damn well you did. I could see that even as a child. Even before I understood the rest of it."

Raoul gave a faint smile again. "Arabella and Alistair's relationship was in ruins before I met her. If there ever was a relationship on Bella's side. She married him because of the League."

"Sometimes it works out."

Raoul met Malcolm's gaze. "As you say. But not in their case. At the time, I thought Arabella had been simply a prize Alistair wanted to win. That he didn't care, either. But it was far more complicated than that. So I suppose, given what I shared with her—I do feel a certain amount of guilt. Not that it changes the fact that he's a formidable enemy, opposed to everything we stand for, and also a direct threat to all the people I love."

"And trying to kill you."

"Yes, I may understand his reasons better, but I can hardly be in charity with him on that score."

Malcolm frowned. "I'm not sure it does explain his reasons better. I mean"—he dug a hand into his hair—"his jealousy may be part of it. But he could have tried to have you killed anytime these past thirty years."

"He did at Dunboyne."

"But then he didn't try again, as far as we know. The first glimmering we got of it was in Italy. After Alistair disappeared. When Julien told us the League were trying to hire him to kill you."

"That was partly an attempt to draw out Julien."

"But they really were trying to have you killed. Have tried. Something shifted."

Raoul took a sip of whisky. "Are you suggesting Alistair wants me out of the way because of something I know? The same thing that made him stage his death and disappear?"

"It's one explanation. He might think Arabella told you about Marie Antoinette's diamonds."

Raoul frowned. Alistair and Dewhurst had used the diamond necklace to bring down Cardinal de Rohan and had inadvertently helped bring about the French Revolution. Arabella had used the information to blackmail Alistair into helping Raoul escape Ireland after the United Irish Uprising. "He might. But if she had, it probably would have been right after I left Ireland. Over twenty years ago. He made no effort to kill me at the time—despite having tried just before at Dunboyne."

"He might have been afraid Arabella would use the information if he did."

"Fair enough. But he didn't try after she died. And that's obviously not what made him run. At least, not unless there's more we don't know. Or he was afraid the whole thing was going to unravel."

"No. But it could be something else. Something you don't realize you know."

"God knows it wouldn't be the first time I've been unaware of something relevant."

"He's been targeting a group of enemies. You. Hubert. Glenister. Beverston. Smytheton. Glenister and Beverston and Smytheton are because he's trying to get control of the League. But you and Hubert are more complicated. I think he feels it's the key to his coming back. And it's the key to his coming back because it somehow gets rid of the reason he had to run in the first place."

"We've all done it," Raoul said. "Oh, not faked our deaths—well, except for Julien—but run. Left the country."

"And we did it because we were afraid of secrets coming out."

"In '98 it was because I feared being arrested. My actions weren't particularly secret."

"Well, Julien was afraid of being arrested. I was afraid Mel would be arrested if the truth came out. I was afraid you would be too. That's why the regent's pardon made it safe to stay. Whatever the potential repercussions, neither of you risks arrest. Unless you do something else."

"And I don't think fear of embarrassment would have made Alistair run on its own. So whatever he's running from, he must fear arrest too. Perhaps that's why he's so keen to help the king's case against the queen."

"You think he wants a pardon as well?"

"Is that so surprising? He may even have been inspired by what Fanny did for us."

"Christ." Malcolm dug a hand through his hair. "It doesn't put us any closer to understanding what he did. Though I suppose one could argue we'd be better off if he got his pardon. Presumably then he wouldn't have reason to attack you and Hubert. I wouldn't count on it, though."

"No. And it hardly changes our tactics in the queen's case.

I'm not confident this will shift the political center in Britain, but even the chance that it might is worth pursuing. More to the point—and speaking as someone who has cause to be grateful to the king—the queen has been badly used. And to rake her over the coals for her own actions, given the king's very public actions, seems the height of hypocrisy. Aside from the fact that it would have been much better if the king could have remained with Mrs. Fitzherbert."

"It's a personal battle turned into a political one."

"Marriages are political units, in a sense. To that degree, standing up for the rights of a wife is an important political statement."

"And the trial is a circus."

"That too."

Malcolm pushed himself to his feet. "Go back to Harry and Cordy's with Mel. I'll see you there. There's someone I have to speak with without delay."

CHAPTER 42

Julien opened the door of Carfax House himself. His gaze darted over Malcolm's face in the light of the candle he held. "Has Pierre taken a turn for the worse?"

"No word about Pierre. Which I assume is good. We're all all right," Malcolm stepped into the Carfax House hall and pulled the heavy door to. "How long have you and Gelly known Alistair is alive?"

The realization settled in Julien's eyes. Fear for his comrades gave way to the concern of a general who learns his secret headquarters have been discovered. "Come into the study."

Julien threw open the door, set down the candle, lit a lamp, poured a glass of whisky, and put it in Malcolm's hand. Malcolm took a drink and realized he had downed half the glass. Julien put a hand on his shoulder and pressed him into one of the two armchairs in front of the desk, poured himself a glass of whisky, and sat in the second chair. "How did you work it out? Or did someone tell you?"

"Alistair told me."

Julien's hand froze, midway to carrying his glass to his lips. "Christ. I've been telling Gelly for months it was too dangerous. But I thought we had more time. And I own I was more worried you'd tumble to it yourself."

"Yes, as usual, everyone seems to have overrated me. But Raoul worked it out. You'd think by now I'd be used to being the last to know." Malcolm took another drink of whisky. "Did you tell Gelly?"

"No, she told me. Belmont told her."

"The New Year's before last. That's why she ran from Dunmykel."

"Alistair wanted to see her. She wanted to see him and see if it was really true. She was improvising. She was terrified of your learning the truth."

"What the hell did she think would happen? That Alistair would go on playing these games indefinitely? That he'd just disappear back to wherever he'd been hiding?"

"I've been saying much the same to her. At first we were trying to learn more of his plans. But it was obvious you were going to have to know eventually."

Malcolm thought of the last time he'd seen Alistair with Gisèle, before Alistair's supposed death. He'd had to go round to the Berkeley Square house to discuss something with Alistair, and Gelly had been leaving Alistair's study, tossing a smile over her shoulder. For a moment, an answering indulgent smile had lingered on Alistair's face. "Alistair was always fonder of Gelly than of Edgar and me. But he must always have known she wasn't—"

"You, of all people, must realize one can be a parent in all ways without having sired a child. I understand that far better now than I did two years ago. I think Alistair likes to think of Gelly as his daughter. He always has. Perhaps because she reminds him of Arabella."

As often, Julien had likely shot close to the truth. "Surely he worries that she'll betray him—"

"He's not a fool, so I assume so. But I think the fact that she's seen you and that you—and O'Roarke and Mélanie and the others—fairly obviously hadn't known he was alive plays to her advantage."

"And for much of the past ten years Gelly wasn't particularly happy with me."

"Yes, she's played that to her advantage as well."

Gisèle would do that well. But—"My God, if he learns the truth—"

"You've always known the League's tumbling to her was a risk. I actually think Alistair's feelings for her protect her."

Malcolm's fingers tightened round his glass. "People who are betrayed can turn angry."

"I don't think he'd hurt her."

"*Think.*"

"She's not with the League most of the time anymore. And we're not talking about a naive civilian. This is Gelly." Julien sat back in his chair, glass cradled between his hands.

Malcolm studied his friend. "You're scared."

"Petrified. How could I not be?"

"You could go back to pretending not to care about anyone."

"I don't see how that would help." Julien took a drink of whisky.

"What does Alistair want?"

"I'm not sure." Julien's fingers tightened round his glass. "Despite Gelly's and my best efforts. But I'd say he wants to regain what he lost."

"What I have."

"Partly."

Malcolm took a drink of whisky. Perhaps the only thing he and Alistair shared a taste for. "I suppose I should appreciate the irony. What Carfax did to you, I've done to Alistair."

"Hardly the same, unless you've been blackmailing Alistair to spy for you."

"We're going to have to—"

"You don't have to do anything, Rannoch, as long as Alistair remains in hiding. There's a reason he left. And a reason he hasn't reclaimed what he'd call his. Which is at least half Arabella's."

"And what's that reason?"

Julien sank further into his chair. "We still don't know precisely."

"Edgar knew."

Julien grimaced. "Yes, he must have done."

"And Alistair knows you killed Edgar."

"We don't know that for a certainty. But yes, I suspect he does. It's one of the many reasons I've been staying out of the League's way since Edgar's death. Since I killed Edgar."

"Alistair was hard on Edgar. But he recruited him into the League. I imagine—"

"Yes. I don't expect Alistair is happy with me. But he's hardly the first or last person to be angry with me."

Malcolm frowned into his whisky glass. "Does Fanny know?"

Julien drew in and released his breath. "I'm not sure. I have no reason to think she does."

"But?"

"I can imagine Alistair's reaching out to her."

"Yes." Malcolm's fingers tightened round his glass. "So can I."

Julien got up and splashed more whisky into both their glasses. "Close as we've got to Alistair, his motives remain a mystery."

"When did you last see him?"

"Before the business with Glenister. Before Edgar. After that, my allegiance seemed too in the open even to play games. Officially I had to pull away from Gelly."

"Why did he turn on Glenister?"

"Considering we now know he seduced the man's wife and got her pregnant with an heir almost three decades ago, I think it's plain they were never the friends we thought. But I don't know. Save that he's seemed to be trying to get rid of all his enemies lately."

"Including O'Roarke. And Hubert. He's trying to make it safe for him to come home?"

"I think so."

"But O'Roarke wasn't a threat to him in the old days. Neither was Hubert that we know of."

"No. It has to do with why he ran—and no, I don't know why. Gelly and I've been doing our damnedest to discover it for most of the past two years."

Malcolm hesitated. A knife blade twisted in his chest, but he had to ask. "Did Alistair—did he ever say anything about Edgar?"

"You mean about why he went to work for the League?"

"About why he did anything."

"I didn't know he was working for the League until you did. If I had, I'd have warned you."

"Would you? Even then?"

"Among other things, if I hadn't, at some point you'd probably have told him about the League. And Gelly's role in it. Can you imagine? Think of the risk."

"Yes, that's a point." Malcolm scraped a hand over his hair. "I almost did tell Edgar about Gelly when he first came back from France. I think we were fortunate we were in the midst of the Glenister investigation. I knew I had to put everything off until we got through it."

"If it weren't for Edgar, the investigation wouldn't have been going on. At least, not the Annabel Larimer part." Julien watched him a moment. "He was your brother, Malcolm. No one can blame you for not suspecting him."

"Are you saying you wouldn't have suspected a brother if you'd had one?"

"I rather shudder to think what any brother I might have had would have been like. But I can imagine underrating a brother as an agent and at the same time trying to protect him." Julien hesitated again. "If Edgar hadn't forced my hand by trying to kill you, I'd still have been hard pressed to let him live."

"You think I wouldn't have been as well?"

"Yes, but you wouldn't have acted on it."

"I might have planted him a facer. At the very least. I still don't know how I'd have managed to meet him with equanimity."

"You would have done. You're one of the best agents I know. And perhaps the absolute best when it comes to hiding your feelings."

"Compared to O'Roarke and Mélanie and you?"

"We're all somewhat adept at it. But you're the best at taking yourself out of the equation."

"After I learned what Edgar had done to Kitty, there was no going back for us. And no going forwards. I might have managed to meet him with civility, but only because I couldn't let him see we were opponents. Anything warmer between us was over."

"But he was still the boy you grew up with. We grew up with."

"I didn't know the boy I grew up with." Malcolm tossed down a drink of whisky. "Nor did you."

"You knew part of him."

"That's what Mel tried to say. But what I thought I knew was a lie. It's not like Mel. In fact it's the opposite. Because, for all the lies, I knew her. The core of her. That's why we are where we are now."

"You're where you are now because you're a decent person, and she's the mother of your children," Julien said in a quiet voice. "You'd be where you are now with a woman you knew far less well than Mélanie."

"That depends on how you define 'where we are now.' We might be in the same circumstances, but we wouldn't have the relationship we do. No matter how we appeared on the outside. Whereas, I didn't know Edgar at all." Malcolm frowned, thinking of Edgar's quick dismissal of life's complexities, his tendency to idealize women until they fell from their imaginary pedestals. "Or I didn't give enough credence to what I did know. And I didn't see what should have been obvious."

Julien stretched his legs out. "It wasn't obvious to me either." His fingers tightened round his glass. "And I wasn't blinded by being his brother. Or by his connection to Kitty, until much later." He turned his glass in his hand. "He got angry when he was crossed, even as a young boy."

"A lot of children do. Most, at times. Certainly my two."

"And my three. But not to that degree. They pull back. Or forget what it was about. Edgar could be single-minded. I can't say I saw where it might lead, but I noticed."

"Which is more than I did."

Julien took a sip of whisky, his gaze on Malcolm. "There are things we'll probably never understand. People we'll probably never understand. I've accepted that's true of my father. It's perhaps the only thing I've accepted about him. It wouldn't stop me from throttling him either, should he walk in the door. I know enough to know I have no respect for him. Nothing would change that. But I can't say I understand him as a person." Julien frowned at his glass. "I'm not sure I *want* to understand him. But I'll admit to still puzzling over him."

"I expect I'll always be puzzling over Edgar."

"I understand. And I don't expect this to stop you. But your puzzling over him is more than Edgar deserves."

Malcolm gave a short laugh. "I don't do it for Edgar. It's more for myself. Because I need to understand."

"Yes, that's you, Malcolm. That's been clear from when you were boys too."

"Perhaps because I'm singularly slow to do so."

"On the contrary. You're far more insightful than I am. But I wonder sometimes if seeing something from another's view makes it harder to act against them."

"I'm not sure I could see things from Edgar's view. Save that I can understand it seemed unfair to him that I had—have—what in his mind should have been his inheritance."

"You also have the respect of a lot of other people. Including Alistair."

Malcolm froze in the midst of setting down his glass. "Alistair had nothing but contempt for me."

"Alistair knew your abilities. I don't think he'd have been nearly so hard on you if he hadn't done. I remember Edgar's losing his temper when you climbed the Old Tower at Dunmykel faster."

"I was more than a year older. Edgar was a much better athlete than I was, eventually."

"Even so."

Malcolm forced his fingers to unclench round his glass. Before he smashed it. "You think that was why Kitty—"

Julien's own fingers turned white. "I think what Edgar did to Kitty was pure violence and in no way your responsibility. You can't blame yourself."

"But Edgar was jealous."

"Edgar was jealous. What he did with the jealousy is on his head."

"I should have—"

"No."

"Christ, Julien. She was the woman I loved. We had a stupid quarrel, and I went off, and my brother brutalized her. At least in part, perhaps, because of me. Tell me you could ever forgive yourself for that."

"I'm not in the habit of thinking of forgiveness in terms of myself. But put like that—I have at least a glimmering of what you mean."

Malcolm ran a hand through his hair. "I haven't said that to anyone else. Not to Mel. Not to Kitty. I can't."

"No. I understand." It was said simply, the sort of platitude one offered after a confidence. And yet it had the unmistakable, bone-deep ring of truth. "I'll own I can't forgive myself for not having seen it one of the times I was in Lisbon," Julien added. "And been able to interfere somehow. Kitty would say I'm being a fool. That I can't control everything and it wasn't my responsibility."

"And yet Kitty would have much the same response if the same had happened to you."

Julien gave a faint smile. "Perhaps."

"Carfax—Hubert once talked about the games Alistair played with Edgar and me. I didn't see it that way growing up, but looking back, I suppose it's true. And Kitty's had to pay the price."

"Kitty hasn't let it define her."

"No, she's too strong for that. But there's been a price."

Julien's expression hardened. "It would be unpardonable to ask her to talk about it. I hope I've made it clear that she could if she ever wished to. But of course, I can't intrude. I wouldn't wish to. It's an intolerable feeling, though. That I couldn't do anything then. That I can't do anything now."

Malcolm drew a breath and voiced the question that had to be asked. "Do you think Alistair knows that Edgar was—" He couldn't say Leo's father. It wasn't true, not in any understanding Malcolm had of the word father. "Do think Alistair knows about Leo?"

The tautness of Julien's body told Malcolm the question had been gnawing at him just as much. "I don't know. I hope to hell not. Because I've begun to suspect lately that family—however he defines it—means a lot more to Alistair than I would have thought."

Odd how chilling it could be to realize that someone cared for family. But then, anything to do with Alistair could be chilling. "You think he'd want—an heir?"

"I don't know. But for Alistair to be anything to Leo is unthinkable. I'm not letting him anywhere near my family."

Malcolm nodded. "I'm distinctly relieved he doesn't want anything to do with Colin and Jessica. Did Alistair talk about Sandy Trenor?"

"Not about being his father. But then, he hardly made confidences to me. But given his interest in Sandy, I think we can assume that's at least one truth he knows. We already knew Trenor was at risk from the League."

Julien watched him a moment. His gaze was steady, unyielding, yet oddly soft. "You have a father who loves you, Rannoch. That's not anything to discount. Much as I've discounted it for most of my life. What's more—and don't you dare tell O'Roarke I said so—he's someone you can proud of."

"Yes." Malcolm felt some of the tension drain from his shoulders. "That protected me from Alistair when I was a boy. More than I consciously understood at the time. It means even more now. And of course, I'm an adult and Alistair doesn't have any hold on me."

Julien stretched his legs out and contemplated his toes. "I disliked my father as much as you dislike Alistair, I think. The only difference is I think he really was my biological father, little as that means. But I can't say he doesn't have any hold on me. Or that it wouldn't be challenging if he walked back in through the door."

"I never claimed Alistair's return wasn't challenging. But I should be past the emotions involved."

"That's what I meant. I don't think one ever is. And it's not a sign of weakness to admit it."

"I don't worry about seeming weak."

"You handle it much better than most of us."

"You don't *have* to worry about it. You've never seemed weak. "

Julien gave a rough laugh and swallowed the last of his whisky. "You don't know the half of it."

CHAPTER 43

$\mathcal{L}$aura looked at her husband in the small circle of light cast by the candle on the night table. She was sitting up in bed in their bedroom at Harry and Cordy's while Raoul perched on the coverlet. "I understand why you couldn't tell me."

Raoul gave a faint smile. "Do you? I seem to have an appalling number of secrets."

"Well, that's a given. As it is that we all have them. But this would have been hard for me to keep from Malcolm and Mélanie. And you needed to tell Malcolm first."

"That was my plan. I was working out how to do so. Not for the first time, Alistair stole a march on me."

Laura tilted her head back and studied her husband's face in the flickering light. "It can't be easy seeing him again. Confronting a ghost."

His gaze slid to the side. When it came to his past with Arabella, she was still an outsider. "Harder for Malcolm. But, yes. It brings up memories. Memories that seem a bit different in light of things I've learned since Alistair's supposed death.

And then there's the fact that if it weren't for Alistair, I probably wouldn't be alive today."

Laura smoothed his hair off his forehead. "In that sense, I'm inestimably grateful to him. Though perhaps more so to Arabella for blackmailing him into it."

"There is that. Though in fairness to Alistair, he stuck to his bargain."

"Malcolm won't fight him for anything. At least, not anything tangible."

"No. Which isn't to say losing Dunmykel and Berkeley Square wouldn't cost him. But Malcolm would be the first to say he doesn't believe in inherited privilege. Let alone privilege inherited from someone who isn't his father at all."

"Arabella's money helped buy Dunmykel, as I've heard it. And Arabella left her stamp upon it as much as Alistair."

"True. She's very much present there. But Malcolm wouldn't fight for it. Yet if it were simply a matter of his stepping aside and Alistair's regaining everything, Alistair would have done it. Or never have disappeared in the first place. There's more to why he disappeared, and more to what he needs from coming back, and we seem to be in the middle of it." His brows drew together.

"What?" Laura said.

"I'm used to trying to gain advantage in a shadowy game where people shift from side to side. But at least the overall objectives of both sides—or all sides—are more or less clear. In this case, we're trying to outmaneuver an enemy whose goals we don't understand. Which makes it damnably hard to predict their next move."

∾

JULIEN FACED his wife across their bedchamber. The lamplight fell over her face and warmed her skin. "Gelly told me in confidence."

"I understand," Kitty said.

"If so, you're a damned sight more understanding than I think I might be in the same circumstances."

"We always said we'd have secrets."

"This is a rather significant one. And it touches on things we share."

"It goes back to before we met. Or, at least, to before we were a couple. And you and Gisèle were working against the League before you met me. Loyalty often comes down to choices, as Raoul says."

"I didn't put loyalty to Gisèle or Arabella before loyalty to you." The words came out more quickly than he intended.

"No, but you had promises to keep to them. Too many people knowing a secret can be dangerous. If I'd known, working so closely with the others, it would have been difficult. It must have been difficult for you."

"By God, it was." He watched Kitty longer. "You're taking this very well."

"I'm trying. Mind you, I'm frustrated I didn't know. And kicking myself for not working it out." Kitty tightened the tie on her dressing gown. "How's Malcolm?"

"All in all, not quite so much of a wreck as Gelly and I've been fearing. Perhaps we should have realized that given what he's been through a little thing like a man who made his life a misery's returning from the dead wouldn't destroy him."

"Malcolm has a remarkable ability to handle—everything." She tugged at the amber silk again. "This is going to change everything."

"Yes." Julien crossed to his wife's side and took her in his arms. A fragile bulwark against an uncertain future. "It can hardly fail to do so."

"MALCOLM." Alone at last in the bedchamber they were sharing at Harry and Cordy's, Mélanie studied her husband. So many things she might say would be an intrusion. And even now she wasn't sure he'd want her to intrude.

"I'm all right, Suzette." Malcolm shrugged out of his coat and gave a bleak smile. "Funny, I haven't called you that in ages, have I? Must be remembering the days when Alistair was still alive. When we thought he was still alive." He dropped the coat on a chair. "Oh, Christ, I'm not all right. But there's no fixing it."

"It's too soon to find a way forwards."

"Someone we thought was dead is alive. That should be a cause for joy. I never wanted Alistair dead. I wasn't happy when I thought he was."

"Quite the reverse, as I recall." He'd drawn away from her in those days. Retreated into a past she'd still been struggling to understand—that she couldn't say she fully understood to this day. And into the insular world of the British beau monde to which he'd been born, however he might rebel against it, and to which she'd always be an outsider. "Of course, at that point we didn't know he'd tried to have Raoul killed. Or would try to have Raoul killed, I suppose. We didn't know about the League."

"No. Though I still can't say I'd have wished him dead. But there's no denying—"

"It was simpler when he was? There's no shame in saying it, Malcolm."

"No, and his return does present challenges. Which is really what's important. He's not my father, after all. I can say it clearly now, thank God. He's not anything to me in biology, and certainly not emotionally. We scarcely had a relationship when I was growing up. Or when I was grown. Assuming I can claim to be grown. His return shouldn't matter. Any more than the return of Trenchard or any of our other opponents would matter."

"Well, Trenchard's return would certainly complicate things."

"Fair enough. Much more than Alistair's." Malcolm came up to her and took her in his arms. "It shouldn't matter, but of course I have all sorts of feelings about Alistair, and he's Edgar's father, and Gelly may in some ways think of him as a father even though she's working against him. And he owns this house and Dunmykel and so much of what we have. That's tiresome, but we went all the way to Italy and survived. We can survive in a different part of London if we have to. It's foolish of me to dwell on feeling like a fraud."

"My darling." Mélanie slid her arms round him. "You're the furthest thing from a fraud. But I can understand your feeling that way. I own I feel a bit odd myself at the idea we've been living in his house the past three years. We made it our own. And it turns out—"

"It isn't ours at all."

Her mind shot to their bedchamber at home, the walls she had had moved to make the room bigger and the dressing room smaller, the soft gray paint she had carefully considered, the framed theatrical prints. As well, perhaps, that they weren't home tonight. "You'd think as spies we'd be used to living a life that isn't precisely ours. We can be happy somewhere else."

"Of course."

She reached up to touch his face. "Malcolm—what Alistair thinks of you doesn't matter."

"I decided that before I left Harrow."

"It's one thing to know it, another to feel it, I think. I've always hated him for what he did to you. It took me a long time to understand it." And she still wasn't sure she did.

"I was a boy. I'm not anymore. Whatever Raoul thinks. And I have people who love me. I should be reasonably immune to Alistair."

Something at the back of his eyes told her that he knew he wasn't entirely. But also that he wasn't going to share that with her. She should understand. There were still things she couldn't or wouldn't let herself share with him. She firmly believed a certain amount of personal privacy was vital in a marriage. Which didn't mean she didn't feel a small pang.

"Darling, everything you've built is still yours. Not the house, your seat in Parliament, the articles and speeches you've written, the life we've created."

"Of course. Though it looks as though we may have to find another location for the school."

She smoothed his hair. The school for children who couldn't get a good education otherwise that they were starting with Laura and Raoul, and Harry and Cordy, and Julien and Kitty meant a great deal to all of them. Most of their friends had contributed one way or another. "We can do that."

He nodded. "Haddon Park might work. I got it from Arabella. We have far more than we need."

"We have each other, that's the most important thing. Oh, dear, that sounds a dreadful cliché. But it's true."

"I shouldn't feel so—as though I've lost my equilibrium."

"For heaven's sake, darling. Even if Alistair were a distant acquaintance, this would shake us."

He dragged a hand over his face. "I suppose—as little a relationship as we had, as distant as we've always been, I can't deny that he helped shape me. By his very absence."

"Legal fathers matter in our world. And by accepting you, he took on the relationship."

"Given that he was married to Arabella, he didn't have a lot of choice about accepting me." Malcolm paused. "I understand more now about how he felt about her. At times I can almost feel sorry for him."

"So can I. It doesn't negate my other feelings."

Malcolm grimaced. "Feelings don't matter in this."

"There's a time I'd have been the first to say that, darling, but I think one ignores them at one's peril."

"I'm not saying we should ignore them, but the important thing is what we do next. We still face a threat from the League. Perhaps a greater threat now that we know Alistair is behind the faction trying to take it over."

"Trying to take over his own organization."

Malcolm frowned. "Difficult to make sense of Alistair. But I suspect what's happening with the League has to do with why he disappeared."

"And what he wants to do to come back."

CHAPTER 44

*B*everston regarded his youngest son across the study in which he had been having confrontations with his children for as long as he could remember, from nursery squabbles to school incidents to uncomfortable reports from Oxford. "I'm going to marry Nerezza," Ben said.

Beverston returned Ben's regard across the desk. "An excellent idea. I was wondering when you'd get round to it. Have you asked her yet?"

Ben blinked. "Sir?"

"Your restraint is commendable, Benedict, and I honor you for it, but it can't be comfortable for the two of you to continue as you are."

Benedict colored. "That's not—"

"Nothing to be ashamed of, lad. Though I wouldn't have wanted to discuss it with my father either."

Benedict lifted his chin. In that moment, he looked far older than seemed possible to the man who had held him as a baby. Wasn't it only yesterday he'd been going off to Eton? "I love her."

Beverston nodded. "Yes, I don't doubt you do."

Benedict frowned. "I wasn't sure you'd admit you believed in love."

"A year ago, I might not have admitted I did. A lot's changed in the past year. You've changed. I'm proud of you, lad."

Benedict blinked. "Sir?"

Christ. To have one's own child surprised one was proud. "You've shown yourself willing to take actions and make hard decisions. And as Nerezza's husband, you'll be better positioned to protect her."

Benedict scanned his father's face as though it were a draft map of uncharted terrain. "You don't mind?"

"Why should I mind?"

Benedict opened his mouth, then closed it, as though overcome at the impossibility of repeating the things his father might object to in his beloved without slandering his beloved himself.

"You love her." Beverston moved round the desk and put a hand on his son's shoulder. "I'd like you to be happy. I think you can be, with Nerezza."

Benedict met his father's gaze, at once man to man and father to son. "I know I can be."

"Then go to it." Beverston squeezed his son's shoulder and released him. "I'll settle things with your mother."

"WHAT CAN WE DO?" Harry asked.

They were gathered in Harry and Cordy's breakfast parlor, sharing the news of Alistair's return. Harry's gaze locked on Malcolm's face with none of the usual quips about being left out of the action.

"Possibly give us a place to stay." Malcolm reached for his coffee. "Though it hasn't quite come to that yet. Meanwhile, can you go to Bow Street and update Roth on Edmund Blayney? I was supposed to meet him this morning, but I should talk to Danielle Darnault. Who I'm quite sure knew Alexander Radford's identity. And to Aunt Frances." He looked at his father.

"I haven't talked to her," Raoul said.

Malcolm gave a quick nod. He was still a bit raw when it came to Raoul and Alistair. "I sent a note round to her and Archie, but I'm not sure how early they'll be up."

"How long can you stall him? Mr. Rannoch." Cordelia frowned into her coffee cup. "This is going to take a lot of getting used to."

"Tell me about it," Malcolm said. "So long as we don't have the memoirs, Alistair can't expect us to turn them over."

"That's a point," Laura said. "If—"

She broke off as the door opened and Frances and Archie came into the room.

"You're up early," Malcolm said.

"The twins have little respect for the fact that their parents have been out late." Frances scanned Malcolm's face. "How bad is it?"

"You'd best sit down," Malcolm said. "This is going to take some time."

Frances and Archie listened in silence, as they had listened to so many shocking stories in this family. Archie's face went white. So did Frances's. But not with quite the shock Malcolm would have expected. When Malcolm finished, Archie's gaze went to Frances, but Frances looked at Malcolm. "We need to talk."

Malcolm inclined his head.

⁓

FRANCES REGARDED Malcolm across Cordelia's parlor, to which they had withdrawn without the others. Not for the first time, she found herself quite unprepared for what she had to discuss with her nephew. "I've never asked you to forgive me, have I?"

"I don't see why my forgiveness should be needed. Whom you love is your own business."

"When a person I let myself love is wantonly cruel to another person I love, it rather changes the dynamic."

Malcolm leaned against a pretty satinwood table, his gaze steady on her face. "I don't know that there's any 'letting' involved when it comes to loving. One can't make oneself love someone or stop loving them. You always defended me from Alistair. Until I was thirty, I thought you cordially disliked him. Rather proving your instincts for the spy game long before you started playing it."

Frances could read the care with which her nephew was choosing his words. It would be so much easier if he was still a boy who could be comforted with a hug—a hug that would soothe them both. "Alistair came to see me at the ball last night."

Malcolm's fingers tightened almost imperceptibly on the polished wood of the table. "Yes, I rather thought he might have done. At the ball, or some time recently."

"I had to think before I could tell you."

"You're not the only one. Gelly and Julien have known for over a year. Raoul has for a few days. What everyone seems to be losing sight of is that how this affects me is the least of it. We still have someone trying to take control of the League and bring down a number of people in the process, and also inter-vene in the queen's trial and tip the balance in Parliament. We now know that person is Alistair. That doesn't change the need to stop him. Though it does make teasing out his motives more complicated." He studied Frances. "Did he ask you to do anything?"

Frances spread her hands over her lap. "He wanted my help intervening with Prinny—the king. To get him an audience. He said"—she hesitated—"he said if I could do it for Mélanie and Raoul, I could do it for him."

Malcolm folded his arms across his chest. "Did he say why he needed a pardon like you got for Mel and Raoul?"

"No." Frances's fingers tightened at the questions about Alistair's motives she had been asking herself since their meeting.

"Or offer any suggestions as to how you could secure one for him?"

"He said"—Frances's fingers scraped against the silk of her gown as she recalled Alistair's words—"that he had information that would be of great value to his majesty. I assumed he meant Danielle Darnault's memoirs."

"But Alistair doesn't have them. Not unless he's lying, and while he's fully capable of lying, I don't see why he'd have offered to trade me Dunmykel and Berkeley Square for something he already has. He could have been assuming he'd be able to get the memoirs, but it seems early to try to arrange to talk to the king about them. Unless Alistair is the one who took the part of the memoirs Brougham bought. According to Brougham, there's information in them about the queen. What did you tell Alistair?"

"That I had to think. Which was perfectly true."

"Good." Malcolm's gaze settled on her face, the gaze not of a nephew but of a spymaster. "I want you to tell him you'll help him. And find out whatever you can."

CHAPTER 45

"Humphrey—" Barbara Beverston set down her rouge brush and stared at him. "We don't even know where that young woman came from."

"Does that really matter?" Beverston asked. "You've seen how good she is for Ben."

Barbara frowned. Her green eyes were what had first drawn him to her, when he'd been scanning the year's crop of debutantes, after his parents made it clear it was time he chose a wife. "I've seen that Ben is besotted with her."

"It's lasted too long to be calf-love. Ben's shown he's in earnest." Which was something Beverston wouldn't have quite admitted to believing in until recently. "Nerezza has as well."

"You like her."

Beverston gave a wry smile. Nerezza was a number of things to him he couldn't possibly put into words with Barbara, for all there were few illusions in their marriage. But in the end, perhaps it did come down to that. He liked Nerezza. "Yes, I do. She'll be good for Ben."

Barbara's penciled brows knotted tighter. "Benedict is still very young."

"He knows what he wants. Roger did too, though you know I had my doubts at the time about that too."

"And I told you to let him have what he wanted."

"Precisely."

Barbara reached for the cup of morning chocolate on her dressing table. "Mind you, I had my own concerns. I didn't quite see what Dorinda would grow into."

"No. For that matter, I didn't see what Roger would grow into."

"Poor Humphrey." Barbara took a sip of chocolate and set the cup down. "But you can't expect your children to necessarily agree with you."

"No, I quite accept that. I always did, but more so now."

Barbara smoothed the silk of her dressing gown. The pale blue put him in mind of one she'd had when they were newly-weds. "We were both happy when John proposed to Diana," she said.

They didn't talk about John much. And there was still a great deal about him Barbara didn't know. At least not from her husband, and Beverston doubted from anyone else, though of course one could never be sure. "Diana was the perfect daughter-in-law."

"Or so it seemed."

"We were right about that. John just wasn't the perfect husband."

Barbara studied him. For a moment, Beverston had the sense that she was aware of things she didn't want to admit to. "Still, Diana was a model wife. She's a very good mother. This girl—"

"Nerezza."

"Nerezza." Barbara drew out the Italian syllables. "She's the sort a young man Ben's age dallies with. Gains experience. And then after a few years he goes on and makes a proper marriage. Like—"

"Like we did?"

Barbara gave a twisted smile. "We haven't done badly."

"I like to think not. I don't know that I've made you very happy."

Barbara paused in the midst of reaching for her chocolate again. "What on earth has marriage got to do with happiness?"

"A great deal, from Ben's point of view."

"Precisely why he's in no fit state to enter into it."

"Or precisely why he should."

Barbara clunked her cup back into its saucer. "What on earth's happened to you, Humphrey? You're sounding quite unlike yourself."

"One can still learn a few new things after fifty."

"Such as?"

"That one's children's being happy matters rather a lot."

Barbara shook her head. "Marriage is always a bit of a gamble."

"So it is. For myself, I'd say I've been more fortunate than most. I'd just like to make sure our children have enough security."

"Humphrey—" Barbara's frown gave way to a look of concern. "You aren't ill, are you?"

"No, nothing like that. Just contending with a few past reckonings. And not quite sure where that will take us." Beverston crossed to his wife's side. Closer than he often got these days. Except on occasion. "You and the children will be all right. You're well provided for. And there's no reason for any of this to touch you." He reached out and touched his fingers to her cheek.

Barbara caught his hand. "It's the League, isn't it?"

Beverston felt himself go as still as if he'd turned to ice. "What do you know about the League?"

"For heaven's sake, Humphrey. I didn't think you ever thought me a fool."

Beverston held the gaze of the woman to whom he'd been married for over three decades.

"It's a dangerous business," she said. "You needn't tell me about it, but if my wishes count for anything, I'd appreciate it if you had a care."

He squeezed her hand. "I wasn't sure it would matter to you."

"Oddly enough, I find that it does."

"Well, then." Strange how words from one's own wife could mean so much, when he'd long thought there was little more than civility between them. "That's something."

"More than something." Barbara's fingers tightened round his own. "Be careful, Humphrey."

Beverston, for the first time in perhaps a decade, lifted his wife's hand to his lips. "I will."

◊

"How long have you known?" Archie asked in a quiet voice.

Frances met her husband's gaze. The gaze of the man she had trusted and let into her heart and her life as she had no other man before. "How do you know I knew?"

"I don't, of course." Archie leaned against the same satinwood table where Malcolm had stood earlier, arms folded, legs crossed at the ankle. "I'm the first to admit one can be sure of few things. But I knew Alistair. Better than most of our group—except you, of course. I have a glimmering of what you meant to him. And he seems to want his past back. He wanted Gisèle. I suspect he wants you too."

"You can't imagine he'd have had a prayer of getting me."

"There again, I've learned not to say never. But it's not a question of what I think he might achieve, but of what he thinks. Alistair has always tended to think very highly of himself."

Frances locked her fingers together and stared down at her

wedding band. "He found me in the garden at the ball last night." She met Archie's gaze. She'd never thought to feel she was pleading with him for understanding. "He asked me to keep his secret. He asked for my help approaching Prinny."

Archie returned her gaze. His own was steady, without judgment, but also without the reassurance she found she craved. Like a child. Archie had never treated her like a child.

"We've never talked about it," Archie said. "We've always agreed the past is in the past, and it seemed an intrusion. It wasn't anything to do with us. What place Alistair occupied in your heart was your own business. I've always abhorred jealousy. At the merest whiff of it, I'd give my mistress her congé and be off like a shot. I had no interest in being with someone who didn't want to be with me. Easier to leave than to be the one left. And if one convinced the world—and oneself—that one had been growing bored, any tang of embarrassment or hurt melted away. But then, until you, I've never been in a relationship where my feelings were engaged on this level. I can't say I ever felt I had to come first with you. What we have is different from what either of us has shared with anyone else. I rather prided myself on being above the sort of jealousy that the younger set might feel. But I confess it was one thing to be comfortable with Alistair's feelings for you in the past. It's rather different to face the prospect of your choosing between us in the present."

"Archie. You can't seriously think it's a case of that."

"No? When you chose to be with me, you thought Alistair was dead."

"I can't say I ever chose to be with Alistair, precisely. I just couldn't get rid of him."

"Exactly."

"I'd never have thought of building a life with Alistair."

"But it's a bit simplistic to reduce love to that, isn't it? One doesn't just conveniently fall in love with people one could build a life with."

Frances looked into her husband's eyes, a hundred moments, declarations made and even more declarations neither of them could put into words chasing through her mind. "You've always said—" She broke off, not quite able to say it. How odd to be sitting here, swathed in pintucked silk, with a man with whom she had shared all sorts of intimacies, and feel stripped naked.

"I've always said I'd never fallen in love properly before you." Archie put out a hand and tucked a curl behind her ear. His fingers lingered against her cheek for a moment, but then he drew his hand back instead of leaning in for the kiss that usually would have followed. "And it's true, barring schoolboy infatuations not worthy of the name. So I suppose I only have your word for it that love isn't convenient."

"I can't claim to have much proper experience of love. But— no. I thought I was in love with Dacre-Hammond, and he was hopelessly unsuitable for building any sort of life with. Not because he was ineligible in any way, but because we had too little in common to forge anything but the trappings of a Mayfair marriage. Alistair—I didn't even like Alistair. If we'd tried to have any sort of sustained relationship, I suspect we'd have been a worse disaster than he and Bella were. Assuming that's possible."

"My love." Archie's gaze lingered on her face. "You and Alistair did have a sustained relationship."

"Well—yes. But not the sort one can call anything like something one would build a life on."

"Rather proving my point that they aren't the same thing."

Frances folded her arms across her chest. "I told myself so many times it had to stop. I think Alistair did too. I was rather disgusted with myself for desiring him, but I could admit to it. What it took me years to admit was that I cared about him. Which made me that much more disgusted with myself."

Archie dropped down in front of her. "I can't say I ever fell in love with a League member, but I worked with them enough to form friendships. I won't pretend to understand Alistair or to make excuses for him, but I could appreciate his keen understanding. And I'm quite sure he—cared—cares about you."

Frances glanced away. "We went away together. Before he died. Before I thought he died. I thought it was a coincidence we had that time together. Now I think he was saying goodbye."

"Yes, I imagine he was." Archie sat back on his heels. "He's Chloe's father, isn't he? And Allie's?"

Frances looked back at her husband. "I think we both know it takes more than congress between the sheets to make someone a father. But yes, in terms of pure biology, he is."

"Has he—No, I suppose that isn't any of my business."

"Has he asked about them? No, not in so many words. I've never even told him definitely that they're his." She drew a breath, rather regretting the wording. Archie was Chloe's father now in all the ways that mattered.

"Judging by what he's been doing, I rather think he may have an interest in anyone or anything he suspects is his." His gaze moved over her face, as though he was examining uncharted terrain. "You once said exclusive rights were something demanded by colonial powers, not consenting adults."

Frances felt herself color. "I told you I used to think that, which is a rather different thing. Before I met you."

Archie gave a faint smile. "Yes, I appreciated the point. It does seem one should be able to be adult enough not to cavil at a relationship that isn't exclusive. I've tried it myself a few times. It's less comfortable than it seems it should be. Or perhaps I'm simply less broadminded than I think. But I could manage to make such a relationship work, at least for a time. I couldn't now." He pushed himself to his feet. "If you want to be with Alistair, I won't try to hold you, Fanny. I understand if you need time to sort out your feelings. But I won't share you."

Frances pushed herself to her feet. "When have I implied in any way that I wanted to be with Alistair?"

Archie's hands settled on her arms. "You haven't. Perhaps it's my own fear talking. Or my sense of what he means to you. But this isn't just about you and me and Alistair. We're locked in a struggle with Alistair and the League. I know which side I'm on. But I don't know that it's fair to ask you to oppose Alistair."

"Don't you dare accuse me of letting my feelings cloud the issue."

"I wouldn't dream of it. But we all know about complicated loyalties."

Frances gripped her husband's elbows. "I do as well. But I know which side I'm on. I know who I want to be with. I chose you, Archie, and it had nothing to do with your being a safe choice I could build a life with. I love you. I can't do without you. The fact that it's quite comfortable for us to live together is a pleasant side effect."

Archie smiled for the first time in their conversation and bent to kiss her.

Frances returned his embrace and settled into his arms. They were all right. For the moment. She wasn't going to push it as far as to ask if he believed her.

MÉLANIE FINISHED FASTENING a fresh dressing to Pierre Ducroix's shoulder. "No sign of infection. You're recovering well, Monsieur Ducroix."

Pierre smiled. His gaze was clearer than it had been the previous night. "I'm indebted to you, Mrs. Rannoch. I seem to have the strength to do nothing but say thanks. And I owe thanks to a great many people."

"You need your strength to recover. Which you will."

Mélanie closed her medical supply box and smiled at Danielle, who was sitting on the opposite side of the bed.

"It's difficult to think beyond the moment," Danielle said. "But I believe Mr. Rannoch has questions for me." She looked at Malcolm, who was standing at the foot of the bed. "And I think I owe him answers."

CHAPTER 46

"I understand you didn't want to tell me the truth about Alexander Radford last night," Malcolm said, when he and Danielle had withdrawn to a small sitting room across the passage from the bedchamber Pierre occupied.

Her eyes narrowed with recognition and perhaps relief. "Julien told you."

"No. We returned home to find Alexander Radford—Alistair Rannoch—in our library."

She drew a breath that cut the still air in the room. "If I'd had any suspicion—"

"Yes, everyone's been saying that if they'd had any suspicion, they'd have told me sooner, which doesn't do away with the fact that I was going to find out at some point, and that I was quite able to handle it, and keeping it secret was foolish. However, that isn't the issue at the moment. The issue is what Alistair wants."

Danielle folded her arms across her chest. "I would like to know that myself. What did he tell you?"

"He didn't. Not precisely. He's trying to cover up a past I don't understand."

Danielle's brows drew together. "I got close to him on Carfax's orders. The former Carfax. I expect you know that by now."

"Yes."

"Alistair was plotting with the Duke of Trenchard then. A complicated scheme to make Trenchard prime minister. I was able to get some information. Though not as much as I'd have liked. I heard later that Alistair had been killed in England. I had no reason to doubt it. Until I went to Venice and met a man calling himself Alexander Radford."

"What did he tell you?"

"That he'd found it convenient to disappear. I said I understood. That if he wished to hide from the world, I had no reason to reveal him."

"Did he seem to believe you?"

"As far as I could tell. Of course, I had no thought of going to Britain at that point, and I don't think he was actively contemplating a return to it in the near future. In truth, when I wrote about him in my memoirs, I had no idea how much interest those pages might arouse. I was thinking about Pierre and jotting down everything I could think of that might help. I wasn't thinking about—wider issues at all."

"I can understand that."

"Can you, Mr. Rannoch?" She tilted her head to one side with a faint smile. "You're a generous man."

"We've all been trying to navigate a shifting world. Especially since Waterloo. Did Alistair give you any explanation for why he'd disappeared?"

"No, and it seemed safer for me not to know."

Malcolm nodded. "You wrote a chapter about Henry Brougham."

Danielle dropped into a worn petit-point chair. "I wrote chapters about a lot of people." She pleated a fold of her blue gown between her fingers. "In general, it's easy to say that people who whisper secrets across the sheets deserve what they get. But I felt qualms about Brougham."

"The chapter you wrote about him has gone missing. It's possible Alistair has it."

"Devil take it. I'm sorry."

Malcolm dragged a ladder-back chair close to Danielle and sat across from her. "He talked to you about Princess Caroline. The queen."

"He mentioned her relationship with Bergami. Some details of their living arrangements and how open they were. He was concerned about what she was risking." Danielle plucked at a loose thread in her cuff. "Princess Caroline obviously trusted Brougham. I should have given more thought to what I might be doing to another woman."

"Alistair wants all the memoirs. But he may be trying to barter that chapter to the king."

"Damn it." She snapped off the loose thread. "Having written the memoirs as insurance, I suppose I am well served if someone else tries to use them to insure his own future. I didn't think of it at the time, but I can see the value in that chapter. When I wrote them, I didn't anticipate where we are now."

"None of us did."

"If anyone can outthink Alistair Rannoch, I would imagine you can."

"I wouldn't know where to begin." Malcolm leaned back against the hard slats of the chair. "You were close to Tsar Alexander."

She raised a dark, finely arced brow. "I don't know that I'd say close. I was his mistress for a bit. Though I doubt I was the only woman he was sleeping with."

"Is he in the memoirs?"

"Yes, though I'm not sure how much interest that would hold for your colleagues in Britain. I can't claim he betrayed international secrets to me. In fact, he told me rather less of interest than Brougham did."

"James Blayney was trying to acquire information about Tsar Alexander's visit to England six years ago."

Her brows drew together. "That certainly wasn't in the memoirs. I was in Vienna then, and not too long after, I went off to have Ilia."

Which might support that Blayney's interest in the events of six years ago was driven by what he knew or suspected about Pendarves and Julien, rather than by the memoirs. Still—"Did the tsar ever say anything to you that might explain why his time in England would have interested Blayney?"

"No. That is—" She adjusted the locket she wore on a black velvet ribbon round her throat. "He told me once that Castlereagh and Metternich and Talleyrand thought they were so clever negotiating behind his back, but that they had no idea he had sources of his own. Who had been particularly helpful when he was in Britain. Which I took to mean he had at least one highly placed British agent. But he gave me no hint as to who it might be."

"Mrs. Rannoch." Edmund Blayney got up from his desk as Mélanie appeared in the doorway of his study. "Are you satisfied with Pierre's progress?"

"Very much so. There's no sign of infection, though he'll be weak for some time. He's sleeping again, and I understand little Ilia is napping as well. Mademoiselle Darnault is speaking with Malcolm. I was hoping I might have a word with you."

Edmund met her gaze. "I saw you looking at Pippa's fan last night."

"Yes. I know you're friends. You grew up together."

"My brother and I grew up with all the Langdon children."

"And Pippa came to see you last night."

Edmund's mouth twisted with acknowledgement. "I'm a journalist, not a playwright like you. I can't imagine a convincing story that would account for why she'd have paid a social call at such an hour."

"Oh, in a play it would certainly not have been a social call. One has to make choices with drama in mind."

Edmund gestured to two straight-backed chairs in a patch of sun by the window. "You'd better sit down. After last night, an explanation is the least I owe you. And on the whole, I'd rather have the chance to give you the truth. Or at least my version of it. It seems odd now, but there was a time when the differences between Pippa's world and mine didn't seem so great."

Mélanie sank into a chair, adjusting the folds of her chestnut lustring skirt. "I know a bit about those differences, having married into this world."

Edmund Blayney gave a twisted smile as he sat opposite her. "My brother never got over it. I managed not to care, much of the time. But there was no denying the difference it put between us. The things that weren't possible."

"Such as marrying Pippa Langdon."

He drew a measured breath. "Marriage was never a possibility. We met in London again after Pippa was married. It seemed harmless. Spending time together. I don't think either of us realized the danger until—I am all too well aware of how dishonorable my actions were."

"I don't believe much—if at all—in honor, but I don't know that being in love can be called dishonorable."

"It couldn't go anywhere. We should never have let it happen. I should have—"

"I'm quite sure Pippa wouldn't let you take all the blame."

He gave an unexpected grin. "No, she wouldn't. I should say I'm sorry it ever happened, but God help me, I'm not. What passed between us was ours. But that my brother ever was able to use it, that I gave him power over Pippa—or power to try to use over Pippa—"

"I imagine Captain Blayney was a challenging younger brother."

He gave a rough laugh. "I don't seem very grief stricken, do I? The truth is I don't think it's really sunk in yet that Jamie's gone." He dug a hand into his hair. "It's scarcely been a day, and I've been consumed by the practical implications and waiting for Bertrand to bring Pierre. I expect it will hit me like a gut punch, and even now I have moments when all I can do is see him as a lad. Climbing a tree without fear. Talking his way out of a beating. Shifting the blame onto me, on more than one occasion. He got by on charm from a very early age. I found it more amusing than anything, when we were young. And occasionally frustrating—not possessing a great deal of charm myself, I tended to confront the consequences of my actions head on. And as I was something of a rebel, there were consequences. Mostly I preferred to face them. Part of rebelling was being openly defiant."

"I can see that."

He sat back in his chair and regarded her for a moment. "You seem like a woman comfortable with your situation, Mrs. Rannoch."

The words shot through her. "I've learned to be. It hasn't always been easy. I've been fortunate to be able to shape my situation to my wishes, to a large degree."

He inclined his head, and for a moment she had the sense he understood a great deal more than she'd admitted. "Jamie charmed the senior Lord Pendarves. We both benefited from his kindness. Without my education, I wouldn't have the life I have now. And Oxford meant a great deal to me. I went in with ideas. I developed them. Even when I disagreed, it helped me think. It wasn't until I was out of university that I realized I had something that would make me happy with life, whereas

Jamie seemed doomed to be dissatisfied. These recent years, I've mostly seen him when he came to me for funds. I bailed him out a few times. To the extent I could. Which wasn't a great deal. In general, I did my best not to think about Shropshire."

"Until you saw Pippa?"

He gave a twisted smile. "Pippa wasn't Shropshire. Pippa was Pippa. Always has been. I can't say I ever forgot her, because I don't think I ever could, but staying away from her I managed not to think about her every waking moment. It was our rotten luck we encountered each other again."

"It's not my business and strictly speaking not relevant to the investigation, but I'm not sure Pippa would say it was rotten."

"Probably not. She has a kind heart beneath the sharp tongue, that for some reason she has always been determined not to let anyone see. But it can hardly be said to have made either of us happier."

"Do you wish it hadn't happened?"

His fingers curled round the arms of his chair. "For her sake, how could I not?"

"And for your own?"

"God help me, no. I could live on those memories for the rest of my life."

"Then perhaps it's not the ending that makes a relationship worthwhile or not. Though I don't know that your relationship with Pippa Haworth necessarily needs to have an ending."

His head shot up. For a moment she caught a spark in his gaze that might have been hope. Then his mouth curled. "You're a clever woman, Mrs. Rannoch, with a great deal of sense it seems. And a remarkable ability to see beyond the confines of our world. Your first play shows your insights into human nature. And your belief in happy endings. But, given the first, can you really see the second for Pippa and me? Can you imagine a viscount's daughter married to a newspaper publisher, living above a print shop, unable to go out in polite society?"

"I can imagine it. How well it would work would depend on Pippa. She's given me a sense she doesn't think much of polite society."

"Mrs. Rannoch, surely at this point you've seen that living in polite society and rolling one's eyes at it but still being able to go where one pleases and see one's friends and family is a world away from being exiled from it completely. From the little I've seen of your husband, he falls into the first category. But however remarkable he is, would you want to see him consigned to the second?"

"We lived in Italy for several months." It was not something she talked about easily, but it seemed important, for reasons she could not quite articulate, to make her case to Edmund Blayney. "We weren't sure we'd be able to return. Though we were comfortably situated."

"But you worried about him."

"I did. But he'd say he far preferred our isolation in Italy to the alternative."

Edmund held her gaze and nodded. "Having seen you together, I imagine he did. You share a life. What Pippa and I had was a moment's madness. It's one thing to be dissatisfied with one's life. It's quite another to throw it over for a life that's materially more challenging."

"You love her." After a few minutes' conversation with him, Mélanie had no doubt of that.

"My dear Mrs. Rannoch. I love her far too well to put her through the consequences."

"I can understand that. But surely you're far too intelligent a man not to let her decide for herself."

His gaze narrowed. "You're deadly, Mrs. Rannoch."

"Thank you."

"I'm hardly cut out to be much of a husband, even to someone not accustomed to the life Pippa is."

"Oh, well. I certainly wasn't cut out to be a wife."

"And did you find it easy?"

"On the contrary. But overall it's been worth it. It is worth it."

"Because your feelings have endured. As have your husband's."

"We've both worked to ensure that they do."

"But there are no guarantees."

"No."

"And if the feelings don't endure? And one faces the fact that one is—"

"Trapped?"

"That one's trapped the person one loves in an untenable situation."

"It's a risk. Of course, being without the person one loves can be just as untenable."

"That assumes you can be sure of love."

"Oh, love's the last thing you can be sure of. I can't claim to understand any of this, Mr. Blayney. Or to have answers or wisdom to offer. Every family is different. But I do know from my own experience that one can stumble into happiness. And that it would be foolish not to seize it with both hands."

"I knew you were a brilliant woman from your writing, Mrs. Rannoch. After a half-hour in your presence, I see that you are kind. And fortunate in your life. But perhaps before you counsel Pippa and me to seize happiness, you should ascertain if either of us is a murderer."

CHAPTER 47

Frances pushed the door of Cordy and Harry's library to. "Damn."

"Quite." Raoul got to his feet as though he'd been waiting for her. Which he probably had.

She shut her eyes for a moment and drew a breath that strained her corset laces. "I'm sorry. But there's no one else I can talk to about this as I can to you."

"Yes, that's why I'm here."

She put her hands over her face, then dragged them away. "I know which side I'm on. Archie and Malcolm don't seem entirely convinced."

"Archie and Malcolm are being cautious. Archie is perhaps wary of being hurt."

"I wouldn't hurt him."

"Not intentionally."

"Do you trust me?"

"Trust is a complicated term."

"Oh, for God's sake. Stop playing word games." She strode across the room. "And stop being a spymaster."

"I've told you before, Fanny. I'm always a spymaster."

"Well, right now, I need you to be my friend." She gripped the edge of a console table.

Raoul came up behind her and put his hands on her shoulders. "I'm sorry, Fanny. I hope I haven't forgot how to be that."

"You know damn well you haven't." She turned in his arms and clung to him for a moment. "I love Archie. I don't want to be with anyone else. I'm afraid of Alistair. I'm afraid of what he could do to Malcolm and to all of us. But when he first revealed himself to me last night—I was happy."

"I don't think anyone could blame you for that."

"I don't think Archie would understand it. Given that he just gave me permission to leave him for Alistair if I wanted to."

Raoul frowned. "When happiness is hard-won, one can fear losing it."

Frances frowned. "Surely he realizes—"

"How would you feel if the only other woman Archie had loved suddenly turned out to be alive?"

"I'd—you may have a point." Frances drew back and pushed her fingers into her hair, heedless of the pins.

"I can't say I like Alistair," Raoul said. "But at times I feel sorry for him."

Frances shot a look at him. "I didn't take him to bed out of pity."

"No. But it makes him more complex than I used to think. And I don't deny his brilliance."

"I don't think I've ever understood him."

"Well, people one doesn't understand can be endlessly fascinating. Look at me and Bella. Speaking of which, if Bella walked through the door, I'd be confused and angry at her for making us all mourn her, and, above all, overjoyed to see her. But it wouldn't for a moment make me consider leaving Laura. And not just because it would be dishonorable."

"I believe that. But do you think Laura does?"

"You'd have to ask her."

"Bella's a damnable ghost to have to confront," Frances said. "And sometimes the ghosts we can't see are harder than those we actually confront. At least, that's what I thought until I saw Archie's reaction to Alistair."

"I'LL SEE you in Berkeley Square." Malcolm kissed Mélanie's cheek in front of the *Clarion* print shop. "Odd, we haven't really been back there since so much changed." He righted his hat and set off down the street before Mélanie could respond or try to gauge his mood. He was going to see Hubert. She was going to the Tavistock Theatre to talk to Pendarves's lover, Jack Tarrington.

Mélanie watched her husband vanish down the street, then turned, when a slender figure in a gray gown and a claret-colored spencer caught her gaze across the street. She met the woman's gaze and saw her go still. Mélanie waited until a hackney and a farm cart trundled by, then crossed the street. "You could just go in and talk to him," she said.

Pippa Haworth gave a faint smile. "I confess it's not the first time I've walked by and not gone in, in recent years." Her face grew serious. "Is Edmund in trouble?"

"No. That's not why Malcolm and I are here. You'd have to ask Mr. Blayney to tell you more, but I imagine he would, if you asked. I understand you're quite close."

Pippa drew in and released her breath. "He told you."

"Perhaps we could talk." Mélanie glanced down the street. "That coffeehouse looks respectable. If you're willing to risk a bit of scandal?"

"Can you doubt it?"

The entrance of two fashionably dressed ladies drew a few raised brows in the coffeehouse, but the clientele of journalists with notebooks and clerks and tradesmen tossing down quick cups of coffee kept to themselves and did not ogle them. They found a table at the back and ordered coffee. It was Mélanie's third cup of the day and, given the amount of sleep she'd had, she suspected she'd need more.

"I've been very slow," Mélanie said. "I was quite sure the first time we spoke that you were protecting someone. I said as much to Cordy and Kitty. And it was also clear to me you were far more familiar with Edmund Blayney's work and current life than the rest of your family seemed to be. I should have put the two together long since."

Pippa tugged off her gloves. "I shouldn't have said so much about Edmund. Or perhaps I should have realized you'd tumble to it all and told you the whole then. But I was terrified of what it might mean for him. Edmund flirts enough with arrest as it is."

Mélanie set her own gloves down atop her reticule. "My husband has a great deal of sympathy for Edmund Blayney. As do I. Raoul O'Roarke—who it is no secret is Malcolm's father—counts Edmund as a friend."

"Yes. I've heard Edmund speak highly of both Mr. O'Roarke and Mr. Rannoch. None of that will protect him in an investigation. As I think you yourself would be the first to admit."

"That's true." Mélanie added milk to her coffee—oh, for a bowl of café au lait—and took a welcome sip. "One can never be sure what an investigation may uncover. But it's also true that holding information back can be just as dangerous. Because it can send investigators down pathways after things that aren't central to the investigation."

"Is that what Edmund's and my relationship is? Something that's not central to the investigation?"

Mélanie set down her cup. "You tell me."

Pippa gave a rough laugh. "Edmund was always—not the love of my life, my best friend. I told you I'd half admired Jamie when he scrambled up trees with impunity. That was true, so far as it went. But most of the time I didn't notice him because I was talking with Edmund. We read. We laughed. The truth is I'm much more of a bluestocking than I'd have let on after I made my debut."

"I'm not surprised. Cordy is too."

"Yes, that's one of the reasons we became friends. We didn't censor our conversations, whether that meant scandal or Suetonius or David Hume. Or Mary Wollstonecraft. Then Edmund went to university and didn't come back as often. I missed him terribly, though I'd have said I was missing the person I could talk to better than anyone else. Not the man I—"

"The man you love can be the person you can talk to better than anyone else. In fact, it's rather amazing when that's true."

"Yes." Pippa smiled, then frowned. "That is—I'm not sure I've ever properly understood either one." She reached for her coffee. "We kissed once, the Christmas I was seventeen. It was— rather shattering. At the time I wasn't completely sure if it was because I'd never been kissed before. Edmund apologized and said he wouldn't for the world damage our friendship. Which made me think he didn't want to be more than friends. If I'd had a scrap of sense, I'd have realized he was being honorable and thrown myself at him and insisted we elope. Or perhaps I was sensible. I'm not sure Edmund wanted to be saddled with a wife then. Or ever. In any case, I went off to London for my season, as was expected. For a supposed rebel, I've done what was expected far more than one would think. Needless to say, no man could compare. I wasn't even interested in falling in love."

"Because you already were?"

Pippa shot a look at her. "Yes, though I didn't quite admit it to myself at the time. I didn't understand love. Good God, I'm two-and-thirty and I still don't understand it. Haworth drove a dashing curricle, and could make me laugh, and seemed as though he'd give me freedom more than most. Which, in fair- ness to him, he did. I didn't have to be chaperoned—which was quite a novelty for the first year—and I presided over my own household, even if the housekeeper was a bit of a tyrant. I had a baby, and I didn't let the nursemaids tyrannize over the nursery, which was taken as quite as rebellious as climbing trees and wearing scarlet silk my first season. I read Edmund's articles whenever I could. Partly because they interested me. And partly because they were a way to be close to Edmund. And then, one day, we met—at a lecture, of all places. On abolition. He walked back through Green Park with me afterwards. We agreed to meet again in the park. It seemed unexceptionable. He was a childhood friend. We shared interests. And it *was* unexceptionable on the surface, though my thoughts were anything but. And then, not the first time we met, not the second, but the third, we crossed over a line. And I could scarcely imagine ever going back."

Pippa turned to the thick leaded-glass windows, as though the memories were too private to share. Mélanie knew the feeling. "The next weeks were the happiest and most uncomfortable in my life. I'd never been so happy as I was when we were together. But even lost in madness—and it did feel like madness, the most exhilarating madness I've ever experienced —I knew we couldn't go on. Oh, I'd have left Haworth. Without a second thought." She bit her finger. "I should miss him more now he's gone. Instead, I'm sorry he didn't have someone who loved him better. But I'd have run off with Edmund and lived shunned by society. In fact, that sounded rather heavenly. I'm not sure how it sounded to Edmund. We never talked about it. Because we both knew I wasn't going to leave my children. My child." She cupped her hands round her coffee cup. "I only had one, at that point. That was what ended it."

"Your daughter?"

"No. That is, not my first daughter. When I realized I was pregnant with the second."

Once again, she should have seen it coming and hadn't. "Did you know who the father was?"

"Yes. Haworth and I—Suffice it to say, yes." She tossed down a swallow of coffee. "Edmund said we could go away together. That he'd do whatever it took. But that he understood my decision. Because of course going away together would have meant giving up Cynthia. My first daughter."

"I understand. At least, as best I can, never having faced that situation." Not quite. Though losing her children had been one of her greatest fears before Malcolm knew the truth.

"I couldn't give up my daughter. Which meant Edmund had to give up his child. It was damnable. We both knew it. And so we separated. It was a mess and and neither of us can bear goodbyes, so we didn't say them. At least not proper ones. We simply stopped seeing each other. It felt brutal. Edmund went to France. He said he couldn't bear to stay and watch. I was miserable. I saw Jamie at the theatre. God help me, I thought, I'm already with child, what do I have to risk?"

"And perhaps it felt like a way to be close to Edmund Blayney."

"Perhaps. Though they could scarcely be more different." She rubbed her hands over her face. "It couldn't really even be called an affair. It was only a handful of times over less than a month. But of course Sophia tumbled to it. That woke me up. I hadn't given up Edmund only to lose my children in any case. I focused on what I needed to, which was making things work with my husband. Haworth—I managed to make him believe the baby was his. Or at least enough he didn't ask questions. Especially when it was a girl. I owe him rather a lot, actually for not making more of a fuss. It's one of my fonder memories of him."

"It must have been beastly," Mélanie said with genuine feeling.

"Yes. Though I have only myself to blame. Of course,

Edmund may be relieved to have escaped having to attempt to form a family."

"He hasn't asked about his daughter?"

"He made it clear he knew he couldn't think of her as his. I hadn't talked to him properly in years. Until I went to warn him last night. He—I got the feeling he didn't want me there."

Mélanie curled her fingers round the warmth of her cup. "There was a great deal going on last night. Which is only tangentially related to Jamie Blayney's murder. But having spoken to Edmund Blayney very recently, my advice would be that you should speak to him without delay."

Pippa's gaze flew to her face, with all the anxiety of a schoolgirl in the throes of first love.

"I'd be the last to claim relationships are easy," Mélanie said. "But as I told Mr. Blayney, I do believe that when happiness is possible, one should seize it."

Pippa tossed down the last of her coffee and snatched up her gloves and reticule. "I'm sorry, Mrs. Rannoch—"

"Go," Mélanie said.

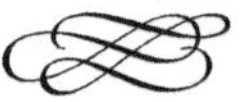

CHAPTER 48

"Good God." Hubert grabbed his spectacles, which were sliding down his nose.

Malcolm folded his arms across his chest. "You sound surprised."

Hubert pushed his spectacles back into place. "That's because I am."

"It never occurred to you?"

"Did it occur to you?"

"No. Not precisely." Malcolm dragged a chair over and sat opposite Hubert's desk. "Not at all. But I'd been questioning Alistair's death. Without quite putting together the implications. And I don't have your sources of information."

"You overrate me. And underrate yourself."

Malcolm sat back in his chair. "You've been investigating the League."

"So have you. I admit a lot of things about Alistair's death didn't add up. And given what I knew about Julien's supposed death, perhaps I should have been quicker to see it. But I wasn't."

Malcolm sat back in his chair. "So it seems I'm a fraud. Like you."

"Not precisely. Not unless you knew Alistair was alive and blackmailed him into staying away."

"An unwitting fraud, then."

"You're too astute to waste your energies on your own role, Malcolm. We have to focus on what Alistair wants. And how to stop him." Hubert tented his hands together. "You think he has some of the memoirs?"

"I think he may have the chapter about Brougham. Which probably has the most damning details about the queen. But he wants the rest. And he claims he's willing to trade me quite a bit to get them."

"I'm glad to hear you didn't go off on a moral high horse and tell him you'd never make a deal."

"I'm not quite so stupid. As long as the memoirs are missing and he wants them, we have a hold on him. Of course, if he thinks there's a chance in hell I'd give him the memoirs, he doesn't know me."

"Alistair never knew you. If he had, he'd have played his whole life differently."

"I was never more than a footnote to Alistair's life."

"Which was possibly his greatest mistake." Hubert spread his hands on the desktop. "Where do you think the memoirs are?"

"I don't know." That was true. But there were some pieces of the investigation Malcolm hadn't updated his former spymaster on. Such as Danielle Darnault and Pierre Ducroix's relationship and whereabouts. "We'll keep looking." He pushed his chair back. "Sir?"

"Yes?"

"Why do you think Alistair disappeared and is now so desperate for a pardon? What did he do?"

Hubert aligned the papers on the desk before him. "I don't know."

"Really?"

Hubert's gaze locked on Malcolm's own, opaque behind the spectacle lenses. "Really."

❦

PIPPA PAUSED OUTSIDE THE WINDOW. Edmund was in the print shop again, but slumped in a chair, head thrown back, not in the midst of producing the paper. She didn't knock this time. She stepped into the shop and closed the door behind her. Edmund's head jerked up. His gaze locked on her own.

"I'm sorry," Pippa said. "I thought we needed to talk some more after last night, and I wasn't sure you'd come to me."

Edmund's chair scraped against the floorboards as he pushed himself to his feet. "My apologies."

"Don't be silly, Edmund. When have you stood when I came into a room our entire lives?"

"Any number of times when others were present."

She took a step forwards, then paused, studying him. "That's always been our problem, hasn't it? We did fine on our own. It was being round other people that muddied things up."

He gave a wry smile. The sort one gives at a beloved memory. "Difficult to live one's life without other people."

"Of course it is. And I can't imagine you, in particular, would do so. No ignoring the world when what keeps you going is trying to change it. But I think we've both learned to cope with the world's chatter. To ignore the part that's most destructive."

"Pippa—" Edmund moved to the cabinet, pulled out the flask and glasses again, again poured two glasses of whisky. "I'm sorry, I know it's early. The house is in a bit of chaos just now. Difficult to brew tea." He seemed to take unusual care topping off each glass to the desired height. He crossed to her side and put one into her hand. "Circumstances brought us back together. Whatever Jamie was, I'm sorry for his death, and I'm sorry for the damage that's been done to others. But, God help me, I'm not sorry it brought us together." He picked up his own glass and tossed down a swallow.

"Well, then," Pippa said. "We're in agreement."

Edmund's fingers whitened round his glass. "Things ended badly between us. This gave us a chance to put some of that right. We can look back on our past without bitterness. At least, it's that way for me."

"I was never bitter," Pippa said. "Well, only towards myself. Well, perhaps a bit towards you at the beginning."

"Honest Pippin." Edmund gave a faint smile. "I'll own to my own share of bitterness. And more than a little guilt. And regret that we'd wrecked it. But now we've got the memories back."

"And I'm grateful for that. But—" Pippa swallowed, took another drink of whisky, tightened her grip on her glass. "I don't see why they have to be just memories."

Something shot through Edmund. Fear? Hope? Wariness? "Because we still live in the world, Pippin. And the world still matters. In both our lives. The investigation gave us something to share. But can you really imagine our sharing our lives?"

Her fingers tightened round her glass. "Are you saying you don't want me here?"

He drew a ragged breath. "It's complicated just now. There were reasons I needed you to leave last night. Reasons outside what's between us."

"Yes, I understand, and you needn't tell me just now. But other than that, do you not want me here?"

"*Wanting* has nothing to do with it."

Pippa glanced round the print shop and then up at the ceiling to his rooms above. Which she'd never seen. "I don't know how much room you have, but I expect we'll need more. Perhaps we can take over the flat next door. Or we could live in Brook Street and you could keep the shop here, though I quite see that would be difficult with having to get out the paper late at night. I own I don't much care for the idea of my husband's constantly slipping from my bed to go set type. And I think the girls would like to help, but taking them back and forth in the middle of the night seems complicated."

For an instant she saw a spark in his eyes that could set fire to damp wood. Then his gaze closed, as though an iron curtain had been set before a flame. "Pippa. Pippin. Love of my life. You have no idea what that means to me. But even before you were married, even before Jamie, even before my politics rendered me a social pariah—we lived in different worlds."

"Don't be silly, Edmund. If we'd lived in different worlds, we wouldn't have played together. I spent more time with you as a child than I did with my parents."

"Children can play together without really inhabiting the same world. Your father loved Jamie—but do you think he'd have let Sophia marry him?"

Pippa's breath caught in her throat. "That's different. Papa was old-fashioned."

His gaze lingered on her face like the brush of fingers that was at once a caress and a farewell. "Your father understood the world we live in. I didn't agree with him about a great many things. We'd no doubt be at odds were he still alive. But he was a good man, who loved his children. He wanted the best for you. And the best didn't include marrying Jamie. Or me."

Her insides burned, as though she'd tossed down the last of her whisky. "You can hardly claim to agree with his thoughts on that, given how you differ about the course of the world. I loved my father, but I certainly don't agree with him. About any number of things. You can't tell me you disagree with him about the world in general, but agree with him when it comes to his family?"

Edmund drew a breath that echoed across the room, like the scrape of sandpaper. "The world needs to change. But individuals don't change all at once. I know what you deserve. And I know what I can offer you."

"That seems rather presumptuous. And while I can't claim to know your circumstances, surely at this point it's at least as much a question of what I can offer you."

"Pippa, you can't think I'd take advantage—"

"And you claim to believe in equality of the sexes. Women take advantage of their husbands' circumstances all the time. Granted we don't have a lot of other options for making our way in the world. But given what you're trying to do to improve the world, I'd think you're entitled to take all the advantage you can get."

"For God's sake, I wouldn't—"

"That's quite your own affair. But I'm very well able to take care of Cynthia and Katie and myself. You wouldn't find us a burden."

"Maddening woman. That's not what I said."

"What you said was a lot of idiotish twaddle, so I'm doing my best to ignore it."

"Pippa." Edmund set down his glass. His hands closed on the edge of the table, as though he was trying to anchor himself. "I know how brave you are. I know you could make do in almost any sort of privation. I know your courage. But can you imagine I'd want to put you through the consequences of—anything permanent between us? Through losing—"

"What? Vouchers to Almack's? I find it tedious, and whatever you say, I'm quite sure Cynthia and Katie would too when they're grown. Going to Mayfair balls? I expect we'd still be invited to some, but I don't really care."

"Not even if they're hosted by—"

"My sisters? Or my sister-in-law? I don't think they'd cut us entirely, but that's their choice. One could say Sophy's wanted to be rid of me since we were in the nursery."

"You think I could live with that? Separating you from your family?"

"You think I could live without you?" The words tumbled out without thought. She gripped the edges of her chair. "I suppose that's silly. Of course, I can live without you. I've been doing it for five years. And, of course, you can live without me; you've been doing it for the same. But I don't *want* to do it. And I flatter myself that you don't want to, either."

"For God's sake, Pippa—"

She pushed herself to her feet, crossed to his side, took his face between her hands, and put her lips to his own. His mouth tasted of whisky and memories. His arms slid round her and then hardened, melding her to him. He let out a harsh breath and his fingers sank into her hair. Her hat and a hail of hairpins thudded to the floor. The sound thundered in her brain like the call of victory.

He lifted his head, wonder in his gaze. He had a shaving cut along his jaw. "Pippa—"

"Unless you don't want us," she said. "And I do mean 'us.' It wouldn't really work if you weren't prepared to be a father, or at least an uncle. I fully realize that's a great deal to take on. And of course, the girls mean everything to me because they're my daughters, but I understand it doesn't follow that they'd mean the same to you, whatever the circumstances of Katie's conception, and perhaps you don't want children—"

"Pippa." He caught her hand in his own. "Even without Katie's being my daughter, can you imagine I wouldn't love any child of yours? And I've always thought of Katie as my daughter, even when I couldn't claim her. That's the hell of it."

The floor tilted beneath her feet. "Oh. Well, then." She scanned his face. "I won't pretend it isn't quite a transition, being a parent, but it really does make life better in so many ways. At least, I think so. Oh, dear, I'm babbling. Edmund, for God's sake, stop worrying about what I'd be giving up by marrying you, and start thinking about what I'd be giving up by *not* marrying you. I'd be giving up *you*. Which I don't think I can bear, having found you again." She scanned his face. "Unless you don't want to get married? I own that would be a bit odd, but if you don't, I suppose we could live together—"

"Pippa, don't be an idiot," he said. And folded her in his arms.

CHAPTER 49

Raoul sank into a chair in Harry and Cordy's library and looked at his friend. "It's a lot to adjust to."

"For all of us." Archie's gaze fastened on Raoul's face. "We're still in the midst of an investigation. I imagine sitting in Cordy and Harry's library is the last place you want to be."

Raoul returned the gaze of the man who was possibly his best friend. Unless the distinction belonged to Fanny. "I think I'm precisely where I most need to be right now." He leaned back in his chair. "Given that I didn't realize about Fanny and Alistair, I'm not sure what insights I can lay claim to. But I've known Fanny since she was fifteen. I've seen her with you. It's not a relationship I've seen her have with anyone else."

"No, I'm sensible enough to know that." Archie stared at the tip of his walking stick. "That doesn't necessarily answer the question of what she wants."

"You can't seriously think Fanny would leave you."

"No. This may sound odd given her first marriage, but she takes her promises seriously. At least, certain promises.."

"One can love more than one person. I've never doubted that. It does change a bit, though, when the two people are there at the same time. Or perhaps it makes it clearer." Raoul hesitated. There were some things he didn't speak about to anyone. But then, Archie was a friend like few others he had. No others he had, in point of fact. "Laura and Mélanie are quite good friends."

Archie returned his gaze. They'd talked about a lot, but never talked about this. Not in so many words. "Laura and Mélanie were friends before Laura was your lover. And I think Laura knows what Mélanie is to you. And what she isn't."

"Granted. But I don't think Alistair means what he used to to Frances."

"I suppose we'll find out, one way and another." Archie turned his walking stick in his hand. "I never thought of myself as the jealous sort. But then, I never had much cause for jealousy."

"Nor did I, but I've certainly been capable of it. When I was with Bella and knew we hadn't made promises to each other. I confess to feeling a twinge when I learned about her affair with Carfax—Hubert. I felt a twinge with Margaret and Desmond, even though our marriage was effectively over and a part of me was relieved." He'd even felt a twinge with his own son over Mélanie, though he wasn't going to say so, even to Archie. "I felt a twinge with Laura's William Cuthbertson."

"I remember your watching him dance with her. But I don't think he's been Laura's Colonel Cuthbertson for some time."

"So I know, on some level. It doesn't make the twinges go away." Raoul shot a look at Archie. "Even long after Arabella died, when I briefly thought you'd been her lover. Which I wouldn't have blamed you for."

Archie's gaze shot up. "I wouldn't—"

"You'd have been well within your rights. I had no claim on Bella."

"Our friendship gives you a claim on me."

Raoul met his friend's gaze. "Thank you."

Archie inclined his head, eyes steady on Raoul's own. After a moment he said, "What do you think Alistair wants?"

"You know him better than I do. You worked with him. You even had the illusion of being friends."

Archie frowned. "I can't claim to have known him. Even in my very early days in the League, when I was amusing myself and didn't quite know what I was into. I knew enough to know we didn't have much in common. I thought he was a bit of a poseur. I tried to get to know him better after I went to work with Arabella against the League. But for all he was at the center of a large organization given to excess and indulgence, he was a difficult man to get close to. I always thought he was jealous of Glenister. Long before we knew he'd seduced Lady Glenister to win a bet. He was cleverer than Glenister, but Glenister had the title. And the fortune, in those early days. And I always thought Alistair was jealous of you. More than either you or Bella realized. I'm sure he was jealous of Hubert when he learned the truth."

"You think that's why he's moving against Glenister and Hubert and me now?"

"I think it's part of why he was trying to bring you down at Dunboyne. It may be part of what's going on now, but there has to be more to it. The reason he's disappeared. The reason he wants a pardon. And he's after Smytheton as well. I don't think Alistair was ever jealous of him."

"No, but Smytheton was involved in Alistair's getting me out of Ireland. I keep going over that, but I can't think of what Alistair could be afraid would be revealed about it now."

"Alistair loved Arabella. Assuming one can say he's capable of love."

"There are different types of love."

"Quite." Alistair twisted his walking stick again. "But I think he loved Fanny, too."

Raoul looked sideways at Archie. "Yes, so do I."

"Do you think he wants her back now?" Archie asked, gaze on the walking stick.

"I'm not sure about that. But I don't think Fanny wants to go back to him. I don't think Fanny ever was *with* him, precisely."

"I remember the duel Alistair fought with Harleton. Harleton was the one who challenged Alistair over Fanny. Alistair claimed to be amused over the whole thing. As though Harleton was behaving like a schoolboy to care. But I caught him looking at Harleton once, not long after, when we were all drinking port at White's. And I'd say Alistair felt more than a twinge of jealousy." Archie was silent for a moment. "She kept it secret. Seeing him."

"Only for a few hours."

"We drove home in those hours. Looked in on the children. Got into the same bed. Woke and breakfasted with the children. I knew something was bothering her, but I never dreamt—"

Raoul watched his friend. "You've kept things from her."

"So I have. It's a given we keep things from our spouses, as we all say. But—"

"None of them has involved a former lover."

"No. And of course, she had a right to keep it to herself, to try to sort through what it meant. She owed Malcolm an explanation before she owed me one. But I can't help wishing—that she'd wanted to tell me."

"She probably would have, eventually."

"And the damnable thing is now I'll never know."

MALCOLM STEPPED over the threshold in Berkeley Square. Beneath the familiar fanlight, onto the familiar checkerboard marble tiles, the staircase his children slid down in view across the hall. Odd to feel like an interloper in one's own home. But then, it wasn't really his home. It never had been.

"Is Mrs. Rannoch back yet?" he asked Valentin.

"Not yet, sir. Mrs. O'Roarke is upstairs with the children. But you have a visitor waiting in the library. Mr. Benedict Smythe. He's most anxious to speak with you."

Ben stood by the library table, hands clasped behind his back. "Nerezza and I are betrothed."

"Congratulations." Malcolm clapped him on the shoulder. "That's wonderful news." And particularly welcome today.

"We have Father's blessing too. Which I didn't need and didn't expect. I was prepared to go forwards without it. But I have to say I'm glad to have it."

"Your father can be surprising."

"But you don't look surprised."

"He said something to me about it. I'm never quite sure of anything your father says, but he convinced me he wanted the two of you to be happy."

"He said he'll talk to Mama. I'm hoping she'll come round as well."

"I imagine she will."

Ben nodded. His face was suffused with wonder, but also uncertainty. "It's all I've wanted since I met Nerezza. I was afraid she wouldn't agree, for all sorts of reasons. I still can't quite believe it's real."

"Not surprising." Malcolm hesitated. Ben was looking at him as though expecting him to have some sort of advice. He struggled to come up with something that wasn't a platitude. "Marriage takes work. And I'd be lying if I said there weren't challenges. But I think you have every chance of being very happy. You've already proved how devoted you both are."

"Thanks." A grin broke across Ben's face. "I know I can't be happy without her, and I hope I can make her happy."

"I don't know that one person can ever make another happy. That's something we have to find for ourselves. But the right partner can certainly help. It's quite clear you're both happier together."

"I hope so." Ben shifted his weight from one foot to the other. "See here, Rannoch. I'm not—That is, Nerezza's the first woman I've loved."

"Not surprising, at your age."

"Yes, but I haven't—" Ben glanced to the side. "I mean, I never liked the idea of dalliance. Not really fair to the girl involved. And I didn't want—well, I did want to, of course, at times, but it also seemed so cheap. So I haven't—I can't say I'm experienced. I'm not experienced. Not in the least."

For a moment, Malcolm was thrown back to himself at much Ben's age, his mind at war with the confusing impulses of his body. "You're to be commended for your restraint. You certainly have a lot of time to explore such things."

"Yes, but Nerezza—I wouldn't say these things, but I know you won't judge her. I know you know that one shouldn't judge anyone, man or woman. She's—she's more experienced than I am. I expect you're not surprised."

"Not entirely," Malcolm said.

Ben stared down at his hands on the brown-veined marble of the table. "I told her it didn't matter. And it doesn't, not in the least. It's in the past, and what I care about is our future. But it does mean—when we—when we're together as husband and wife—Nerezza will know a great deal more than I do."

"Not necessarily a bad thing. I mean, for one of you to be more experienced than the other."

Ben frowned, as though he'd translated a difficult passage and wasn't sure he'd got it right.

Malcolm drew a breath, sifting through his own past—and Mélanie's—unsure of how much to share. "That is, there's a great deal to be said for discovery, but sometimes it's easier if one of the explorers has—trod the path before, so to speak."

Ben colored, but his gaze still showed a concentration that went beyond embarrassment. "Yes, but—"

"Usually it's the man? True, at least based on assumptions. But there's no particular reason it should be."

"But—" Ben hesitated, shifted his weight from one foot to the other. "I want to make Nerezza happy."

Fears from his own past shot through Malcolm's head. Standing in his sitting room in Lisbon on his wedding night, wondering if he should knock on his wife's door. Qualms and questions he still sometimes had. "My dear fellow, Nerezza is madly in love with you. I can't imagine anything that happens on your wedding night changing that."

Ben flushed. "I'm afraid it won't be what she'll expect. I haven't precisely told her—"

"Perhaps you should."

Ben's gaze jerked to Malcolm's face, wide with horror. "Good God."

"I admit I'm not sure I'd have been able to do so myself." Malcolm hesitated again, the past welling up in his throat. "I understand your qualms. I wasn't very experienced on my own wedding night."

Ben's gaze went wide with embarrassment, but also with relief. "But you weren't—that is, you had—"

"Yes. A bit." Leaving aside that he had been without experience with Kitty, and that hadn't gone badly—at least, not the part in bed.

Ben nodded, gaze on his hands. "I'm afraid I won't know what to do."

"I think you'll find it comes naturally."

Ben's gaze shot to his face. "You're very comfortable talking about it."

"Oh, I wasn't for years. Not at all. I'm still not."

"A lot of fellows are. I remember boys at Eton who already had women in the village."

"A lot of fellows are comfortable boasting about their exploits. Or what they claim are their exploits. That's not at all the same thing."

"Do you think so? I never thought of it that way. I've never really talked to anyone—that is, I couldn't to my father. I thought about talking to Roger, but even that—"

"Different with one's family." Malcolm drew another breath. He was going to have to get used to this. Colin would have questions in another fifteen years. Or ten. "I can't claim to a great deal of knowledge. But don't be afraid to ask me questions. If nothing else, you may find my lack of knowledge reassuring."

Ben gave a shy grin. "You're very kind."

"My dear fellow. You may find it comforting to talk with someone who's as uncertain as you."

"You're going off to investigate again, aren't you?" Leo reached across the Carfax House breakfast table for another piece of toast. They were gathered for a late morning repast.

"I'm afraid so," Julien said. "But we'll have dinner with you tonight, one way or another."

"Can we all go the Rannochs'?" Timothy asked.

Kitty met Julien's gaze across the table. "Possibly. The Rannochs are even busier than we are. But we'll probably be there later today."

Leo and Timothy nodded. Investigations and missions were part of ordinary life in their experience. What they couldn't know was how much even the unconventional framework of their lives had been shaken the previous night. Julien was still coming to terms with it himself.

Kitty wiped Genny's face. She was feeding herself porridge and had managed to get most of it in her mouth. Julien refilled

Genny's milk cup. He was watching her take a careful sip when Cam, the second footman, came into the room.

"Lord Pendarves has called, my lord. He's in the library."

Julien pushed back his chair. "Papers for me to look at. It shouldn't be long."

But when he went into the library, Pen greeted him with a white face. "I went to get my notes from six years ago to bring you. But they're gone."

CHAPTER 50

Malcolm saw Ben from the house himself. He was halfway up the stairs to see Laura and the children when he heard someone at the door. He ran back down the stairs and waved to Valentin that he'd get the door. He opened it to find Lord Molyneux on the steps. "I'm sorry," Molyneux said. "I imagine you're in the midst of a lot."

Malcolm bit back a laugh at how very true that was. "Not so much that I can't talk. Come in. We don't stand on ceremony, as you see."

"Thank you." Molyneux's tone was level and matter-of-fact, the tone he would use to ask if they could discuss strategy over a bill. But in his contained face, his gaze was that of a man stepping over a precipice.

He sat opposite Malcolm on one of the Queen Anne chairs in the library, but hesitated, hands on his legs. "I don't quite know where to begin."

Malcolm had no wish to betray Phoebe Molyneux's confidence unless it was absolutely necessary, but he needed to persuade Molyneux to talk, and, like Pendarves, Molyneux was not the sort who would speak of personal matters easily. "I assume this is about the Blayney investigation."

Molyneux inclined his head.

Malcolm leaned back in his chair. "We already know your wife grew up with Captain Blayney."

Molyneux's mouth tightened. "Blayney was in the Peninsula by the time I married Phoebe. I don't believe I even heard of him until we were at Drury Lane two years into our marriage and I noticed my wife staring at a man who had come into a box across from us. In a way I'd never seen Phoebe look at anyone before." For a moment, in the gaze of this settled, sober politician, Malcolm saw a flash of the desperate longing of Kit Montagu or Benedict Smythe or Sandy Trenor in the throes of first serious love. Molyneux swallowed as though his throat hurt. "One doesn't ask such questions, but from when we first met, Phoebe made it clear that she had no interest in romantic overtures. I could not but suspect that meant some unhappy past love. When I saw her looking at Captain Blayney, I was quite sure that was the case, and that Blayney was the man in question. But of course, I couldn't ask. Later, Blayney came up to us in the grand salon. Phoebe introduced him as a childhood friend. We spoke briefly. My attention was claimed by an acquaintance. I noted Phoebe and Blayney speaking longer, but of course I could not ask her about it either."

Some husbands wouldn't have hesitated. But Molyneux appeared at once too restrained and too sensitive to intrude on his wife's history. And perhaps also to express his own feelings to his wife.

"We saw Blayney a few times, at various events," Molyneux continued. "I greeted him as an acquaintance. I saw Pendarves and Prescott and Sophia and Pippa do the same. It would have felt like a violation of my wife's privacy to ask questions of her family about a friend. I don't know how much Phoebe spoke with him. I didn't have a meaningful conversation with him until some seven days since. When he called on us. At a time when I believe he could have known Phoebe would be from home. He—made some rather extraordinary claims about my wife."

"And asked you to ensure his silence?" Malcolm said.

Molyneux leaned forwards, brows knotted. "He wanted to know if I knew anything about Pendarves's work with the Russians six years ago."

"You were in London then." Malcolm could remember Molyneux at events during the Allied sovereigns' visit to Britain.

"Of course. Difficult to avoid it. I remember Phoebe's saying she hadn't seen her sisters and brother so many nights running since they'd left home. Balls, receptions, Ascot. We even all tramped down to Oxford for the tsar and the others to get honorary degrees." Molyneux grimaced. "Prescott drank too much, and I found him being sick in the Prussian delegation's retiring room. Reliving his undergraduate days. But I was hardly going to share details with Blayney, who was clearly looking for more gossip. You're a husband, Rannoch. And the father of a daughter. You must understand my feelings towards a man who had behaved so towards a young girl who was little more than a child. Let alone towards the woman I—towards my wife. I am not a man of violence, but it was all I could do to avoid planting the man a facer."

"It would be distressing for your wife, should the events be brought up, but they are in the past, and she is comfortably married now—"

"It's far more than that, Rannoch." Molyneux drew a hard breath. "Blayney threatened to claim that my eldest son isn't mine. That he fathered Freddy."

"That must have been horrible to hear."

"It—" Molyneux's hands curled inwards. "Yes."

"Did you believe him?"

"Not at first. I said I was hard put to avoid planting him a facer. At that, I did. I knocked him to the hearth rug. It was very satisfying, but not particularly helpful. He was undeterred. And I—it is difficult not to wonder."

"Did you ask your wife?"

"Good God, Rannoch. It's not something we could discuss."

"Not even after you knew about her past with Blayney? You could say you needed to know the truth to protect her." Malcolm had once said something similar to Raoul about Mélanie.

"It would—it would seem to violate what is between us. And, in a sense, it doesn't matter. My son is my son, whatever the circumstances of his conception."

"I honor you for that."

"And slander about his birth could hurt him and his mother and his brother, whether true or a fiction. I don't want my son to grow up doubting that he's the rightful Lord Molyneux. I don't want my younger son to feel that his brother's title should rightfully be his."

Malcolm thought of his own brother. "I completely understand. But the need to protect your children is perhaps something for you to discuss with your wife. Even if you don't wish to ask her for the truth."

"How the devil am I supposed to do one without doing the other?" Molyneux sat back in his chair. "Your pardon, Rannoch. You evidently speak much more freely with your wife than I do with mine."

"It's not my business to ask," Malcolm said. "And not directly relevant to the investigation. But does your wife know how you feel about her?"

Molyneux drew a hard breath. "Phoebe's my wife. She knows the respect and affection I have for her."

Malcolm studied the emotion behind Molyneux's carefully contained expression. Like a dam that can't quite contain the raging water behind it. "But does she know you're in love with her?"

Molyneux's gave shot to Malcolm's face, then away. "You seem to be blessed with a happy marriage, Rannoch. Phoebe made it clear to me from the start that she had no interest in romantic overtures from me. I married perhaps later than I should have done. I should perhaps have married a woman closer to my own age. I arguably should not have married a woman for whom my own feelings could generously be described as 'foolish.' But having made the mistake of doing so, I can at least attempt not to embarrass us both with a public display."

"Your wife's response might surprise you."

Molyneux gave a twisted smile. "You're a kind man, Rannoch, and that's an agreeable fairy tale. I still remember the first time I saw Phoebe. On the terrace of her parents' house. She was wearing a white frock with a green sash, and her hair was coming loose from its pins because she'd just run up from the garden. I was—it sounds absurd for a man with my lack of romance to use the word 'bewitched,' but that's how it felt. I should have left it there and contented myself with the memory."

"I have a friend who would have once said much the same. He and his wife are now madly in love. To use a phrase I generally avoid. Perhaps more relevantly, they're happy."

Molyneux gave another twisted smile. "Fairy tales do happen, though I wouldn't have taken you for a man who believes in them. But just because fairy tales can happen doesn't mean they invariably do. In fact, I think we can at least acknowledge that they're the exception."

"But as men who strive for change, I think we can both acknowledge that the possibility of the exception is what keeps us going."

Molyneux gave an unexpected, if rather bleak, laugh. "Given

your politics, I should have known you were a romantic, Rannoch."

"So my wife claims. I claim any tendency to believe in fairy tales in the family is on her side. At least, when it comes to the adults. But I have learned one can be a fool not to reach for the possibility of happiness."

"I could agree with that. But that assumes it is possible. I'm not sure Phoebe's been happy since I married her. I understand the reasons better now I know about Blayney. I'd like her to be happy. But I'm quite sure if she can find that happiness, it will be despite being married to me, rather than because of it."

Molyneux stared out the window for a moment. "You've been through Blayney's papers. Did he leave anything about Phoebe?"

"Not that we've found. But his papers had been searched before we got there. We have reason to believe Blayney was engaged in an elaborate blackmail scheme. And that someone else has taken it up since his death. There's no reason to be sure your wife's past is part of it. But you should be prepared."

Molyneux gave the contained nod of a commander accepting news of suspect enemy troop movement. "I appreciated your arguments for your anti–capital punishment bill, Rannoch. I see myself as a man of peace. I didn't kill Blayney. But if he walked into the room now, I'd be lying if I claimed I wouldn't want to murder him."

❧

"Mrs. Rannoch." Jack Tarrington looked up with a quick smile, his auburn hair falling over his forehead. Was the flash of calculation in his gaze her imagination?

She returned the smile and dropped down on the worn green-room sofa beside him. "I thought everyone in the company called me Mélanie by now."

"But I haven't been in one of your plays yet." Jack grinned. "I know there's a lot happening in society just now. And you're busy with an investigation. I hope it isn't impossibly selfish to say I hope that isn't delaying the next play too much."

"I don't think a writer can ever be asked for her next work too often."

"May I get you some tea?"

"Yes, thanks." Nothing like tea to put the conversation on a comfortable footing. At least in England. In Italy it was wine. Not for the first time in the past few hours, Mélanie wondered if it wouldn't have been better for one of the men to undertake this. But she could speak to Jack as a fellow company member. And as an outsider, to a degree, at least. Even if she couldn't share the full truth.

She took a sip of the strong, pungent, slightly bitter tea they brewed at the Tavistock. "I'm counting on you in the play. But it's actually the investigation that brought me here."

Jack's fingers froze on the chipped handle of his cup. "I haven't followed it closely, but it seems very far from the Tavistock. Unlike the last one."

"Yes, so we thought. But James Blayney, the unfortunate man who was killed, grew up on the Pendarves estate. And I understand you are friends with the current Lord Pendarves."

Jack took a drink of tea, fingers not shaking. He was a superb actor. "Yes, Pendarves has paid visits to the green room from time to time and we've spoken. I thought he was a bit stuffy at first, but he's got some good ideas and we're closer on some matters of reform than one would think. We've also had more than one argument, but he's good natured about it, I'll give him that."

"I know a bit about how challenging it can be," Mélanie said.

"What?"

"Having political differences with the person one loves."

Jack stared at her. "Mrs. Rannoch—"

"Mélanie. And Lord Pendarves already told Julien. Lord Carfax. We have no desire to tell anyone else. But I need to know about your recent quarrel with James Blayney."

He glanced away. "Damnation."

"The more quickly we can discover the truth, the safer Lord Pendarves will be."

"That rather depends on what the truth is, Mrs. Rannoch. Mélanie."

"Fair enough."

"And so by not talking, I make it look as though I have more to hide? Until that night I only knew Blayney vaguely as a face in the green room. Until he appeared in my dressing room with the most damnable threats."

"Did he ask for money?"

"No. And I've heard the talk that he'd been trying to sell an opera singer's memoirs. But he didn't try to sell me papers. He wanted me to get papers for him."

"Papers belonging to Lord Pendarves?"

"Some notes from six years ago, when the Russian royals were here. He was afraid Pen would refuse to hand them over. He said if I could get them, he'd leave us alone."

"And so you took them?"

The gaze Jack turned to her was slashed raw. "It wasn't my ruin I was afraid of. It was Pen's."

CHAPTER 51

*P*ippa came into Cordelia's sitting room with her usual direct smile. "I'm amazed to see you up and dressed after giving a ball last night. And I'm sure you have a dozen things to do."

"That's precisely why I'm up and dressed. Giving a ball is the least of it. I never sleep much during an investigation." Cordelia met her friend's gaze and echoed the smile. "You look well." In fact, she hadn't seen Pippa's gaze so bright since their first season. Maybe not even then.

"I've been to see Edmund Blayney." Pippa hesitated. Then her smile deepened. "We're betrothed."

"That's wonderful," Cordelia said with genuine enthusiasm. "I know you've known him for a long time."

"Far better than I've admitted to you." Pipped gripped her hands together. "We should talk."

They moved to the settee by the windows, and Pippa told Cordy about her history with Edmund Blayney. Without elaboration but also, seemingly, without holding a great deal back. "I should have told you the whole thing when you first told me

Jamie had been killed, but I wasn't sure then how it would play out. Which doesn't make me seem like a very good person."

"It makes you seem prudent. It's difficult to think clearly in such a situation. And you were protecting the man you loved."

Pippa tilted her head to one side, her gaze clear and candid. "I told Mrs. Rannoch you must despise me. I think that must be doubly true now, Cordy."

"What on earth makes you think that?"

"For following a path I'm very sure you regret yourself."

"That would be presumptuous of me, to say the least. Your case is very different from mine."

"I betrayed my husband with a man I'd loved before I married."

"Well, among other things, you didn't run off with him and create a flagrant scandal."

Pippa glanced to the side. "It might have been more honest if I had done."

"I didn't have children at the time. But aside from that, George was—is"—sometimes it still caught Cordelia by surprise that her former lover was still very much alive and could at some point come back to disrupt their lives—"a very different man from Edmund."

"Do you think that justifies betraying a husband? The quality of the lover involved?"

"I think that's part of it. As well as the quality of the husband. Harry didn't deserve what I did to him. But Harry himself says he wouldn't have wanted to stay with me if I didn't love him. My mistake—at least, my worst mistake among many—was loving the wrong man. I can't presume to know, but from what I have learned, I suspect you may not have done that."

"Wrong?" Pippa gripped her elbows, her nails digging into the sleeves of her claret-colored spencer. "We hurt each other. Because we both knew we were never going to be happy with a relationship built on a lie. So you could say everything about Edmund's and my relationship was wrong."

"Except how you felt about each other."

"There is that." Pippa glanced to the side, gaze fixed out the window. "I wouldn't not have what we shared for anything. My husband never knew. At least, I don't think he did. And I don't know that he'd have cared much. Except, perhaps, injured pride. Which can do a lot of damage. Prescott was upset about Sophia, though he's hardly been the most faithful husband himself. I saw him with a new mistress just this morning. At least, I assume she was a mistress. A trim little blonde with a curvy figure. She looked more like a lady's maid than a Mayfair lady, though one can't always tell. She was holding his arm in a way that implied they knew each other well, and they went into a coffeehouse, which most ladies he might have been walking with wouldn't do." She drew a breath. "I used to meet Jamie at a coffeehouse. But I wore a veil and went in a side door. God, that sounds sordid."

"Love affairs have to be secret by nature. The places I met George—" Cordelia gripped her hands together, though it was a relief in an odd way to talk about George.

"I don't think I was the only woman Jamie brought to this coffeehouse. They seemed to know him well. There was a room there that was practically his. In fact, I caught sight of him near there about a week since, crossing the street. At least, I think it was Jamie. I was too far away to be sure, and I had no desire to speak to him."

Cordelia's mind leapt from George to the present. "Where's the coffeehouse?"

"Near Charing Cross. Why?"

"We need to go to Berkeley Square."

~

"PEN'S NOTES from 1814 were stolen." Julien slammed his hat and gloves down on the library table with unusual force. He might be capable of lethal violence, but he rarely made a move that wasn't contained.

"Does he know when?" Malcolm asked.

"The last time he saw them was just after Blayney tried to blackmail him into giving them up. So it could be any time in the past week." Julien strode to the fireplace. "I should have gone to get them last night. I almost did. But then I got the reports about Danielle."

"It was more important that you followed her," Malcolm said.

"Not really. Not that I'm not glad to have been there, but you and Mélanie had it in hand."

"The papers might have been gone already."

"Maybe. Probably." Julien scraped a hand over his hair, also a rare gesture. "You're right, it's unlikely they were taken in the few hours in between. Still." He took a turn about the hearth rug.

"Stop prowling about, Julien." Kitty came into the room. She had taken their children up to Laura and the rest of the children. "It won't solve anything."

Julien turned to his wife with a rueful smile. "Caught. I just don't like being a fool."

"Even if you'd somehow tumbled to the importance of these papers from 1814 the night of the murder, they'd likely already have been gone." She set her gloves and reticule on the library table with a control that was in marked contrast to Julien. "Mind you, I'd be a bit more sanguine if we knew precisely why Blayney wanted those papers, and what they might have to do with you."

"Danielle Darnault says Tsar Alexander told her he had a highly placed British agent who was helpful during his visit to Britain," Malcolm said. "Which isn't necessarily surprising. But I wonder if this agent was the source of the information Pendarves thought Julien betrayed."

Julien frowned. "And that's why Blayney was so interested in Pen's notes from the Russian visit in 1814? Because he thought they'd reveal who this agent is?"

"It would explain Blayney's interest."

"Without his necessarily having any suspicions about Julien and Lord Pendarves," Kitty said. "I must say I find that thought rather comforting. Assuming the word comforting can be applied to anything in the past two days."

"Pen says a draft of a letter from Castlereagh to Metternich went missing during the tsar's visit," Julien said. "He thought I might have taken it, which I didn't."

"I remember," Malcolm said. "There was a lot of concern, but it never surfaced."

"If this agent showed it to Tsar Alexander, Alexander wouldn't have said anything. That would have exposed his agent and ended his flow of information."

"No," Malcolm agreed. "But it would have contributed to the frosty relations between Britian and Russia."

"It doesn't explain who has the papers now," Julien said.

"I strongly suspect Alistair—or Alistair's agents—took Brougham's chapter of the memoirs," Malcolm said. "It's possible he's behind the theft of Pendarves's notes as well."

"So Alistair Rannoch is interested in this Russian agent from six years ago?" Kitty moved to one of the Queen Anne chairs, dropped into it, and pulled Julien down beside her.

"Assuming Alistair had wind that someone highly placed in Britain was spying for the Russians, I have no doubt he'd be interested," Malcolm said. "It's just the sort of thing he likes to make use of. Of course, it's possible the agent was a League member, and Alistair wants the papers to cover up his colleague's complicity. No end of options with the League."

"I keep feeling we're missing something." Julien draped an

arm round Kitty, brows knotted together. "I should talk to Pen again. If—"

He broke off as the door opened to admit Harry and Roth.

"We were going to have a pint," Harry said. "Then we thought we'd get a jug and bring it back here. I thought everyone could do with it." He held up a jug of stout. His gaze went to Malcolm, not for long, but Malcolm sensed how concerned his friend was about him.

"As always, your instincts are superb." Malcolm went to the drinks trolly. Rather than go to the kitchen or ring for Valentin, he poured the stout into whisky glasses.

"Brougham's kitchen maid reports a flour delivery they weren't expecting three days ago." Roth took an appreciative drink of stout. "The day after Brougham got the papers. She thought the manservant had forgot to tell her, but when I questioned all the staff, it seems quite clear no one ordered it." He dug out his notebook. "The description isn't much help. Brown hair, tanned skin, average height, average build. 'Older,' but neither of them is a day over five-and-twenty, so that could mean thirty."

"He's probably a hired agent, in any case." Malcolm took a drink of stout. It didn't necessarily help, but it certainly didn't hurt.

"Do you know who might have hired him?" Roth asked.

"I think I do." Malcolm took another drink of stout and told Roth about Alistair.

Roth listened in silence, gaze not leaving Malcolm's face. "That's a great confidence."

"Better if you know." And at this point, Malcolm had few secrets from Roth. Well, aside from the fact that his wife and father had been French agents.

"So Alistair Rannoch may have a chapter of the memoirs," Roth said.

"And is trying to negotiate with the king over them. But he still wants the rest of the memoirs."

"And these notes of Lord Pendarves's from 1814—"

"We still can't work out precisely where they fit in," Julien said. "Perhaps—"

He broke off as Mélanie ran into the room. She paused on the threshold and took in the crowd. "I'm glad you're all here."

"Harry and Roth brought stout." Malcolm gave his wife a glass.

"Thank you." Mélanie took a drink. "I saw Jack Tarrington. He took Lord Pendarves's papers. Because Jamie Blayney was threatening him. He gave them to Blayney the night before he was killed."

"So presumably the notes from 1814 are with the memoirs," Malcolm said. "Wherever Blayney hid them. Unless one of the searchers found them before we did. Although at least we know Alistair hasn't found them."

Valentin came into the room. "This just came for Mr. Roth." He handed Roth a paper.

Roth slit the paper open and frowned. "It's from Wilkins, the patrol I had watching Mrs. Blayney's house in Chelsea. He hadn't seen her since shortly after he arrived. He went to talk to the kitchen maid to make sure she was all right. The maid was evasive, and then one of the children came in and said their mother was gone. Apparently, she slipped out last night. Deliberately avoiding Wilkins. He's trying to pick up her trail, but wanted me to know."

"She could have a lot of reasons for going off secretly," Malcolm said.

"Yes. Wilkns also says the little girl claimed she'd seen another man watching the house. I should—"

The door burst open again to admit Cordelia, followed by Pippa Haworth. "We think we know where Captain Blayney may have hidden the memoirs."

CHAPTER 52

Pendarves looked up in surprise as Julien and Kitty came into his library.

"Sorry," Julien said. "At this point, there isn't time to stand on ceremony. I don't believe you've met my wife?"

"Lady Carfax." Pendarves inclined his head.

"Lord Pendarves." Kitty smiled. "I know this is awkward, but it needn't be. And at this point, we need to focus on the investigation."

Pendarves's gaze shot between them. "Is there news?"

"Six years ago," Julien said. "You said you thought I'd taken a draft of a letter from Castlereagh to Metternich about the Russian situation."

"Yes, though now I think about it, that wouldn't have really made sense, with your working for Carfax. He could have just asked Castlereagh."

"Believe me, there are any number of things Castlereagh wouldn't tell Carfax and any number of reasons Carfax might have stolen papers relating to Castlereagh." Leaving aside the fact that Julien had actually been working for Talleyrand. "But as it happens, I didn't take the letter, as I told you."

"I believe you. It's probably tucked at the back of a drawer somewhere."

"I don't think it's that. We have reason to believe the Russians had a highly placed British agent at the time. Which raises the question—who else might have had access to the papers?"

~

THE THISTLE COFFEEHOUSE was tucked away on a small court. The sort of respectable yet anonymous place a man might choose to meet a lady with a reputation to protect. Long ago, before she'd married Malcolm, Mélanie had gone to similar places on missions where spycraft had crossed into amorous encounters.

She and Malcolm had come alone to investigate. Julien and Kitty had gone to talk to Pendarves, and Roth and Harry had gone to Jamie Blayney's lodgings to see if Mrs. Blayney was there. A handsome but tarnished brass chandelier swayed from the ceiling as Malcolm opened the door to let her in. A collection of tradesmen and clerks and dark-coated men who might be bankers or attorneys were gathered at the tables. Mélanie saw more than a few white cockades and a variety of scurrilous cartoons, mostly mocking the king and cabinet, in the newspapers spread on tables as she and Malcolm threaded their way to the bar. A woman stood behind it, tall, probably in her midthirties, with stylishly dressed dark hair. She wore a well-cut gray gown and a white muslin tippet.

"What can I get you?" Her tone was polite but guarded.

"Information," Malcolm said. "We understand James Blayney frequented your establishment."

Her eyes narrowed. "Come out of curiosity about a murdered man? Or—" Her gaze shot between them. "Are you the gentry that work with Bow Street?"

"We're assisting them," Mélanie said. "We understand there was a room Captain Blayney often engaged here. When he was entertaining a guest privately."

"I'm sure I don't—"

"You needn't worry about protecting reputations. One of the ladies Captain Blayney brought here told us."

"I run a respectable establishment—"

"I'm sure you do," Malcolm said. "We just need to see the room." He set a purse on the bar.

"It's the third door at the top of the stairs. But someone else just went in there."

Mélanie and Malcolm didn't even look at each other before they made for the stairs.

Malcolm flung open the door. A woman stood in the corner, next to an oak bed that took up most of the room. A piece of paneling was dangling from the wall and she was reaching behind it. "Here now, I've taken this room."

"Mrs. Blayney," Malcolm said. "Perhaps I shouldn't be surprised to find you here."

She spun round, clutching an armful of papers she'd snatched from the compartment she'd uncovered in the paneling. "These are mine. They were my husband's. I'm his heir."

"So you are. But they were only his by theft."

"You don't even know what they are."

"It's over, Mrs. Blayney. You aren't going to leave the room with them."

A door at the back of the room opened. "Step aside, Rannoch. Give me the papers, Mrs. Blayney." Lord Prescott leveled a pistol at Malcolm and Mélanie.

Mrs. Blayney gave a squeak of alarm, but her fingers tightened on the papers. "They're mine."

"They're valuable. I can pay you well for them."

Malcolm edged in front of Mélanie. "You'd best give them to him, Mrs. Blayney."

Mrs. Blayney stared at Malcolm. "You want me to give up the papers?"

"That seems the prudent course of action, though I'd suggest you insist he give payment first."

Prescott shot a glance at Malcolm. "What game are you playing at, Rannoch?"

"You seem to care about the papers rather more than I do." Malcolm folded his arms, which made more of a shield for Mélanie. Unfortunately, it also made it harder for her to see. "I hope you have a purse on you."

With the look of one who fears he is being duped but can't see how, Prescott drew a purse from inside his coat and tossed it over the floorboards to Mrs. Blayney. Mrs. Blayney snatched it up and pushed the papers across the floor. Prescott bent to retrieve them. He tried to hold the pistol steady, but his arm wavered. Malcolm sprang across the room and knocked Prescott to the ground. The pistol went off. The ball buried itself in the paneling. Mrs. Blayney screamed. Prescott hit Malcolm in the head with the pistol. Malcolm grabbed Prescott's hand and forced it to the floor. The pistol skittered away. Mélanie snatched it up. Prescott kneed Malcolm in the groin, stumbled to his feet, grabbed the papers, and ran out the door he had come through.

Malcolm pushed himself to his feet and ran after. Mélanie followed, down a twisting staircase and out into a yard overhung by close-set buildings. Prescott was halfway across the yard. Malcolm snatched up a rock and threw it at Prescott. It caught him in the shoulder. He stumbled. Two men ran into the yard. One grabbed Prescott as he stumbled. The other snatched the papers clutched in his arms.

Malcolm hurled himself on the man who'd grabbed Prescott. The three of them fell to the cobblestones. Mélanie sent the spent pistol hurling end over end at the man with the papers. It caught his knee, not hard, but enough to slow him. She grabbed a piece of wood from the ground, wishing she had the umbrella from when she and Harry were attacked.

Footsteps pounded and shadows shifted. Two figures ran into the courtyard. A fair-haired figured slammed a fist into the jaw of the man with the papers. A cloaked figure grabbed the papers as the man fell. Mélanie took two steps before her mind registered that it was Julien and Kitty.

"Catch." Kitty threw her the papers.

Mélanie caught them and turned to see a knife flash in the hand of the man who was grappling with Malcolm and Prescott on the ground. Malcolm grabbed the man's knife wrist. Prescott was pinned beneath him. Mélanie ran to them and stepped hard on Malcolm's opponent's shoulder. The man screamed. Malcolm wrested the knife from him. It was smeared with blood, but Malcolm appeared unhurt. Malcolm pushed himself up on his knees, the knife now at the throat of his opponent. "No sudden moves."

Kitty had another knife, probably her own, at the throat of the man Julien had hit. Julien ran over and held the recovered knife on Malcolm's opponent while Malcolm got to his feet. Then they both hauled Malcolm's opponent up. Prescott had gone silent. It was only when they had Malcolm's opponent on his feet that they saw why. Blood was seeping from his chest and his eyes had the fixed stillness of death.

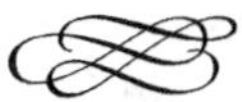

CHAPTER 53

"They've given a very vague description of the man who hired them." Roth scrubbed at his face with tired hands and accepted a cup of coffee from Mélanie in the Berkeley Square library, where they were all gathered. All except Raoul, who was still with Frances and Archie, and Laura, who had left to join him.

"Whoever hired them was probably an agent," Malcolm said.

"For the League?" Cordelia asked. "I mean, for your—for Alistair?"

"Probably. But it's possible the various people who've attacked us in the last two days are working for different people. All after the memoirs."

"The two men are in Newgate," Roth said. "As often happens, I have no very great faith we'll be able to keep them there once official pressure comes to bear."

"And Mrs. Blayney?" Cordelia asked.

"She's gone home under a Bow Street escort." Mélanie set down the coffeepot. "She says she decided if whatever papers her husband had were so valuable, she wasn't going to lose out, so she went to London to look for them. James Blayney had taken her to the Thistle once early in their marriage and engaged the same room where he took Pippa Haworth later. She remembered a spot that would make a good hiding place. She doesn't seem to have had anything to do with Prescott."

"How did Prescott end up there at the same time?" Harry asked.

"I'm not sure," Malcolm said. "But I suspect he had someone watching Mrs. Blayney's house in Chelsea in case she made a move. That person followed her to London and alerted Prescott to her whereabouts."

"And Prescott was a Russian agent?" Cordelia blew on her coffee.

"At least in 1814," Julien said. "And for who knows how long after. The irony is he doesn't seem to have been Danielle's lover."

"Molyneux told me he found Prescott in the Prussian delegation's retiring room at Oxford six years ago," Malcolm said. "Supposedly being sick, but I suspect actually looking for information. Mademoiselle Darnault doesn't even seem to have known he was a Russian agent. But there was enough in the memoirs for Blayney to piece together that Prescott was a spy. He wanted Pen's notes from six years ago for more proof. But he tried to blackmail Prescott with what he had. And Prescott wasn't prepared to pay Blayney forever over something that was far more damaging than a love affair. I also think Grace Arbuthnot is the golden-haired woman Pippa Haworth saw with Prescott. She seems to have transferred her attentions to Prescott before or after Blayney was killed. If it was before, she may have told Prescott that Blayney would be at the Chat Gris."

"Have you told Sophia Prescott?" Cordelia asked.

"Mélanie and I went with Jeremy," Kitty said. "She was as self-contained as when we spoke with her yesterday. I have a feeling Sophia rarely lets herself appear uncontained. And yet I also suspect she grieved more for Captain Blayney than she will for her husband."

"What did you do with the memoirs?" Harry asked.

"Returned them to Danielle on our way here," Malcolm said. "She burned them. Pippa Haworth was there as well, with her daughters. And Edmund Blayney was smiling in a way I wouldn't have thought possible when I met him two days since. Pippa left to go to her sister when we told her about Prescott. But you could tell how happy she and Blayney are."

"Some good has come out of this," Cordelia said. Then she bit her lip, and Mélanie felt the cloud of Alistair's return descend over the room.

Mélanie got up to refill the coffee, mostly as a distraction seemed needed. While she was pouring, Raoul, Laura, Archie, and Frances came into the room.

"You've missed the excitement," Malcolm said. "Though from your faces you've had excitement yourselves."

They exchanged glances. Laura pulled a packet of papers from inside the bodice of her pelisse. "I believe these are the papers Henry Brougham bought from James Blayney."

Relief shot across Malcolm's face. Along with myriad questions.

"Alistair gave me a way to contact him last night," Frances said, sinking into a chair and accepting a cup of coffee. "I sent word to him this afternoon. The message went through a tavern and then a haberdasher's but Raoul and Archie were able to trace it back to where Alistair is staying. I met Alistair in a quiet part of Green Park an hour since."

"Don't tell me he actually gave you the papers," Cordelia said. "I know he wanted you to make an arrangement with the king—"

"No." Frances took a sip of coffee. "Alistair trusts me more than he should, but not that much. But our meeting got him out of his lodgings."

"And you were able to take the papers?" Roth looked between Raoul and Archie.

"No, Archie and I distracted the people Alistair had watching his lodgings." Raoul sat on the settee beside Laura. "Laura got in disguised as a laundry maid and managed to steal the papers."

Malcolm grinned at Laura. "First Carfax and now Alistair. You're quite brilliant at this."

"They both underestimated me. Neither was as on their guard as they should have been."

"More fool they." Raoul kissed her hand.

"So it seems the case is more or less resolved," Roth said. "At least—"

"Alistair isn't resolved at all," Malcolm said. "But that's our problem."

"It's all your friends' problem," Roth said. "And I suspect it will lead to more issues for Bow Street, one way or another. In any case, I'm here to help."

Malcolm met Roth's gaze for a moment. "Thank you. For now, we have to wait to see what his next move will be. I suspect we won't have long to wait. And meanwhile, the trial's about to resume."

"Don't remind me." Julien stretched out an arm along the back of the sofa, fingers brushing Kitty's shoulder. "I'm not looking forwards to all the days of hearing intimate details bandied about. If we have to discuss bedsheets and which positions are most compromising, I'd much rather hear from novelists than lawyers. Though I imagine Brougham will be more entertaining than the prosecution." He looked at Malcolm. "Whatever the state of the trial, I'm here when needed."

"Thank you." Malcolm picked up the coffeepot and refilled Julien's cup. He cast a quick glance round the library, and Mélanie could tell he was wondering how long it would be theirs. "I am quite sure you are going to be. All of you."

"We've never ended an investigation with so much not ended at all." Kitty closed the nursery door on the sleeping boys.

"No." Julien straightened up from settling Genny, also sound asleep, in her cradle. "I'm well-served for bemoaning the lack of a challenge. I wouldn't have wished this on Malcolm and Mélanie for anything."

Kitty went to her husband and slid her arms round him. "At least neither of your friends proved guilty. Danielle and Pierre Ducroix seem to be headed for happiness. I hope Lord Pendarves and Mr. Tarrington can get past Mr. Tarrington's giving the papers to Captain Blayney."

"So do I. Pen's proud. But he's learned tolerance, I think, since I first knew him. Of himself and of others." Julien put up a hand and toyed with one of her ringlets. "Kitkat—"

"Yes?"

"I don't want to be with anyone else. I can't really imagine it."

"Yes, you said as much, right before you asked me to marry you. I suppose you could have changed your mind since, but I flatter myself I'd have noticed something of the sort."

"Witch." He tilted her chin up. "It doesn't matter if it's a man or a woman. It's that it wouldn't be you."

Kitty smiled, gaze on his own. "That's rather lovely, Julien. I'm not worried about your past. And I'm not worried about anyone else in your future, man or woman."

"If David married a woman, he'd be denying who he is. At least, he would be if he tried to have a real marriage with her. I'm not."

"I can't imagine your denying who you are, Julien. You have too much sense of yourself." Kitty slid her fingers into his own. "We were going to confront this at some point. With one of our pasts or the other. We'll no doubt have to confront it again."

"Probably." He drew their linked hands to his mouth and kissed her fingers. "I'm not concerned about your past either. If

I was going to be jealous of anyone, it would be of one of my best friends."

Kitty felt herself go still. Odd for all they'd been through, they'd never talked about Malcolm directly. "You don't have to worry about Malcolm."

"I'm not." He gave a crooked smile. "Not now, anyway. I'll own when you first came to London, I was conscious of some feelings I wouldn't quite admit to, which should have been a massive clue to my feelings for you. I even warned Mélanie against you."

"I doubt Mélanie needed the warning."

"Mélanie was rather more sensible than I was."

Kitty hesitated, but even though they rarely put such things into words, more needed to be said. "If I hadn't contemplated a life with Malcolm, I might not have been able to imagine one with you. But that doesn't mean I have any doubts about where I'm happiest. Or where I belong."

"Yes, well, there was a lot we both didn't know at that point." He hesitated himself. "I'll admit to being a bit hurt you hadn't contacted me, now we were both in the same country again."

Kitty ran her free hand over his hair. "Darling idiot. Didn't it occur to you that I was afraid of seeming as though I was making demands?"

"Since when have you been afraid of anything?"

"I was a widow with three children. I thought you'd run a mile."

He held her gaze in the flickering candlelight. His blue eyes had turned to onyx. "One of those children was mine."

"I suppose that was part of it. I was a bit afraid of your learning the truth about Genny."

Julien's gaze shot to the cradle, then back to her. "You wanted to keep me away from her? I could see that. I hardly seemed a likely father."

"No, not that. I'd seen you a bit with the boys in Argentina.

You were good with them. Amazingly so. But if you'd known about Genny and hadn't wanted to be her father—that would have been the end. I couldn't have dallied with you." She looked at him, her voice rough against her throat as she framed the words. "The children are the center of my life. It wouldn't have worked if you hadn't been all in. And I didn't think you could be."

"And so you pushed me away."

"Easier than having you push me away."

"As if I would have done."

"Julien, you have to admit you aren't the easiest person to read."

"Fair enough. Especially considering I couldn't articulate my feelings to myself."

Kitty looked down at their still-clasped hands. "But I knew."

"What?"

"To reach out to you when I needed you."

"You needed my fighting skills," he said in an even voice that accepted the memory of that terrible night.

"That's true. But I needed more than that. And I think I knew I'd get more than that. I needed someone I trusted." Her fingers tightened involuntarily over his own. "And though I wouldn't admit it, a part of me already trusted you."

A quick spark lit his gaze. "Yes, I still can't get over that."

"Didn't you trust me?"

"That's different. You're you."

"I'm hardly the most trustworthy person."

"Or you don't admit you are."

"Pot calling the kettle. Though it was easier, in a way, before we were married."

"Easier?"

Kitty studied their threaded fingers. "There was nothing holding us together. So if we stayed, it was because we wanted to."

He released her hand so he could slide his hands up her shoulders and link them behind her back. "You can't imagine I don't want to stay with you."

"No. But sometimes I'm aware of the pressures of the roles we've assumed. And I know you. You take our commitment seriously."

"My sweet." He tilted his head so his mouth was inches from her own. "I took it seriously before we were married. Before we agreed we were exclusive. At least in theory, before we'd agreed." He frowned.

"I know," Kitty said, memories of troubling moments from that time sharp in her mind. "At the start I assumed we weren't. Of course, at the start I was waiting for you to decide you'd had enough of domesticity."

"Idiot." He kissed her nose. "In fairness, I assumed the same— not about my growing tired of domesticity, but about our being exclusive. Because it wasn't really a word in my vocabulary." He drew back, frowning in consideration. "And I do think I could manage if we weren't. But I don't think I'd *like* it."

She tilted her head back. "I told you I didn't have time for anyone else. Which is true. But surely you know I don't *want* anyone else."

"I hope not." He kissed her, lightly but he let it linger. "At moments like this I tend to be reassured."

Kitty leaned into the kiss. "So if we encounter an ex-lover of mine—"

"I'll be completely understanding." He slid an arm behind her shoulders and let his mouth drift to her earlobe. "Or at least do my best to make you see me that way."

"Darling wretch." She kissed him back.

He looked down at her with a crooked smile. "Loving someone opens one to all sorts of fears and hurts. No doubt that's part of why I avoided it for so long."

"As did I. Though I wasn't so heartless as not to care at all."

Kitty regarded her husband, the man she in some ways knew better than anyone else on earth, and yet in others was still learning to decipher. "And I don't think you were either."

~

Malcolm bent to scratch Berowne, who was curled up at the foot of his and Mélanie's bed. "All in all, more's settled than I thought would be at the start of the day."

"A splendid way of thinking of it." Mélanie closed the nursery door.

The children were all asleep, though Malcolm expected there would be more questions in the morning. He felt his wife's gaze on him. "Darling—" Mélanie said.

"No." Malcolm stroked Berowne under the chin, then tugged at his cravat. "There's much to be talked of, but not tonight. I think the only way through the mire is one step at a time." He unwound a fold of linen from round his neck. "With everything else that happened, I never told you. Ben came to see me. He and Nerezza are betrothed."

"Oh, I'm so glad." Mélanie smile was quick and genuine. "I was afraid Beverston would interfere."

"So was I, but apparently Beverston's given his blessing. Though Ben says the lack of his father's blessing wouldn't have stopped him, and I believe him."

"And rather nice that they told you first."

Malcolm stripped off the neckcloth and dropped it in the laundry basket. "I'm sure they mean to tell all of us shortly. Ben came to me for advice."

"About proposing?"

"No, he's already done that, and Nerezza's already accepted." Malcolm undid his top waistcoat button. "About the wedding night."

"Oh."

"Yes, that was my reaction." Malcolm continued on the waistcoat buttons. "Apparently he's even less experienced than I was."

"Well, that needn't be a bar to anything. I hope you told him."

"Mmm. I tried."

Mélanie dropped down on the edge of the bed. Her brows drew together. "Does he know that Nerezza—"

"Is more experienced? Yes. That doesn't bother him. Except that he's afraid he won't—er—meet her expectations."

"Nerezza must know he isn't overly experienced."

"It's not quite like admitting one can't ride a horse." Malcolm coughed at the analogy.

"No, it has all sorts of feelings and expectations bound up in it. It'll be much better when they actually get to their wedding night. They won't have to think so much."

"We were lucky," Malcolm said.

"Darling—" Mélanie drew a breath. Malcolm saw her hesitate, as though the words were caught in her throat. "Our wedding night was remarkable."

He gave a quick laugh. "That could mean a lot of things."

"You know perfectly well what it means." She came up to him and slid her arms round him. "That may be the first thing that was honest between us."

He smiled down at her. "I was terrified."

She scanned his face. "Malcolm—" He saw her hesitate, as though debating whether to put into words something she wasn't quite sure of. Or perhaps wasn't sure she had the right to know. "Kitty was your first, wasn't she?"

"Kitty was my first." He picked up one of her hands and kissed it. "You were my second. And last."

"You're a quick learner."

"Yes, well, all things considered, it was probably as well for us you had more experience than you let on."

Mélanie choked, a sound between tears and laughter. "Oh, darling."

"Statement of fact. Though I couldn't quite say as much to Ben." He pictured Ben's earnest, concerned face and then Nerezza staring at the bowl of roses the night before. "It's not easy."

"Making love?"

"Marriage."

"Oh, well. Yes. It can shake monarchies and governments and overturn empires. It can leave people deserted in Chelsea or miles apart in the same house in Mayfair, as we've seen just in the past two days. It can create more secrets and lies than the most elaborate spy mission."

"Or it can be a spy mission." Malcolm smiled into his wife's sea-green eyes.

"That too." She looped her arms round his neck and reached up to kiss him. "But with the right person, it's certainly worth it."

HISTORICAL NOTES

Danielle Darnault is fictional, but her memoirs are inspired by the real-life memoirs of Harriette Wilson and her attempts to blackmail a number of her former lovers, including Henry Brougham and the Duke of Wellington.

Many of the things Emily Cowper and Harriet Granville say in the book come from their letters chronicling the amazing months of Queen Caroline's trial. See Mabel Airlie's *Lady Palmerston and Her Times* (London: Hodder and Stroughton, 1922); Tresham Lever's *The Letters of Lady Palmerston: Selected and Edited from the Originals at Broadlands and Elsewhere* (London: John Murray, 1957); and Edward Frederick Leveson-Gower's *Letters of Harriet, Countess Granville, 1810-1845* (London: Longmans, Green, and Co., 1894). Kenneth Bourne's *Palmerston: The Early Years 1784-1841* (New York: Macmillan, 1982) has excellent information on Palmerston, his relationship with Emily, and the Brougham/Caro George affair.

The tumultuous marriage of George IV and Queen Caroline, and George's efforts to secure a divorce will continue to feature in the adventures of the Rannochs and their friends.

A READING GROUP GUIDE

A READING GROUP GUIDE
The Westminster Intrigue
About This Guide
The suggested questions are included
to enhance your group's reading of
Tracy Grant's *The Westminster Intrigue*

.

1. Marriage is a theme of the book, from the marriage of
   the king and queen to the marriages of the central
   characters. Which couple in the book do you think
   has the strongest marriage, and why?
2. Which couple in the book faces the greatest
   challenges to their marriage, and why?
3. Did Alexander Radford's identity surprise you? If
   not, why?
4. What do you think lies ahead for Pippa Haworth and
   Edmund Blayney? How do their chances of happiness
   now compare with when they were younger?

5. Do you think Jamie Blayney loved any of the Langdon sisters? If so, which of them, and why?

6. Why do you think Alistair Rannoch disappeared? How will his return continue to impact Malcolm and Mélanie?

7. What do you think lies ahead for Nerezza and Ben?

8. We see several characters confront their relationships with ex-lovers in the course of the book. Which relationship do you think is most threatened by an ex-lover, and why?

9. Julien says Mélanie went undercover as the perfect wife and is just coming up for air. Do you agree with him? What are the implications for her relationship with Malcolm??

10. Compare and contrast Alistair's return from the dead with Julien's.

11. What do you think lies ahead for Danielle and Pierre?

12. Which of the central characters do you think has changed most by the end of the book? Why and how?

13. What do you think lies ahead for Pen and Jack Tarrington?

ABOUT THE AUTHOR

Tracy Grant studied British history at Stanford University and received the Firestone Award for Excellence in Research for her honors thesis on shifting conceptions of honor in late-fifteenth-century England. She lives in the San Francisco Bay Area with her young daughter and three cats. In addition to writing, Tracy works for the Merola Opera Program, a professional training program for opera singers, pianists, and stage directors. Her real life heroine is her daughter Mélanie, who is very cooperative about Mummy's writing time. She is currently at work on her next book chronicling the adventures of Malcolm and Mélanie Suzanne Rannoch. Visit her on the Web at www.tracygrant.org

Cover photo by Kristen Loken.

www.ingramcontent.com/pod-product-compliance
Lightning Source LLC
Chambersburg PA
CBHW060301100726
47907CB00002B/233